JUN 05 2011

Strong at the Break

OTHER BOOKS BY JON LAND

*Published by Forge Books

STRONG
AT THE BREAK

A CAITLIN STRONG NOVEL

Jon Land

A Tom Doherty Associates Book
New York

STRONG AT THE BREAK

Copyright © 2011 by Jon Land

A Forge Book
Published by Tom Doherty Associates, LLC
175 Fifth Avenue
New York, NY 10010

www.tor-forge.com

Forge® is a registered trademark of Tom Doherty Associates, LLC.

Library of Congress Cataloging-in-Publication Data

Land, Jon.
    Strong at the break / Jon Land—1st ed.
      p. cm.
    "A Tom Doherty Associates book."
    ISBN 978-0-7653-2337-8
    1. Texas Rangers—Fiction.   2. Militia movements—Fiction.   I. Title.
  PS3562.A469S76 2011
  813'.54—dc22

                              2011011542

First Edition: June 2011

Printed in the United States of America

0 9 8 7 6 5 4 3 2 1

For International Thriller Writers,
keepers of the flame

ACKNOWLEDGMENTS

Welcome back to those who've been with me before and welcome to those visiting my fictional world for the first time.

Speaking of which, this isn't a great time for the publishing world. Never an easy business and now a nearly impossible one and that makes me appreciate the Tor/Forge Books family all the more, starting at the top with Tom Doherty and Linda Quinton, dear friends who publish books "the way they should be published," to quote my late agent, the legendary Toni Mendez. Paul Stevens, Justin Golenbock, Patty Garcia, Karen Lovell, Phyllis Azar, and especially Natalia Aponte are there for me at every turn. Natalia's a brilliant editor and friend who never ceases to amaze me with her sensitivity and genius. Editing may be a lost art, but not here, and I think you'll enjoy all my books, including this one, much more as a result.

Some new names to thank this time out, starting with Lindsay Preston and Jeff Buck, who were instrumental in guiding me through the complexities of drug smuggling over the United States–Canadian border. (We're actually doing a nonfiction book on the subject together that will be every bit as riveting a thriller as my fictional ones. Check back at www.jonlandbooks.com for updates or drop me a line at jonlandauthor@aol.com.) Many thanks also to Michael Anthony and his terrific book *Mass Casualties** for the seed that gave birth to one of *Strong at the Break*'s key subplots. My friend Mike Blakely, a terrific writer and

Mass Casualties: A Young Medic's True Story of Death, Deception, and Dishonor in Iraq by SCP Michael Anthony, Adams Media, 2009.

musician in his own right, taught me Texas firsthand and helped me think like a native of that great state. The help I received in researching right-wing militia groups is too voluminous to detail and came from those who mostly asked that I not use their names, so I'll respect those wishes.

Finally, I'd be remiss if I didn't thank all of you who've written and e-mailed me about how much you enjoyed the first two tales in the Caitlin Strong series. Rest assured the third does not disappoint. Excited? I am, so let's turn the page and begin.

P.S. For those interested in more information about the history of the Texas Rangers, and to see where a lot of my info comes from, I recommend *The Texas Rangers* and *Time of the Rangers*, a pair of superb books by a great writer named Mike Cox, also published by Forge.

The world breaks everyone, and afterward, some are strong at the broken places.
—Ernest Hemingway

PROLOGUE

He may not win the laurels,
Nor trumpet tongue of fame,
But beauty smiles upon him,
And ranchmen bless his name.
Then here's to the Texas Ranger,
Past, present and to come,
Our safety from the savage,
The guardian of our home.
—from an anonymous poem
    written by a Texas Ranger
    in West Texas, 1897

MIDLAND, TEXAS; 1990

"How much longer we gonna sit here, Dad?" Caitlin Strong asked, fidgeting in the old truck's passenger seat.

Jim Strong turned his gaze from Pearsley's Tackle and Gun Shop across the parking lot toward his thirteen-year-old daughter. With her next birthday just weeks away, Caitlin had seemed to sprout overnight. The little girl gone, replaced by a young woman with the same wavy, raven-colored hair as her mother. The thought brought a lump to Jim's throat. Memories of his late wife, gone for a decade now, had grown no easier to bear with the passage of time.

"Not long," he managed, returning his gaze to what locals referred to simply as the "Tackle and Gun," a one-story bunker of a building with a flat roof plagued by broken downspouts that left water stains streaked in blotches down its beige exterior. The gravel parking lot offered only a single shady area courtesy of a grove of bigtooth maple trees standing alone against the otherwise sparse land. But the early afternoon sun had risen high enough to overwhelm them, the truck fast becoming a sauna.

"That's what you said, like, an hour ago," Caitlin told him, making no effort to hide her displeasure as she continued to sit with her shoulders slumped.

"But I mean it this time."

Caitlin sat up all the way, into the hot swatch of sunlight streaming in through the windshield. The old truck's interior always smelled rusty and s̶ ̶ ̶ ̶ ̶ hen it heated up, though she wasn't sure why. "This is some kind ̶ ̶ ̶akeout, ain't it?"

"Isn't it," Jim corrected.

"Grandpa always said ain't."

"Grandpa never had the benefit of your education, Caitlin."

Her father turned toward her and Caitlin noticed the light sheen of perspiration coating his cheeks, a bit thicker along his forehead. The sun could've been to blame, she supposed, except his seat was on the truck's still shady side.

"I thought we were going fishing," Caitlin said.

"We are."

"Not sitting here in this parking lot."

Neither as colorful nor elaborate as his legendary father, Earl Strong, Jim Strong was also not nearly as prone to telling Caitlin of his Ranger exploits. Of course her granddad's tales had been of days past, wild adventures from the heyday of the Texas Rangers. But all that had ended when Earl Strong died peacefully just short of ninety years old a few months back. His passing had left Caitlin with only an old aunt on her mother's side, who watched television with a magnifying device wedged in front of the screen, for a babysitter. So Jim Strong had resolved to stay closer to home and pretty much had, except for the stretch when he and fellow Ranger D. W. Tepper led the takedown of a cultlike group of fanatics known as the Church of the Redeemer here in Midland.

"This is about that church, *isn't* it?" Caitlin prodded from the passenger seat.

"Might have called themselves a church," Jim Strong told his daughter, his cheeks reddening with the suppressed rage that accompanied his most angry moments, "but tips we got had girls not much older than you being bedded by men could've been their grandpas. Walking around in robes, figuring themselves to be holier than holy, all led by a man the state's been after for not paying taxes on account of he calls himself a reverend."

"Maxwell Arno," Caitin said.

"I tell you that?"

"I've been reading about him. Says he made the ch.   sleep in bunkrooms and use outhouses. Wanted to train them a   ay from the sin of modern conveniences. That's a quote."

"Is it now?"

"You bet."

"Well, the Rangers raided Arno's complex outside of Midland after learning he was stockpiling guns and ammunition in an old storm cellar. What I saw in there made my stomach turn, and that's the God's honest truth. Girls not much older than you already carrying babes in their swollen bellies. Girls who . . ."

Jim Strong stopped suddenly and turned back toward the Tackle and Gun. The sun cleared the rest of the bigtooth maples and cast shadowy stripes across his face, making the sweat glow. His neck looked thin and knobby, his Adam's apple suddenly like a golf ball he'd swallowed.

"You're still angry, Daddy," Caitlin said after holding her words in briefly. "Why's that so if you shut this place down?"

"'Cause Max Arno got away."

"I read that too. You figure he's coming here?"

"I figure he might."

"What else, Daddy?"

Jim Strong swung toward his daughter. "Now how'd you know there was something else at all?"

"Don't know," Caitlin shrugged. "Just do. Know what Grandpa would say?"

"What would he say?"

Caitlin sighed deeply before continuing. "Dog poo's about impossible to get off your shoe no matter how much you rub. Even when it's gone, the smell's still there, like, forever."

Jim Strong smiled slightly, a bit sadly, in spite of himself. "I seem to recall him saying that very thing to me. But that doesn't stop you from still rubbing."

"You got another tip, didn't you?" Caitlin asked her father.

"Probably nothing," said Jim Strong. "Figured I'd best check it out."

"Just you."

"It's my fight, Caitlin."

"Why?"

"Got my reasons," Jim Strong said, the sadness he'd managed to chase away returning to his eyes.

Caitlin nodded. "Guess that means it's *our* fight now."

That's when the white cargo van pulled into the parking lot. Caitlin watched her father tense behind the wheel, leaning all the way forward into the sun. His eyes squinted. The left side of his mouth twitched and his hand involuntarily swayed to the Springfield model 1911 .45 caliber pistol holstered on his hip. He watched as the van found a space and two men who looked like football players emerged, surveying the scene. Apparently satisfied, they opened a side door of the cargo van and Caitlin watched Maxwell Arno emerge into the sunlight, accompanied by a boy about her age who must've been his son, Malcolm.

"Stay here," her father ordered, reaching for his door latch. It stuck briefly and Jim Strong had to shoulder it open. "I'll be right back."

"Daddy—"

"Not now, Caitlin," he said, all his focus drawn to Maxwell Arno, his son, and the two giants walking toward the Tackle and Gun on either side of them.

Caitlin rolled down her window as her father crossed the truck's hood, making straight for Arno with his .45 out now, hammer thumbed back. She took her eyes off him long enough to pop open the glove compartment and extract the old Colt her granddad had given her, making Caitlin promise never to tell her daddy. Something had made her hide it there before they set out early that morning, all oiled and loaded. Now she eased it from the dark confines, cocking the Peacemaker's hammer while she reached for the latch on her door.

"That'll be far enough, Mr. Arno," she heard her father say. Jim Strong had come to a halt a good fifty feet from Maxwell Arno and his giants, a tough shot with a pistol for anybody but the best, like him.

The two giants swung, hands dipping quick into their jackets. Arno turned just after them, easing his boy behind him and smiling almost placidly. Caitlin, strangely, saw only him, the giants reduced to spectral blurs at the edge of her vision. Arno's skin was milky white, his hair all slicked back save for a stubborn cowlick strung across his forehead that made him look like a child. Even his smile was innocent, likely bred of the constant cajoling of parishioners, followers, and especially donors he needed to be beholden to him.

"It's *Reverend* Arno, Ranger," he said, recognition flashing in his eyes when they fell on Jim Strong, who was holding his .45 dead on him.

"Tell the Frankenstein brothers there to bring their hands out from their coats slow and empty, Mr. Arno."

In the frozen moment that followed, Caitlin felt herself climb out of the truck onto the steamy, hard-packed gravel that baked her feet through her sneakers. Her granddad's old Colt felt so heavy in her hand she wondered if she'd be able to raise it, even with the help of all ten fingers. Funny how it never felt so heavy when she hoisted it at the range. Well, not funny really. She edged a little forward, angling herself so as not to be directly behind her father so she'd have a clear shot if it came to that.

If it came to that . . .

She wished her granddad were here now to help her bring the gun up and keep it steady. Stand behind her and cup his hands around hers the way he'd done on the range since she was eight. None of that today, though. It was her and her daddy and nobody else. Jim Strong was crazy if he thought she was going to leave him on his own, thirteen or not.

Maxwell Arno grinned. "Why don't you tell them, Ranger?"

"I just did," her daddy said. "And I don't see them complying."

"You walk out of this now, you walk out of it alive," Arno told him, so confident and unruffled he looked as if he had doused himself in baby powder.

"Too late for any such thing, given there were plenty of children hurt while under your care."

Maxwell Arno's gaze found Caitlin, a leering grin stretched across his face. "That your daughter back there holding a gun looks like it came from a model kit?"

Jim Strong stiffened, but didn't turn. "I imagine it is."

"Then maybe you shouldn't be the one telling me how to tend the children in my flock."

"Your flock's done and gone, and you, sir, are a wanted man."

Arno bobbed his head from side to side, as if to acknowledge Jim Strong's words. "This could get ugly, Ranger."

"It's already ugly, 'cause you made it that way. I'm placing you under arrest here and now, Mr. Arno. How that happens from this point is up to you."

Caitlin wanted to get her granddad's Colt up and ready to fire. But it wouldn't budge, almost like somebody was holding it down, keeping her out of firing position. Her feet felt as heavy as the gun, sneakers melting into the gravel, Caitlin unsure whether the sizzling she heard in her head was real or not.

Time froze up again. Nobody moving except those exiting the Tackle and Gun to scamper their way to safety at the sight of what was transpiring. Caitlin found the eyes of Malcolm Arno before his father pushed the boy back behind him.

Then the old Colt slipped from her sweaty grasp. She felt it dropping, heard the clunk when it hit the gravel. Her daddy almost turning when the giants yanked the pistols from their jackets, one a little behind the other. Jim Strong shot that one first, the other managing to get off a single wild shot that wouldn't have been good from twenty feet never mind fifty, before her daddy plugged him too. But both men righted themselves fast, wearing that bulletproof stuff for sure. So her daddy opened up again, pouring the last six bullets from his .45 so fast Caitlin could barely distinguish the crackling sounds in her ears.

She watched the giants' faces explode in bursts of blood, bone, and foamy spray that looked like dark, dewy mist. They keeled over on either side of Maxwell Arno, looking like felled trees bracketing another about to be cut down. But then Caitlin saw the pistol flash in Arno's hand, sunlight glinting off both it and the smile suddenly filling his face.

"You used all eight, Ranger," Arno told Jim Strong, who still held his .45 in a single hand before him.

Caitlin watched her daddy's other hand dip back under his jacket. "I'm gonna ask you to drop the gun, Mr. Arno."

"Or what, Ranger? Or what in the name of the Almighty Lord do you intend to do with an empty gun?"

In her mind, Caitlin measured off the distance to retrieving the Colt. Bringing it up and firing in a single swift motion just like the legendary Earl Strong, greatest Texas Ranger of them all, had taught her. But everything about her remained stiff and tight, her granddad's Colt roasting on the gravel a million miles away.

"Maybe you didn't hear me," Max Arno was saying, but he didn't say anything else.

Caitlin saw her father's hand twitch, that's all. Then she realized it was suddenly outstretched, empty before him, and Max Arno was looking down at his own chest that had the hilt of a knife protruding from it. Both his hands went to the blade as if to yank it free, then locked up. He looked puzzled, fading eyes finding Jim Strong one last time before he crumpled at the waist like an old rag doll and collapsed to the pavement, gaze starting to glaze over.

His son dropped with him, clinging, afraid to let go. The boy wasn't crying, wasn't speaking, just shaking his father as if to wake him up, to no avail, of course, since his locked-open eyes told Caitlin he was dead for sure.

The boy's eyes, meanwhile, met Caitlin's and for a moment she saw the shock, terror, and innocence that made her almost feel bad for him. Then those same eyes filled with a deep cold hatred that wouldn't let go of her until they swept above the pavement, perhaps in search of a loosed gun to grab.

But her daddy was there too fast, kicking the stray pistols aside while never losing grasp on his own in which he'd jammed a fresh magazine. Not a clip, her granddad had taught her, a magazine, although she couldn't explain the difference.

Then Malcolm Arno dropped down atop the body of his father, wailing hysterically. Just a boy again, suddenly lost and alone in a world that had just changed horribly for him.

. . .

Caitlin stood there in the hot sun, searching for her breath until her daddy sidestepped her way, never really taking his eyes off the three dead bodies and one crying boy. She tensed, having no idea what to expect under the circumstances while knowing she was in a heap of trouble.

Jim Strong crouched to retrieve her granddad's old Colt and Caitlin watched him ease the hammer forward and then dump the six bullets out into his palm. Pocketing them, he reached toward Caitlin with his free hand and stroked her hair gently. She collapsed into his arms, hugging him tight, tighter even than she had after Earl Strong's royal funeral, when it finally dawned on her there'd be no more trips to the shooting range or tales of the Texas Rangers told at her bedside.

"Let's get you back in the truck, little girl."

"That's what Granddad used to call me," Caitlin said, looking up at her daddy and swallowing so hard it hurt.

"Well," Jim Strong said, kind of sadly, "I expect it's not as true as it used to be."

"Daddy?" she started, looking back toward the crowd now surrounding the bodies and thinking of the way Malcolm Arno had looked at her.

"Yeah?"

"Nothing, I guess. 'Sides I'm sorry."

Jim Strong cupped her head in his big hand that smelled like gun oil. "It's me who's sorry," he said, forcing a smile. "Guess we're gonna have to put that fishing trip off until tomorrow."

"What is it you're not saying?" Caitlin asked, eyes narrowed on her father. "I can always tell, you know."

Her father didn't bother denying it, shrugging. "Just like your granddad there."

"So what is it?"

Jim Strong looked over and held her stare. "Some things don't really need saying, Caitlin."

She could see the hurt in his eyes, something biting into him down deep that left his expression looking like he'd swallowed a bad piece of meat. Jim Strong didn't keep many secrets and those he kept stayed locked deep down inside him where no man, woman, or girl could pry them free.

"Whatever you say," Caitlin relented.

But she didn't mean it, not really, as her dad turned away wiping a tear from his eye.

Part One

Nowhere, perhaps, could one find such an assemblage of extraor-dinary and eccentric characters, as were to be met with in a Texas Ranger company. Here, men from all ranks and conditions of society were brought into contact. Here was the old, scarred hero of many a sanguinary Indian fight, whose head, for many months at a time, had not known the shelter of a roof, but whose only covering had been the "blue vault," and whose only food such as his trusty rifle had furnished him.
  —Putnam's Monthly Magazine of American Literature, Science and Art; September 1857

I

From the street the house looked like those nestled around it in the suburban neighborhood dominated by snow cover that had at last started to melt. A McMansion with gables, faux brick, and lots of fancy windows that could have been lifted up and dropped just about anywhere. The leaves had long deserted the tree branches, eliminating any privacy for each two-acre spread had the neighbors been around to notice. Problem was the neighborhood, part of a new plot of palatial-style homes, had been erected at the peak of a housing boom now gone bust, so less than a third were occupied.

Caitlin Strong and a Royal Canadian Mountie named Pierre Beauchamp were part of a six-person squad rotating shifts in teams of two inside an unsold home diagonally across from the designated 18 Specter, the marijuana grow house they'd been eyeballing for three weeks now. She'd come up here after being selected for a joint U.S. and Canadian drug task force looking into the ever-increasing rash of drug smuggling across a fifteen-mile stretch of St. Regis Mohawk Indian Reservation land that straddled the border.

Beauchamp lowered his binoculars and made some notes on his pad, while Caitlin looked at him instead of raising hers back up.

"Something wrong, Ranger?"

"Not unless you count the fact I got no idea what we're trying to accomplish here."

"Get the lay of the land. Isn't that it?"

"Seems to me," Caitlin told the Mountie, "that the DEA got that in hand already. You boys too."

"It's task force business now. We need to build a case for a full-on strike."

"You telling me the Mounties couldn't have done that already, on their own?"

"Not without alerting parties on the other side of border, who'd respond by dropping their game off the radar, eh? When we hit them, the effort's got to be coordinated and sudden. That doesn't mean two law enforcement bodies working in tandem, it means two *countries*. And that, Ranger Strong, is never a simple prospect."

"So we've got to tell both sides what they know already."

Beauchamp shrugged. "Put simply, yes."

"I guess I'm just not cut out for this sort of game," Caitlin said and sighed.

The thunk of car doors slamming froze Beauchamp's response before he could utter it. Both he and Caitlin had their binoculars pressed back against their eyes in the next instant, watching six big men in black tops, black fatigue pants, and army boots approach the grow house from a dark SUV lugging assault rifles and what looked like gasoline cans.

"Uh-oh," said Beauchamp.

"Hells Angels?" asked Caitlin, following a bald pair of black-garbed figures who looked like twins.

"Yup."

"What exactly they doing here now, while there's people and drugs still inside?"

The Mountie moved his gaze back to her, his expression flatter than she'd seen in the three weeks they'd been working together. "Only one thing I can think of."

2

The DEA's lead agent, Frank Gage, drove Caitlin out to the St. Regis Mohawk Indian Reservation first thing when she reached St. Lawrence County in upstate New York, her unpacked bags stowed in her motel room. They turned off Route 37 down a bumpy road formed of cracked pavement lost to the snow the farther they drew into the woods. March was the absolute dead of winter in these parts, and Caitlin had never seen so much snow and ice in her entire life, enough of it to make the trees sag under its weight.

"Peak of the season, this road's got more snow than you can imagine," he said, finally snailing his car to a halt in a clearing that opened into a picturesque, white-encrusted scene of a frozen river that somewhere contained the border between the United States and Canada.

Caitlin followed Gage out of the car and down a slight embankment atop snow that crunched underfoot before hardening into ice. Her boots had the wrong tread for this kind of ground and she found herself slipping, unsure exactly of where the land ended and frozen water began beneath them.

"Welcome to the source of our problems, Ranger," Gage told her.

"Where's the border exactly?"

"There isn't one. That's the problem," he said, pointing across the vast whiteness to the woods on the other side. "That's Canada over there, but it's also part of the Mohawk Reservation on their side of the border too."

Caitlin followed Gage's gaze and spotted an old Indian man cutting a hole in the ice. He had a fishing pole resting on a foldout chair behind him; if he was aware of their presence, he chose not to acknowledge it.

"Who's that?"

"Old tribal cop. A legend in these parts who hates the druggers almost as much as he hates us. Comes pretty much every day to catch his dinner. Locals say he might be as much as a hundred years old."

Caitlin watched the old man plop down in his chair and ready his pole over the perfectly circular hole he'd fashioned in the ice.

"That all makes this a virtual sovereign nation the Canadian authorities are reluctant to violate even more than we are," Gage said, picking up where he left off before Caitlin had been distracted by the old Indian. He turned toward her, breath misting in front of his face. "More drugs come into the country over this and other frozen rivers, what we call 'ice bridges,' than any other spot in the country."

"Excluding Mexico."

"No, Ranger, not excluding Mexico at all, no offense to you."

"None taken," Caitlin said, trying to make sense of what the DEA man was telling her.

"We estimate fifty-five billion dollars a year in drugs now comes in through Canada. Compare that with forty-five, maybe fifty, through Mexico."

"You telling me we been fighting the war on drugs in the wrong place?"

"I'm telling you that over the past five years or so a new front's opened up in that war and you're looking at it. Starts with the grow houses, pharma and meth labs organized throughout Quebec and parts of British Columbia by the Hells Angels."

"Same biker gang we got?"

"They operate on both sides of the border. An elaborate network of fully franchised businessmen backed up by the usual armed sons of bitches riding Harleys. Angels are responsible for manufacture and shipment across Mohawk land here with the Natives' full blessing, since plenty of them end up as major distributors of the product themselves. I'll show you the homes of some of the biggest suppliers later. Goddamn mansions sitting just down the road from shacks generally unfit for human habitation. Tribal dealers use runners to sell their product to networks loyal to Russian organized crime throughout New York, Ohio, and Michigan. And that's just for starters since it doesn't even include the truckloads bound for other suppliers."

"You've sold me on the severity of the problem," Caitlin told him, feeling the wind sift through her hair. The air was bitingly cold, the bright sun offering a measure of respite, though not very much. "But I don't really see how the Texas Rangers can help you solve it, sir."

"Rangers can't; you can."

"Come again?"

"You've become a real authority on the subject, Ranger Strong."

"Not by choice, I'll tell you that much."

"All the same, you've been fighting your own war on drugs for more than two years now."

"Sure, back where it's smuggled in through tunnels dug out of the desert floor or old irrigation lines. Where I come from, we still got drug mules carrying product in rucksacks or on the backs of donkeys."

"While up here," picked up Gage, "it's driven by the truckload across frozen rivers by men who speak French instead of Spanish. You can see what I'm getting at."

"Not really, sir, no."

"Problem's the same; only the language and geography's different."

"I speak Spanish, not French."

Gage gave her a longer look this time. His thinning hair blew about in the stiff breeze, exposing a swatch of bald patches. He smoothed it back into place as best he could, but then a fresh thrust of wind tousled it once more.

"Only language drug people speak is money. Accents don't matter a whole hell of a lot to them. Where we're at now is the planning stage. Trying to handle this piecemeal's gotten us nowhere. What the task force is putting together is an overall strategy, kind of a master plan."

Gage had continued to kick at the gathered snow, revealing a deep symmetrical, crisscrossing pattern cut in the ice. Caitlin followed the pattern farther out onto the ice, convincing herself it ran from one side of this frozen swatch of the St. Lawrence River all the way across to the other.

"What is it?" Gage asked her.

"These trucks of yours carry enough weight to need snow chains?"

"Never thought about it."

Caitlin rose from her crouch, brushing the snow from her gloves. "You should, sir. What we got here looks to be big freight jobs running on double tires with only the outer ones chained. You're talking about some haul if it's drugs they're carrying in those cargo bays."

Gage finally looked up from the chain marks and studied Caitlin for what seemed like a long time, long enough for her to note his cheeks had gone cherry red in the cold while his nose remained milky pale, like his whole face was out of sync.

"I'm operating on a shoestring here," he told her. "Six agents, some locals and state cops out of New York, the Royal Canadian Mounted Police, a tribal policeman, and now you."

"Well, now that makes me feel a whole lot better."

"It's like this," Agent Cage explained. "The growers buy homes at foreclosure sales mostly across Quebec and British Columbia as well as outside Toronto and other venues. They pretty much gut the interiors to turn them into grow houses for an especially potent strain of marijuana known as BC Bud. The head growers get all the soil laid down, seeds planted, lighting and environment set up and turn things over to immigrants to handle the tender loving care."

"Did you say immigrants?"

"I did indeed, Ranger. Chinese mostly, totally beholden to the druggers for their very lives after being smuggled out of their home countries. A separate syndicate charges a fee to get the immigrants into Canada and then turns them over to the druggers to work off the rest with a ticket to the good old USA when the time comes. Poor bastards can see the American Dream across the border and will do pretty much anything they're told."

"My granddad arrested plenty of Mexican runners in the thirties bringing marijuana and black tar heroine across the border for pretty much the same reason."

"Hard-core druggers have certainly made a life's work out of feeding on desperation, haven't they? By the time their pigeons realize they've signed on to a sham, fear keeps them in line." Gage shook his head, thin wisps of hair shifting with it. "Not much changes."

Caitlin looked toward the vast expanse of land across the frozen river that looked postcard pretty and very small in the distance, thinking about another front opened in a war they were already losing. "In this case, it just gets worse."

3

"What do you mean?" Caitlin asked Beauchamp, watching the black-garbed figures heading up the walk to the front door, three of them lugging the gasoline cans.

"Didn't Agent Gage explain what the Angels do to the houses once they're done with them, once the mold sets in?"

"Burn them to the ground. Only this house hasn't been harvested. No mold yet, nothing like that. And there's still people inside."

"Meaning . . ."

"Jesus Christ," realized Caitlin, binoculars still glued to her eyes, "they're on to us."

"It does seem that way, eh?"

Caitlin moved closer to the window in response. "How many immigrants we got in that house?"

Beauchamp checked his notebook, flipping back a few pages. "Seven, by my count. I recognized two of the Hells Angels, the big bald ones with those arrow tattoos painted on their skulls: the LaChance brothers. They're from your side of the border in Michigan but wanted for murder in Canada too."

Caitlin lowered her binoculars and watched the Mountie fumble for his cell phone. "Then how 'bout we go arrest them?"

But Beauchamp had the phone at his ear. "We gotta call Gage first. See how he wants this handled."

Caitlin was already on her feet, pushing the blood back into her legs, taking her mind to a distant, yet familiar place. "Only one way it can be handled, Mountie."

"He's not answering." Beauchamp's eyes flared in the room's thin, ambient light. "I've heard the Rangers are the next best thing to Mounties."

"Funny," said Caitlin, "I've heard almost the same thing."

Standing now, Caitlin pressed her binoculars back against her eyes and focused on the grow house. She caught splotchy glimpses of some of the Angels spreading the gasoline about, dousing everything in their paths. There were glimpses too of the biggest ones, the American LaChance brothers, smacking a few of the Chinese around, ignoring their protestations since clearly they held no more value than the lumber and furnishings about to go up in an inferno.

"They're gonna burn those Chinese along with everything else," Caitlin said and pushed back her jacket to expose her holstered SIG Sauer nine-millimeter pistol.

"Then what are we waiting for?" Beauchamp asked her, pocketing his phone and ripping out his pistol in its place.

4

QUEBEC; THE PRESENT

Caitlin slid across the icy street, the wind and cold feeling like bramble shrubs brushing against her cheeks. Beauchamp was heading around to the rear of the house, their plan to trap the Hells Angels inside in their cross fire. Her heart had steadied to a slow, rhythmic pounding, her breath steady and a bit rapid. She felt her ears perk up, her vision suddenly able to pierce the night like a cat's, seeing the world the way she would through a rifle's crosshairs.

A gunman's cloud, her granddad had called it. The first time Caitlin had experienced violence firsthand had been in the parking lot of the Tackle and Gun in Midland, when she'd stepped out to join her father with Earl Strong's Colt heavy in her grasp. After that day she'd resolved to never let the same hesitance and fear conquer her again, and truth be told, it hadn't. Thing was, violence, when it did come, was normally a sudden thing, as unexpected as it was unpredictable. Walking into firestorms like this was rare indeed, and time slowed to a crawl the moment she reached the grow house's front yard, clinging to the shadows.

Caitlin lived every breath, every thought, every glimpse through the home's windows with the naked eye. Going up against eight men was bad odds for sure, especially when they were spread through the house, which made taking them all by surprise impossible. The air misting with frost and moonless sky would keep them from seeing her approach, but once she and Beauchamp started blasting, stealth would be forfeit.

Crack!

The booming report of a heavy pistol shot smacked Caitlin's ears like a baseball bat slung against a wood beam. She recorded a muzzle flash at the distant edge of one of the windows just crossed by one of the LaChance brothers. She felt herself picking up the pace, surging into the neat slivers of light sifting out through the windows. SIG raised and ready when she came to the nearest, a bay offering the best view inside of an unfinished great room rich with dark figures slithering about, locked down as targets in her mind.

It was no different from what Jim Strong must have felt when he climbed out of their truck to finish things with the Reverend Max Arno once and for all. He knew what was coming then just as she did now.

Almost to the window glass . . . Caitlin's mind cataloging placement and movement, the calculations as instinctive as her motions now . . .

There was glass to consider, what it did to the trajectory of bullets, bending them all over the place, and how that had to be anticipated in the shots that were about to start flowing.

Caitlin didn't remember pulling the trigger. There was recognition of one of the LaChance brothers about to put a bullet from his hand cannon, a long-barreled Magnum, into another Chinese man before she fired her SIG twice through the glass. The first shot grazed his shoulder, spinning him around. The second, already reprogrammed to account for what she'd learned from the first, took him dead center in the face, throwing him backward into the wall directly beneath the spray of gore from the exit wound that painted the wall.

As the Chinese man LaChance had been about to shoot crawled desperately across the floor, another Hells Angels swung toward the bay window glass, firing without a clear target. She emptied the magazine's remaining eleven bullets to drop him, his bullets getting no closer to Caitlin than the glass sprayed outward to smack her like hailstones, a few shards leaving their stinging mark through fabric or against exposed skin.

She was slamming a fresh magazine home when a shotgun-wielding Angel whirled into position before the window. Ready to fire when Pierre Beauchamp's first bullets punched him through what was left of the bay window's glass from the rear of the house. Caitlin could see the Mountie twisting to his right, gun angle changing before a blast fired by a Hells Angel out of her line of vision staggered him. She could see Beauchamp's gun go flying, the Angel who'd shot him crossing into her view, stealing sight of the now unarmed Mountie from her.

Damn!

The bay window's integrity had been pretty much ruptured, so the rest of it should give way without a fight. Lots of things could have flashed through Caitlin's mind in that moment, but what stuck was standing in the parking lot of the Tackle and Gun, her granddad's big Colt too heavy to raise much less fire.

She'd seized up because she'd been thinking, and any gunman worth his weight in blood and shells will tell you that there was no place for thinking in gunplay. Not now, not ever. So outside this house where people were dying, Caitlin launched herself into a leap she didn't remember taking until she smashed through the remaining glass into the kill zone.

5

QUEBEC; THE PRESENT

Caitlin landed on her feet, stumbling and churning as the floor went icy beneath her boots, coming up as she dropped to meet it. The fall saved her from a barrage of automatic fire instead, sprayed by the Hells Angel who'd been about to finish off Beauchamp. She fired up into him, twisting across the floor until she heard him gasp and looked up to see blood cascading from this throat.

There was no time to check on Beauchamp, not now, especially when Caitlin heard the *poof!* of flames catching, unsure whether a round or a match had been the culprit. Either way, gulping up the gasoline fueled their rise, and the empty great room was cast in an eerie orange glow. A wash of fire came at her and Caitlin backpedaled desperately, jacking home her third and last magazine. Doing a mental count of the downed Angels in her head and thinking of the five surviving Chinese she still needed to get out of here. Two darted past her for the door, one burning his hand on a knob superheated by the burgeoning flames. But he still managed to yank it open and cold air washed into the room, further fanning the fire that had begun to melt the thick snow surrounding the house.

Caitlin started forward, holding a sleeve against her mouth, fighting not to retch for the watering it would bring to her eyes, when one of the Angels she thought she'd killed found his feet and his gun. Silhouetted against the flames, holding a hand against his neck to stanch the blood leaking through his fingers.

Bang! Bang! Bang!

Not his bullets, though. They were the damn Mountie's, good old Beauchamp firing his pistol through a back window before he dropped to his knees in the snow outside.

Caitlin pushed herself into motion again. She had no real knowledge of the interior's layout. The pungent skunklike smell of freshly grown marijuana plants thickened in the air, and she stepped over the body of a second Chinese en route to a gutted section of the home that contained shiny foiled arrays of house plant pot laid out like a cornfield or orchard. The stench came close to overpowering her until figures dashed down the nearest row, slicing toward her, and Caitlin held her fire long enough to see it was another three Chinese, the last according to her rough count, taking flight.

Another Angel lurched out from the same row in their path. Caitlin shot him before he could get off a single round himself, shot him five times, but he still kept coming. Barreled straight into her when she jammed the SIG into his face and fired, drenched instantly by the spray of blood, bone, and brain matter. The faceless Angel fell atop her and

Caitlin shoved him off, feeling about the muck-ravaged floor for the gun she'd somehow lost hold of.

The marijuana in this section of the grow house had caught now, tentacles of flames reaching for the ceiling, which darkened to black and then began to peel away. Caitlin coughed up a storm, the watering she'd been desperate to avoid in her eyes playing havoc with her vision, though not enough to keep her from seeing the huge figure that had appeared before her down the row.

The second LaChance twin, big and bald as his brother with matching hand cannon in hand, his arrow skull tattoo pointing directly at her. Caitlin spotted the SIG just out of her reach in the same moment he did. Both of their minds measured off distances, concluding there was no way she could reach it before he shot her dead. He hesitated in that moment as flames licked the air around him.

Go for it, his hateful eyes urged her, *go for the gun*. And he wanted for her to do just that. Prolong the enjoyment of the kill, convinced the SIG held Caitlin's only chance.

But it didn't.

The smoke kept LaChance from seeing her hand dip under her jacket just as her father's had twenty-plus years ago, coming out with the very same knife that had killed the not so reverend Maxwell Arno. It was airborne before LaChance could react. Sped forward on an upward angle and found his throat, lodging actually on a forty-five-degree angle directly under his chin. LaChance coughed out a horrible gurgling rasp before going down, eyes wide as cue balls, his whole body smoking as the flames converged to swallow him.

Caitlin found her feet, heard herself coughing. The flames were thicker here in the part of the house this LaChance had set fire to first. But gagging sounds mixed with soft whimpers told Caitlin her count had been off. There was one more Chinese inside, after all, and damn if she was gonna go through all this and leave him inside to die.

It turned out to be a her. Caitlin knew the air was too smoke-rich to breathe anymore. So she sucked in one last deep breath before following the sounds to a young woman curled up in a fetal position amid the charred wood and toppled marijuana stalks that smelled like mold and roadkill skunk baking on the blacktop.

Caitlin's lungs burned. She felt the heat of the floor through her boots. The spreading flames nipped at her, stealing the path to the nearest window and making her wonder if they owned her for good.

6

SAN ANTONIO; THE PRESENT

"What happened next?" Captain D. W. Tepper asked from across his desk at Texas Ranger Company D headquarters in San Antonio a week later.

"Heat pressure had already blown out all the glass so I grabbed the girl, closed my eyes from the burning, and headed toward cold air."

"Smart move."

"Never been so scared in my whole life, being inside a fire like that. Six of the Chinese got out. Two didn't. I went out to tend Beauchamp."

"Your field dressings saved that Mountie's life was what I heard."

"I got lucky none of his wounds was a bleeder. You know the strangest thing?"

"What?"

"The way the heat of the flames melted all that snow. By the time I dragged Beauchamp clear, the yard was down to bare brown ground. We watched the roof and walls collapse before the fire trucks even got their hoses primed. I'll never forget that stench for as long as I live. Give me a gunfight any day over that."

"Speaking of gunfights, report I got from up north recommends I suspend you."

"What'd you tell them?" Caitlin asked him. She swept the long black hair from her face and felt the beginning of a burn on cheeks still getting used to the Texas hot spring sun again. It seemed she looked older than she had just a month back when she left, and Caitlin blamed it on the cold air turning her face to parchment. Her arms were missing their tone from lost time in the gym, and the dark eyes that always seemed too big for her face looked smaller, as if unable to see as much as they had when she left. She'd missed the road, the Texas towns that fell in her patrol, being able to define the job by the moment instead of letting the job define her. She was five-foot-eight in bare feet, and a good inch more than that in boots, but her return left her feeling considerably shorter after the weeks away.

"That I warned them what was gonna happen when they requested you. Far as I'm concerned, they got only themselves to blame. I gotta figure this drug task force wasn't ready for the shit storm that follows wherever you go." Tepper leaned forward. "Tell me something, Ranger. You ever gone anyplace you didn't kill somebody?"

"Wounded Mountie's doing just fine," Caitlin told him from the other side of the desk. "Hell of a man too. I'd ride with him anytime."

Tepper smacked his lips, his expression taking on the scowling tilt of a man who'd just swallowed something bitter. "They're claiming one of the Hells Angels you shot was an informant."

"Didn't stop the bad guys from making our stakeout. And if there really was an informant planted inside the Angels, why didn't we get at least some kind of warning?"

Tepper started working his finger in and out of the furrows of his brow. "I ever tell you about the time me and your daddy came up against an Angels chapter in Abilene?"

"No, sir."

"Was like this. They were mixing up some badass crystal meth, to be pushed by their California brethren, out of a slab house looked like it was ready to drop straight down to hell. House was guarded by other Angels making little effort to disguise their presence, figuring nobody'd ever dare mess with them. So your daddy gets the idea we should show up in the guise of vacuum cleaner salesmen to get us close enough to where we needed to be without making a fuss.

"So we stop at Sears to pick up the most state-of-the-art machine they had. Pull our truck over innocently enough and up we walk with badges in our pockets and guns holstered far enough back to hide. We lug that vacuum up the walk and one of the Angels who smelled like he'd rolled himself in shit stops us halfway. Two others show themselves, and we start acting all scared, begging off until we had all three zeroed.

"Then your dad and I whip out our guns, the three bikers stupid enough to draw theirs, and the shooting began. So I twist aside to steady a shot and trip right over the vacuum. Got off two shots with no idea where they went, while Jim Strong dropped all three bikers.

"All of a sudden, a blast plume near blows the roof of the house clean off. I'd later realize the shots I'd squeezed off tripping over the vacuum had gone right through the walls and punctured a tank of acetylene or some other meth ingredient, making the whole lab go boom. Your daddy and I were standing there when the biker chemists come crashing through the door, stripped down to their skivvies thanks to the heat of the lab inside what used to be the house.

"Kicker is one had a pistol jammed down his undershorts which he proceeds to reach for as he darts out across the lawn, looking like he's grabbing for his pecker. I swear I heard your daddy laugh and before either of us could shoot the biker, dumb son of a bitch that he was, blows off his own johnson. Ranger, you never saw such a mess in your whole life."

Caitlin noticed a video game called "Outlaw" featuring a Texas Ranger of old on the cover still wrapped in plastic atop Tepper's desk. "That about reliving old times?"

"Bought it for my grandson in the hopes it'll take his mind off wanting to learn how to shoot for real."

"How old is he now?"

"Twelve. Still rather have him blasting away at make-believe bad guys than shoot real lead into cardboard cutouts."

"My granddad started taking me to the range when I was eight."

"Playing with guns instead of dolls, in other words."

"They never made a holster for Barbie, D.W."

Tepper leaned forward and interlaced his fingers, making them look like twisted pencils. "That's good, since I need you to talk to a soldier patient over at the Intrepid Center for Heroes."

"I'm barely in the door, Captain, and my suitcase is still in the car. Why you giving this to me?"

" 'Cause you worked on the grounds way back when in that other life of yours. Figured that gave you lay of the land."

"I worked out of Brooke Army Medical Center as a therapist and counselor."

"Same grounds, same vets."

"The Intrepid specializes in burn victims and amputees from Iraq and Afghanistan. Things they can do with prosthetics make you feel you're in some Arnold Schwarzenegger movie."

"See, you just proved my point. Kid says his life's in danger and he needs to talk to somebody fast. I took the call myself, and there's nobody better to take things from here."

"Shouldn't he be talking to the army instead?"

Tepper cleared his throat and swallowed down some phlegm. "He says the army's the ones that want him dead, Ranger."

7

SHAVANO PARK; THE PRESENT

Cort Wesley Masters sat in a chair next to his sixteen-year-old son Dylan, the boy positioned in a way that kept his face hidden by his wavy black hair. He kicked at the cheap rug on which the chairs were perched in front of Thomas C. Clark High School principal George Garcia's desk, seeming determined to slice through the nap with the heels of his boots.

"We take truancy seriously here, Mr. Masters."

"So do I, Mr. Garcia. I assure you of that much."

Garcia moved his eyes briefly to Dylan before continuing. "Your son, apparently, doesn't concur."

Garcia was a gaunt man wearing a wide tie that further exaggerated the length of his neck, Adam's apple bobbing over the knot. He had coarse graying hair and droopy eyes that made him look tired all the time. Same height as Cort Wesley, but all told a man he could break over his knee. His office was plainly furnished with surprisingly sparse walls adorned by neither framed diplomas, awards, nor school pictures. Just a few portraits of clowns that matched both his penholder and Post-it dispenser.

Cort Wesley tried to keep his eyes off them.

"I told you there'd be severe repercussions if Dylan missed any more time," Garcia was saying, "and now here we are."

"Where's that exactly?" Cort Wesley asked him.

The principal wasn't afraid to hold his stare, and Cort Wesley respected him for that. The harsh intensity of his charcoal-colored eyes was normally enough to make any man turn away. Cort Wesley wasn't cut or buffed by bodybuilding standards, but his shirt did little to contain the width of his shoulders or the knobby bands of muscle up and down his arms. He'd taken to wearing his hair shorter these days, because it was easier to take care of and made him feel he had the same control over things he'd enjoyed back in the military. A million years ago, sure, but Cort Wesley liked to think he could pull off the same stuff today he had back then, although mostly these days that entailed raising a pair of boys he'd met only two years before. Hell, the goddamn Iraqi Republican Guard he'd come up against in the Gulf War had nothing on one teenager and another just short of that milestone.

"I'm afraid Dylan's missed too much time to legitimately make up all his work," Principal Garcia was saying. "His grades have slipped badly and his teachers are at wit's end in dealing with missed classes and assignments." Garcia took in a deep breath, as if he was considering something he'd already decided. "I see no way we can promote him to senior under the circumstances."

Cort Wesley glanced over at his son, Dylan's dark eyes aimed downward now. He was wearing a long-sleeved shirt he'd picked up at some mall store filled with blown-up pictures of half-naked boys showing off their torsos. He'd bought a pair of hundred-dollar jeans there that were already fraying at the bottoms where they hugged the lip of the boots Caitlin Strong had bought him for his fifteenth birthday a year back when he still seemed like a kid.

Garcia looked like he was reluctant to lean forward, nothing to bring himself any closer to Cort Wesley than was absolutely necessary. "I wanted to have this meeting now while there's still time to place him in a Catholic or private school situation that can better accommodate his needs."

"The hell with th—" Dylan started to say until a stare snapped his way by his father froze the words.

"You mind giving me a minute with Mr. Garcia alone, son?" Cort Wesley asked him, trying to sound as if Dylan had a choice.

The boy stood up, shifting his jeans so the boot heals wouldn't snare the cuffs. "Don't call me that," he said and stormed out the door.

8

SHAVANO PARK; THE PRESENT

Cort Wesley listened to Dylan's boots clacking out of the room, waiting for the sound to drift off before resuming. "How much you know about me, Mr. Garcia?"

Garcia looked trapped between breaths and thoughts. "I read the papers, watch the news," he said, like a man drawing his words in longhand before letting them out.

"Then you know my family's been through an awful lot and my son through more than most men see in their lifetime. I'm hoping that warrants an exception here."

"If I could, Mr. Masters," Garcia said, his remark ending in a shrug.

"I used to be a soldier, Mr. Garcia, and one thing the army taught me was the man in charge can do whatever he wants. You know, chain of command, and you, sir, are the head of that chain here. Sure, I know you got the school board and superintendents to answer to, but this being a purely academic matter makes me figure you can make any decision you see fit."

Something changed in Garcia's expression, his face flattening and squaring as if the view before him had changed in an instant. Almost made Cort Wesley turn to see if someone else had entered the room.

"You fought in the Gulf War," he said finally.

"Yes, sir, I did."

Garcia looked like a driver realizing he's going the wrong way, looking for a spot to make a U-turn. "I lost my wife three years ago in Iraq."

"I'm sorry, sir."

"She insisted on reenlisting. See, she was in the Gulf War too. I-Corps, the intelligence branch."

Cort Wesley nodded, wondering where Garcia was going with this.

"When my wife got back, she told me things I guess she wasn't supposed to. Some of it was about something she called Team Bravo, an elite Special Forces group that was in Baghdad quite a ways before that first war started. My wife told me Team Bravo's job was to turn as many of the Iraqi army's elite cadre as they could and assassinate the ones they couldn't. A kind of reinvention of the Phoenix Project from Vietnam."

Cort Wesley just looked at him, Garcia holding his stare now.

"Everything I've heard about you, Mr. Masters, tells me you were part of this Team Bravo."

"There a reason why you're bringing this up?" Cort Wesley asked him, not bothering to deny it.

"Because, if you don't mind me saying, a man who can handle that can surely handle a sixteen-year-old boy with his hormones bursting out of his pants who's lost his way for a time."

"Lemme tell you, Mr. Garcia, compared to raising boys, my war experience was a walk in the park. You got kids yourself, sir?"

The principal shrugged, then shook his head regretfully. "My wife and I kept putting it off. Always thought there'd be more time until there wasn't. Something always came up, got in the way. You know, Mr. Masters."

"I suppose I do."

"You got yourself a fine boy there and you have my sympathies over this rough patch he's going through. If he turns things around, I'll find a way to keep him at Clark and get him promoted, make it work somehow."

"Thank you, sir. Truly."

"It's my wife you should be thanking, Mr. Masters. I'm making the offer out of respect to her and her service. And yours."

"I appreciate that more than I can tell you," Cort Wesley said, but he could see the principal's expression was twisted in something between pain and uncertainty. The same way he'd looked when talking about his wife moments before. "Something else, sir?"

"My wife said the members of Team Bravo didn't leave after the Gulf War ended."

Cort Wesley met Garcia's stare, saw the longing and emptiness that had taken root there. Ordinarily he never talked about his war experiences with anyone, not even Caitlin Strong. But he figured he owed something to this man for going out of his way to help Dylan.

"Folks in Washington wanted to make sure they didn't have to go back and finish the job with Saddam, so they wanted it finished for them with a bunch of help on the down low," Cort Wesley told Garcia. "Trouble being they backed out after the wheels had already been set in motion, leaving a lot of brave Iraqis concentrated in the south hung out to dry. That was the end of things far as I was concerned, Saddam's Republican Guards slaughtering people we'd lit a fire under, kind of like the Bay of Pigs all over again. I came home disgusted, sir, and the taste of it still lingers."

Garcia's features relaxed.

"I'll tell you something else, Mr. Garcia. Our contact in intel was a woman who was as smart and loyal as they come. Never did get her name; she was just a voice at the end of a comm line. But I know she was as disgusted as I was by how things turned out. I can't say it was your wife for sure, but in all my years of service I never did deal with any other woman in I-Corps."

A placid look fell over Garcia's expression. He looked like a man who'd just let out a long, easy breath as he stood up slowly and extended his hand across the table. "Thank you, Mr. Masters. Thank you."

Cort Wesley rose to take it. The principal's grasp felt weak, his expression gone dour as if he doubted his own wisdom. "Like I said, sir, it's me who should be doing the thanking."

"Mr. Masters?"

Garcia's call turned him back around halfway to the door. Cort Wesley watched the principal start a hard swallow, then not quite finish it.

"When she got back, there were nights my wife couldn't sleep. The good ones she'd read a book. The bad ones she'd lay there sobbing and I felt weak and worthless because I couldn't do anything."

Cort Wesley shrugged. "Sounds like the way I feel about being a parent sometimes."

This time Garcia finished his swallow, a man searching not for words but answers no one had been able to provide him. "Least your boy's alive, Mr. Masters. You can take comfort in that."

9

SAN ANTONIO, THE PRESENT

"Thanks for coming, Ranger," Mark John Serles said to Caitlin from his wheelchair in the snack room on the second floor of the Intrepid Center for Heroes at Fort Sam Houston, currently unoccupied except for them.

There was a clock on the wall, its second hand sputtering through its circle with a loud ticking sound Caitlin thought for a moment might be Serles's heart hammering. That's how anxious he looked, as if his nerves were held together by baling wire that bit down every time they tried to relax. He kept fidgeting in his wheelchair, his head cocked to the side as if he were hearing other voices.

Serles squeezed the arms of his wheelchair. Caitlin noticed he was rocking slightly back and forth, making her feel almost woozy from following him. She'd worked with enough wounded veterans, amputees included, to not let her stare drift to his stumps, the kid's legs ending just above the knee.

The Intrepid Center for Heroes sat adjacent to Brooke Army Medical Center on the grounds of Fort Sam Houston. Built entirely with privately raised money, much of it by the radio host Don Imus, the center was likely the most advanced rehabilitation center in the world for amputees and burn victims. Its modern, four-story structure contained every amenity imaginable including state-of-the-art equipment, lap pool, physical therapy centers and some of the best counselors and therapists America's wounded had ever known. Living facilities adjacent to Intrepid were available for families, along with transitional housing for recovering vets returning to the world with their disabilities.

"I'm from right here in San Antonio myself," Serles resumed after a long pause. "I wasn't sure if you knew that."

"No, I didn't."

"No reason why you should with this place counting broken troops from every state in the good ole US of A inside its halls."

Serles tried to finish his remark with a smile but barely got his lips to move. An uneasy silence fell between them, the small talk waning, and Mark John Serles took to rolling his wheelchair back and forth instead of just rocking it. Information D. W. Tepper had been able to gather put it that the kid had been a medic in Iraq working at a field hospital, a bunker-rich world encased in concrete. Kid had been all of twenty when he deployed and just past twenty-one when an IED blew his legs off.

"I asked for you specifically, you know," Serles resumed.

"Didn't know that either, no," Caitlin said.

Serles was drumming the chair's arms nervously now, jittery eyes cheating toward the doorway. Caitlin watched him squeeze the chair's arms every time someone in uniform walked by.

"Is there another place you'd rather talk?" she asked him.

"No place's safe for me. Not here, not anywhere. Being from Texas, I've heard of you—everybody has." Serles's eyes grew distant, then quickly regained their focus. "You worked here for a time, right?"

"Across the way, actually, at Brooke Army Medical Center."

"With folks like me?"

"Somewhat. That was back a few years after my husband went over."

"What unit?"

"Civilian consultant."

Serles pondered that briefly. "How's he doing?"

"He died."

"I'm sorry."

"Had nothing to do with the army, not the war even."

"Ma'am?"

"Long story, Mark," Caitlin said, taking easily to calling the kid by his first name.

"I used to go by M.J. until it started making me feel twelve years old all the time."

He started rocking again, lapsing into silence with eyes aimed downward. The fact that he'd lost his legs above the knees made fitting effective prosthetics harder with a less certain result. Mark John Serles still wore his hair military style with the sides trimmed tight to the scalp. Other than that, though, the kid could have passed for sixteen easier than twenty-one. He had dark puppy dog eyes big enough to hold hope, sadness, and fear at the same time.

It was the fear that interested Caitlin the most. It seemed to make him hold his eyes wide and virtually unblinking, shifting suddenly toward a sound as simple as the refrigerator kicking back on or a sudden rush of footsteps past the lounge's open door. His fingers she'd noticed drumming on the arms of his wheelchair now clenched the padding, as if to tear it back.

"This building was being constructed when I was at Brooke," she said, breaking the tension that had settled between them. "Can't believe the progress they've made with prosthetics in just those years."

It was true. Entering the building today, Caitlin had seen kids not much older than Mark John Serles walking on two prosthetic limbs as well as she did with flesh and bone. If they'd been wearing slacks instead of shorts, she never would've even known.

"I got a couple more surgeries scheduled before I get mine," said Serles. "But they've already started the fitting process. I just want them to give me my life back."

"And they will."

"Not if somebody else takes it away first, Ranger," Serles said, the fear plain in his eyes again. A pair of uniforms stopped just beyond the doorway and the breath seemed to clog up in his throat.

Caitlin slid her chair farther under the table to be closer to him. He seemed about to continue when a trio of therapists entered the room and moved to the coffee station. Once again, she could see Serles's features seize up, torso tightening and hands squeezing the arms of his chair hard enough to make the veins rise from the surface.

The therapists mixed cream and sugar into their cups and took their leave, smiling at both Caitlin and Serles on their way out the door. But this time Serles didn't seem to relax, his lower lips trembling when he resumed.

"I'm scared, Ranger. I try not to sleep at night because it's the only time I'm alone. Stay up reading or watching TV. Because I figure that's when they'll come."

"Who?"

"Army, government—I'm really not sure. Missed their chance at me in Iraq, so they'll be back for sure."

Caitlin felt something like needles pricking at the back of her neck. "They came at you after you drove over that IED?"

Serles's gaze froze on hers, as he shook his head. "Was them that set it."

IO

Baghdad; four months earlier

The man was drenched in blood. Shot by a sniper through the throat, it was a wonder he was alive and being prepped for surgery. Had it been one of those busy times at the concrete-encased hospital, when the wounded came in droves after a bombing, firefight, or mortar attack, he would've likely been triaged into a pool of those unlikely to make it and thus treated last. This was a slow day by those standards, though, and the man was the only active patient waiting beneath the harsh glare of the fluorescent lights overhead. A recent mortar attack had loosened the housings on several of them, the bulbs now cocked at odd angles that left some of the room cloaked in shadows and the rest bathed in a dayglow brilliance that actually burned Mark John Serles's eyes.

The field medics had done a marvelous job of stanching the blood flow and keeping the victim alive this long. He wore dark fatigues, more stylish than functional, and no dog tags. Civilian, then, though Serles knew he could just as easily been CIA, since the city was still swimming with spies. Or even a journalist.

"Who is he?" Serles asked the field medics who'd brought him in and were finishing up their paperwork.

"We don't know," the one holding the clipboard replied. "Wasn't carrying any ID."

Serles could see the man's pockets had been turned inside out. "Wasn't carrying *anything*?"

"He was cut down just outside the Bafra Market—"

"Green Zone?"

"Last time I checked. Anyway, a hundred people could've passed him before we arrived." The field medic scrawled out his signature and lowered the clipboard to his hip. "Iraqis like souvenirs."

The field medic handed him the clipboard and Serles signed it, formally taking possession of the victim. The hospital treated civilians as well, most of whom were Iraqis caught in cross fires or wounded by terrorist bombs. Those were the toughest days in Serles's mind. What a bullet did to a body was nothing compared to the ball bearings or ground glass stuffed in those homemade bombs or suicide belts. Once ignited the debris and fragments reached supersonic speeds that could cut a body in half or render it utterly unrecognizable, little more than a steaming pile of flesh and gore. Sometimes the civilians brought here were somewhere between the two, something Serles's medic training program back stateside hadn't exactly covered.

He'd been in country for nine months now, the experience much worse and entirely different from what he'd been expecting. He was prepared well enough for the operating room, and the prospect of helping to save lives made the terrible sights, sounds, and smells tolerable. In the OR, working amid harried, overburdened, and overstressed doctors, his contribution was vital. Often the literal difference between life and death.

It was the rest of the time that was seldom anything but bad and often much worse. Serles's first supervisor was incompetent, played favorites, and couldn't make out a simple shift schedule worth a lick. There were times when he worked sixteen hours straight, had four off, and came back for sixteen more. Got to the point where he had to chew gum in the OR during surgery just to keep himself awake, the docs figuring he was a slacker when his head kept bobbing up and down.

Serles learned quickly about the army chain of command and what happens when you disregard it. The procedure was to complain to the superior officer fucking up and wait for him to punitively punish you for complaining, which of course made things worse. Wait another three weeks for things to get no better, then tell the regular inspection team about it so they could dress the obstinate asshole down. Him making them promises he had every intention of disregarding and then punishing you again. In the army nobody got fired, almost nobody got demoted or reassigned, and superiors or supervisors were seldom disciplined.

The training never covered that either.

Serles figured he had no choice but to adjust to the constant change in his sleeping patterns, even that exacerbated by the regular mortar attacks that sent base personnel scurrying for the bunkers. He thought maybe the insurgents were timing the attacks for his sleep periods since they always seemed to come during those rare times when he finally slipped off soundly.

The bunkers themselves, cement shelters about four feet high and maybe fifteen feet long, were scattered at strategic points on the grounds. Enough room inside for about twenty people and you quickly learned to program the location of the nearest one into your brain no matter where you were on the base.

Serles got used to the percussion of the shells when they impacted, got so he could tell exactly where on the base they landed. Worst thing was being crammed into a bunker, after being roused from a rare deep sleep, and waiting for the all-clear signal. Sometimes it took more than an hour to come, and he would emerge bent, cramping, and with nerves too jangled to get back to sleep. It was a cycle of deprivation from which it proved impossible to find any semblance of rhythm or routine.

Serles tried keeping a diary to maintain the track of time and keep himself sane, but it only made him more depressed. He had a girlfriend back home, but there were nights he couldn't even keep her picture straight in his head. It kept dissolving to be replaced by a patient who died in the OR, gazing up at him in death, or the smirk of the incompetent asshole supervisor who reveled in making him miserable.

Serles had been on duty for fourteen straight hours, looking forward only to completing his shift in two more, when the sniper victim was brought in. While the victim's blood was being typed and the OR readied, Serles was alone with the man. He started to figure he worked for Blackwater or some competing outfit. Private military. Then the man's eyes opened, filling with fear as they met Serles's.

"You've been shot, sir. You've lost a lot of blood but they brought you to the best field hospital in Baghdad and we're gonna fix you up for sure."

The man tried to speak, but only a gurgle emerged. Then he moved his head slightly, Serles watching the man's tongue switch from one side of his mouth to the other.

"They shot me," he wheezed in what barely passed for a whisper.

"I know that, sir. An Iraqi insurgent sniper did the deed, but today's your lucky day 'cause he didn't kill you."

"No . . ."

That and the terror plastered over the man's face got Serles's attention.

"No," the patient repeated, loud enough to be clear now. "Wasn't an Iraqi." He swallowed as best he could. "An American."

"An *American* shot you?"

The semblance of a nod.

Serles fished the notebook he'd been using for a diary from his pocket. "What's your name, sir?"

"Kirk . . . en . . . dale."

Serles wrote that down, spelling it phonetically. "What outfit you with, sir?"

"American . . ."

"I know that much."

". . . intell—"

That was as far as he got before a gurgling rasp sucked up the rest of his words.

"Intelligence?"

Kirkendale nodded.

"All right, the OR's almost ready. I want you to stop talking now. Save your strength."

Kirkendale shook his head very slowly, twice. His eyes beckoned

Serles closer, close enough to smell his blood and the dry stench of his labored breath.

"One-four-seven . . . eight-six-three."

"What was that, sir?"

"One-four-seven-*dash*-eight-six-three. You need to write it down. Please."

Serles retrieved his notepad from the gurney where he'd laid it and jotted down the numbers. Easy sequence to remember, but he read them out loud again and Kirkendale nodded, spitting up some blood as he forced out his next words.

"Alpha, Delta, Charlie . . . Operation . . . Rising . . . Dawn."

Serles wrote that down too, then looked back to see Kirkendale's body had gone still and his eyes had locked open.

"Oh shit . . ."

11

San Antonio; the present

"My notebook disappeared a couple days later," Serles picked up. "I didn't think much of it, not until . . ." The rest of his words got cut off in his throat, swallowed down like bile.

"Take your time, sir," Caitlin urged.

The kid tried to smile. "I ain't no 'sir,' Ranger."

"You are to me, Mark. You served your country and paid a terrible price for it."

His eyes lost all their gleam. "That's what I need to get to now."

"The IED?"

Serles half nodded, as close as he could come to completing the gesture. "They sent me on an errand, me and a guy named Donleavy who we called Donkey for short. Pick up some medical supplies at the airport that were late being delivered. Weird thing being that I'd just inventoried the supply closet and there was plenty of the very same stuff they'd sent us to get. I didn't think too much of it at the time because there's no figuring any rhyme or reason to the way the army does things. Halfway there, the IED got us on the freeway. Weird in itself, since the insurgents had started setting their IEDs in parked cars a while back, more effective that way."

Caitlin remained silent, no idea what to say to prod the kid on.

"Now here's where things get really strange," he continued on his own. "We could see other Humvees up ahead of us cross the very same spot. Then we go over it and *boom!*"

Serles began to tremble when he said that, his hands squeezing the armrests of his wheelchair while his mouth continued to quiver. He tried to swallow and ended up sighing instead.

"Woke up with what was left of the Humvee turned on its side and I didn't even think I was hurt. I mean, I didn't feel any pain, just figured my legs were stuck instead of blown off, and was counting my lucky stars when I glanced over at Donkey and saw him cut clean in half in the driver's seat. That's when I looked down below my own waist."

The kid took some time to settle himself, starting to sob a bit, and Caitlin adjusted her chair so she could lay a hand over his arm. She felt him tense under her grasp and then relax slowly.

"It's all right, Mark. Take your time. Nowhere else I gotta be right now."

"Can you call me M.J.?"

"Sure . . . M.J."

He met her gaze, his eyes frightened and detached, the horrors of that place all coming back to him. "You have any idea how many IED victims we treated in the OR?"

"Quite a few, I'd imagine."

"Got so you could recognize the mark of the damn things. They were crude mostly, homemade and packed with whatever shit the damn insurgents could stick into them. No two victims were alike but the wounds were always, *always*, a jagged mess. But Donkey, like I said, had been cut clean in half, the wound half cauterized by the time I looked over at him. And my . . ." The kid couldn't say it, couldn't say "legs." "The wounds were clean and symmetrical. Even left and right. That sound like a crude bomb to you?"

"Not at all, M.J."

"No, it don't. Sounds like a shaped charge. Strictly American military ordnance."

"No chance the insurgents could've gotten their hands on a few?"

"If they did, Ranger, this was the only time I ever saw evidence of it. I don't think anybody else saw what I was seeing, even the doc who saved my life. It all slipped out of my head, lost in a morphine fog. But then it started coming back soon as they weaned me off. Tried to tell myself that it was something I'd conjured up from the shock, except the more my mind cleared, the more I was certain it was a shaped charge that had killed Donkey and blown my legs off."

"Donkey just being along for the ride."

The kid tilted his head to the side. "Didn't I tell you? He was working the same shift when they brought Kirkendale in. Donkey was the only one I told."

Caitlin kept looking at the kid for what seemed like a long time after that. Didn't need to write it down because it was something she was never going to forget.

"Have you told anyone else about this since you've been back, M.J.?"

"No, ma'am. Not even my counselor or PT—that's physical therapist. Didn't want either of them writing me up for a psyche evaluation."

Caitlin rose, the kid's eyes following her as she felt her BlackBerry buzz in her pocket. "You mind if I take this?"

Serles shook his head and Caitlin lifted the phone from her pocket, Cort Wesley Masters's number flashing in the ID box.

"Dylan's gone," Cort Wesley told her, before she had a chance to say hello.

12

Through the lobby's glass entry doors, Caitlin saw D. W. Tepper standing in the shade cast by the Intrepid building. She joined him outside in the early-spring heat and watched him stamp a cigarette out under his boot.

"Captain?" she said, stopping just short of him, something all wrong about his being here.

Tepper handed her a sheet of paper that was already dog-eared and smelled of tobacco. "This came in a few minutes after you left. No one else has seen it yet." And then, as if feeling the need to say more, "It's about your friend Masters."

Caitlin read the single-spaced type running nearly the whole page beneath Texas Department of Public Safety letterhead. The piece of paper shook in her hand, as if ruffled by the wind.

"This can't be right."

She looked up to see Tepper's weary eyes boring into her. "Maybe so. But it's gotta be handled all the same, Ranger. And that means by the book." Tepper stopped and looked down at his crushed cigarette, shaking his head. "I figured you deserved a heads-up."

"Masters just called me. His oldest son's missing."

She could see Tepper's expression tighten, the deep furrows seeming to fill in a bit. "We talking foul play?"

"Could be," Caitlin told him, elaborating no further as thoughts churned in her head. "I just don't know for sure yet."

Tepper smacked his lips, watched the piece of paper in her hand flapping about until she folded it back up. "Not a good idea you handling this, Ranger."

Caitlin stuffed the paper in her pocket, holding Tepper's gaze the whole time. "It is if you want to avoid bloodshed, sir."

PART TWO

They stood upon the western frontier like towers of strength.
They fought whatever came in the shape of a foe to the Lone Star
flag, no matter what the disparity in numbers.
                                   —*The Austin Daily Statesman*, 1874

13

MIDLAND, TEXAS; THE PRESENT

"Latest arrivals are here, Mal," the voice of Jed Kean told Malcolm Arno over his cell phone that doubled as a walkie-talkie.

Arno rose from his desk, an exact replica of his dead father's since the original had been confiscated by the FBI and never returned. That was back when the Church of the Redeemer had been based on a beautiful stretch of land not far from this very spot. But the government had seized that too and sold it off after charging his father with tax evasion and dumping all his worldly possessions for pennies on the dollar to raise what they falsely claimed he owed them.

Arno was bigger than his father, broader too. The Church of the Redeemer was dead and gone all right. From its grave, though, had risen the group Arno had named the Patriot Sun, perfectly fitting for the circumstances of its background and founding. It hadn't been the scope of Max Arno's vision that had ultimately gotten him killed by a Texas Ranger, it was the lack of vision. He simply hadn't gone far enough, probably because the times hadn't called for it.

But these did. Simple as that.

Malcolm Arno came out from behind his desk in the Midland complex's main office building. Spread out over the rest of his four-hundred-acre spread were expansive quarters for his men and their families, training facilities, an armory, athletic facilities, farm and grazing fields, shops, stores, a meeting hall that doubled as a church, even a movie theater. Arno had done it all on his own, picking up where his father had left off and then some. The seizure of Maxwell Arno's possessions and property had left Malcolm penniless, a thirteen-year-old boy named a ward of the state and sentenced to life in a series of foster homes before ultimately landing in a juvenile detention facility. It was there, while he lay awake at night amid the stench of boy sweat, stale farts, and unwashed clothes, that he began planning for the day that was now within his reach. Not the specifics, mind you, just the broad parameters of a new world that would exceed even his father's vision as it excised the very forces that had destroyed him.

Located on the city's outskirts, and far from view of the buildings stretching for the clouds on Midland's skyline, the Patriot Sun had purchased the abandoned land of a mothballed air force base from the government for a princely, eight-figure sum in keeping with Texas real estate values. There wasn't much left but crumbling pavement, scrub, and dilapidated buildings bracketed by shut-down oil fields with their rusted derricks still in place. Arno had gutted it all and erected a fortress encampment in its place, both self-contained and defensible; lessons learned from his father's mistakes at the Church of the Redeemer.

When they fled through the old root cellar, his father promised Malcolm they'd be coming back to reclaim what was theirs. They'd bide their time and grow stronger, he said. The Church of the Redeemer was just too far ahead of its time. The country wasn't ready for them yet.

But it was ready now.

Malcolm Arno stepped into the dry scorching heat and walked along the cobblestone path inlaid amid the luscious grass fed by underground sprinklers. He'd brought in the same Israeli scientists who'd made a paradise out of parts of the Negev Desert to do the same here in the arid plains of West Texas. The buildings had a rough, unfinished hue about them, their simplicity belying the bulletproof glass and reinforced walls that could help the compound withstand even the most concentrated attack. The complex was also outfitted with a series of massive generators that could supply uninterrupted power for weeks at a time.

The steady hum of air-conditioning compressors cooling the class-rooms, meeting and training centers, living quarters, and offices sounded like music to Arno, testament to all he had built. The complex grew much of its own food and raised both live- and feedstock that were slaughtered right on the premises for meat. Only thing Arno cared about was being able to hole up here a long time if it came to that. Beat back anybody the State of Texas could throw at him, Rangers included. Succeed where his father had failed.

He continued on toward the Intake Center, passing the fully stocked medical clinic behind which sat the single building on the grounds that was guarded twenty-four hours a day. Only Malcolm Arno's most trusted advisers, captains of the Patriot Sun, knew the truth of what lay behind those walls. The many who worshipped him, the few who truly understood him, the media who tried to explain him had no clue of that building's contents or purpose. The strange sounds that often emanated from within its double-thick concrete walls were ignored by the residents, Arno's minions who accepted his word as dogma because he spoke for them. Offered them a voice amid a country that had stopped listening to their anger and protestations. This world was their refuge, their solace from that which had disowned and disavowed them by losing sight of all that was good and right. This world was their hope, just as it represented the hopes of millions more like them.

A man who looked as wide as a beer keg and as tall as a telephone pole stood at the entrance to the Intake Center, his shadow thrown back against the door it nearly equaled in scope. At six-foot-two, Arno was only four inches shorter than the bigger man but only half as broad seemingly. This in spite of the fact that he had begun a ritual of push-ups and pull-ups to both pass the time in juvie and toughen himself up to the threats and attacks of the boys who thought they ran the place.

Jed Kean's jet-black hair was thick and greased back, which made Arno run a hand through the thin locks he combed straight forward to better disguise the gaps in his scalp. Jed's father, a member of the Church of the Redeemer, had finally taken a sixteen-year-old Arno in to live with his family. From that point, he and Jed had been like brothers and Jed had stood by his side every step along the path not just to reclaim the Reverend Max Arno's legacy but also to exceed it.

He had joined Arno on the endless road of revival meetings and talks before groups that still displayed the Confederate flag. Kean had been with him in dark, dingy basements where he spoke to men sitting in folding chairs amid clouds of cigarette smoke and stale air that stank of mold and sweat. Arno building his base from the ground up, laying his foundation, learning to speak for a forgotten and disregarded segment of America. The building of funds came slowly, starting with a simple passing of a hat that came back empty as often as not. But the attention garnered was priceless and had led directly to the windfall that had allowed the Patriot Sun to be. Kean was also one of the few to be intimately aware of those details.

"You're gonna be real happy with this batch, Mal," Kean said, grinning. "Cream of the crop and I don't use the phrase lightly."

The big man led him through the door of the Intake Center and down a short hallway that opened into a single waiting room. Three Mexican girls sat inside on chairs, all between fifteen and sixteen just brimming with potential.

"Once we get 'em cleaned up, they'll be the best ones yet," said Kean.

Arno moved his eyes from one to the next and back again. "I do believe you're right on that account," he agreed, holding his gaze on the one he'd already decided to take first.

"Doc's checking out the fourth girl right now," Kean told him. "But trust me, boss, these three are the pick of the litter. Goddamn sugar plum fairies dropped down from the sky. Don't speak a word of English neither."

"News ain't all good, Jed. Man we sent to Galveston missed his chance with that judge."

Arno watched the big man stiffen, the color seeming to bleed from his face. "Told you to let me handle it."

"Might just do that, Jed, after I sit in with the doc for a time. Make sure he doesn't miss anything."

"Extra pair of eyes is always a good thing."

"Just get yourself ready to travel, Jed, and program your GPS for Galveston."

14

Cort Wesley Masters was waiting at the curb when Caitlin screeched her SUV into the drive set before the Thomas C. Clark High School. He was inside before she'd come to a complete stop, saying "Let's get going" with enough heat steaming off him to singe the upholstery.

"What the hell happened, Cort Wesley?" she asked, driving off with him still working the seat belt assembly into place.

"Dylan ran away, that's what happened. I'm here for a meet with the principal and he took off in my truck while I'm fighting to keep him enrolled. Learner's permit and all."

"Keep him enrolled?"

"Guess you don't know everything now, do you?"

"Might help if you'd tell me."

"Meaning you'd have to be around for me to do so, 'stead of gunning down bad guys north of the border as well as south now."

"Word travels fast."

"I've been keeping in regular touch with your captain."

"Get back to Dylan."

"Just drive me over to the nearest rental place and you can go about your business, Ranger." Cort Wesley studied her briefly, then resumed. "It's clear you got something else on your mind and I don't want to be a bother here."

Caitlin's thought of the single sheet of paper folded up in her pocket and dialed her emotions down a notch, focusing on the matter at hand. "Hell with that, Cort Wesley. My business is Dylan right now."

"This is between me and him, Ranger."

"Then consider me your chauffeur." Caitlin hesitated at the next intersection. "Where we going exactly?"

"Head south on the interstate. Some back roads after that."

"Mexico?"

"Mexico."

"You call the cops?" Caitlin asked him.

Cort Wesley looked like he couldn't believe she'd even posed the question. "I called you."

"What about Dylan?"

"His phone's going straight to voice mail. Turned off so you can't locate him by GPS."

"What kind of head start's he got?"

Cort Wesley checked his watch. "An hour now. Bit more maybe."

"Guess we both know where he's headed."

"You casting blame on me in that statement?"

"Why, 'cause you never took him down there to see Maria Lopez like you promised?"

A year before, Dylan had saved the life of a runaway Mexican girl named Maria Lopez, who'd been part of a group of kidnapped girls being ferried to a worksite outside San Antonio. Problem was the man he'd saved her from turned out to be behind four hundred serial murders of women across the Texas-Mexico border, embroiling both the Texas Rangers and Cort Wesley Masters in a battle with drug cartels and a renegade Mexican colonel. The embroilment ended with a host of bodies being downed and Dylan emerging with a chip on his shoulder he dared the world to knock off. Facing down one of the deadliest men ever born, as close to the spawn of Satan as the world would ever see, had imbued the boy with a bravado and hardness that had come to define too many of his actions and thinking. That attitude had made school an afterthought and had led inevitably, Caitlin knew, to today's actions.

"I've been busy too, in case you haven't noticed," Cort Wesley told her.

"South of the border, right?"

"Why you looking at me that way?"

"What way is that?"

"You got something to say, just say it."

"I think you should have stayed clear of Mexico," Caitlin said, the words feeling like ground glass in her mouth. "You're not exactly popular with the *federalés*, one Major Batista in particular."

"You ever know something like that to stop me?"

"No, that might actually take some honest thought."

Cort Wesley stopped looking at the road ahead of them and turned to glare at her. "You know what takes some thought? Figuring out how many Americans still got legitimate business south of the border they're too scared to conduct given the danger involved."

"So they pay you to make them feel safe."

"Where's this headed, Ranger?"

"You kill anybody in Mexico?"

Caitlin watched him freeze up, his features locking as his chest stopped its quick motions in rhythm with his nervous breathing. She drew the folded-up piece of paper from the pocket of her jeans.

"You're wanted for murder down there, Cort Wesley. And I'm supposed to bring you in."

15

San Antonio; the present

Cort Wesley crushed the piece of paper she'd handed him into a ball without reading it. "What is this exactly?"

"Letter to the Mexican authorities from Austin saying the State of Texas is going to comply with their extradition request."

"Simple as that?"

"Why don't you tell me how simple it is?"

Cort Wesley looked away from her and squeezed the balled-up piece of paper tighter in his fist. "What happened down there had nothing to do with the services I was providing businessmen."

"Well, it had to do with something."

Cort Wesley rotated his gaze between Caitlin and the road ahead. "Shouldn't you be turning around?"

"Be a good idea if I did. Somehow I don't think driving into a country where you're wanted for murder's a very good idea."

Silence settled between them, Caitlin deciding to wait for Cort Wesley to make the next move.

"Man I killed was a runner for the Juárez cartel," he said finally.

"Simple as that?"

"Not really, no."

"So why don't you explain the complexities to me?"

Cort Wesley returned his focus to the road ahead. "We gotta take a right just up ahead."

"Get off the main roads."

"That's the idea."

"Just in case anybody else is fixing to track you down?"

"Because this is the way Dylan would have gone," Cort Wesley told her.

"This is the route you and your dad used to run stolen appliances across the border," Caitlin realized, once her SUV's tires thumped off the main road.

"Used stuff nobody was gonna miss anyway."

"Except for the pieces that disappeared from new construction in those gated communities."

"Took the gate once too."

Something in Cort Wesley's tone made Caitlin realize something. "You told Dylan about those days, didn't you?"

Cort Wesley's eyes narrowed ahead into the blinding sunlight. "This road leads to a border crossing my dad and I used to use." He looked over at her, his expression bled of emotion, his mind somewhere else entirely. "It was always Dylan's favorite part of the story."

Caitlin squeezed the wheel tighter. "Tell me something, Cort Wesley. You ever think about keeping your promise to take him to visit that girl?"

"Yeah, plenty of times." Cort Wesley took the deepest sigh Caitlin could ever remember, sounding more like a crackling sob in the end. "But I couldn't, Ranger. I couldn't."

"Why's that?"

"'Cause Maria Lopez was killed two months ago."

16

It felt to Caitlin like someone had kicked her in the gut. She'd gotten bad news before, plenty of times, but never something that came through unfiltered on a direct line to a place deep inside herself very few could make stir. She looked from Cort Wesley back to the road, squeezing the steering wheel so tight the leather wrapping squeaked.

"Car accident," Cort Wesley continued a bit farther on, how much Caitlin couldn't say. "Maria and her parents were all in the front seat of her father's truck, none wearing seat belts when a car running from the police struck them broadside."

"Two months ago and you didn't say a word?"

"Dylan loses his mother two years back, what am I supposed to tell him?"

Caitlin spun her gaze on Cort Wesley and held it so long she nearly veered off the road. "I wasn't talking about him, I was talking about me."

"Some things you gotta bear alone. That sound familiar?"

"No."

"It should, Ranger. You've said as much to me maybe a hundred times. 'Lone Wolf Caitlin' they ought to call you, the way you keep walking away from anything that can take you from your guns."

Caitlin swallowed hard, stung by her oversight. "You know why we get along so well?"

"Do we?"

"Figure of speech. It's 'cause we both like living in a vacuum while the world keeps trying to suck us out."

"I've got no idea what you're talking about."

"Bearing our pain alone. Must run in the family. My father was the same damn way. Unlike my granddad, he didn't relish telling me his tales of being a Ranger, all the gunplay and the like. There was only one time I pried the whole story of something out of him and that was different."

"Why?"

"Because I was there."

17

WEST TEXAS; 1990

"I need you in West Texas, Ranger," Ranger Assistant Commander Maurice Cook said to Jim Strong from across his desk at the State Capitol in Austin.

"My duffel's packed in my truck as always, Commander."

"Might need two since this assignment could keep you away for a time."

Jim waited for Cook to continue. He was a big man with thick forearms that kept him from buttoning the cuffs of his dress shirts. Cook was also one of the best-educated men who'd ever served the Rangers in an executive capacity, boasting a law degree along with several others that all came with fancy initials. That education had helped him spearhead a move to restructure and streamline some of the Ranger hierarchy and, if rumor became fact, he'd soon be succeeding H. R. Block as Senior Ranger Captain, Chief of the Texas Rangers.

"Ever hear of the Church of the Redeemer?" Cook asked finally, his words slightly slurred by the pinch of tobacco packed between his cheek and gum.

"Yes, sir, and none of it good. Heard enough to figure that place is something just short of the devil's playground."

"Well, we're setting up a task force to see to the group's end on direct orders from the governor, and I'm assigning you to head it."

"I'd like to take D. W. Tepper with me if I could, sir."

"Son, you can take the Lord Jesus Christ Almighty Himself if it helps put the Reverend Maxwell Arno behind bars."

"He was my second choice, sir."

Cook grinned and rose to shake hands. He'd taken Jim Strong under his wing some years back and, as a result, Jim had found himself involved in some of the highest profile Ranger cases since the start of his career. He'd been dispatched to the Rio Grand Valley in 1966, four years after becoming a Ranger at the age of thirty, when the United Farm Workers struck for higher wages, setting off a firestorm of violence. He'd been on the front lines when a criminal named Fred Gomez Carrasco led inmates in an armed takeover of the Walls Unit, where Texas's most violent offenders were housed, in Huntsville State Prison in 1974. He'd been part of the Ranger team that secured the release of thirteen-year-old Amy McNeil in a bloody gunfight with her kidnappers in Alvarado in January of 1985.

Jim Strong might have been pushing sixty in 1990 but he looked ten years younger and acted twenty. He could still shoot with the best of them, and the craggy lines that had shown up on his brow and patches beginning to darken under his eyes did nothing to diminish the tight bend of his stare or the stature with which he carried himself. His father had died a few months before and his passing seemed to fill Jim with a renewed vigor, as if he was channeling the legendary Earl Strong and, by connection, had become the owner of Earl's famed exploits as well as his own. He'd married late in life and had his daughter, Caitlin, even later, testament to the fact that for Jim Strong life truly had begun at forty.

Cook let go of Jim's hand but held on to him with his stare. "Ranger, if half of what we hear about Arno and this church of his are true, we've got ourselves a genuine mess on our hands. Best to deal with it before the spill widens, and with these rumors of Arno stockpiling weapons, that spill could end up running red."

"Not on my watch, Commander."

Cook grinned, his lower lip drooping lower than the upper thanks to the Skoal wedged in there. "Report whenever you see fit. Anything you need, Austin will provide."

What Jim Strong needed most, though, was someone on the inside of the Church of the Redeemer, a group notorious for tightly screening its membership and maintaining vigilant security precautions against precisely what Jim was planning. Before leaving for Midland, he studied the list of the church members who worked outside the grounds and cross-matched the names with criminal complaints and convictions. Sure enough, Max Arno had been beyond cautious with his selection, but the name Beth Ann Killane popped up for an altogether different reason: her son Danny was due to start his sentence at the Abilene juvenile detention facility in three weeks time for shooting two classmates with a pistol at his high school, located between the towns of Midland and Odessa.

The fact that the victims were Latino would-be gangbangers who'd chosen to bully Danny in order to prove their toughness made some impression on the court, but not enough to prevent Danny from being sentenced to a two-year stretch. Because his was a violent crime, he'd be placed with boys even worse than the bangers who'd terrorized him. Latinos and blacks for whom juvie was a joke and rehabilitation was an opportunity to make your bones before you even returned to the outside. Kill or maim a fellow inmate and they could get their gang tats the day of their release instead of waiting months to be initiated.

Beth Ann Killane, Danny's mother, was a church member who worked at Pancake Alley, a coffee shop off I-20 in Odessa—pretty much an institution in those parts. So as soon as he hit town, Jim Strong began showing up there for breakfast every morning, Stetson in hand, cinco-pesos badge pinned to his lapel, and model 1911 .45 holstered on his hip. He made sure to exchange conversation and small talk with her, lingering well after his third or fourth cup of coffee was drained and morning paper long folded over in the hope the opportunity arose to enlist her help.

Beth Ann seemed to be growing more edgy by the day, the clock ticking ever closer to her son's incarceration that would either kill or break him. One morning a week into Jim's routine, she was refilling his cup when the pot of coffee dropped from her grasp and exploded on the floor, dousing his pant legs with scalding liquid.

"I'm a mess," she moaned, soaking up the coffee with a combination of paper towels and dishrags. "I'm just a mess."

"Sit down across from me and calm yourself, Beth Ann," Jim said in as soothing a voice as he could imagine. His own wife had been gone for going on eleven years now and he'd learned to live without a woman's company in any but the most distant circumstances. Beth Ann Killane smelled of coffee grounds right then, but most mornings she smelled of lilac-scented body lotion and flowery shampoo. If she wasn't so sad and did more with her hair than just shampoo it, she'd be quite attractive, as the pictures he'd seen of her boy attested.

"My break doesn't start for another twenty minutes."

Jim Strong looked around the mostly empty diner and cast the owner a nod, his eyes saying the rest of what needed to be said. "It's been extended today."

She took the chair across from him.

"Now why don't you tell me what's eating you up so, ma'am?"

The story of her son spilled out like somebody broke off the spigot. It flowed nonstop for twenty minutes, every detail, nuance, and tragic turn. Beth Ann finally broke down at the end of a tale in which she laid the blame for her son's plight squarely at her own feet, hands ringing her face to save it from dropping all the way to the table. "My poor boy, my poor boy . . ."

Jim Strong reached across the table and laid a hand on her arm. Her skin felt hot and moist, the hairs standing up straight.

"I could look into your boy's case, if you want."

"It's not good, I'm afraid," he said, when she sat down across from him the following morning. Watching Beth Ann Killane deflate, her hope draining like the contents of an air mattress, made him feel as low as it got. But he was a Ranger with a job to do. "Your son's case is ironclad. He shot those boys down and the jury reckoned it was justifiable only to a point. Now I do believe the fact that jury was nine out of twelve Hispanic gives you grounds for appeal if—"

"We gave up that right based on the prosecution agreeing to put him in a juvenile facility instead of Huntsville."

"Oh," said Jim Strong as if he didn't know that when, of course, he did.

"So there's nothing you can do."

"No, ma'am."

"Nothing at all?"

Jim held her gaze. In the thin light of Pancake Alley, thanks to a number of roof panel–covered bulbs that had blown, her face looked darker in the places where tears had streaked it. "Well, that depends." He lowered his voice and slid his chair around closer to her, looking up. "See, there might be something I can do for Danny, but it would depend on you doing something for the Rangers. After he looked into the matter, my captain mentioned that you're a member of the Church of the Redeemer."

"I am," she said.

"There's no other way to put this, so I'm just gonna say it direct." Jim paused, waiting for Beth Ann's eyes to hold his before resuming. "If you were willing to provide the Rangers some information on the church and the Reverend Maxwell Arno, I believe my captain would be able to intervene on your son's behalf."

Beth Ann stiffened. "The church has been good to me, Jim."

"I'm sure it has. What this comes down to is a choice, Beth Ann: that church or your boy. I wish it weren't that simple but it is, since whoever comes out of Abilene in two years will bear no resemblance whatsoever to Danny if he walks out at all."

Beth Ann broke down, the tears streaming down her face beyond a napkin's ability to even slow them.

"I apologize for the harshness of my words, but you need to hear this straight," Jim told her, while she was still weak, "so you can make your choice with a clear head." Then he reached over and took her hand in his, something he'd neither planned nor expected. "You tell us what we need to know about Reverend Arno and his Church of the Redeemer, and I will pick up your son's unconditional pardon, signed by the governor, in Austin myself."

Beth Ann looked at him, hope sifting through the mist coating her eyes.

"Here's the way I look at things," Jim told her, really meaning what he was about to say. "You can get yourself another church, Beth Ann, but you can't get yourself another boy."

18

"Truth is, I don't know much of the rest of the story," Caitlin finished.

"As I recall, this Killane woman was the only victim of the Ranger raid on the compound," Cort Wesley told her.

"She was at that."

Cort Wesley nodded, leaving things there. "What about Beth Ann Killane's boy, Danny?"

"Never served a single day in Abilene. And, true to his word, Jim Strong picked up the papers himself in Austin."

"Why am I not surprised?" Cort Wesley was looking at Caitlin differently than he had been. "You got any idea how much the boys miss you when you go off on one of your spaz outs?"

"Spaz outs?"

"That's what Luke calls them," he told her, referring to his twelve-year-old son.

Caitlin realized she hadn't thought of Luke at all since hearing the news about Dylan. "Where is he? Who's watching him?"

"Some neighbor friends of ours. Their boy's the only one who can stand up to Luke in those damn video games." He stopped, stiffening a bit before he resumed. "So what happens, you deliver me to the folks in Austin on this extradition beef?"

"You wanna give me a reason why I shouldn't?"

"You haven't heard the whole story yet."

"Why don't you tell me?"

"Would it matter?"

"To me, yes."

"But not the folks in Austin."

"Extradition request came from the governor of the province in Mexico personally."

"I must've cut into his profit margin."

Cort Wesley looked back toward the world beyond the windshield. The dry desert roads had left a layer of dust across the windows, speckling his face where the sun hit it and giving it the look of dark blips amid the light.

"Dylan blamed me for not giving him Maria Lopez's letters or sending his," he continued. "Started mailing them from the post office on his own. I gave the mailman a bottle of Jack Daniel's so he wouldn't leave them in the mailbox when they got returned."

"So now he's heading to Mexico to find a girl who's dead and a man wanted for murder down there is chasing him." Caitlin started to shake her head, then stopped. The balled-up piece of paper was lying by Cort Wesley's boot atop the carpeted floor mat on the passenger side. Something played at the edges of her consciousness, something she couldn't quite see yet. "Who was this Juárez drug dealer, Cort Wesley?"

"Doesn't matter now."

"The hell it doesn't."

"Telling you's not gonna make this extradition order go away."

"Maybe I'd just like to hear the rest of the story."

Cort Wesley cast his gaze back out the windshield, not really seeing anything. "I killed him because I couldn't take Dylan down there to visit Maria Lopez."

"I don't think I follow."

Cort Wesley swung back toward her. "Yeah, you do, Ranger."

And then Caitlin realized, something cold wrapping around her insides and tightening. "Tell me I got this wrong, Cort Wesley."

All emotion slid off his expression and he held her gaze for what seemed like a very long time before responding. "That drug dealer never would've served a day in jail for killing Maria and her parents in that car crash, Ranger. I didn't figure I had much choice."

19

Dylan watched the last of the sun sink behind the mountains, feeling suddenly tense and scared. He'd been driving for twelve hours straight, no stops other than a pair of bathroom breaks and one to get a burrito and soda. He'd turned off the main road south toward Matehuala when construction slowed traffic to a crawl, his dad's truck climbing into the Sierra Madre Oriental, where a misty shroud from the colder temperatures at this elevation swallowed the road and made every twist of the wheel a dangerous proposition.

Up until that point, for a good stretch of the way, it seemed he'd been driving into the sun, feeling its rays soaking him through the windshield. The heat dissipated as it sank behind the mountains only to reappear when he ascended a narrow two-lane up the Sierra Madre. From there he watched the last of its rays bleed amber downward, only to disappear before reaching the ground. Then the truck entered the soupy mist of the mountains that swallowed all light. The temperature seemed to drop twenty degrees, the last of the day sucked into the ether of some transitional realm between life and death.

For a good part of the drive, Dylan imagined Maria in the passenger seat next to him and spoke to her out loud, alternating between English and Spanish.

"My dad's gonna knock me silly for running off like this," he said, picturing himself taking her hand in his and squeezing tight, "but I know it's worth it. I haven't been able to think of anything else for months now and I don't really want to. I can't wait to fall asleep so I can dream about you, then I hate waking up 'cause you're not there anymore."

Dylan swallowed hard, a thick lump having wedged itself in his throat.

"When I used to babysit my brother, he and this friend of his used to grab my arms and pull me in opposite directions. That's what I feel like now. I love my dad, girl. Can't say it out loud to him, of course, but

I love him all the same and I hate running off like this. But I know he'll understand, 'long as I don't mash up his truck or something."

Dylan smiled at that, looking toward Maria and sighing deeply when she wasn't there, as silence reclaimed the cab.

The world finally cleared when the road dropped into Altiplano with only a straight route remaining through the state capital of San Luis Potosí before he reached Matehuala. Maria had written him all about the city in her letters, so much so that Dylan felt he knew the place already. Her parents had moved there shortly after her return because work was more plentiful. Her mother had ended up getting a job as the cashier at a car wash, while her father was hired as assistant chef at a restaurant adjacent to Matehuala's tree-covered central plaza. He guessed the city of 78,000 was fairly typical by Mexican standards for its beautifully restored buildings and period architecture. Maria had written that she liked Matehuala a lot more than San Antonio and the bigger Mexican cities she'd seen, wrote that she liked the fact that it was quiet and nobody knew who she was or what she'd gone through up north. She never told him anything about the other kids, boys or girls, and Dylan read each of her letters dozens of times.

He knew she was doing well in school because the last few letters had been penned, at least partially, in English. Dylan figured she spoke it a lot better now, leading him to redouble his efforts at learning Spanish in school. His dad was all over his case about bunking class and hanging out with his friends, but Cort Wesley Masters didn't get the fact that he was consumed by his thoughts about Maria. Sitting in classrooms was a portrait in misery, impossible for him to stop his mind from wandering to her and feeling the inevitable stirring in his jeans.

His friends made it tolerable, understood what he was going through. Still, he hadn't told a single one of them what he was doing because he'd made the decision on an impulse that confused him even now. Confused him because he'd just run out of the school, the boots Caitlin Strong had given him clip-clopping across the pavement and his backpack shifting back and forth from its slung position over his shoulder. His gym clothes were stuffed inside along with a pair of sneakers that became a godsend during the long drive, for which God had not made boots.

"I know Caitlin can track me by my cell phone," he said out loud again, words aimed toward the empty passenger seat. "So I left mine back at school and bought a throwaway kind. Don't know why I bothered since you don't even have a phone. I thought about calling Caitlin a few times to explain myself and ask her to do likewise to my dad, who's likely tearing down walls somewhere right now he's so pissed."

Dylan smiled at the image, then felt his eyes moisten with tears and lapsed back into silence. He knew his dad well enough to be sure Cort Wesley Masters would be coming after him, figuring he'd given Dylan the lay of the same land the boy could cover in his sleep. But Dylan already had his spot to cross the border picked out, and it was nowhere near any of the ones his dad and grandfather had used in their smuggling operation in times long past.

Half the drive south was spent fighting the lump in his throat and the urge to turn the truck around and head home. Every time he got as far as looking out for a spot in the shoulder wide enough to handle the swing, he thought of Maria and knew he'd come too far to do anything but keep going. Too far after ten miles, after fifty, and after a hundred. Too far in his mind from the moment he'd climbed up behind the wheel of his dad's truck and gunned the engine with the spare key attached to his ring.

Still, the lump was there, along with a stubborn temperature needle that kept climbing and climbing. Dylan ended up shutting down the AC, leaving his jeans matted to the upholstery and his long black hair feeling like a damp dishrag making a puddle on the kitchen counter. The more he tried pushing it back off his face, the more it strayed forward, heating up his skin and moistening the shirt collar it seemed to steam bake.

He stopped to get gas and snacks at a one-pump station on the outskirts of Altiplano and, having not slowed to grab cash in Texas, stuck his ATM card in an old machine with dust sandblasted into its steel. The machine wouldn't work, then wouldn't spit his card back, and the rail-thin woman inside behind the counter was no help at all, so Dylan stormed out, slamming the screen door behind him with all of eight bucks left in his pocket.

Back on the road, he greeted the first signs for Matehuala with the rise of tears to his eyes. He swabbed them with a forearm shed of his long-sleeve shirt, but it was too wet to do much good.

What the fuck have I done here?

The stubborn rashness of his thinking had reached a point where it seemed like somebody else had been doing it for him. Dylan slowed the truck through the steamy night, palmed his throwaway cell phone, and thumbed the keypad. Just thinking of dialing his dad gave him shivers and sent rocks sliding through his mouth. Caitlin Strong would be with his dad by now for sure, the two of them likely hot on his trail. His head start was worth something, though not very much. It wasn't like they didn't know exactly where he was headed; Maria's letters had come with return addresses, after all, and Matehuala wasn't hard to find. And just what was he supposed to do with no ATM card now? Eight bucks wasn't going to get him much farther than this.

Without his own cell phone in hand, Dylan had to reconstruct Caitlin's number in his head, feeling his heart start to hammer his chest as he pressed it out.

20

MEXICO; THE PRESENT

"Don't tell my dad it's me, okay?" Caitlin listened to Dylan say.

"I hear you, sir."

"If you do, I'll hang up. I'll swear it."

"I never disobey an order from a superior," Caitlin said, Cort Wesley driving now and busying himself with the road.

"I messed things up good, Caitlin."

"We've all been guilty of that from time to time. Mexico seems to bring it out in folks."

"Like you torturing those drug mules who shot your partner?"

"I don't recall ever telling you any such thing."

"My dad did. You sure he can't hear me?"

"Not a lick, Captain."

"He told me when I asked him why you quit the Rangers for a while. Made me promise not to tell that he did."

"Guess you just broke it. Now where you wanna meet once I'm back home?"

"I'm somewhere in Altiplano. I want this over, Caitlin. I want to go home."

Caitlin heard Dylan sniffle on the other end, imagined him swiping a hand across his nose. "We can arrange for that much I'm sure."

"I could drive on another hour, two maybe. Meet up with you in Matehuala. It's where you're headed anyway."

Cort Wesley shot her a glance at that, his eyes telling her he'd figured things out. "Is that Dylan, 'cause if it is . . ."

Caitlin held a hand up to keep him quiet and away from the phone. "Do you trust me, Dylan?"

"My dad onto us?"

"Do you trust me?" she repeated, instead of answering him.

"More than anyone."

"Then just stay put wherever you are and let us come to you. You need to trust me, that I'll explain everything as soon as I get there."

A deep sigh filled the line, followed by a clacking Caitlin figured was Dylan clicking his teeth together, a habit of his for as long as she'd known him. Cort Wesley kept glancing over, glaring at the phone clearly ready to snatch it from her grasp.

"All right, Caitlin," Dylan said finally. "I'll pull over in the next parking lot."

"Someplace with light. And people."

"I know the drill. I'm not stupid."

"Think I've figured that out by now."

"I don't wanna talk to my dad right now, but tell him I'm okay."

"I will."

"Caitlin?"

"I'm here, son."

"Don't let him shoot me."

She smiled in spite of herself, the gesture seeming to relax Cort Wesley slightly. "That's a promise."

Another pause followed.

"Whoa, what's this?"

"Dylan?"

"Something's going on up ahead."

"Say that again."

"Something's happening up ahead. Like an accident or something."

Caitlin felt herself tensing, straining forward against the bonds of the passenger seat's shoulder harness. "What?" She was conscious of Cort Wesley's slackened gaze tightening again, electricity dancing off his skin, the SUV slowing involuntarily.

"Couple cars look like they been in an accident. No, a truck and a car. I gotta slow down."

Both Jim and Earl Strong had told her you never know where a feeling comes from but to never disregard one. "No!"

"Huh?"

"Get the hell out of there! You hear me? Get the hell out of there!"

A pause.

"Dylan?"

"There's a truck behind me. I'm boxed in."

"Shit!"

Cort Wesley grabbed for the phone. "Lemme talk to my son, goddamnit!"

Caitlin jerked her BlackBerry away from him, pushing herself against the window. "Get your ass out of there! You hear me, boy?"

"There's men coming toward the truck. I think they're cops. They're waving me out, Caitlin."

"Jesus Christ . . ."

"Give me the goddamn phone!" Cort Wesley demanded, veering the SUV onto the shoulder, twisting it to a gravel-rattling halt. He flailed at Caitlin, iron grip locking on her wrist.

"Lock your doors, son!" she said, not about to let the phone leave her ear.

"They're locked."

"Pull a U-ey, whatever it takes. Just get your ass out of there!"

"I can't!"

"All right, tell me where you are. Be as specific as you can."

"I don't know the name of the road. It slopes out of the Sierra Madre, maybe halfway between Altiplano and Matehuala. They're at the door. I think I'm—"

Crack!

The sound of glass shattering split her eardrum, sounding impossibly loud.

"Dylan!"

A thump followed, Dylan's cell phone hitting the truck floor or passenger seat.

"Dylan!"

Then came the struggle, the screams. And nothing.

21

Mexico; the present

They found Cort Wesley's truck dumped in a marsh, the shit stripped out of it. Mexican state cops, mixing with locals out of Altiplano, milled about in the muck and shook the mud from their shoes and pant legs. They were there when Caitlin and Cort Wesley finally pulled up to the scene after a miserable two hours spent winding their way through the mountain-heavy, mist-laden darkness, trying to find the road on which Dylan had ended up.

Caitlin had called Captain Tepper and he, in turn, had called the Department of Public Safety, who had reached out to the police in both Altiplano and Matehuala. She harbored few expectations anything would come of it, so she was frankly surprised when Tepper called her back with news of the truck being found another thirty minutes from their current position.

"You should've let me talk to him," was all Cort Wesley could say as his feet churned through the muck.

Caitlin let him have his rage and studied the scene around her. The *federalés*, Mexico's infamous national police force, were on the scene as well, in the process by all accounts of taking control of the investigation while the local cops continued to linger near the truck.

A *federalé* captain approached Caitlin halfway between her SUV and the truck, seeming to ignore Cort Wesley. "I am Captain Sanchez," he said in excellent English. "I'm afraid there's no sign of your son."

"He's my son," Cort Wesley said, before Caitlin could say anything at all.

"And who are you?"

"I'm a Texas Ranger," Caitlin interrupted, flashing her identification. "I came down with the boy's father here to bring him home."

"We'd like to see the truck, if you don't mind," Cort Wesley cut in, his feet disappearing as he waded through the muck toward it.

Sanchez backpedaled to keep his pace, eyes shifting between Cort Wesley and Caitlin as if to determine which he should be addressing.

"What are your people telling you, Captain?" she asked Sanchez.

"Skid marks up on the road indicate the boy lost control of the truck. Ended up down here in the ditch after banging it up a bit."

"That how you explain the broken driver's side window?" Cort Wesley pushed.

"The door's jammed. The boy could have knocked the window out to escape."

They reached the truck, both Caitlin and Cort Wesley gazing inside the cab.

Cort Wesley grabbed the rubber sill and squeezed, not seeming to care about the glass fragments digging into his skin. "That how the glass ended up inside, instead of out, Captain?"

"What the boy's father means to say," Caitlin picked up, "is that we were in touch with the boy just before he was taken."

"Did you say *taken*?" the captain asked her.

Caitlin nodded. "He was describing what sounded like a staged accident before him, this truck here getting boxed in from the rear."

Sanchez didn't look convinced. "You believe he was *kidnapped*?"

"We do."

Caitlin eased up next to Cort Wesley so Sanchez could see her tracing a neat line over the air even with the smashed window's perimeter.

"See how there are no shards left attached to the framing?" She waited to make sure Sanchez did. "That tells me they used a special tool made with a conical-shaped hardened steel head to crack out the entire window. A random attacker would've likely used a simple hammer or rock. Whoever did this has done it before."

Sanchez traced the line her finger had made with his eyes, still not looking convinced. "You believe this boy was targeted?"

"As a kid driving a truck alone through the middle of Mexico, yeah, I think he was targeted for his vulnerability. That a recurring MO in these parts?"

"Excuse me?"

"MO—modus operandi. Like a pattern."

"Kidnapping?"

"Kidnapping."

"No more than in your American cities."

"This isn't a city, Captain."

"But the boy was on his way to one, *Señorita* Ranger."

"Cut the crap, will you?" Cort Wesley snapped, glaring at the captain with a pair of dark eyes glistening with moisture. "We all know what happened here and my guess is you, or somebody you know, knows exactly where my son can be found. So just tell us, or call whoever you have to so we can go pick him up and get ourselves home."

The quiet assurance of Cort Wesley's voice was as unsettling as it was chilling.

"Why would you think I'd know such a thing, *señor*?" Sanchez asked him.

"Because *federalés* are corrupt as hell."

"Oh boy," Caitlin muttered.

"Not all of you, but plenty choose to pad their pockets with some look-the-other-way money in times like this." Cort Wesley leaned back inside the truck through the busted-out window glass and spotted some snack wrappers on the passenger seat and an unfinished soda, diluted by melted ice in a cup holder.

"My guess is they had a spotter wherever he picked up the food," Caitlin chimed in, before Cort Wesley did any further damage to their cause. "Man must've called in Dylan's location and general appearance. Maybe the spotter's face is on a security tape or somebody at the store will remember him. Either way that's your first clue."

"Second is to throw a stone at that group chewing cigarettes over there," Cort Wesley added, gesturing toward a smoke cloud that had formed atop a group of five stiff-spined officers. "Whoever it hits can likely tell us exactly who has my son."

"My superior is en route now, *señor*," Sanchez said dismissively. "You can voice your suggestions to him."

And he walked away, leaving Caitlin and Cort Wesley at the truck with the local police officers for want of a crime scene unit.

"I don't think this had anything to do with you," Caitlin said to him. "I think it was random."

"That scares me more, Ranger. Makes me wonder how I'm ever going to get him back. We've got lots of enemies down here."

"And a few friends, Cort Wesley. I get a few minutes, I'm gonna call one of them straightaway."

Cort Wesley gazed at his wrecked and stripped truck reflectively, perhaps picturing Dylan still behind the wheel. "What the hell was I thinking?"

"What, in not telling him the girl was dead or that you killed the man who did it?"

"Kid had a right to know," Cort Wesley said, not really answering her question. "That got lost somewhere in the equation." His eyes filled with self-loathing. "Me letting him write letters to her weeks after she's in the ground. Great fatherly work." Cort Wesley shook his head. "Could this night get any worse?"

Caitlin saw a pair of camouflage-colored SUVs pull to a halt on the road above the ditch and a host of men climb out in unison.

"Oh, shit . . ."

"What?"

"It just did."

22

"If it's not my old friend the Ranger," said the stout *federalé* major whose nametag identified him as BATISTA. He grinned. "Didn't I warn you never to return to Mexico again?"

Caitlin fought not to look back toward the shadows where Cort Wesley had retreated. "I'm here on a personal matter, Major."

"So I understand, el Rinche. But that does not change the terms on which I released you from custody last year in Juárez after you and your outlaw friend nearly destroyed the city."

The last time they'd met had been in the wake of what had become known as the Battle of Juárez, already reaching mythic stature among the common people of Mexico. Batista was most interested in the location of the man who'd made it all happen, the former Venezuelan assassin Colonel Guillermo Paz. Paz had a hefty price on his head in four countries, not the least of which was Mexico thanks to the drug gangs against which he'd gone to war and ultimately laid waste to.

"You know I'm still looking for the big man, Ángel de la Guarda, a legend to the people who don't know any better," Batista told her. "I know his real name is Guillermo Paz, an ex-colonel in President Chavez's secret police. They say he's starting to build his own secret army somewhere in Mexico now."

"Then if I were you," said Caitlin, "I'd want to be somewhere else when he finishes."

Batista grinned at her insinuation. "There's no place for vigilantes in my country, any more than there is in yours." A smirk fell over his features. "Then again, that's what the Texas Ranger code is based upon, *sí*?"

"Just how bad do you want to find out, Major?" Caitlin asked him.

Cort Wesley fought himself to remain silent through the exchange, relieved Batista hadn't noticed him or made the connection yet. Even from ten feet away, the oily stench washing off Batista was so strong it nearly made him gag. A combination of dried sweat, unwashed clothes, and something that reminded Cort Wesley of cooking grease. He turned away to distract himself, looking off toward the local Mexican cops who continued to battle each other for who could blast the most tar into his lungs. One met his gaze and looked away; didn't just look away, but actually shuffled farther back amid the group with fear evident through the smoke rising from his lips.

Cort Wesley angled his eyes to trail the cop, taking all of him in. Noticing he was wearing slip-on, ankle-high boots instead of the standard variety his *compadres* wore laced over their trousers.

Dylan's boots, the pair Caitlin had gotten the boy for his fifteenth birthday from Allen's Boots in Austin. She'd made the drive to pick them out, not trusting the Internet.

And then, before he could think further, Cort Wesley felt himself in motion.

Batista never noticed Cort Wesley slip past him, and by the time Caitlin did it was too late. Before the cops could react, he was on all six of them with a flurry of blows so quick and blinding that the smoke cloud barely moved. He whirled into the cops in a fashion more befitting a ballet, unleashing moves too fast for the mind to make record of. His hands swept around, dovetailing and curling back for strikes that blended from one to another. His feet whipsawed, slicing into knees and kicking out legs. The cops were standing and then they weren't, all left writhing in the mud as Cort Wesley stooped over one and yanked off his boots, Dylan's boots, in the last moment before the *federalés* converged and swallowed him.

Caitlin pushed past Batista, finding herself in the midst of the fray with no memory of passing any distance. Shielding Cort Wesley as best she could. Saw gunmetal flashing in the spray of stilled headlights from the road above and came up just short of drawing her SIG, having the presence of mind to consider the utter disaster a gunfight here and now would yield.

The best she could do was keep herself between Cort Wesley and the *federalés* so their bullets would hit her instead, the move forcing the hesitation she'd hoped for. Long enough for Batista to make his way over yelling, "*¡Parada! ¡Parada!* . . . Stop!"

The major's pistol, though, was out and steadied by that time, hard to tell whether aimed at her or Cort Wesley, but ready to fire either way.

23

MATEHUALA; THE PRESENT

"It's been a long time, Ranger," Fernando Lozano Sandoval, now chief of the Chihuahua State Investigations Agency, said the next morning. His bodyguards flooded the lobby of Matehaula's Las Palmas Midway Inn moments before he entered, setting up a perimeter both inside and outside the building.

"Thanks for coming," Caitlin told him.

"A man is eternally in the debt of someone who saves his life. Now, let's get some breakfast."

A year before, Caitlin had rescued Sandoval from drug cartel assassins dispatched to Thomason Hospital in El Paso to finish the job they'd started in Juárez. They'd remained in contact ever since, trading both information and mutual admiration. Sandoval had lasted longer than any Mexican official with the *cajones* to take on the cartels, becoming a virtual phantom in the process. No one knew where he lived, and one legend said he slept in a different place every night. Another insisted that the government had built an elaborate network of tunnels beneath the country that Sandoval and other officials now used to get around without ever showing their faces. Caitlin figured the mythology suited Sandoval well, and he exploited it to the fullest in his capacity as the country's chief drug enforcer.

Caitlin had checked into Las Palmas after following Batista and his *federalés* to the local barracks in Matehuala. Cort Wesley would be incarcerated there until such time that his formal extradition was secured, if he managed to live that long. Only the more expensive cabana rooms were available at Las Palmas, so she booked one and reluctantly accepted a hotel "runner" to guide her across the spacious grounds bisected by bike paths, phoning Sandoval on his private number to set up this meeting as soon as the door was closed behind her.

"I've heard about your most recent exploits north of your country's border," Sandoval continued, taking the seat across from her in the hotel restaurant and crossing his legs to expose his sockless feet shoed in white Italian loafers. "It would seem America's drug problems are not limited to Mexico, eh?"

"Unfortunately, no. But it's a problem down here I needed to see you about."

"So you explained, so you explained."

Sandoval looked much better than the last time she had seen him, weak from blood loss and pale with fear. He wore an elegant cream-colored silk suit that exaggerated his tanned features even more. The hair she recalled as limp and thinning in the hospital had regained its luster and shape, styled without a single black strand out of place. He was a picture of health and confidence in stark contrast to his status as the number one enemy of the primary cartels operating out of Juárez and Sinaola.

Caitlin imagined the restaurant would normally be bustling with activity by now, but Sandoval's bodyguards had subtly emptied it of other diners and kept new ones out so he and Caitlin could have the place entirely to themselves for the duration of their meeting.

"I notice your suit looks finely pressed," she told him. "I figure you had to drive through much of the night to get here and just changed into it."

Sandoval's shrug confirmed her suggestion. "I wanted to be more presentable than the last time we met."

"You're as brave a man as any I know, sir. That makes you presentable no matter how you look."

"I haven't slept at home in a year or seen my children in six months. When I speak with people like yourself, fighting the same war I'm fighting, I know my sacrifice is worth it." Sandoval's dark, deep-set eyes sought hers out, as he poured both of them glasses of fresh-squeezed orange juice from a pitcher. "You risked everything in Juárez last year."

"We're both just doing our jobs."

"Our friend Colonel Paz, the people's guardian angel, received the credit."

"Deservedly so, sir." Caitlin leaned a bit forward. "Is it true he's building his own army down here?"

A smile played at the edges of Sandoval's lips, enough to answer Caitlin's question before he responded. "I wouldn't know."

"Of course not."

"But you didn't ask me here to rehash politics and old times."

"No, sir, the truth is I'm here about the other man who was with me in Juárez: Cort Wesley Masters."

Sandoval ran a perfectly manicured finger across the bridge of his nose, as if to join his eyebrows together. "I understand he is in custody, wanted for the murder of a Mexican national."

"A drug dealer from the Juárez cartel who killed a family while fleeing the police not far from here a few months back."

"I'm sure there's more to it than that, Ranger."

"There is. You just don't need to hear it."

"But I need to arrange for Mr. Masters's release, is that it?"

"There are extenuating circumstances."

Sandoval weighed her words, nodding. "The *federalés* are loyal to anyone who pays them. I have ample funds in my budget to secure Mr. Masters's release. I hear Major Batista is hoping to install a swimming pool in his yard this year." Sandoval leaned forward and lifted a breakfast pastry from the basket centered on the table. "But the warrant for Mr. Masters's arrest and extradition request will remain."

Caitlin nonetheless felt her chest relax, her breaths coming easier. "I understand."

"Then help me to understand what brought the two of you back to Mexico like this."

"Mr. Masters's son was kidnapped down here last night."

Sandoval stopped just short of biting into his Danish and laid it down upon his plate, expression suddenly somber.

Caitlin leaned forward to shrink the distance between them. With the restaurant all theirs, she didn't have to lower her voice but did anyway. "How bad is it?"

"The theft of our children is the real scourge of Mexico, Ranger. It has increased tenfold in the past year, better organized and capitalized."

"Capitalized?"

"We do not believe the leaders of the ring are Mexican."

"American?"

"All indications point to that, yes." Sandoval slid closer to the table and lowered his voice. "Utterly reprehensible, I know. You have my apologies."

"Sir?"

"It is a terrible place in which I find myself."

Caitlin looked in his eyes, the sadness and embarrassment building in them, and knew. "You're letting it go on."

"The slavery rings aren't my department."

"In other words, you're looking the other way."

"We have a war to win, not a battle. Our resources are already stretched too thin, and the slavers are everywhere."

Caitlin fought not to sound as angry as she felt, tucked her hands into her lap to keep Sandoval from seeing them clench into fists. "I'm just interested in one of their victims, sir."

Sandoval raised his coffee toward his mouth. "The slavers operate numerous safe houses throughout my country. The closest is twenty miles from Matehuala."

"You telling me Dylan Torres is there for sure?"

"If he was taken from the road between here and Altiplano, yes. But he won't be there long. It's just a way station, the subjects are seldom in residence for more than a week." Sandoval looked about the restaurant as if to confirm they still had it to themselves, then jotted something down on a piece of paper and slid it across the table. "I think this is where you'll find what you're looking for."

Caitlin pocketed the paper without opening it. Considering the whole ugly process splashed the bitter taste of bile up her throat. She swallowed it down with some orange juice that burned all the way to her stomach. Her heart thudded and perspiration was starting to mat her denim shirt to her skin, soon to soak through in patches. Her hand trembled as she laid the glass back on the table, fitting it into the same ring of condensation.

Sandoval rose, taking the rest of his Danish with him. "I've already spoken with Major Batista. It took a much bigger pool than I was expecting."

"I'm in your debt, sir."

"No, Ranger, it's I who will always be in yours." He finally took a bite of his Danish and licked the remnants of icing from his fingers. "But if Mr. Masters runs afoul of our law again, I won't be able to help him."

24

GALVESTON, TEXAS; THE PRESENT

Judge Walter Weems stepped out of his house into the scalding air. April in Texas shouldn't have been this hot, much less this early in the morning, and he was sweating by the time he entered his garage, his beloved Cadillac Deville Sedan centered comfortably in the dual bay.

He climbed in and stowed his briefcase on the passenger seat, having completed his review of the briefs from opposing counsel on a host of motions filed in the past few days. It was amazing any justice ever got done at all, given the unconscionable delays. But justice had to be done here. A defendant named Sylvester Rodart had allegedly blown up a woman's health center, killing two nurses, a doctor, and a nineteen-year-old girl there only for a consultation. Forget "allegedly," since Rodart's high-powered attorneys weren't disputing the facts in evidence at all, choosing instead to argue justifiable homicide. Not just because of all the fetuses snuffed out inside what had been the clinic, but also those that would ultimately follow. Rodart's team wanted to introduce pictures of aborted fetuses into their defense, the subject of the briefs weighing down this entire case.

Truth was Weems had already decided to rule for the prosecution's motion to exclude, and pretty much everyone knew that, based on the rulings he'd already issued on this case. The photos were inherently prejudicial, immaterial, and downright exploitative. Weems had caught hell

in the press for following the law on this case and a movement was rising up against his reelection on those grounds, led by the Texas Tea
Party folk he detested with all his being. Let the bastards do whatever
they wanted. He was seventy-three, just about ready to spend more time
with his grandkids anyway. Take his wife on their first real vacation in
twenty years, while the whole damn country went to hell.

Weems closed the Deville's door, wishing he'd remembered to leave
the windows open. He was certain he'd dragged the stink of the court-
house into the car with him the day before, had bagged his suit as soon
as he got home instead of just balling it up for the dry cleaner. Listening to Rodard's lawyers wax eloquent on their client's heroic character
in the service of God honestly made him feel dirty, and Rodart himself
had a stench like rotting catfish rising off his skin and clothes strong
enough to infest the entire poorly ventilated courtroom. The man was
so oily his flesh actually shined under the lights, as he sat there day after
day at the defense table with a smirk painted over his features. Weems
wanted to take a fire hose to him to wash the man clean, but had settled
for an early adjournment.

Weems stuck his key in the ignition and turned, already reaching
up for the rearview mirror that looked strangely out of place.

BOOM!

The wash of flames that devoured him seemed to come through the
air-conditioning vents, Judge Weems's last thought being there was
something was very out of place indeed.

25

MIDLAND, TEXAS; THE PRESENT

Malcolm Arno had emerged from his private home on the grounds only
after the morning news shows reported the death of Judge Walter Weems
in what was already being called a homicide. Arno couldn't wait for the
on-scene reports from the judge's house where the remains of his body
had still not been recovered.

He loved the morning, the cool bite to the air before the heat rising off the Texas desert set in. Instead of things smelling burned and baked, the sweet scents of chaparral and mesquite washed in from the scrub brush and bramble blowing across the desert floor—at least for a time, before the sun scorched the day and the scent of ground oil rubbed itself into the air.

Once, a long time ago, Midland had been a small town dominated by farming and ranching. That all changed with the 1923 discovery of oil in the Permian Basin, when the Santa Rita Number One well began producing in Reagan County, followed shortly by the Yates Oil Field in Iraan, Texas. Seemingly overnight, Midland was transformed into the hub of the West Texas oil boom, not nearly as widespread as that of the East, but even more plentiful on a per acre basis. A second boom period began after World War II with the discovery and development of the Spraberry Trend, still ranked as the third largest oil field in the United States by total reserves. And the legacy of black gold wasn't finished with Midland either, not by a longshot. Another boom period occurred during the 1970s, thanks in large part to the energy crisis doubling and then tripling the price of oil. Malcolm Arno had often heard it said that Texans should thank not God, but Richard Nixon and Jimmy Carter for their riches. And he knew that even today the Permian Basin produced one-fifth of the nation's total petroleum and natural gas output.

Arno had heard old oil workers say that they could never get their nostrils or lungs free of the oil slick that coated their nasal passages and throat to the point that they tasted and smelled its rich, tarry scent long after they'd left the fields. It was the same here in Midland today. By afternoon, once the sun hit the top rung of its ladder, the air would carry the permanent texture of oil, like a brand. The same stench the old oil workers complained about being forever imbedded in their lungs clung stubbornly to the air. You couldn't see it and it might not show up in any trace metals and minerals, but it was there all right, reeking its way through the hottest points of the day.

Not now, though, not in the morning refreshed by the night's taking the air back for a time. Arno stopped near that outlying building set farthest back on the Patriot Sun grounds, recognizable from the darker shade of roof since it had been laid well after the others. He nodded at

the two guards who respectfully nodded back, making a show of stiffening themselves at their post. The soundproofed walls hid all but a few
muffled sounds from within, and Arno enjoyed listening to those
sounds for the comfort they provided. Testament to his power and plan,
a symbol of his ability to go beyond his father's work and seize the man-
tel Reverend Max Arno hadn't lived long enough to take.

"Mal?"

He'd been so preoccupied he hadn't even noticed Jed Kean coming
up right alongside him.

"Good morning, Mal."

"That it is, Jed, thanks to you," Arno said, slapping the big man in
his back. "Glad to see you made it back from Galveston safely. Gonna
be a fine day."

"Better even than you think," Keen said, grinning from ear to ear.

"You got my attention, Jed."

"How'd you like to settle an old score?"

"Got plenty of those, don't I?"

Kean slid a little closer to Malcolm Arno and laid a powerful hand
gently on his shoulder. "None bigger than this one."

PART THREE

In 1875 Leander H. McNelly, the toughest, meanest Texas Ranger of them all, was in the middle of a raid into Las Cuevas, Mexico, to retrieve stolen cattle when the U.S. Secretary of War sent him a cable telling him to retreat. McNelly sent back a telegram telling him to go to hell.

—Lonestar Legends

26

"So what do you think, Padre?" Guillermo Paz asked the young priest who'd just arrived at his compound.

"Impressive," he nodded, looking up into the big man's eyes. At six feet tall himself, the priest wasn't used to looking up at anybody, but Colonel Paz had him by what looked like a foot, maybe a few inches less. The Colonel wore camouflage fatigues over boots that looked bigger than circus clown feet. His hair was long, black, and shiny with grease. His uniform top seemed painted onto a torso shaped and layered like banded steel. Colonel Guillermo Paz, the priest thought, looked as if someone had drawn him as a character in a comic book or graphic novel and then lifted it off the page. "Especially under the circumstances."

Paz had begun the tour of his makeshift training base in the recently erected "church." Just a tent basically, filled with folding chairs, a plywood altar, and makeshift confessional with curtains instead of doors and a mini blind separating the priest from his confessor. It might not have been much, but Paz regarded it as the showpiece of the camp. Once the site had been chosen, nestled close enough to the mountains to disguise its presence from the air, Paz had begun making the arrangements for weapons, ammunition, cots, bedding, water, power facilities, and living accommodations. The process had gone remarkably smooth. Paz was convinced that the next phase of his life had been "preblessed" by God himself. Acquiring the living accommodations had even been a snap once Hollis Tyree, a billionaire Paz had never met yet was intimately acquainted with, supplied the camp with a whole series of FEMA trailers salvaged from a certain mothballed worksite up in Texas's Tunga County.

His "recruits," meanwhile, had been selected for him, culled from regular army, Zeta Special Forces, a few foreign national volunteers, and numerous civilians who'd talked their way here with no clue what they were getting themselves into. They had no idea that Colonel Guillermo Paz, formerly of the Venezuelan secret police and once one of the most feared assassins in the world, only trained soldiers if there was war in the offing for them.

"Hey, Padre," he said to the young priest, "what do you say we take the new confessional out for a spin?"

Once inside, Paz settled his vast bulk onto a simple stool that creaked under the strain. He was immediately grateful for the curtain since it allowed his legs to spill out onto the floor beyond. He wasn't worried about being interrupted since his troops had only shaken their heads at the church's construction. They didn't understand that the best soldiers needed to believe in a higher power. Otherwise their task was pointless and unguided.

Paz waited for the young priest to take his place and the mini blinds to peel open. "Bless me, Father, for I have sinned. It has been one year since my last confession."

"A long time, my son."

"Yeah, well, I've been on the run for a while. Looking for my place in the world, you might say."

"And have you found it?"

"I'm here, aren't I? Kind of a unique situation we've got, I'm sure you'll agree. But the reason I wanted to talk to you was I had a dream about my Texas Ranger last night."

"*Your* Texas Ranger?"

"Long story, Padre." Paz looked for something to carve his name into, settling on the plank floor and going to work with the heel of his boot on the P. "Let's leave it for another day. Suffice to say for now that she changed my life and I saved hers in return. In this dream she was right here in Mexico for the beginning of another war."

"War?"

"Figure of speech," Paz told the priest, having a difficult time cutting his boot heel through the plank in a discernible pattern. "You believe in witchcraft, Padre?"

"No, my son."

"You should. My mother had the gift of the *bruja* and I must've inherited it from her. It wasn't a dream last night so much as a vision. There were guns and blood with Caitlin Strong right in the center of it all."

"Caitlin Strong?"

"My Texas Ranger."

"A woman . . ."

"Thing is, Father, that dream brought it all home to me. The purpose for this army I'm building out here. The war we're going to be fighting."

"I wasn't told anything about a—"

"I brought you here," Paz interrupted, "because I want my soldiers to understand it's a lot easier to fight with God on your side than on the other's side."

"God does not choose sides, my son."

Paz finished the P as best he could and started in on the A, switching from his right boot to his left. "No offense, Padre, but that's a crock of shit and you know it. God *does* take sides and I'm living proof of that, since he chose mine. I started listening to him lots better the day I left my own country for the last time, realized home isn't a place so much as a state of mind. You ever read Aristophanes?"

"Can't say that I have."

"He wrote 'A man's homeland is wherever he prospers.' Well, I've been prospering pretty much since I first met my Texas Ranger. But I thought our time together was finished, until I had that dream last night. Her standing with guns ready again."

"About to wage war," the priest said, his voice cracking.

"For sure. It's gonna be big and bloody, and I need to get my army ready quicker than expected. I never cared much for causes until I crossed paths with her, but those causes keep bringing us back together."

The priest hesitated, Paz listening to his suddenly labored breathing. "Would you like to give your confession now, my son?"

"Just did, Padre," Paz told him. "Because with all the killing that's coming, it pays to get started a little early."

27

San Luis Potosí, Mexico; the present

The address Sandoval gave Caitlin in San Luis Potosí was located down an alley adjacent to the famed San Francisco church in the city's downtown section, formed around open-air plazas and dominated by colonial architecture.

"Why here?" Cort Wesley asked her from a plaza that sat diagonally across from the head of the alley. "Why not hide this place around the skyscrapers outside the city center with a million people to use as camouflage?"

"Because it would stick out too much and upset the kind of people you can pay off to maintain it here."

Cort Wesley had been standing in the sun but his face was red and hot from more than that. The Mexican police, led by Major Batista of the *federalés*, had first refused to release him to Caitlin's custody and even refused to let her see him.

"How far you wanna push this?" Caitlin asked.

"Why, *señorita*, I'm not pushing at all, just doing my job," Batista had said smugly, grinning. "You should rethink your attitude."

"It's not my attitude you should be concerned about," Caitlin said, leaving it at that.

Batista finally relented an hour later. From the humbled look on his face, Caitlin guessed he'd received another phone call from Sandoval in anticipation of just such a tactic. To save face, he insisted on confiscating Caitlin's pistol—hardly a problem since she carried a pair of back-ups in hidden compartments tucked inside her SUV. Cort Wesley looked none the worse for wear, just more pissed and frustrated than the previous night. Strangely he didn't look tired, although Caitlin couldn't imagine him sleeping a single wink.

"Tell me something good, Ranger," he greeted.

Caitlin did just that, explaining the information Sandoval had provided that would take them to San Luis Potosí. Once on the road, she handed him a .40 caliber SIG that was a sister version of the standard Ranger issue nine-millimeter pistol. Since arriving in the city, they'd both walked down the alley twice, cataloging everything while not stopping or lingering too long anywhere near the address of the building in which Sandoval had indicated Dylan was likely being held.

Cort Wesley had just returned from his pass down and back the smoothly layered stone walk, and Caitlin could see his skin seeming to crawl with a slight quiver.

"Don't worry, Ranger, I didn't storm the place and I didn't shoot anybody, least not yet."

"That's a load off my mind," Caitlin said, her meaning clear as she held his stare.

"You want me to say I'm sorry for killing Maria Lopez's murderer?"

"How'd it go down?"

"How do you think?"

"That you gave no thought to the fact you could be throwing your life away."

"Right then I didn't care."

"That's the problem, Cort Wesley. You should have, instead of easing your own guilt over never taking Dylan down here to visit the girl."

Cort Wesley shook his head. "Look who's talking."

"Come again?"

"I'm talking about taking justice into your own hands. Specialty of both of us now."

"Difference being at least I've got the option of making an arrest."

"Not in Mexico you don't, Ranger. Or maybe you forgot your previous trips down here, like the one that took you out of the Rangers for a spell."

"Difference being none of that led to an extradition request."

"Could have, on multiple occasions." Cort Wesley held his hands out before him in a conciliatory gesture. "Look, right now let's just get Dylan. We can deal with all the rest of this later."

"That's what I'm afraid of."

Wearing his hair trimmed shorter disguised the increasing graying at the temples and further exaggerated the breadth of his already wide shoulders. Today Cort Wesley's neck looked rigid and knobby with muscle that seemed to run in layers under his shirt, vibrating in rhythm with his pulse.

Caitlin turned her gaze down the alley. "What'd you make of the place?"

"Building's got three stories and a basement. Starts and finishes flush with the structure on either side, like they were all connected at one point. Near as I can tell there's entrances in both front and rear and maybe through the basement if it's still joined up to the others on either side of it."

"You make that blind man across the way?"

"Tin cup and all," Cort Wesley nodded. "A spotter for sure."

"I didn't make anybody else."

"Me either, Ranger. Could be one in a third-floor window but I didn't linger long enough to look. No security camera or guns in evidence, and that's a relief." He stiffened. "Now how we gonna get ourselves inside exactly? I'm happy to go in with guns blazing, but I don't know what you promised that Mexican friend of yours."

"That we wouldn't . . ."

"Figures."

"So long as he could supply us with what we needed to avoid it."

"And did he?"

Caitlin smiled.

28

In public restrooms just down the street from where they'd left the SUV, Caitlin and Cort Wesley changed into the dark blue Mexican *federalé* uniforms provided by Sandoval.

"How many guns Sandoval figure we're looking at?" Cort Wesley asked, standing at the head of the alley again.

"Half dozen at the most, and only a couple practiced enough to give us any trouble."

Their plan, what there was of it, was simple. The *federalé* uniforms would give them access to the building where they'd confront one or two of the prime guards. They'd instruct those men to bring them whoever was in charge. From there, without a keen insight into the building's layout or exactly who they'd be facing inside, things would play out based on the moment, and Caitlin expected Cort Wesley could be counted on to keep his gun stilled until there was no other choice.

They could assume that the old building, once a prominent hotel during Mexico's nineteenth-century heyday, would still be broken up into a series of smaller rooms. Dylan would likely be in one, another dozen or so kids occupying others probably congested on a single floor. Lighting may have been a prime indicator in determining the precise placement, except that from the outside all the windows looked the same, and daylight stole anything that might've differentiated one room from another.

"Your friend Sandoval say anything about drugs?" Cort Wesley asked, pulling the words from his own throat as if he dreaded the answer.

"Not a word."

" 'Cause isn't that how they get kids like this to do their bidding, turn them into whores and sex slaves?"

"The eastern European gangs maybe. But they're operating the parlors themselves. The kids moved through Mexico are placed with consolidators and brokers for sale or placement with third parties."

"So they gotta keep 'em clean, feed them well. Hell, maybe they converted one of the floors into a goddamn spa."

Caitlin remained silent, watched the sweat starting to dapple Cort Wesley's blue uniform top.

"Consolidators and brokers," he said, repeating her words suddenly.

"Yeah."

Cort Wesley snorted out some breath. "I might just shoot every last one of them."

Caitlin approached the entrance behind Cort Wesley and watched him pound the heavy wooden door with his fist.

"Federal Police!" he said in Spanish, loud enough to disturb some tourists passing by. "Open up!"

"We're supposed to be here to collect a bribe," Caitlin reminded, "not stage a raid."

"Must have forgot," Cort Wesley told her and pounded the door again. "And I don't think subtlety scores you many points with people like this."

"No one's answering."

Cort Wesley drew the .40 caliber SIG Caitlin had given him. "Gotta figure they'd want to avoid a commotion."

"They're gone," a voice said from behind them.

Cort Wesley and Caitlin turned to see the blind beggar seeming to stare their way.

"They're not answering because they're gone."

"You *saw* them leave?" Caitlin prodded, starting across the alley's smooth stone floor.

The beggar took off his sunglasses, staring right at her as he winked. "I saw no one come. Since I got here this morning, no one comes. People always come."

Caitlin and Cort Wesley exchanged a worried glance. "Last night then," he said, before she had a chance to.

"You're not *federalés*."

"No," Caitlin acknowledged, "we're not."

The beggar's eyes were dull and dark, squinting against the sudden wash of light. He remained silent until Caitlin slipped a ten-dollar bill into his tin cup. Then he grinned, showcasing a front tooth lost entirely to a silver-shaded filling.

"Last night then," the beggar resumed. "They were still inside when I left after midnight." He rattled his tin cup. "Business was good last night."

"What time did you get here this morning?"

Silence.

Caitlin dropped another ten into the cup.

"I always get here at nine, in time for the first of the morning tour buses."

"You've seen them coming and going," Cort Wesley said, suddenly looming over the beggar.

"I sit here every day. And they come and go." He shrugged.

Cort Wesley yanked a picture of Dylan from a cargo pocket of his uniform trousers. "You see this kid come?"

The beggar grinned, didn't look at the picture.

"You wanna eat that cup of yours, *amigo*?"

"Then I wouldn't be able to tell you anything, would I?"

Caitlin stuffed another ten home.

"More," said the beggar.

"Don't push your luck," Caitlin advised.

The beggar finally took the picture from Cort Wesley's grasp, squinting again as he regarded Dylan's face framed by long black hair. "Last night, they brought him in."

Cort Wesley snatched the picture from his grasp. "He's my son."

The beggar didn't seem to care. "Then I feel sorry for him, *señor*, because he has gone to the devil along with the rest of the children brought here."

Cort Wesley crouched down, even with the beggar's eyes. "Where'd they take my son and the others?"

"I don't know."

"How much you want?"

"The money doesn't matter. I don't know."

Caitlin eased Cort Wesley back a bit, thought her hand might come away numb from the current surging out from his nerve endings to his super-heated skin. Still, she managed to stuff a twenty-dollar bill into the cup this time.

"How many children?"

"Six to eight at a time. Never here very long. They come, leave after a few days or a week, while more come."

"How many men?" asked Cort Wesley.

"Four, maybe five on average. It varies. By the day, the week." The beggar stopped, then started again almost immediately. "But Gort was here last night. I saw him."

"Gort?" Caitlin repeated.

"I call him that because he looks like the robot from the science fiction movie, the one in black-and-white, about the world standing still, big and bald. Except he had paint on his head."

Something scratched at Caitlin's spine. "Paint?"

"You know like a . . ."

"*Tatuaje?*"

"Yes, *tatuaje!* A tattoo!"

"Of what?"

"I don't know, like an airport runway."

Caitlin felt a chill. "Or an arrow?"

Recognition flashed in the beggar's eyes. "Yes! I'm almost sure, almost."

Caitlin stiffened, feeling Cort Wesley look at her the way she'd just been looking at him, the electricity dancing off her skin now instead.

"You know this guy, Ranger?" he asked her finally.

"Kind of," Caitlin answered, turning his way. "I shot him dead up in Canada."

29

"He and his twin brother both," Caitlin continued, still reconstructing the memories. Both her dad and granddad had told her gunfights slip away from you the same way dreams do. A mechanism of the mind to deal with the kind of violence that was part and parcel of a gunman's life. "Their name was LaChance. Transplanted American Hells Angels out of Michigan who were part of a drug-smuggling operation on the U.S.-Canadian border to rival what's coming out of Juárez."

"You're telling me this big bald guy who showed up here last night . . ."

"Same description, right down to the tattoo."

"So, what, you saying this guy's a *ghost*?"

Caitlin turned back to the beggar. "The big man—"

"Gort."

"Gort. How often was he here?"

The beggar frowned, trying to fix the answer in his brain. "Once a week, maybe twice. That's why it was strange to see him last night, because he'd been here the night before."

"He showed up after the boy was brought in?"

"*Sí*, Gort came after I saw them bring the boy inside."

"But you left before Gort came out again."

"Then everyone was gone when I returned this morning."

Caitlin stuffed another bill into the beggar's cup and moved aside, already wielding her BlackBerry.

"Who you calling?" Cort Wesley asked her.

"Expert on ghosts, one in particular," she said, punching in the exchange for Royal Canadian Mountie Pierre Beauchamp.

"*Bonjour*," Beauchamp greeted.

"It's Caitlin Strong, Mountie."

"Well, howdy there, Ranger," Beauchamp said, doing his best impersonation of a Texas drawl.

"How you healing?"

"Be back at work soon enough, behind a desk anyway, but they tell me my days of riding a horse are done."

"I didn't know you rode."

"I don't. Just trying to make you feel more guilty, eh? They're giving me a medal, you know."

"No, I didn't. Congratulations."

"The final report of our raid makes me sound like Rambo. No mention anywhere of Mrs. Rambo, though."

"Less complications that way."

"I don't imagine this is a social call."

Caitlin held her gaze on Cort Wesley as she continued. "Those LaChance twins have a triplet, Mountie?"

"Yup. Goes by the name of Buck. Just as big and even meaner. We pinned a murder rap on him a year back and he hasn't been seen in the province since."

"That's because he's relocated himself to Mexico, moving kids instead of drugs."

Caitlin could hear Beauchamp breathing in the pause that followed. "What the hell have you got yourself into this time, Ranger?" he said finally.

"Damned if I know, Mountie. You get yourself better, you're always welcome in Texas."

"I think I'll pass on that, if you don't mind. Fighting alongside you once is enough for any sane man. And, Ranger?"

"I'm still here."

"How many are you going to gun down this time?"

"As many as it takes, Mountie." Caitlin ended the call and looked back at Cort Wesley. "It's time we took a look at the inside of that building."

30

"You got that look about you," Caitlin said as they moved about the now abandoned building that had served as a way station for kidnapped children about to be sold as sex slaves.

"What look is that?"

"Way you're holding your eyes and moving like you got an M-sixteen in hand instead of a pistol. Like this was Iraq instead of Mexico."

"Dylan's principal raised that very same subject yesterday."

"You never talk about Iraq with anyone, Cort Wesley."

"And I didn't with Garcia. He figured it out all on his own."

Caitlin stopped at the foot of the stairs. "How's that?"

"How's not important. Point is part of it had to do with what happened after the war, the team I was part of hitching our wagons in the southern part of the country to help start a revolution aimed at toppling Saddam. Whole thing was CIA all the way, right down to the weapons drop. Then good ole Washington dropped the ball instead. Goddamn Bay of Pigs all over again and a bunch of innocent people got slaughtered on account of that."

Caitlin remained silent.

"I never felt so helpless in my life, Ranger. Watching it all unfold made my skin turn inside out, and I swore I'd never feel that way again. Now I do, only worse."

"We'll find Dylan, Cort Wesley."

Cort Wesley arched his back, sending a crescendo of crackling noises up his spine. "You don't sound so sure of that."

"I'm just getting started," Caitlin said and started up the stairs toward the second floor.

The lock on the front door was rusty and old, easily picked with a simple credit card. The smell of air freshener, something flowery and sweet, had greeted them as soon as they got it open. Already dissipating to allow the stench of mold, wood rot, and stale body odor to reclaim the air.

The first-floor furnishings were simple, confined mostly to a long, wide space that had once been the lobby when this building was a hotel. There were a few desks and tables strewn about with no particular rhyme or reason, as if someone had laid them down because there was space to do it. A thin layer of dust covered the tops of all, except for the parts that were covered by something else. Fast-food plastic, balled-up candy wrappers, soda cups layered at the bottom with melted ice, crumpled paper bags and cans of cheap beer with stray liquid roasting and stinking— all evidence of men on watch, on guard, living on nutrients purchased from any number of kiosks or eateries lining the plazas that dominated the city's old downtown. Men who'd left in a hurry after making no attempt at all to disguise their presence.

At this point Caitlin couldn't have even said why she'd come inside with Cort Wesley in the first place, once learning the building had been emptied. She supposed it had something to do with getting the scent; that's what her daddy and granddaddy had called it, and she recalled Jim Strong spending the better part of a day at the Church of the Redeemer compound after the Ranger raid had emptied it and Max Arno had gotten away. He had described it as feeling the place out. Touching, smelling, seeing, sensing. Fire up his instincts and let them turn the trick. Anyway, it must have worked. What else could have made him show up at the Tackle and Gun in Midland just a few hours before Arno and his son?

So that's why she was inside the place now. Getting the scent, hoping some fact registered in her subconscious that would lead her to Dylan.

She'd been, what, three years younger than him that day Jim Strong had shot it out with the last remnants of the Church of the Redeemer? In retrospect, Caitlin figured her childhood had ended then and there. Wasn't what she'd seen so much as taking Earl Strong's old Colt from the glove compartment, feeling its cold weight as she climbed out of the truck into the parking lot, because in that moment she'd had every intention of using it if need be. She guessed that's why her father hadn't been cross with her, apologizing about their missed fishing trip and promising to start fresh again the next day, as if the very intention that had driven her from the truck could've been blotted out, erased from memory, that easily.

Of course, things didn't work that way. Caitlin didn't feel appreciably different, any different really, after that day, but she was. She started going to the range more and more, abandoning the old Colt in favor of a succession of revolvers and semiautos that felt lighter and surer in her grasp. Finally settling on Smith & Wesson's Model 59 Nickel 9mm Parabellum that seemed molded to her hand. It was the first double-action pistol with a double-stack magazine, featuring an alloy frame. A bit heavy at two pounds but perfectly balanced. Her dad gave her one on her fourteenth birthday, the trip that had begun in Midland finally coming to an end.

"I can't stand feeling helpless like this," Cort Wesley said as they mounted the stairs carefully, pistols palmed. "Like back in Iraq, standing on the sidelines, not a damn thing I could do as the people I was supposed to help got massacred by the Republican Guard. I'm sorry I never told you about that before."

"Things we keep inside ourselves make us who we are, Cort Wesley," Caitlin told him, thinking again of watching her father kill three men in that parking lot.

The hotel was smaller on the inside than it appeared from the out. Just ten rooms on the second floor, five per side, all the doors open now but with padlocks affixed to the exterior frame and bars fastened across the windows. And where lavish furnishings of the time had once been were nothing more than bare cots with thin covers and buckets layered with human excrement and urine, filling the hall with a putrid stench that would become intolerable once the sun superheated the building's interior.

"They must've left in a real hurry," Caitlin noted.

"Doesn't look like something that was planned either, does it?" Cort Wesley added.

Caitlin didn't feel his question needed an answer, knew what was coming next before Cort Wesley resumed.

"I think they broke this place up because of Dylan. He gets here, somebody calls LaChance. Then they're in the wind."

She gave him a long look. "I never heard you sound scared before, Cort Wesley."

"I know my son, Caitlin. Goddamn hothead just like his old man. He goes off on somebody, maybe the guy overreacts. Uses a knife or a gun."

"Haven't seen any blood anywhere and neither have you."

"It's a big place, Ranger."

Caitlin looked inside another of the rooms, checking the bucket stinking in the corner with hand pressed over her mouth and nose. "And they got mules to clean up the shit. LaChance doesn't get the call and hoist anchor just because somebody made a mess."

"What then?"

"Let's keep looking."

31

San Luis Potosí, Mexico; the present

Cort Wesley checked every room on the second and third floors, holding his breath as he inspected the contents of each of the buckets.

"Figure Dylan's would be empty," he explained, "considering he couldn't have been here very long."

Caitlin moved into one of the third-floor rooms ahead of him, freezing in the doorway. "This is the one," she said, as he came up behind her.

Caitlin watched Cort Wesley's emotions twisting his features into coils of rope. "How do you know?"

She shrugged. "Nothing I can say exactly. You live with two Texas legends with more than seventy years of Rangering between them, you learn to trust your instincts."

Cort Wesley checked the room's bucket. "Empty," he said, as if to confirm her words, en route to a more thorough check of the room starting with the walls and floor. "If Dylan was here, he'd leave some sign to let us know."

Cort Wesley went back to his careful scrutiny. Caitlin joined him in checking the other side of the room from floor to ceiling, for what exactly she didn't know.

"Here," Cort Wesley said suddenly, crouching on the floor just short of the bed. "What's this look like to you?"

Caitlin knelt alongside him, studying a scratchy figure in the wood. From a standing position, it appeared to be a simple scuff or sign of wear. Closer up, though, it had the look of something haphazardly cut into the surface. Caitlin could fit her thumbnail in with plenty of room to spare, meaning whatever had made it was substantially thicker and sharper.

"Could be a 'D,'" she noted.

"Never mind could be. It's a 'D' all right. Carved with a belt buckle."

The two of them picturing Dylan working the floor with his buckle, smart enough to get rid of the wood shards and shavings in the process and leave the letter small enough so it wouldn't stand out to anyone not looking for something like it.

"Kid's always thinking," Cort Wesley said, as much to himself as Caitlin. "That's what always seems to get him in trouble."

Caitlin continued tracing the letter's outline. "Not this time. How long you figure it took him to do this?"

"Not much more than a couple minutes."

She shook her head, finally rising. "Still doesn't make any sense I can see."

"Unless they figured out who he was."

"So what, even if they did? He's the son of a Texas outlaw, not a Texas Ranger. What the hell would that matter to them?"

Caitlin had no answer, the whole scenario baffling to her. What you couldn't see scared you more; what you could see never scared you at all. Or so went Ranger teachings since the days they patrolled the badlands prowling for renegade Indians or Mexican invaders.

"You think your friend Sandoval might know something else that can help us?"

"If he did, we'd already know it."

Cort Wesley's eyes narrowed, the color flushing from his face. "You trust him?"

"Dylan was long gone by the time we met this morning," Caitlin replied, getting his meaning.

Cort Wesley began pacing the room, the way both he and Dylan always did when their nerves got the better of them. "I'm at wits' end here, Caitlin."

"My dad once ran lead on a kidnapping of a young boy out of Kilgore. All the evidence pointed to an ex-con who did a ten-year stretch in Huntsville for having his way with one about the same age. Locals leaked his name to the press and a lynch mob mentality set in. As a matter of fact, neighbors were dragging the guy out of his house when Jim Strong showed up and faced them all down without even drawing his gun."

"I imagine there's somewhere you're going with this."

"Turns out the boy was hiding in the basement of his own house. Pulled off the whole thing just because he wanted to meet a real live Texas Ranger. My dad found him thanks to a trail of potato chip crumbs from a leaky bag the kid grabbed from a kitchen cupboard. Came close to putting the boy over his knee, then just gave him an autograph, took his leave, and that was the end of it."

Cort Wesley looked like he was waiting for more, then just shook his head.

"Something else we might want to focus on here, that's my point," Caitlin elaborated for him.

"Like what?"

"Why they closed up shop so fast. Gotta figure it's 'cause they figured out who Dylan was and who'd be coming after him. That's why the mules called LaChance and he hightailed it down here."

Cort Wesley could picture his oldest son sticking in the damn Mexicans' faces. Telling him who his dad was and what he'd do to them. Maybe throw in something about being best friends with a Texas Ranger as close to a modern-day gunfighter as there was.

"Is that supposed to make me feel better?" he asked Caitlin.

"It should. Could be they blew town 'cause they're scared. Could be they're trying to figure a way out of this."

"Could be they're gonna ask for the whole Texas treasury to let the boy go."

"Either way, it means he's alive and is gonna stay that way, Cort Wesley."

He shrugged, weighed her thinking, and conceded the logic of it. "I can't leave Mexico without him, Ranger."

Caitlin nodded grudgingly. "I know."

"I don't want you hanging around. I want you back in Texas checking on how a Hells Angel like LaChance figures into this."

Caitlin looked Cort Wesley in the eye, saw uncertainty and hope fighting for control. "Maybe give me a chance to wipe out the whole family line."

"A service to humanity, Ranger. Kind of like what I did in Juárez."

Caitlin let his comment hang in the air between them. "You can't work this alone, Cort Wesley."

"You got an alternative to suggest?"

"I just might," she told him.

32

MEXICO; THE PRESENT

Dylan felt the van rattle over the rut-strewn road, tires hammered by its worn-out shocks. His jaw ached from the jarring thumps and bumps, and the sack smelling of old vegetables the big bald guy with the tattoo on his skull had tucked over his head scratched at his skin, leaving it hot and itchy.

The big bald guy had studied his learner's permit, looking at him as if trying to match his face to a nonexistent picture.

"Your daddy's Cort Wesley Masters."

"And if you let me go now, he might not kill you."

"He and this Texas Ranger he's been fucking."

Dylan bristled at how he said that, the way his eyes gleamed. "She'd kill you for just putting it like that."

Strange how it wasn't hard for Dylan to summon the bravado needed to talk that way. It came easy, natural, even with the heavy hammering of his heart against his chest through the bone dryness that had consumed his mouth. He'd kept his cool for the duration, save for the moments when the fake cops came for him in his father's truck and he fought back feebly like a girl. He hated the feeling of being overpowered, of having hands that smelled like ass all over him, smudging his skin as they yanked him out into the night. Dylan thought he was going through the window, but then they got the door open and, next thing he knew, he was on the pavement with a boot pressed down against the back of his neck.

He thought of his own boots in that moment, the ones Caitlin had given him splayed sideways in the backseat, being left behind in the truck. Knew he'd never see them again, which made him feel too young, too sad, and very scared.

The fake cops had stood him up and one kicked him in the balls for good measure, laughing when Dylan doubled over and dropped back to the ground clutching himself. His balls still ached even now, seemed swollen the way they were pressing up against the crotch of his jeans. He hated the way he smelled and his hair felt like a dust mop atop his head.

I'm sorry I lost the boots, Caitlin. . . .

He'd say that after she came and rescued him, her and his dad. He'd been stupid to run away and even more stupid to let himself get taken this way. So Dylan resolved to act smarter. Think himself a way out of this instead of letting his brain seize up and surrender to panic. Use the anger, his dad would tell him, focus it.

But that wouldn't help him now. His hands were bound behind him with those plastic cop cuffs that squeezed his wrists so tight they hurt. His legs were free, only with no hands to use or eyes to guide him, they weren't about to do him much good.

Dylan had the sense they were headed north, all the thumping and bumping telling him they were avoiding the main thoroughfares and using back roads instead. He kept his focus peeled forward on the front of the van, listening to the voices for any clue they might yield. He was certain there were only two people up there. He could identify one of them, a fat shapeless mess of a man, by his voice, and had the other pinned down to one of three others. He hoped it was the man with the limp since, if he did manage to get free, fleeing a lard ass and a gimp made for good prospects indeed.

The problem was the bald guy with the tattoo of an arrow on his scalp. His eyes were like black marbles stuck in his head, full of purpose and loathing. They never seemed to blink when he was staring at Dylan, sapping more and more energy from the boy with each second his stare lingered. He glared at Dylan from the doorway of the stinking room his kidnappers had stuck him in, Dylan somehow retaining the presence of mind to cover the "D" he'd carved in the floor once the door rattled open.

It was still hours later before the other men came to fetch him. One of them gave him back his sneakers while another stood in the doorway looking at him differently than they had before.

"We go now," the fat, shapeless mass of man said, while the one with a limp made sure Dylan could see a knife the size of a tire iron sheathed to his belt.

Dylan laced his sneakers. As soon as he was finished, Fatty fastened the plastic cuffs on him and, with the gimp, led him through the putrid building down a set of creaky stairs that smelled of wood rot. Dylan couldn't say how long ago that was exactly, a bunch of hours anyway. He couldn't say how he knew but he was pretty certain the bald guy wasn't far away either. Maybe following in his own car.

Or maybe it was just his imagination, spurred by the ache in his balls and stomach soured by the stench of the sack roasting his face and sticking to his skin from the sweat.

Dylan focused on what he'd do when they finally stopped, seeing it in his head so when it came for real the motions would feel practiced, rehearsed. He imagined he had his dad's Glock or Caitlin's SIG, blasting away at the assholes and punching red holes in them.

In the end, though, the fantasy retreated and he was just a kid in a foreign country without a gun, a knife, or a video game bonus round tied up in the back of a van. Suddenly the fat guy and the one with the limp seemed as big and bad as they really were, and Dylan Torres, son of the most feared man in Texas, was a scared kid who just wanted to be home.

He felt himself sobbing and tried to stop. But the tears came anyway, seeming to tighten the sack's hold on his skin as the van bottomed out and bounced back up again.

33

Cort Wesley watched Guillermo Paz step out onto the rooftop terrace of El Rincón de San Francisco restaurant, the eyes of the few diners willing to brave the heat for the beautiful view listing toward his massive frame. Paz's boots clacked atop the smooth tile floor, his bulk big enough to block out the nearby San Francisco church's cupola and bell towers from this angle until he reached the table.

"I'm glad to see you again, outlaw," Paz greeted, extending his hand.

"You mind not calling me that, Colonel?" Cort Wesley said, taking it and feeling his own hand swallowed up in the grasp.

"Perhaps you'd prefer your former military rank."

Cort Wesley continued to match Paz's firm grasp, not about to break it until he did. "Don't recall us ever discussing that subject."

A smile flirted with Paz's lips, as he eased his hand back. "We didn't have to."

"The unit I was a part of wasn't big on rank."

"Mine in Venezuela either. But someone has to be in charge."

"Lieutenant's close enough, then."

The two men remained standing, facing each other from across the table set off to the rear of the terrace against a waist-high retaining wall the same mauve stucco as the building's exterior. The architecture matched that of the nearby church from which the restaurant took its name.

"You've heard what I'm doing down here," said Paz.

Cort Wesley nodded. "Something about an army."

"And from what the Ranger told me, Lieutenant, you might well need one."

Paz had called Caitlin back immediately on a number routed through a satellite-processed dummy exchange.

"I knew you were down here, Ranger."

"How's that exactly, Colonel?"

"Wish I could tell you. Sometimes I just get a sense of things, especially when it pertains to you, usually in my dreams."

"This doesn't pertain to me exactly."

"Who then?"

"Cort Wesley Masters. His son's been kidnapped," Caitlin said and proceeded to explain the rest.

Silence filled the line for several moments after she'd finished, not even Paz's breathing loud enough to break it.

"This is just the beginning, you know."

"Of what?"

"Another battle that will see us fighting side by side."

"Is it true what I heard, Colonel?"

"What did you hear?"

"That you're raising an army down here."

"I've been raising armies my whole life, Ranger."

"I heard about this one from a *federalé* commander who seemed more than a little terrified about the prospects. Then I asked a very powerful man named Sandoval to confirm it for me."

"And what did he tell you?"

"Nothing, but that was enough."

"Enough to what?"

"Back to Cort Wesley Masters's son, Colonel."

"You wouldn't be calling me if it were just a kidnapping. You'd have the boy back safe now and already headed home."

"He was taken by a sex slave ring somehow connected to a Hells Angels chapter operating out of Quebec. The place Sandoval sent me to retrieve him had been cleared out and fast, Dylan included."

"Dylan being the outlaw's son, the one whose mother I killed in my former incarnation."

"All true, Colonel."

"You don't believe this kidnapping was random, do you?"

"I believe it stopped being random when the kidnappers realized who they'd grabbed. That changed their plans."

"So you need to find out how. And why."

"Right now all we need is the boy back. That's where you come in, Colonel."

"I changed my mind," Cort Wesley was saying, after he and Guillermo Paz had finally sat down. "I like outlaw better."

"I can't help you find your son . . ."

Cort Wesley started to rise.

"But I can help you get him back."

Cort Wesley sat back down. Paz was wearing civilian clothes that fit him snugly, as everything else did. Sweat shined through the torso and glowed off his face like the oil that matted his long black hair into braided ringlets swimming all the way to his shoulders.

"By finding the men who took him instead," Paz finished.

"What do you need from me, Colonel?"

"Forgiveness."

Cort Wesley stared at him instead of responding.

"For taking the life of this boy's mother," Paz continued.

"Forgiveness isn't mine to give."

Paz leaned forward across the table, his chair creaking from the strain. "I've already made my peace with God for what I did, but not with you. I never said I was sorry. But I don't expect you to accept my apology."

"Then why bother giving it?"

Paz's eyes held Cort Wesley's and wouldn't let go. "The Ranger told me about the drug dealer you killed in Juárez."

"There a place for that in this conversation, Colonel?"

"Only because you're sorry about that now, just as I'm sorry for what I did then. Regret is not healthy, outlaw, but it's human."

"Wish I had it to do all over again, if that's what you mean."

"Wouldn't matter," Paz told him. "You'd do the same thing, just as I would. We can't change who we are, our very natures, from moment to moment. We can only learn from our actions, our mistakes, and move on."

"Well, I might be moving on right to a Mexican jail."

Paz shook his head. "Something else in our natures, outlaw: we survive."

"For now anyway," Cort Wesley told him.

34

Captain Tepper was waiting in his office when Caitlin arrived just after dark. He sat drumming his fingers on the desk blotter. Caitlin noticed the tips were stained brown and an ashtray layered with ash and cigarette butts sat just off the blotter.

"Maybe it's time to quit again, D.W.," she said, drawing Tepper's gaze to her.

"More likely time to move on to bourbon, Ranger, the hell you're causing me."

"This about Cort Wesley?"

"I got the whole state of Texas crawling up my ass about why we haven't brought him in yet."

Caitlin had left Cort Wesley her SUV and taken a flight back to San Antonio that routed her from Ponciano Arriaga International Airport in San Luis Potosí through Mexico City on AeroMéxico Connect. She slept fitfully for the brief duration of both flights and landed early evening in Texas, still trying to figure out how a drug ring operating on the U.S.-Canadian border was connected to a child slavery ring operating in Mexico.

"What'd you tell them?" Caitlin asked Tepper.

"That we were working on it."

"True enough." Caitlin took the chair angled in front of Tepper's desk, hating the stale smell of Marlboros that hung in the air. "Why do the Mexican authorities care so much about a single dead drug dealer all of a sudden?"

"Remember I told you the extradition request was signed by the governor of the province?"

"Yes, sir."

"Turns out the dead man was his brother-in-law." Tepper paused to let his statement settle. "They take family serious down there, Caitlin."

"So does Cort Wesley, sir. This dealer killed Maria Lopez and her entire family in a car accident while fleeing the police."

Tepper seemed unmoved. He leaned forward, dragging more of the smell of stale cigarettes with him. "I cut you a break on this one, Ranger. You cut my legs out from under me in return, we're all gonna pay the price."

"You want me to arrest Masters while his son is still missing?"

Tepper weighed Caitlin's words, the furrows that lined his cheeks seeming to deepen in contemplation. "Maybe I should take this away from you before Austin takes it away from me."

Caitlin ran her tongue over her upper lip. "I'm betting there's nothing you wouldn't do for your four kids, D.W."

"Well, three of them anyway," Tepper tried to joke.

"Six grandchildren?"

"Seventh on the way. What's your point?"

"Stall Austin, 'cause if anybody tries to bring Cort Wesley Masters in before he gets his boy back, they won't be seeing their kids or grandchildren ever again."

35

San Antonio; the present

Outside, Caitlin steadied herself with several deep breaths before climbing back behind the wheel of her rental car. The interior was stifling, but still smelled of commercial solvent and air freshener, so she opted to drive to the Intrepid Center for Heroes with the windows down. The sky was black and moonless, the air flush with the smell of ozone from an approaching thunderstorm. Heat lightning flashed in her rearview mirror, seeming to chase her down the road.

Caitlin wanted to tell Mark John Serles face-to-face she couldn't help him, that the army shenanigans he was alleging fell out of even the Ranger purview and jurisdiction. She wasn't buying into his story to begin with, figuring all he'd experienced left him seeing shadows even when there was no light to cast them. Her brief experience as a mental health therapist had left her well acquainted with the symptoms of post-traumatic stress disorder, one of which was an overriding sense of paranoia that could lead to a delusional, if not pathological, sense that the world was out to get those afflicted with it. Caitlin figured she might also want to speak to his treating physician at the Intrepid to cue him in on her suspicions. The prosthetic legs that would help the kid walk again in no time were nothing if they ended up bringing him to the wrong place.

Once again, her Ranger ID got her onto the grounds of Fort Sam Houston without delay and she parked in one of the lots adjacent to the center, announcing herself to the receptionist at the front desk with Stetson held respectfully by her side.

"I'd like to see a patient named Mark Serles if I could, ma'am. I believe he's a sergeant."

"Would this be an official visit, Ranger?" the woman asked her.

"He asked me to follow up something on his behalf and I'm here to report on that to him."

"One moment, please," the woman said, tapping out instructions into her computer. When these didn't yield what she was looking for, she tapped out some more. "If you could wait just a few more moments, Ranger."

"Of course," Caitlin said, catching a nervous edge in the woman's voice.

She watched a boy who looked not much older than Dylan emerge through the automatic doors, his running shorts and shirt soaked with sweat from a jog he'd completed in the cool of the night on a pair of prosthetic legs replaced below the knee. He walked past her, smiling with nary a limp. A private in uniform who was little more than a boy too, meanwhile, worked a series of quarters adroitly into a lobby vending machine with one of two prosthetic arms finished in handlike pincers.

The boy caught Caitlin looking at him and smiled too. "Can I get you something, ma'am? I've got a few extra quarters here."

"No," Caitlin said, embarrassed at being caught staring. "But I wanted to thank you all the same."

The boy seemed to understand what she was getting at and nodded, eyes lingering briefly on her badge and Stetson before taking his leave.

"Ranger?"

Caitlin hadn't even noticed the man in a doctor's lab coat coming up alongside her.

"I'm Dr. Gilroy, one of the administrators."

Caitlin's eyes darted up from the nametag pinned to his lapel. "You'd be army, then."

"Yes, ma'am. A bird colonel."

"You do great work here, Colonel," Caitlin told him. "However often you hear that, it's not enough."

"And it means something every time." Gilroy's expression grew taut, the congeniality lost in the furrows suddenly sprouting across his brow. "But do you mind if we speak privately."

"Not at all."

Gilroy led her to a lobby wall set back from a seating area between a pair of towering indoor plants that bled water from their pots. "You're here about Sergeant Mark Serles."

"I am, sir."

"Could you tell me in reference to what?"

"He asked me to check something out for him and I'm here to report on my findings."

"In your capacity as a Texas Ranger?"

Something in Gilroy's tone was beginning to scratch at Caitlin. "That's correct, sir."

"Would you mind telling me what this pertains to?"

"I don't expect you'd violate doctor-patient privilege, Colonel."

"Never."

"Then understand I can't do the same when it's regarding an active Ranger investigation."

"Active investigation?"

"Became that as soon as Sergeant Serles made his call to the local company headquarters. Now, if you could just let me talk to him, I'm sure we can get this cleared up and me out of your hair real—"

"I can't do that, Ranger."

"Pardon me, sir?"

"You can't speak to Sergeant Serles because he was transferred from the center."

36

More scratching and something that felt like a dull thud hit Caitlin in the stomach. "When did this happen exactly?"

Caitlin watched Gilroy consult his steel clipboard, lifting the top open. "Earlier today. This morning."

"You had to check your papers to tell me that?"

"You asked."

"Just seems like something you'd know without needing to look."

"We have a lot of patients here, Ranger."

"But how many of them get transferred, Doctor?" Caitlin continued. "This is a private hospital, isn't it?"

"It was built with privately donated money, but it's a military facility from an administrative and management standpoint," Gilroy said testily, crossing his arms around his steel clipboard.

"Forgive me, sir. My point was our troops come to the Intrepid because you're the best at what you do; in fact, in some cases, the *only* ones who do what you do."

"True enough, thank you."

Caitlin let Gilroy see the concern in her stare. "Then where exactly was Sergeant Serles, a double amputee, transferred?"

"I can't say."

Caitlin felt her muscles growing taut, her skin starting to feel like somebody had slathered Ben-Gay all over it. "Can't or won't, sir?"

"Ranger, what happens inside these walls happens under military jurisdiction."

"Like a kid who got his legs blown off getting pushed out your doors before he could walk through them."

"If you'd like to speak to Sergeant Serles's commanding officer—"

"I'd like to speak to Sergeant Serles."

Gilroy nodded grudgingly. "Very well, then. If you'd accompany me to my office, there are a few forms to fill out."

He put his hand on Caitlin's shoulder to guide her toward the elevators and she shook him off, stiffening even more. "You're not from Texas, are you, Colonel?"

"Very few of us are."

"Then you probably don't realize a Ranger's jurisdiction pays no heed to borders and the like. My granddad chased more than his share of bandits and rustlers into Mexico and my dad made plenty of trips onto army bases to arrest soldiers for what they'd done off them. Where are you from, sir?"

"Florida."

"Well, Sergeant Serles is from right here in San Antonio and that counts for something too."

Gilroy was starting to look impatient. "Not to the army it doesn't."

"Why was Sergeant Serles transferred, Colonel?"

"I don't know, ma'am."

"Doesn't say on that clipboard of yours?"

"The information's classified."

"Then you do know."

Gilroy didn't say anything.

"Who classified it?" Caitlin asked him.

"It's routine procedure with enlisted personnel," Gilroy tried, hoping it would work.

"Nothing routine about getting your legs blown off by an IED or the runaround from somebody who is supposed to care."

Gilroy backed off, as if suddenly aware of the SIG holstered on Caitlin's hip. "MPs are en route, Ranger. Do I have to have them escort you off the premises?"

"Not if you just tell me where I can find Sergeant Serles, Colonel."

An elevator door opened and a pair of uniformed MPs, a woman and a man each wearing a sidearm, emerged and headed straight for them.

"You can't tell me where this boy is," Caitlin said to Gilroy.

"I believe I've made that clear already."

"Then who can? Since you lack the authority, tell me who's got it."

"Ranger, you've gotten all the information you need from me."

Caitlin let the MPs see her looking at them, as she backpedaled for the door. "Yeah, Sergeant Serles is army all right and what happened to him in Iraq may have been way out of our jurisdiction for sure. But he's a Texas boy, born and bred, and when a Texan calls the Rangers for help, we come and keep on a-coming until the job's done. So, Colonel, if you happen to have a change of heart on the subject over to our way of thinking, you know where to find me."

"I do, ma'am."

"And if anything happens to that kid before I talk to him again, I'll figure out where to find you. That clear enough, sir?"

Gilroy mocked a salute. "Crystal, Ranger."

"Long as we understand each other," Caitlin told him, easing her way through the door with eyes never leaving the MPs.

37

SAN ANTONIO; THE PRESENT

Caitlin's blood was still boiling when she pulled out of the parking lot and felt her rental car thump over a speed bump en route off the grounds and into the night. Last thing she needed now was another issue heaped atop her already full plate, but here it was. And she was too exhausted and her thought process too numb to fully consider the ramifications of the now missing Mark John Serles.

What if his story was true?

The question was as impossible to ignore as the answer was increasingly clear. Serles's mysterious "transfer" could only be rooted in the legitimacy of his claims of murdered soldiers and contractors in Iraq for reasons cloaked in shadows and subterfuge.

For now. Because part of the source of Caitlin's anger and frustration lay in the circumstances that had forced her to delay looking into the claims Mark Serles had raised in his story. Maybe if she had acted immediately, maybe if she had offered some kind of protection . . .

Maybe.

Back on I-37, going south down the Pan Am Expressway, Caitlin's mind had started to drift toward possible next steps when the thunderstorm she'd been expecting sprang up, drenching the night and battling the attempt of the wipers to clear the windshield. She slowed her speed, the storm violent enough to make her consider pulling over for a time just before she saw a car parked at an odd angle in the freeway's breakdown lane. The driver's door was open to the blowing storm with no driver in sight.

Caitlin pulled the rental up a safe distance behind the car and popped on her flashers too, hoping they would make at least some dent in the storm. She yanked her arms into the jacket she'd tossed into the car's backseat and climbed out with hood pulled up over her head.

She'd just cleared the car's front fender when her spine tingled, something Mark Serles had told her making her slow.

"Strange in itself, since the insurgents had started setting their IEDs in parked cars a while back, more effective that way . . ."

Memory of those words froze her altogether for just a moment before she began backpedaling. Caitlin had just cleared the front fender of the rental car when a bright flash split the night a split second before a wave of superheated air blew her into the blackness.

38

MIDLAND, TEXAS; THE PRESENT

"Thank you for coming, gentlemen," Malcolm Arno said, as he stepped onto the stage of the complex's meeting hall, into the spill of hot white lights that blinded him to his audience.

No matter. He didn't need to see their faces as he spoke; he knew who they were and multiple greetings had already been exchanged.

"We're all here today because we share the same vision of what America needs to be and where it's gone wrong. Lots of you figure this is something new and different. I'm here to tell you it's not. I'm here to tell you it's been building for a lot of years, from back when I witnessed it firsthand."

A soft murmur spread through the assembled crowd. They were all intimately acquainted with the Texas Ranger raid on Max Arno's Church of the Redeemer and the shootout that had claimed his life days later. Just as they were acquainted with pretty much every incursion by the government into the lives of private citizens, raising a fury that had reached an apotheosis in the time of the current administration.

"There was a time," Malcolm Arno continued, "when what happened at the Church of the Redeemer was a rallying cry for what the country was heading toward. Trouble was not enough heeded that call, and look where that got us. The government has invaded every phase of our lives, and if we don't draw a line in the sand here and now, we won't even have lives left. I called you all here today because it's time to say 'No more!' No more to a godless administration that treats individual liberties like postage stamps. I watched my father die in a parking lot, sat on the gravel next to him while he took his last breath, and I'm here to tell you what I see going on in this country today leaves me with the same empty feeling in my gut.

"But you know something? My father, for all his charisma and brilliance, had things wrong. Sermons and good intentions are nothing compared to bullets and state-of-the-art weaponry. The Texas Rangers took the Church of the Redeemer compound because they wielded pistols, twelve-gauges, and assault rifles. I learned convictions don't carry as far as bullets in making your point and preventing others from stopping you."

The crowd applauded that, a few whistles and hoots of approval thrown in for good measure.

"Washington has to be stopped, plain and simple. Otherwise, my father died for nothing. I still have the shirt I wore that day, all splattered with blood. It's moth-eaten and frayed now, the stains more black than red. Those stains seem to get smaller every time I take that shirt from my closet and hold it up to the light to remind myself. I'll still remember what happened when they're gone altogether, but what about everyone else? The government relies on the fact that we'll talk a lot but not really act. Well, I stand before you today to say that is no longer the case."

The assembled crowd lurched to their collective feet in a rousing ovation that almost embarrassed Arno in its visceral intensity. There were the Brothers of the Revolution, Fathers of the New America, the Sons of the Confederacy forming a twisted family of lost values and fears of massive gun confiscations and secret work camps where those who didn't toe the government line would ultimately end up.

There were the Disciples of Freedom, the Children of Anarchy, the Soldiers of Christ, the True United States, the Army of Tomorrow. All with massive mailing lists and a huge presence on the Web, culled from the rural South, population-starved West, and restless Heartland that together formed the moral center of the country. Both its compass and a mirror to hold up during those times when the liberals made headway with false promises and actions fueled by lies building toward a world where the government ran everything.

"Gentlemen," Arno continued to the faceless assemblage before him, concentrated in only the first three rows of the hall, "we are all soldiers in a war we must win if this country is to survive." Channeling his father now, feeling the great man inside, inspiring him, as his voice rose to a near bellow. "So many don't mind being under the thumb of the government for what they eat, pump, drink, smoke. Taxes keep rising and where does the money go? They tell us they're gonna fix health care and one morning we'll wake up to see them taking over the hospitals and choosing our doctors for us and when we die. My father had had enough twenty years ago, and those twenty years have brought us further down a road to hell itself."

"I say we fry that nigger once and for all!" a Southern drawl voiced.

"I say we should just kill the lot of them while we still have guns to do it," a raspy voice chimed in, to which several others added their assent.

"Guns are no longer our problem, my friends."

"Easy for you to say, living here in a goddamn fortress," a voice blared, "built with your daddy's dollars."

Arno stepped out from behind the podium. "The government took every asset my father and his church ever had. Confiscated it all, even the land and the wood his church was built from after they demolished it. But provenance saw fit to deliver fresh revenue onto my cause and such provenance allows me to share my spoils with you."

"You lost me, Reverend."

"I'm no man of God, my friend. To dare call myself one would be to blaspheme my father's memory and hold myself to an image I can't possibly fulfill. No, violence was against his and any church's teachings. But violence is what we need here and now to reclaim what's ours and reclaim it fast."

The thunderous applause that followed those remarks made Arno think the very walls of the meeting hall were shaking.

"Let me explain," Malcolm Arno continued, seizing the moment to move deeper into the spill of the lights. "You have the desire to wage the war we need, to put a stop to the government steamrolling over our rights and our very being. It's the proper tools you lack, but I'm here to tell you I can change that."

Murmurs slithered through the crowd before him. Arno had purposely timed this speech for after a dinner in which moderate levels of alcohol had been consumed. Enough to get his guests' dander up without turning them into an unruly mob. He needed them with relatively clear heads tonight, needed to send them back to the memberships of the movements and militias they represented to share his vision and his promise. Keep telling their followers what to think after Arno told *them* what to think. Moments like this left him feeling most like his father, channeling the holy preacher born of tent revival meetings and healing ceremonies to which the faithful flocked.

"You think we can win this war by killing one abortion doctor? We can't. We need to kill *all* abortion doctors. You think we can win it by shooting up a Holocaust museum? We can't. We need to burn the building down or blow it up. You think we can prevail by assassinating the president? We can't. Obama's done more for our cause than any man in this room. Made us relevant again. Don't you see? Thanks to him, we don't have to keep our heads hidden in the sand anymore. I'm not talking about wearing white sheets and burning crosses on lawns. No, I'm talking about taking this country back for real and for good. Our movement's gone mainstream. Last thing we want to do is create a martyr for the country to rally around. We've got enough folks in our back pocket and they'll be more once we unleash our fountains of fury."

"That's all well and good," came a voice out of the blur before him. "But just where's all this ordnance supposed to come from?"

"Make me a list," Arno told him. "You want tanks, high-powered machine guns, helicopter gunships? The sky's the limit for us now. We're going to splinter this country right down the middle. Push the piss-ant pussies away and draw more over. There won't be a lot at first, but those numbers will soar and skyrocket. And a hardened ten percent of the country can accomplish a heck of a lot more than a worthless ninety."

The men muttered among themselves, drinking in his rhetoric. Spoken from the heart to men without a cogent feel for words but a firm grasp of the ideals he needed if his father's vision was to be realized.

"We been waiting for this call to arms to come for a long time, Brother Arno," came another voice, lost in a drawl that sounded more Kentucky-based. "I knew your daddy and he'd be pleased as punch by what you're fixing to do."

"But we have to be patient, Brother Eugene," Arno said, addressing him by name. His eyes had adjusted to the lights, the men seated before him captured in a dull haze that obscured their features, rendering them faceless before him. "Can't let our goals be lost in haste or in the small thinking that's plagued us for too long."

"The hell you say? I been planning a goddamn insurrection since you was in diapers."

"But it hasn't come to pass yet, has it? And it won't either, not ever. FBI's so far up your movement's ass, you got them mistaken for hemorrhoids. Before your goddamn revolution can fire a single shot, they'll have you in chains on charges of treason just like happened to the Hutaree up in Michigan and plenty of others too."

"Treason? It's them that should be swinging from the gallows for betraying this country and you damn well know it!"

"You bet I do, but they have the power and always will until we take it from them."

"Revolution," another voice chimed in, "just like the man said!"

"They can't know we're coming," Arno proclaimed just the way his father would have. "They can't know we're there until we're already upon them. Otherwise, they'll crush us. Everyone in this room knows they're just waiting for the excuse. They read our e-mails, bug our phones, monitor our money, plant their agents inside the worlds we build to keep them out. Anyone who so much as clicks on one of our websites gets a file open at the FBI and a whole new batch of friends in Washington watching over them."

"Fuck Washington!"

"*Yeah! Yeah!*" the crowd joined in.

"You wanna fuck Washington?"

"*Yeah!*"

"You really wanna *fuck* Washington?"

"*YEAH!*"

"Then we need to take it over, not storm it. We've got to play their game and play it better. You think I'd be standing before you now if the 2010 congressional races hadn't already got the pot stirring? You think I'd be standing here before you if the writing weren't already on the wall? Well, it is and all we have to do is read it, my friends."

"Didn't bring my glasses," a man with a beard halfway down to his chest said from the front row. "Why don't you read it for me, Malcolm?"

"It says Washington is ours to take, the White House included. Starts with guns, but then moves to a civil war fought with markers and chads and levers."

"What are you saying, son?" asked one of his father's closest disciples who had founded a ministry across the South that now claimed over three million followers, robots waiting to be programmed.

"The next election," Arno answered him. "We're going to elect one of our own as president of the United States."

39

Caitlin was seated on the sill of the rescue truck's open rear door when D. W. Tepper screeched to a halt near the fire engines that continued to douse the burnt-out remnants of the car she'd pulled over to check. He gazed briefly at the bubbled paint and puckered steel of her rental car, its windshield blown out by the shrapnel that had barely missed Caitlin, and just shook his head.

"And you wanna know why I took up smoking again," he said, approaching Caitlin through the night with a barn coat covering his shrunken shoulders and Stetson swallowing a good portion of his face. I-35 south had been shut down entirely, traffic rerouted onto side roads nearly flooded out by the sudden torrent that had spilled from the sky.

"Don't you be blaming that on me, D.W."

He stopped right before her and laid a warm hand on her shoulder. "You are a one-person wrecking crew, Ranger."

Caitlin cast her gaze on the smoldering wreck. "One of the firemen's a reservist who did two tours in Iraq. Said he knows the look of an IED when he sees one."

"You're saying you were targeted personally?"

"I'd say if the shoe fits, Captain," Caitlin said, raising her right foot that was down to the sock, "but the blast blew off one of my boots."

Tepper's features relaxed and then tightened again. "You all right otherwise?"

"My ears are still ringing. Besides that, yes."

Tepper slid up alongside Caitlin and took off his hat. "So who was it did the targeting?"

"You wouldn't believe it."

"Make me."

"I went back to the Intrepid to see the young man you sent me to interview two days back. He's gone. Transferred they said."

"*They* said?"

"Kid told me the army planted the IED that blew off his legs in Iraq. Said it was actually a shaped charge and being a medic I figure he could tell. He was in genuine fear for his life, Captain."

"You didn't put that in any report I saw."

"Didn't have time to file one."

Tepper ran a nicotine-stained fingertip along a deep crevice dug into his cheek. "Make believe you're doing so now."

"Kid claimed it had something to do with a shot-up civilian who was brought into the field hospital where he served as an OR medic. Man's last words were some kind of numerical designation followed by the mention of something called Operation Rising Dawn."

"Mean anything to you?"

"Not yet."

"Not *yet*?"

"They tried to kill me, D.W."

"There you go again with 'they' . . ."

"Okay, the army."

"Oh, shit."

"Sorry, Captain."

Tepper slapped his hat against his side. "Why you always gotta go taking on King Kong? Once, Caitlin, just once I wish you'd pick an enemy that fits behind bars."

PART FOUR

There once was a bank robber by the name of Jorge Rodriguez who lived in Mexico. He frequently crossed the border into Texas to rob banks, and he so frustrated the Texas Rangers that a large bounty was placed on his head. Each time they nearly caught up with Rodriguez he would manage to cross the Rio Grande and be safe in Mexico, where the Rangers were prohibited from pursuing him. One day an old Texas Ranger couldn't stand it any longer. He followed Rodriguez across the border into a little town cantina. He snuck up behind him and put a gun to Rodriguez's temple. He demanded that the now-infamous bandit tell where he had placed all of his stolen money.

"Tell me, now," said the Ranger, "or I will blow your head off, right here!"

But, there was a problem. The Ranger could not speak Spanish! In the bar, however, there was a man who volunteered to overcome this impasse by translating for the Ranger. The translator told Rodriguez exactly what the Ranger had said, and then he asked where he had hidden the money. Fearful for his life, Rodriguez quickly told the translator that the money was hidden behind the third brick at the city well. The translator got a solemn look on his face and said to the Ranger in perfect English, "Jorge Rodriguez is a very brave and stubborn man. He said he would rather die than tell you where the money is hidden!"

—Texas Ranger folktale, 1881

40

"I'm on my way, outlaw" was all Paz said to Cort Wesley over his cell phone. "I'll call you when I get to your hotel."

He'd been sitting in a chair by the window for hours—how many he didn't know, couldn't say. He'd moved to the chair after he grew tired of staring at the ceiling or trying to watch Spanish shows on television. He'd checked into the Hotel Museo Palacio at the corner of Galeana and 5 de Mayo specifically because it was a favorite of Mexican tourists as opposed to American ones. He would've preferred something simpler and less fancy. But Cort Wesley wasn't in the mood for exploring and the hotel's location in the heart the city's historic center meant he could get himself settled fast to wait for Colonel Guillermo Paz's call.

Talk about making a deal with the devil.

But Cort Wesley didn't care. Horns and a tail wouldn't bother him if their owner could help him find Dylan.

It was always times like these that he picked up the scents of talcum powder and root beer on the air, the smells clinging to Leroy Epps, an ex-boxer who became Cort Wesley's cellmate during his stretch in the brutal Huntsville prison known as The Walls. Epps had beaten a man to death in self-defense, but the man had been white and well connected enough to land old Leroy life without parole. Inside The Walls his counsel helped keep Cort Wesley sane and his friendship had been the only thing lending order to the chaos. Epps had died of diabetes that had been diagnosed and poorly treated inside, but that didn't stop Cort Wesley's mind from conjuring the old man up when he needed him the most.

Tonight Epps showed up seated on the edge of the room's bed, staring at Cort Wesley in silence with tired eyes still leaking red onto the whites.

"*You got something to say, champ, go ahead and say it,*" Cort Wesley started.

"*Rather watch you sit there and eat yourself alive, bubba.*"

"*You blame me?*"

"*For being all twisted in knots over your son, no. For shooting down that Mexican rat turd who ran down his girlfriend, that's something else again.*"

"*You sound like Caitlin Strong.*"

"*Guess that makes both of us right then, don't it?*"

"*I've never been good at impulse control, champ.*"

"*Could've fooled me inside The Walls, bubba. You were so cool there the temperature used to drop when you walked into a room.*"

"*Resignation. I knew nothing I did mattered a damn, so what was the point?*"

"*And now what you do does matter.*"

"*So to speak.*"

Epps's big eyes suddenly looked even wearier. "*Gunning down that drug dealer was self-serving, bubba. Tell me I'm wrong.*"

"*I can't.*"

"*You didn't want to tell your boy what happened to his girlfriend until you had squared things.*"

"*I figured that would avoid exactly what's happening now.*"

"*Maybe you should've thought of that when you decided to still keep the truth back from him.*"

"*I just never got around to it.*"

"*Never known you to be scared of anything, bubba.*"

"*That what you think this is about?*"

"*I know it is. Fear that the boy's growing up and slipping away. You tell him about his girl and what you done about it, you're making him a man, and that's what scares you.*"

"*I never felt so goddamn helpless in my entire life.*"

"*Really? I can remember meeting you in The Walls, the most feared out-law in Texas beaten by a system that had fucked him good.*"

"*That was different.*"

"*Really, bubba? How's that?*"

"*I could do something about it, exert a measure of control over the land-scape. Can't do that here.*"

"*And so there lies the problem.*"

"*Being a ghost doesn't give you license to speak in riddles, champ.*"

Epps swept his pale tongue about his parched lips. "*Forgot to take one of my root beers down with me. Wouldn't happen to have one handy, would you?*"

"*No. Sorry.*"

"*No matter. I'll get me one soon as I get back where I be. Anyway, what I was getting at was this: all these changes in your life and you still can't learn to trust nobody.*"

"*I trust Caitlin Strong.*"

"*That's 'cause you know how good she is when it comes to guns and the situations that call for them. You don't trust Dylan 'cause you don't figure he can handle himself similarly.*"

"*With good reason, champ: he's just a kid.*"

"*But* whose *kid, with whose blood pumping through his veins?*"

"*What's your point?*"

Leroy Epps lay back on the bed. He interlaced his fingers behind his head and stretched himself out, bagging his pant legs up so Cort Wesley could see the diabetes-spawned sores that had ultimately killed him with an infection.

"*Well, bubba, you gotta trust this boy to do the right thing in even the worst situation. Not saying he'll be able to get himself all the way out of it, no, but he'll get himself square enough to buy you the time you need. I been looking in on the boy from time to time and, man, if I don't blink twice I think I'm looking in on you, as far as the insides go anyway.*"

"*He's not me, champ.*"

"*Close enough.*"

Cort Wesley's cell phone rang again and he jerked it to his ear, roused from the trance.

"I'm downstairs," said Guillermo Paz.

41

Captain D. W. Tepper glared at Caitlin as soon as she walked into Ruby's Diner where he had breakfast every morning before making the drive from Marble Falls to San Antonio. She moved straight to his booth, noticed the heaping plate of scrambled eggs, bacon, and home fries before him. Untouched.

"Are you trying to make my life miserable, Ranger?"

"What I do now?"

"It's not every day a man gets a wake-up call from the United States Army."

Caitlin remained standing. "They apologize for trying to blow me up?"

"They were more interested in complaining about the holy hell you raised last night at the Intrepid Center, sticking your nose where it plainly don't belong."

"Oh, right, that was *before* they tried to blow me up."

"Army folks told me that kid's transfer was routine."

"They say to where?"

"I didn't ask, 'cause it's none of my business. Yours neither." Tepper looked down at his cooling plate of food and shook his head. "Last time I lost my appetite was on account of a bullet in my side your daddy had to pry out with that knife of his."

Caitlin frowned. "You smell like smoke, D.W."

Tepper dropped his hand down into his lap. "I gotta choose between ruining my lungs or my liver, so long as you're raising hell in three different countries. Man oh man, it's a good thing the USA's got no neighbors to the east or west, or you'd be raising holy hell there too." He ran a hand through the stiff gray hair he still smoothed with Brylcreem. "How you feeling?"

"Head hurts like hell and I can't kick the ringing in my ears, but I can still shoot."

Tepper looked trapped between a breath and a belch. "I'll keep that in mind. Tell me something, Ranger, you ever work with anybody you didn't piss off?"

Caitlin grabbed a forkful of eggs off his plate. "Guess you know who I take after."

"Difference is Jim Strong only pissed me off once."

"Surprised it was that many times."

"I never told you about it, did I?"

"Not that I recall."

"Then it's time you heard, Caitlin. This goes back to the Church of the Redeemer and that Killane lady he turned as an informant. . . ."

42

Odessa, Texas; 1990

"Here's the way I look at things," Jim told her, really meaning what he was about to say. "You can get yourself another church, Beth Ann, but you can't get yourself another boy."

Jim Strong knew in that moment he had won Beth Ann Killane over, knew he'd secured the informant the Rangers desperately needed to put an end to whatever madness was going on inside the Church of the Redeemer. If only half the things they'd heard were true about girls little older than his daughter, Caitlin, sleeping with men and bearing their children, it was enough to turn any man's stomach. And that didn't take into account the very real possibility that the Reverend Max Arno was stockpiling weapons on the site for God knows what down the road.

Jim didn't ask another thing of Beth Ann Killane until he had a pardon letter for her son, Danny, in hand. True to his word, he'd driven personally to Austin to collect it, not about to take no for an answer or accept any bureaucratic delays. The letter, as it turned out, was waiting for him, and he delivered it the next day to Beth Ann at the Pancake Alley diner in Odessa.

"Now," Jim told her, "I want you to take an extra good look at paragraph three here—it specifies this pardon is conditional on you furnishing information on the Church of the Redeemer compound to the best of your ability and knowledge."

"What's that mean exactly?"

"Just what it says."

"And who decides if I've done so to the best of my ability and knowledge?"

"Me, Beth Ann." Before she could voice further protest or question, Jim continued, "And let me tell you something else. This letter here comes with my word attached. That means if those suit-wearing folk in Austin don't keep their word to you, they're gonna have to face me and, believe me when I tell you, that is something they most certainly want no part of."

Beth Ann finally smiled. "Do I have to sign something now?"

"Nope, you just have to talk."

And talk she did, becoming a veritable fountain of information that exceeded even Jim's expectations. Some in the Ranger command suggested the possibility of wiring her up to perhaps get even more incriminating evidence on Max Arno. But Jim dismissed the idea out of hand, certain it would only make Beth Ann nervous and ultimately detract from the contribution she was already making. He'd mounted his argument toward that end, convincing all except his partner, D. W. Tepper, who'd recently joined the task force at Jim's request as his second-in-command.

"Who you protecting here, *amigo*?"

"Just living up to my word, D.W."

"Something in your eyes tells me it's more than that."

"My eyes? Like what?"

"Don't know, on account of it's something I ain't never seen before exactly. Please tell me it's not cause for concern."

"It's not cause for concern, D.W."

"You're not lying to me now?"

"Have I ever?"

Jim wasn't, of course, at least not at the time. Over the course of the ensuing weeks he'd followed the informant's book to a T, making Beth Ann Killane utterly dependent on him and making sure she knew it. Because it was impossible for them to exchange all the necessary information inside the diner, Jim suggested they pretend to be seeing each other socially. He still carried his gun on these occasions but didn't wear his Stetson or Ranger badge.

"See," D. W. Tepper intoned, after Jim tried to explain those particular actions, "I knew it."

"Knew what?"

"That you had eyes for this woman all along."

"Beth Ann Killane?"

"You running any other informants on this case I'm not aware of?"

"I'm just going by the book here, D.W."

"What book is that, *amigo*?"

"The one we learned up at Quantico when we did a month's training with the FBI. Make the informant totally beholden to you, I believe was the way the instructor put it."

"He must have, since I never heard you use the word 'beholden' in twenty years. But tell me, *amigo*, does making a lady beholden include getting her to sleep with you?"

Jim Strong didn't bother hiding his anger. "Take a look at my eyes again, D.W. See how pissed off they look. You want me to pop you one, just keep talking like that."

D. W. Tepper leaned back in his chair, laid his boots gingerly on the table between them and fired a match off the right heel. "Just let me know when I'm proven right," he said, lighting up a Marlboro.

"You smoke too much, D.W."

"So you keep telling me."

"Moving a little slow there. You been in a scrape or something?"

"Met up with Boone Masters in a bar outside San Antone."

"I would've paid to see that one."

"Save the money for Masters's medical bills since I busted him up pretty good."

Jim Strong had been telling the truth: bedding down with Beth Ann Killane had neither occurred nor was his intention at the time. The problem was times change.

Beth Ann's desire to do anything to aid her son's plight knew no bounds. When Jim steadfastly refused to give her a camera to snap off pictures of the complex, she used her drawing skills to provide an amazingly accurate conception of the entire place in perfect scale.

"What about the weapons?" Jim asked, thumbing through her various drawings.

"Sorry, Jim. I've never heard or seen anything about weapons."

He leaned across the table and took both her hands, squeezing them in his. "Here's how it is, Beth Ann. That's the last bit of information we need before we're ready to saddle up and put an end to the misery this man is bringing onto innocent children. But we wanna do it without any loss of life, and if those weapons get out and things turn to shooting, lots of innocent folks guilty of nothing more than looking for something to believe in are gonna get hurt and maybe killed."

Jim let his point sink in before continuing.

"I can control things only up to a point, Beth Ann, and with the Rangers that point is when guns get pointed our way. Best way we can avoid that is to include securing of the guns in our plans to make sure this goes off without a single scratch being suffered by any involved."

"I'll see what I can find out, Jim, but I just don't know. These are peaceful, God-fearing people mostly. They want to build their own lives where the government won't bother them, sure, but I just can't see them resorting to violence."

Jim knew the guns were on the premises, but didn't want to push the issue too far at present. "We've just got to be sure, Beth Ann. The mere possibility means we've got to assume the worst: that the guns are there and someone may overreact and use them. We can't have that, not the Rangers and not the members of the church either."

Beth Ann frowned. "I'll see what I can find out, Jim."

. . .

Beth Ann Killane wasn't exactly an important person inside the Church of the Redeemer. But she was welcomed warmly into the fold and could count any number of folks she was on a first-name basis with to the point where she looked forward to attending the services, retreats, special events, and especially the Reverend Arno's fiery sermons. She endeavored to curry more of his favor by taking charge of the choir when her predecessor's arthritis took a turn for the worse. With the Easter service coming up, this placed her in Arno's company on a daily basis and he began to take real notice of her.

"Sister Beth Ann," he greeted when she was packing up her music sheets one evening.

Hearing Arno's voice nearly sent her leaping out of her skin, but Beth Ann recovered quickly enough to throw on a smile and push the hair back from her face. "Reverend Arno, what a pleasant surprise."

"I wanted to thank you for all your hard work on the church's behalf, sister."

"No thanks necessary, Reverend. I'm pleased to be able to contribute."

"I notice you always come alone to the services. Do you have children, sister?"

"A boy, Reverend."

"No girls as pretty as their mama?" Arno asked, his smile gleaming.

Beth Ann thought his words sounded like someone had slathered them with grease. She fought not to show how revolted she was, based on all Jim Strong had told her, replying, "No, Reverend, just a single son."

"Got a picture of him handy?"

Beth Ann started to fish one from her handbag, then thought better of it. "Not on me, I guess."

"Well, I'm sure if he looks anything like his mama, he's a good-looking boy indeed."

Arno's smile glimmered again and Beth Ann thought she smelled dried sweat trying to push its way through the layer of aftershave with which he always doused himself. In the thin light of the church, he looked merged with the shadows of the candle flames dancing around him. For some reason Beth Ann had the feeling tentacles were about to shoot out of his eyes.

"Our children are our true treasures, sister. Now I'm aware your son's had his problems with the law."

"You . . . are?"

Arno nodded. "Make it my business to be aware of such parts of the lives of the members of my church, especially those who extend themselves for it, like yourself. I raise this because I believe I can help your boy if you let me. The Church of the Redeemer has helped any number like him and I'd be proud to extend myself to Danny on your behalf."

Beth Ann had started to smile, when she realized she hadn't told Arno her son's name. The fact he used it anyway, with so much casual familiarity, left an even queasier feeling in the pit of her stomach.

"I'll keep that in mind," she said with no recollection of ever forming the words. "Thank you, Reverend."

"No, sister," Arno smiled, stretching a hand to her shoulder and rubbing it gently. "Thank *you*."

Beth Ann went straight to Jim Strong's motel room in Odessa from there, shaking up a storm even through her second cup of the coffee brewed from the in-room machine.

"He touched my shoulder," she said, still trying to compose herself, "and I swear I felt scales on his palm, like a darn lizard. I wonder if the Reverend Arno's even human."

"You're doing a wonderful job for us, Beth Ann," Jim said, stroking the same shoulder Arno had rubbed. "Thanks to you, hundreds of folks are gonna be saved from the sickness you've just begun to realize is going on."

Beth Ann looked at him, resolute now instead of scared. "I'm gonna find those guns for you, Jim, and that's a promise."

She'd torn out the pins that normally held up her hair in the nervous frenzy that accompanied her into the room. Jim had never seen it down before and the result was to cast Beth Ann Killane in a totally different light for him. She wasn't wearing her waitress uniform, and the jeans and sweater did a much better job of highlighting the lines and curves

Jim had pretended not to notice before. He reached over and kissed her before he realized what he was doing. Pulled away quick, but Beth Ann reeled him back in for a second kiss even quicker.

"I don't wanna be alone tonight," she said softly, hugging him. "That man put thoughts in my head that make my skin crawl."

Jim Strong hugged her back. "It'll be over soon. I promise."

"Jim?"

"Yeah?"

"Don't let go of me. Promise me you won't."

"I promise."

43

MARBLE FALLS; THE PRESENT

"They slept atop the covers that night," D. W. Tepper told Caitlin, "but underneath them the next. When your father told me, I damn near smacked him upside the head."

"Why didn't you?"

"This was Jim Strong we're talking about. He got something in his mind, it was gonna take a better man than me to get it out. Sound familiar?"

"You're as good a man as they come, D.W."

Caitlin watched Tepper's jowls tighten. "Truth is I didn't blame him a bit. He hadn't been with a woman in the eleven years or so since your mother passed, and if God wanted to drop Beth Ann Killane into his lap, who was I to argue?" He shook his head, gaze going misty. "She was quite a woman to look at, I'll tell you that much. Not when you first laid eyes on her, though. Her beauty kind of grew on you."

"They had an affair?"

Tepper nodded. "Lasted until the day of the raid."

"When she was killed."

Tepper turned his attention back to his food. "I don't like eating with the past as company."

"How'd she die, D.W.?"

Tepper pushed some eggs into his mouth, a slight trail left on the right side. "What I just say?"

Caitlin forked home another mouthful from his plate.

"Aw, hell, order your own, will you, Caitlin?"

She did just that, certain Tepper had gone as far as he intended today with the story of her father's affair with Beth Ann Killane.

"I can't get the connection between a drug ring at the northern border and white slavers in Mexico out of my head," Caitlin said, after the waitress had slid away from their table.

"Start with what you know, Ranger."

"First time I talked to Frank Gage, head of the DEA task force, he took me out to an Indian Reservation in upstate New York and explained how the drug traffic across the frozen rivers has gone off the charts in the past couple years; ice bridges, he called them. Gage suspected a new financial source was behind the surge in traffic up there. Then yesterday I came across the fact that the brother of the two Angels I killed in that Quebec grow house is running kidnapped kids through Mexico."

Tepper forced down some eggs and looked like he was swallowing tacks. "You're a *Texas* Ranger, Caitlin. That doesn't make you the law for the whole goddamn hemisphere." He dropped his fork on the plate. "You get your teeth in something, I swear sometimes you can't even see what you're biting."

"That include the army medic Mark Serles? Strange thing is that I went to the Intrepid last night to tell the kid there was nothing more I could do, that the army had jurisdiction."

"Kind of what they told me this morning."

"Jurisdiction over what exactly? Kid's a wounded soldier, not a criminal. Somebody's hiding something, Captain, and it almost got me blown to hell last night."

Tepper nodded dramatically, curling his fingers together and cracking his knuckles. "So a Texas Ranger under my command gets back from pissing off the *federalés* in Mexico, after getting back from pissing off a drug task force on the northern border, and now wants to piss off the whole of Washington."

"If I have to, yes."

Tepper could only shake his head. "Is there anyplace on this planet that's safe from you?"

"I seem to do all right in Texas."

"Everything's relative, Ranger." Tepper held her gaze briefly before continuing. "You hear from Masters?"

"He's working on a lead."

"Why does the way you just said that worry me?"

Caitlin didn't answer him.

"I talked to my nephew who's a lawyer," Tepper resumed. "He says Masters can fight the extradition in federal court."

"Your nephew have much experience in the area?"

"Nope, but he recommended somebody who does. Real sharp-shooter when it comes to the law. Every bit as tough as a Ranger except he carries a business card instead of a gun."

Caitlin's BlackBerry rang, nothing showing in the Caller ID. "You mind if I take this, Captain? Could be Cort Wesley."

"Go right ahead," said Tepper, digging back into his eggs with his attention remaining on her.

"Caitlin Strong," she answered.

"It's me, Ranger," an anxious voice announced. "Sergeant Mark Serles."

44

SAN ANTONIO; THE PRESENT

Caitlin put the phone on speaker and held it so Captain Tepper could hear. "I've been worried about you, Sergeant."

"I know I caused you some trouble and I want to apologize for that."

"Where are you?"

"Back at Intrepid."

"Back?"

"They moved me across to Brooke for a time. I needed some treatment.

I've been losing it lately, seeing everything but little green men climbing down the walls. I'm sorry for inconveniencing you this way."

"You didn't, Sergeant. It's my job."

"Well, there's no job for you here. I've been letting things get to me, but I'm better now." A pause. "They're gonna start fitting me for my new legs tomorrow."

"Now there's cause for celebration."

"I'm gonna walk out of here, Ranger, and that's a fact."

"I don't doubt it for a minute, Sergeant."

"I don't even remember all the stuff we talked about. I been telling lots of stories to lots of people, and sometimes they roll into each other."

"Hard to keep the facts straight at times, isn't it?"

"Ranger?"

"I'm just making the point that you've been through a hell no one had a right to expect of you. Be a shame if someone was making that hell worse by applying undue pressure."

"I don't think I know what you mean."

Caitlin could feel her neck stiffen with tension, a pounding settling between her still ringing ears. "Anybody making you do or say something you don't want is gonna have to face me sooner or later. That's what I mean."

Silence.

"I appreciate that, ma'am," Serles said finally. "I really do."

"Just keep it in mind, M.J. Texas is a big place for sure, but you'd be surprised at how hard it is to hide all the same."

"Nobody needs to do any hiding as far as I'm concerned. Those things I told you, whatever they were, one thing I'm sure of is that they didn't happen. Truth is I can't remember one lick of how I lost my legs. Guess my mind's gotta make stuff up in order to cope."

"You said they sent you over to Brooke Army Medical Center for a time after we met."

"They did, ma'am," Serles said, sounding clearly embarrassed. "I'd rather not say where exactly, if you don't mind."

"Of course not."

"Because these kinds of things tend to stay with a man, come back and haunt him long after the deed is done."

"I understand, Sergeant," Caitlin told him, her eyes on Captain Tepper.

"I had a nice sit-down with Colonel Gilroy. He's been square with me from the start and no one knows what I'm facing better than him, having been through it himself. So if you don't mind, Ranger, I'd like you to forget our conversation from the other day ever happened. My brain's as busted as my body, but at least they can fix that with the right meds. I feel better already and that's the God's honest truth. I'm sorry for wasting your time."

"Not a waste at all. Just keep our number handy in case you need it again."

"Thank you, Ranger. I truly mean that."

"Thank you for your service and sacrifice, Sergeant. And I truly mean that."

Caitlin heard a quick clacking noise after which her screen flash CALL ENDED and provided the length.

"Well?" Tepper prodded.

"He's lying," she said, the pounding between her ears even worse now.

Tepper gnashed his teeth and blew out enough breath to rustle the daisies that sat in a table vase between them. "I once shot a pitbull got loose from a dog-fighting pen and bit into a boy's arm clean to the bone. Damn thing's jaws stayed fastened tight even after I put five slugs into him and he was deader than Elvis. Ended up prying the dog's jaws open with the jack from my truck." He stopped and rested his elbows on the table. "Question being, do I need to go outside and fetch that jack now to pry you off this?"

"Serles said no one knows what he's facing better than Colonel Gilroy, all things considered."

"I heard him. So?"

"I take that to mean Colonel Gilroy's an amputee too. Except the 'Colonel Gilroy' I talked to last night had all his parts. I'm guessing he was some Washington drone wanted to make sure my investigation wouldn't go any further."

Tepper rubbed his nose with the nicotine-stained fingers of his right hand. "So you figure this Gilroy, or whoever he was, was the one who set up the ambush?"

"Doesn't matter whether he was or not specifically. What matters is why. Mark Serles was telling the truth before. We find out why somebody tried to kill him in Iraq and we'll have our answer."

"And I'm guessing you got an idea where to find it."

"Yes, sir, I do."

45

CONCEPCIÓN DEL ORO; THE PRESENT

Cort Wesley drove Caitlin's SUV with Paz's legs balled up in the passenger's seat, even though he'd pushed the seat all the way back. The steering wheel felt moist under his grasp, and he couldn't find a comfortable temperature level no matter how much he played with the controls. Either too hot or too cold, nothing in the middle. Outside, the open vistas of the Mexican wilderness, baking beneath the sun burning in a cloudless sky, only added to his tension. Nothing to see, nothing that looked any different from the last hour or the hour before that. As if the scenery was moving and the SUV standing still. That's what it felt like to him.

"Where we headed again, Colonel?"

"North."

"You said that before."

"It's still the case." Paz was consulting a handheld GPS device with a digital readout and rigid casing Cort Wesley recognized as pure military ordnance. "For another hundred miles or so."

"It's been two hundred already."

Cort Wesley continued up the two-lane road, passing the endless collection of trucks grinding their way through the sun and heat whenever opportunity allowed. They sped through small towns and villages that sprouted atop narrow patches of flora stitched into the desert or in the shadow of numerous mountain ranges that were an outgrowth of the Sierra Madre or Chowchilla ranges. Except for the trucks and an occasional pedestrian, the only evidence of life was scrub or dirt brush blowing across the rocky, gravel-strewn desert floor that looked white under the unbroken sun that owned the sky. They might have been on the road to hell, for all Cort Wesley knew, the world gone hazy and fried beyond the tunnel provided by the pavement.

"Nice piece of equipment you got there," Cort Wesley said finally, eyeing the GPS gadget now resting on Paz's huge lap. "Not something you can pick up at Radio Shack or Best Buy, is it?"

"Walmart," Paz said simply, before turning to look at him. "You want to know more about the army I'm building?"

"Long drives tend to make me curious."

Paz nodded in concession. "What you need to know is this: three of my soldiers found a pair of men in the town of Concepción del Oro who had your son yesterday."

"But they don't have him now."

"We'll be there soon," Paz said, turning back to the sunbaked world that seemed to sway beyond the SUV's windshield.

With that he jogged the GPS device to a touch screen complete with digital keyboard and tapped in a message. Cort Wesley glanced over, trying to read it, wondering if he was riding into some sort of trap himself and then realizing he didn't trust a single goddamn person in the world besides Caitlin Strong.

"My men found them here," Paz said, as they snailed along Concepción del Oro's main street, formed simply by a number of small markets and meat shops, stores that sold sundries, and others that seemed to cater to the occasional tourist passing through.

That single thoroughfare was built at the base of a hill on which the majority of the residents lived in white adobe-style homes that were uniformly small and single story with roofs the color of red clay. A trio of nearly identical cantinas battled for the business of the town's twelve thousand residents, half of whom lived in the surrounding rural communities. Farmers mostly who trucked their crops to the open-air Zacatecas markets in Mazapil and El Salvador. A collection of plastic and wooden chairs sat empty before each of the cantinas, the patrons chased into the darker cool of the buildings by the oppressive sun. Once the sun sank behind the hillside and nearby mountains, the temperature would drop by twenty, maybe thirty degrees this time of year. For now, though, the street was deserted, as if Paz's and Cort Wesley's very presence had chased everyone inside.

"Which one?" Cort Wesley asked Paz as they slid by the second cantina and approached the third. He was squeezing the wheel so tight the muscles of his forearms pulsed and throbbed.

"As a boy, I watched the priest who taught me how to read and write gunned down by street thugs because he wouldn't pay them off," Paz said, instead of responding. "It was the only time in my life I felt weak and helpless."

"Which bar, Colonel?"

"My soldiers took the two men into the desert where they say they last saw your son," Paz told him. "So you will not have to feel weak and helpless today."

Cort Wesley felt his flesh begin to prick. "They say anything else?"

"I'll let you ask them yourself."

46

SAN ANTONIO; THE PRESENT

"Thanks for returning my call so quickly, Mr. Smith," Caitlin said to the man on the other end of the line, speaking into the hidden microphone on her replacement rental car's Bluetooth device.

"It's Jones here in Washington, remember? And when I see a Texas number on the Caller ID, I start to hyperventilate. Had to catch my breath before I rang you back."

"Glad you decided to anyway."

"Hope I can say the same when we're done."

Caitlin pictured Jones in some innocuous Washington office holding the telephone in a hand more comfortable squeezing a gun or a knife. He went by "Smith" the first time they'd met in Bahrain when he was stationed at the consulate there, then became "Jones" when he returned stateside last year just before they'd met up again in Washington. Jones was a fountain of information that gushed mostly when it suited his needs. But he'd helped Caitlin out twice now when he didn't have to, the two of them both lone wolves while roaming diametrically different territories.

"Need to pick your brain, Mr. Jones," she told him.

"Don't you always? Tell me, Ranger, you kill anyone lately, some badass bikers up in Canada maybe?"

"I see you been keeping tabs on me."

"DEA called to inquire about your credentials. I warned them to shred your file and make believe you don't exist."

"Guess they didn't listen."

"I told them if they brought you in, the lead would be flying. Said you just couldn't help yourself and you weren't one to discriminate either; you just kill everyone in your sights."

"Haven't killed you yet, have I?"

"I've learned to stay out of your kill zone. After Casa del Diablo and Juárez, you're a legend in the circle. Some of the toughest guys with a lifetime of training, as close to James Bond as you'll ever see, asking me if it's all true."

"And what do you tell them?"

"That they're not the only gunfighters left on the planet." Jones's tone turned almost whimsical. "Man, how I miss that world."

"Your ass in a chair instead of a jungle."

"Better to serve you anyway, Ranger. What is it today?"

Caitlin told him the story of Iraq war medic Mark John Serles claiming a shaped charge blew his legs off after a dying spy or contractor muttered something to him while bleeding out.

"Oh boy. You sure he didn't see that in some straight to cable movie on HBO?"

"Maybe one that missed the part about whoever's behind all this trying to blow me up last night."

"They dead?"

"Not yet. Kid gave me some coded designations that sound military. Thought you might be able to help me make sense of them."

"Go ahead, Ranger."

"One-four-seven-dash-eight-six-three, followed by Alpha, Delta, Charlie . . . And then Operation Rising Dawn."

Silence.

"Jones?"

More silence.

"Hey, Jones, you still there?"

"I need you to repeat those— No, goddamnit, never mind. Ranger, how the hell do you keep stepping in this shit?"

Caitlin felt suddenly cold and eased down the window part way to let in some warmth. "What kind of shit is it this time?"

"Where are you?" Jones asked her.

"In a car."

"You're talking to me from a *car*, on a *cell phone*?"

"That's right."

Silence again.

"Okay, Ranger, this calls ends in fifteen seconds. Enough time for me to tell you to go straight to the airport and get on a plane for D.C."

"Look, I got—"

"Seven seconds. I'll be waiting for you there."

"Hey, Jones."

Too late Caitlin realized when only a *click* greeted her.

47

CONCEPCIÓN DEL ORO; THE PRESENT

Paz directed Cort Wesley to the left just past the main drag, banking away from the hillside layered with simple homes. They drove down a one-lane, flattened patch of earth that barely passed for a road, Cort Wesley thinking about returning Caitlin's SUV to her with its suspension shot to hell. The commercials may have shown the thing going off road, but those thirty seconds or so were about the duration it was built to handle such contours in the land.

He kept following the road as it dipped, rose, and flattened some more until the sight of an older model Humvee glowed in the narrowing distance. As they drew closer, Cort Wesley discerned a trio of uniformed men who might have been miniature versions of Paz standing over a ragtag pair who must've been the ones who'd made off with Dylan. God help them if they'd done anything to the boy, or if Paz's silence ended up a harbinger of some very bad news better heard firsthand.

As it was, the only other thing Cort Wesley saw in drawing closer was a pair of holes dug by the two men likely to occupy them if they didn't cooperate to the fullest and, maybe, even if they did. Climbing out of the SUV into the last of the day's heat, Cort Wesley could see one of the men was wide as a tree stump. The face of the second kneeling man was curled in agony, a sweat broken by pain pouring down his face.

"They speak only Spanish," Paz said, suddenly by his side. "I knew you'd want your own answers from them."

"Where's their vehicle?"

"An old van parked alongside the cantina where my men found them. They were inside drinking, looked like they'd been in the desert for the better part of a day and night. My men checked the van and found evidence your son had been held in the rear."

"See your men had them dig their own graves, Colonel."

"Something to pass the time, outlaw," Paz told him, "while they waited for us to arrive."

Cort Wesley kept walking until he was standing before the two kneeling forms, his shadow cast over both of them.

"I'm the father of the boy you brought out here," he said in Spanish. "You're going to tell me where he is or I'll plant you in these two holes myself."

The one who looked in pain was trembling too much to speak. The other, the fat man, swallowed hard enough to steady himself.

"We do not know, *señor.*"

"That's not a good start, kind of start that'll get you dead in a hurry."

"No, things did not go as planned! You must believe me!"

"What happened?"

"You will kill us!"

"Only if my son is dead. Is he dead? If he is, you better tell me now or I'll make it hurt so much you'll be begging for me to kill you."

"We do not know, *señor.*"

Cort Wesley pulled the SIG Sauer pistol Caitlin had given him and racked back the slide.

"We were supposed to meet the other man out here to give the boy to him!"

Cort Wesley forgot about the gun he was holding. "What other man? The big, bald guy—LaChance?"

The fat man looked up into the sun. "I don't know his name, but that is him."

"He took my son from here?"

Silence.

Cort Wesley remembered the gun.

"He was supposed to!" the fat man blared, when Cort Wesley stuck it against his forehead. Eyes squinting at him now. "But something went wrong. . . ."

48

CONCEPCIÓN DEL ORO; THE NIGHT BEFORE

Dylan had to piss like crazy when they finally pulled over, the reduction in heat radiating through the van's one frosted-over window telling him night had fallen. They'd stopped several times to add water or coolant to the engine, Dylan getting to know the grind of the van's hood rising and thud of it being slapped back down into place. And once the damn thing had broken down altogether, leaving him roasting inside for hours bearing the worst heat of the day while the two men worked on the van and argued loudly the whole time. One of them had opened the van's rear door long enough to grab a toolbox or something and then lots of clanking and banging followed as they tried to get the engine started again. He tried to guess their position by the hours they'd been on the road, never hitting even a decent speed and not once letting him out to piss, even when the van broke down, until now.

Dylan heard the rear door being jerked open and felt the wash of a flashlight brighten the world beyond the sack covering his face. He'd been busying himself with getting it loose and almost had it off when the fat one who smelled like unwashed work clothes yelled at him in Spanish.

"*¡Vayamos!*"

They dragged Dylan out of the van and stood him up, yanking off the sack with flashlight aimed straight for his face, so fiercely bright his eyes glued closed from the stinging. He felt a pair of hands holding him up on either arm, the one on the right weaker, almost flaccid, and he guessed that was the man who walked with a bad limp and heavily favored his right side. The two stiffs would be expecting a scared kid so weakened from the long ordeal and grateful to be out in the air that he'd succumb to their wishes and maybe not even notice they stank to high heaven.

Dylan sniffed the air, thinking of how he stank too when the picture he'd been building in his head changed dramatically.

"Water him and make sure he pisses," came a third voice he recognized. "I don't want any accidents stinking up my truck. I got a bunch of stops to make the rest of the way myself."

Dylan finally got his eyes pried open and saw the big bald man with an arrow tattooed down the crown of his skull standing on the other side of a thin culvert that had once carried water and now carried nothing but scrub and dead mesquite. He held a plastic water bottle that he tossed to Fatty, who twisted the cap off and angled it over Dylan's face.

"*¡Abra la boca!*"

Fatty didn't need to tell him to open his mouth twice. Dylan squeezed his lips apart as far as he could and felt the slightly warm water gush over his face, enough finding his mouth and throat to relieve his incredible thirst. Fatty poured fast, probably expecting Dylan to gag, but the boy gratefully guzzled as much as he could until the water backed up and spilled all over his shirt. Only then did he gag, but not much or for long.

The gag gave him some moments to consider the unexpected, since he'd figured only on Fatty and one other—the gimp, as it turned out. The biker guy was a wild card, standing silhouetted by a black pickup with the biggest tires Dylan had ever seen short of a monster truck. Even then the bald man stood well over it, making him nearly a foot taller than Dylan and half that bigger than his dad. There was plenty of stuff tucked in the truck's bed beneath one, maybe two or three balled-up tarpaulins.

"Now make sure he pisses," the bald guy was saying in Spanish now.

So Fatty grabbed Dylan by the shoulder and thrust him forward, aiming him toward the night dropping fast over the mountains. Dylan started walking, a surprisingly hard task along such uneven ground with his hands latched behind him by the plastic flex cuffs that didn't flex much at all.

"Far enough!" Fatty said, after the desert floor dipped into a slight depression.

"You gonna undo my hands?"

"No."

"Then how am I supposed to piss? Come on, I gotta go like a race horse," Dylan continued, not having to feign his squirming. "It's not like I'm gonna run off out here."

Fatty weighed his words only long enough to reject them, then reached around Dylan and unzipped his jeans. He could never remember a time where he felt more uncomfortable than feeling Fatty's heavy, callused hands working him free of his sweat-soaked boxers.

The stream came quickly, blessed relief that dulled that particular agony, along with the constant ache in his balls from the bashing they'd taken last night, though it seemed much longer than that now. He seemed to piss forever, Dylan waiting for the stream to slow before he swung fast toward Fatty and soaked a leg of his filthy overalls with a warm river of piss.

Fatty lurched back, first stumbling and then catching his heel on a rock that spilled him over backward to the ground.

Dylan never saw him hit, because he was already running. Lighting out into the darkness toward the mountains with hands cuffed behind him and dick swinging free of his pants.

"Hey! Hey!" Fatty called.

Dylan tensed. If there was going to be a shot, here's when it would come, while he was still in sight before the darkness swallowed him. He had no real plan at that point, just knew that plunging deeper into the desert where the cool of the night would soften him for the coming heat of the next day and the buzzards wasn't an option.

He thought fast, his mind working just the way his father had described in those rare occasions when he said anything at all about his own experiences. The lights of some nearby town twinkled in the distance but that distance was likely miles and his captors, especially the bald guy, would figure that was his most likely destination.

Nope, they could wait him out under current conditions no matter what plan he picked. If it was just Fatty and the gimp, his options were many. The big bald guy reduced them to none that were much good.

But he had the darkness, and that was something. Lots actually, since there was no better camouflage. Dylan could hear Fatty laboring after him, not sure if it was the breeze or his breathing he heard between desperate pleas to the gimp and Baldy for help.

"¡El huye! ¡El huye!"

The darkness would shield Dylan for a time. As soon as the night gave up the heavy thumping of the big bald guy's boots giving chase, though, he knew his advantage, swinging dick and all, would be short-lived indeed. What that told him was that he better come up with something else and fast.

Dylan's thinking froze, redirected. Because the night wasn't the only thing he had working for him at all. There was something else, if only he could get to it. . . .

49

CONCEPCIÓN DEL ORO; THE PRESENT

"The boy went off into the mountains," the fat man said.

"You never found him?"

Both kneeling men shook their heads vociferously.

"No," the fat one insisted. "We searched all night and most of today. Finally we were so tired and thirsty, we had—"

"I don't give a shit about that. Tell me about your boss, the bald guy."

"He searched with us through the night."

"Left just after dawn," the other man said, speaking for the first time through the pain stretched across his lips. "Said if we didn't find the boy or his body, he'd come back and kill us."

"Then it's a good thing the colonel and I showed up instead, isn't it?" Cort Wesley asked them and watched the men's eyes dare to linger on the massive, sun-blotting form of Guillermo Paz for the first time. He'd stood rigid through the whole exchange, his breathing gradually picking up with a restrained fury etched over his expression. Cort Wesley wondered what he was thinking about. "So, did you find him?" he asked the kidnappers, dreading the answer.

"The boy got away," the fat man said, his voice cracking. "If he was hiding, we would have found him by now."

Cort Wesley gazed into the world of the mountains and endless desert beyond it. If Dylan had doubled back for Concepción del Oro, if he was safe, he would've found a way to reach him or Caitlin. So he hadn't done that, which left only the desert. Frigid at night, steaming during the day. Hiding out under some meager, desperate cover with hands cuffed behind his back. Cort Wesley gazed out into the endless emptiness beyond, trying not to picture Dylan already dead within it. His hand quivered as he thought seriously of taking the SIG from his belt and putting a bullet in the fat man's face. Derive some sense of satisfaction from watching the hollow point shell obliterate flesh, bone, and brains.

"I wanna know how I can find LaChance," Cort Wesley blared instead.

"Who?"

"Your big, bald boss, you stupid fuck!"

"I don't know."

"Somebody contacted him yesterday from San Luis Potosí."

"Not me," the fat man insisted. "The one in charge."

"And where's he?"

"Gone."

"With the rest of the kids you stole," Paz interjected suddenly, the edge in his voice as sharp as a razor's.

The fat man swallowed hard and kept his gaze on Cort Wesley. "I've told you everything I know!"

Cort Wesley gazed out into the distance.

"Are you going to kill me?"

Cort Wesley thought about Dylan heading for the mountains, the boy smart enough to know the only thing waiting for him there was death. So he wouldn't have headed in that direction, at least not for long with all three men pursuing him through the night, leaving . . .

"Jesus Christ," Cort Wesley realized, recalling a slim part of the fat man's tale. "Jesus Christ . . ."

He saw Dylan, thought like Dylan, became Dylan. Moving through the night, taking advantage of his captors' panic over letting him escape.

"LaChance's truck," Cort Wesley heard himself saying, glaring down at the fat man. "Can you tell me anything about the license plates?"

The fat man looked up, as if measuring his eyes for a sign of his intentions, and nodded. "Sí, *señor*, they come from Texas."

PART FIVE

One Ranger is a potent power for good and the Legislature should provide a sufficiently large mobile force that can be sent to points of the state as needed without delay. The Rangers are crime deterrents and we should have an ample supply.
　　　　　　　　　　　　　　　　—Texas state senator J. W. Reid, 1927

50

Caitlin's plane touched down at Dulles Airport in Washington, D.C., late in the afternoon, when the airport was just starting to get busy again. She'd just made an AirTran flight in San Antonio that connected with her Washington-bound flight out of Atlanta with only fifteen minutes to spare. Jones, as wide in the shoulders as ever and back to his military-style crew cut, stood waiting for her at the gate just beyond the Jetway.

"And me thinking only passengers were permitted past the security checkpoints. You make yourself invisible or something?"

Jones clearly wasn't in the mood for humor. "That were possible, I would've made you disappear a long time ago."

"Where we going?" Caitlin asked, falling into step alongside him.

"Washington."

"Thought we were there already."

"Not really."

They drove out to a nondescript office building that overlooked Dupont Circle, its white exterior discolored in some patches and blackened in others by a combination of Metro train exhaust and blowback from an ancient heat exchange system that must've dated to the time of

Lincoln. So plain was the building that it had no doorman, reception desk, or lobby security, and boasted wall-mounted mailboxes an eight-year-old could pick with a piece of his Transformer toy.

"Not much," Jones said, holding the door open for Caitlin, "but we call it home."

"We," she repeated.

Jones shrugged and made sure the door caught behind him. "Press doesn't even know this building exists. Last cameraman to show up came to the wrong address."

"Saved you the trouble of killing him."

"Don't worry, I confiscated his memory card." Jones angled to the right, toward a small coffee shop that was really just a coffee station offering snacks and beverages with a single man behind the counter. "He's mine, don't worry. Let's get a table."

"Something wrong with your office?"

"Elevators in this building are too slow and we're not going to be here very long anyway."

Caitlin let Jones's remark dangle and accompanied him into the snack bar. He made straight to a table set in the rear, placed so those seated couldn't be seen through the windows from the street beyond. Caitlin followed, wondering if the pastries and fruit on display were real or just props. She felt as if she was on a movie set.

"First, I need the name and info on this medic of yours," Jones told her.

Caitlin pulled a piece of paper from the pocket of her jeans. "I wrote it down for you."

Jones took the paper from her, shaking his head. "You carried it with you all the way down here?"

"Yup."

"Haven't I taught you anything?"

"Figured it beat e-mail." Caitlin watched Jones digest the information on her piece of notepaper quickly before tearing it into shreds with a disdainful stare. "This kid in danger?"

"I can't believe the army left him out there this long," Jones said in response. "No wonder they can't manage a war right."

"You didn't answer my question."

"It's out of your hands, Ranger."

"The hell it is."

Jones's eyes narrowed, seeming to change from blue to ice-colored. "You want to help this kid?"

"Damn right."

"Then stop wasting time better spent with the folks who can help you scrape this shit off your shoe."

The look in his eyes was different from the last two times circumstances had brought them together. Jones, for all his bravado, looked uncertain. Jones looked scared.

"One-four-seven-dash-eight-six-three," Caitlin recited from memory. "Alpha, Delta, Charlie."

"Let's start with Operation Rising Dawn."

"Whatever you say."

"Iraq War, first months after we went through that country like shit through a goose. What comes next?"

"This a quiz, Jones?"

"Humor me, Ranger."

"Holding the country together, something you did a lousy job at."

"Point taken. What would we have needed to get it done right?"

"Men. Troops."

"Yes. Now try again."

"Resources."

"Warm."

"Cooperation."

"Warmer."

"Friendlies willing to change loyalties."

Jones pushed his chair a bit more forward. "And how exactly do we manage that?"

"With money."

"Blazing hot, Ranger."

"Operation Rising Dawn," Caitlin repeated.

"All about keeping the country running. Infrastructure, utilities, hospitals, food deliveries—simple stuff like that stops and there is no country."

"But that's exactly what happened."

Jones looked annoyed. "Leave me the floor, Ranger, please. I know full well it ended up as a cluster fuck, thanks to that civilian fool Bremer who couldn't run a hot-dog stand, much less a country. But that doesn't mean Operation Rising Dawn didn't lay it all out for him, step by step, starting with retaining the Iraqi army which, of course, Bremer and his troglodytes chose to ignore. There was nothing wrong with the plan. The plan would have goddamn worked, if he'd simply followed the instructions that came included with the batteries. Just trust me on that."

"Okay. I'm with you so far."

Jones crossed his arms and laid his elbows atop the table. "Now go back to your blazing hot point."

"Money. You'd need plenty of it to keep all those people on, basically employ an entire nation to keep essential services up and running."

"Twelve billion dollars. That was the number we came up with and the amount we sent to Baghdad."

"Twelve billion dollars?"

"In cash. Loaded onto a C-130. I supervised the process myself. Alpha, Delta, Charlie—A, D, C—basically refers to an inventory coding, short for 'Administrative Control.' Standard bureaucratic bullshit."

"And one-four-seven-eight-six-three?"

"What do you think, Ranger?"

"Sounds like a bank account number."

"Close enough," Jones nodded. "A designator for the money itself. The plan was for the cash to be portioned out by Bremer and company, the most incompetent bunch of fools I've come across in my entire career. Watching them make decisions was like watching a blind guy throwing darts: sooner or later you figure he'll hit at least part of the board, but, you know what, in this case they didn't."

Caitlin couldn't believe what she was hearing. "Paul Bremer was in charge of dispersing twelve billion dollars in cash?"

"He was in charge of rebuilding the country, making amends, selling Girl Scout cookies. The twelve billion was supposed to give him the means."

"Supposed to?"

Jones's expression was stone cold. "Because it vanished, Ranger."

51

WASHINGTON, D.C.; THE PRESENT

"Not all of it," Jones continued. "Somewhere around a half. As much as seven, as little as five. Four maybe."

"Vanished."

"Like into thin air, without a trace. Poof!" Jones finished, blowing air though his fingers. "All I can tell you is that we loaded twelve billion under Administrative Control Designation 147-863 into a C-130 and, depending on who you listen to, only a fraction of it made it to Baghdad. Of course, anyone you listen to couldn't possibly be sure because nobody bothered to inventory or count it. They just loaded the pallets straight into transport trucks and headed down the Purple Heart Highway from the airport to the grounds of a Saddam palace Bremer had appropriated so he'd have some place to hang his work boots and take a shit in one of the seventeen bathrooms."

"You don't sound happy."

"Who do you think took the flak for all the bullshit? I've been chasing my tail on this ever since." Jones sat back, looking suddenly more reflective but also bitter, the left side of his face rising in something between a sneer and a scowl. "You recall the name of the dying man who passed the info onto your medic?"

Caitlin searched her memory. "Kirken-something."

"Dale," Jones completed, "Kirkendale. Glad you didn't write that down, anyway."

"He was your man."

"He had an office in a building like this too—let's put it that way."

"Same floor?"

Jones looked like he was fighting a stomach full of acid. "No, a different one. He was a forensic auditor, a glorified accountant really, as good with numbers as I am with bullets. And he had a family. That's why he agreed to go over there to trace the missing money, 'cause of the pay boost. It was only the Green Zone, right? Who dies in the Green Zone? He was weapons trained because he had to be, not 'cause he liked it."

"Wasn't gonna be much he could do about a sniper."

"He was targeted personally, Ranger. His investigation had gotten him places nobody expected him to reach. That made him a risk to the powers-that-be."

"I know the feeling."

"Come again?"

"You're behind the curve, Jones. Last night, somebody tried to blow me up after I found out Sergeant Mark John Serles had been transferred out of the Intrepid."

"Means the force behind the missing money is still covering their tracks." He smirked, seeming to enjoy looking across the table at Caitlin. "Guess nobody told them who they were up against."

"Get back to the missing money."

"Kirkendale and his forensics team were able to back trace eight billion dollars of it. While plenty of that had gone nowhere near where it was supposed to, and assholes like Halliburton had overcharged us to a frightening degree, the missing four was the real problem."

"Where the hell it went," Caitlin followed.

"Exactly, because the options were limited and the more Kirkendale reduced them, the scarier they got."

"How so?"

"When money the military is technically responsible for disappears, where do you look?"

"The military."

"Sure. Bremer was a neo-con, a hawk among hawks."

"Strange criticism coming from you, Jones."

He looked stung by her remark, wrinkling his face in derision. "I like what I do, Ranger, and I'm damn good at it. But when the man at 1600 Pennsylvania tells me to holster my weapon, that's what I do, because I know there will come a time when he needs me to take it out again and I can't do that right if I'm too busy pissing and moaning."

"Back to Bremer."

"I'm not saying he had anything to do with the four billion that vanished, not directly anyway. But it wouldn't have been hard for him, or the Cheney disciples who rode in on the same plane, to look the other way while the money was put to other uses."

"Like what?"

Jones rose fast enough to rattle the table. "Need someone else to fill in the remaining blanks."

"Where?"

"Homeland Security."

52

SAN ANTONIO; THE PRESENT

Cort Wesley stepped into the dark cool of Miguel Asuna's body shop in East San Antonio. Back when Cort Wesley was working for the Branca crime family, this had also served as a chop shop where stolen cars were taken to be disassembled for parts. He'd once heard Asuna boast he could strip a Mercedes in thirty minutes flat.

The way Cort Wesley felt now reminded him both of prison and war; in prison it was the potential of getting shivved that kept him on edge, while in war it was the chance of getting shot. Today it was any lingering stare or flash of recognition that could mean the cops were not far off, ready to bring him in on that extradition beef since Caitlin Strong hadn't. Cort Wesley played out the scenario of what he'd do if confronted a hundred different ways, none of them good.

"Hey, look who's here!" said a big man, as he wiped grease from his hands with a grime-splattered rag.

Miguel Asuna was twice the size of his little brother Pablo, Cort Wesley's late best friend, and by all accounts was still living and working on the fringe of the law.

"It's been forever, Masters," Asuna continued, swallowing his hand in what felt like a giant paw. "What, five or six years?"

"Closer to seven."

Asuna looked Cort Wesley over as if he were considering an estimate on damage. "So you back in the trade, *jefe*?"

"I'm looking for a truck."

"So try Rodriguez Auto Sales up the street."

"I'm in the market for information, not a deal. Big conversion job. Think Bambi turned into Godzilla fit for a monster truck show, but street ready."

Asuna stroked his cheek with a grubby finger, weighing Cort Wesley's words. "Pretty rare vehicle."

"I figure there can't be too many shops in the whole state capable of a custom job like this. Thought maybe you could help me track them down."

Asuna tossed the rag aside and swiped his hands along the sides of paint-splattered work overalls. "My bro always said he owed you, from that first time you saved him from gangbangers."

"He gave me a pair of boots to thank me. Found out later they were stolen."

Miguel Asuna grinned. "Yeah, I remember that score. Just happened to be in the back of a van we boosted. Real nice leather." Asuna's gaze drifted a bit, his eyes moistening in the semidarkness. "Tell you what, Masters. I got a friend, Mike Beardsley out of Laramie. Known for boosting showroom-clean cars for special orders and has also done plenty of custom work in his time. If anybody can come up with the places you're looking for, it's him. You got a cell number where I can reach you?"

53

WASHINGTON, D.C.; THE PRESENT

Jones drove to the FEMA Building on C Street and parked in a red zone.

"Not worried about it getting towed?" said Caitlin.

"We're expected" was all he said in return.

The establishment of Homeland Security had come without a dedicated building to house the amalgamation of departments and bureaus that composed it. The bulk of the offices, Caitlin had heard during a two-week counterterrorism course at Quantico, were contained here at FEMA with the rest scattered where space was available.

A nondescript man, gaunt with his thinning hair tossed about in the wind, was waiting for them before the secured entrance. He wore a dark suit, blue tie, and white shirt, seemingly cut for a man of Kirkendale's mold than Jones's.

"Don't let the outfit fool you," Jones said, as if reading her mind. "Men like this make it possible for men like me to do my job."

"Which is what exactly?"

"Same as it's always been: keeping this country safe. It's the source of the primary threats that have changed. Men like Mr. White are the ones who paint the bull's-eyes on my targets' backs."

"White? You're kidding, right?"

Jones looked as if he were fighting down bile again. "That's his real name, Ranger."

White hustled them through security and into an elevator that accessed only the floors of the building reserved for Homeland. More security awaited when the cab's door slid open, a marine wielding a handheld scanner that somehow confirmed both Caitlin and Jones were exactly who they were supposed to be.

"This way," White said, ushering them into a conference room.

It didn't look as if it had always been a conference room, more like a pair of neighboring offices with the wall knocked out between them. The placement and sizing of the windows looked all wrong to her. The table too seemed out of place. Old, not even refurbished, probably trucked from another floor by movers with high-level government clearances. The table was empty and so were the walls, but wires spooled everywhere, some connected to machines and some in case others were brought in.

White didn't bother offering Caitlin or Jones a chair; they just plopped down into them, as he tried to smooth his hair back into place.

Everything about him reminded Caitlin of a robot, his motions mechanical and formless, his eyes looking more like they'd been raised from a black-and-white still shot until he began to speak, at which point they widened into bursts of intensity.

"Ever hear of Norm Renner?"

Caitlin wasn't sure if she was supposed to answer, but she did. "No, sir."

"Didn't think you had. Renner's from Alaska. Founded an outfit up there called the Alaska Citizen's Militia, this after founding the Michigan Militia fifteen years ago when he lived in the lower forty-eight. That mean anything to you?"

"Michigan Militia was what Timothy McVeigh called home for a time before he blew up the federal building in Oklahoma City."

"I see you've done your homework."

"Just part of the job, sir. And right now that same job has me trying to figure why the army would want to kill a young Texas kid serving as a medic in Iraq over four billion in missing cash."

"Because they couldn't afford anyone finding out where that cash ended up," White replied matter-of-factly.

"That's why I'm back stateside, Ranger," Jones picked up. "Because this is where the biggest threats to the nation's security can be found these days."

"Right-wing extremist groups," Caitlin concluded. "The so-called patriot and militia movements."

"Totally homegrown and extremely dangerous," Jones elaborated. "Bursting at the seams, ever since Obama took office."

"We got our share of them in Texas," she told them both. "Nonviolent for the most part. Lots of bravado masquerading as intention."

"The operative phrase being 'for the most part.' The problem is more and more of these groups are becoming radicalized, not only accepting violence into their ranks, but encouraging and rewarding it."

"Like that abortion doctor."

"That was just a warm-up," Jones said. "Homeland estimates there are over twelve hundred so-called patriot groups now active in this country. They're pretty much scattered all over the place, but, you're right, Texas and California to a lesser degree can claim more than their share. They were all talk for a time but, make no mistake about it, the violence is real and it's escalating. There've been over twenty incidents in the past year, including the murder of a judge in your fine city of Galveston just the other day. And with each incident we see a spike in membership across the board. We can't accurately say how many have now joined up with the kind of extremist groups we're talking about, but that number is estimated to be somewhere around two million. Pretty sizable army, I'm sure you'd agree."

"But what does it have to do with Operation Rising Dawn from seven years ago?" Caitlin asked.

Jones glanced at White before replying. "Follow the money, Ranger."

"You're saying—"

"I'm saying," Jones continued, "that the neo-cons, Cheney's Idiots, count the militia and patriot movements as their most fervent supporters. Their own personal standing army. I'm saying that plenty in the military tend to think the same way."

"Wait a minute," Caitlin started, leaning forward until her torso touched the table, "are you telling me that somebody gave right-wing extremists *four billion bucks*?"

"Maybe not all four billion," White told her, "but a sizable portion."

"Meaning?"

"At least a billion," Jones answered this time. "As much as two, funneled to the kind of people for whom the Civil War never really ended. Make no mistake about it, these people want to take over. They want to be in charge. They see Obama as a tyrant who wants to steal their country from them. They believe he was born either in a foreign country or distant planet. Plenty believe he's the goddamn Antichrist, and I'm not exaggerating, not in the least."

Caitlin let his comment settle. "So what are we looking at? Revolution? A second Civil War?"

"The first Civil War's all the fashion again. Listen to these people describe it, those years weren't much different from your typical reenactment weekend. Only their guns are very real and two billion dollars can buy you a hell of a lot of firepower."

"Kirkendale back-traced the money as far as he could," White picked up. "He could almost pin down the day and time piles went missing.

But he couldn't trace the parties responsible at the top of the military food chain."

"We are very good at what we do," Jones added, lamenting the fact, "make no mistake about it."

"So was Kirkendale," said White, emotion peeking out of his voice for the first time. "He was getting close to the truth. That's why they killed him."

"So the perpetrators are still over there?"

"They wouldn't have to be," answered Jones. "Just their legacy."

"And these militias carry plenty of ex-military men on their rolls," White added.

Jones's eyes took on their familiar flat, unblinking gaze, like he was zeroing in on a target through a scope's crosshairs. "Two million set loose into the streets with two billion worth of bullets can do a hell of a lot of damage, Ranger."

Caitlin moved her gaze between the two of them. "So where do I come in?"

"You said it yourself," Jones told her. "Texas has more than its share of militia groups."

"And you think the money . . ."

"Yes," said Jones, "we do."

White interlaced his fingers atop the dull wood of the conference table. "My team has spent two years tracking bulk arms sales all over the world. One prime common denominator we've been able to isolate is Mexico. Large shipments from dummy manufacturers of merchandise that never existed."

"Don't tell me, shipped to Mexican warehouses with similarly dummy addresses."

"Can't put anything over on you, Ranger," Jones winked, "can we?"

"Been there, done that."

She caught White exchange another furtive glance with Jones. "And that's why you're here," he said.

"Because you think a few billion dollars' worth of guns and ammo are hidden just south of the Texas border."

"For starters."

"Starters?"

"The Mexican stashes only account for about half the guns at most. We haven't been able to find where the rest of them are coming from yet. But the chatter we've been able to latch on to indicates the top of the food chain resides in Texas, all distribution centered there."

"You want my help, you're gonna have to get more specific."

"All right," Jones started, leaning back with hands cupped behind his head. "What do you know about Malcolm Arno and the Patriot Sun?"

54

MIDLAND, TEXAS; THE PRESENT

The four girls who'd been held in the complex's Intake Center were finally cleared by mid-afternoon. Found to be healthy, disease free, of good blood counts, proper height and weight on page one of the report, and something even more important on page two.

Arno had taken a long, slow walk across the grounds on his way to the Intake Center, passing the various one-, two-, and three-story structures that contained the Patriot Sun's adult residences, which also included children up to the age of seven. After that, as had been the case at the Church of the Redeemer, children were segregated by gender in separate dormitory-style housing divided by age in two-year increments. Malcolm Arno agreed with his father that a communal living situation apart from their parents made it easier to indoctrinate children into the true ways of God and His plans for them. Contact with parents was regular but limited so as not to confuse or deter the instilling of values meant to return the country to its purified roots. Since the children enjoyed virtually no contact with the outside world as it was, no distractions were offered that could demean their training meant to build a love for country and community.

Arno lingered longer before the final outlying building. Its contents held the most important feature of the Patriot Sun's future, left over from his father's thinking but updated to appease a more modern sensibility. The world had judged the Church of the Redeemer through a prism of its own contradictory values and misplaced morals. The damn Texas Rangers storming the place like Nazi storm troopers, oppressors riding in under the guise of justice. They had stood in judgment of his father and his teachings to fight the increasing intrusions of government into every facet of life both private and personal.

What a visionary Maxwell Arno had been! He'd seen the erosions of freedom and the gradual growth of government long before others had jumped on a convenient bandwagon. It was sometimes hard to tell, even for his most ardent of followers, what the great man had done to make a point or make a world. Malcolm realizing just before the Rangers had come, that they were the very same thing.

Showered and wearing freshly laundered clothes, Arno finally entered the Intake Center to inspect the latest wares brought up from Mexico, now that they'd been cleared for what was to follow as part of his grand plan. Did that make him a sinner? A saint? More likely something in between, and Arno did not bother judging his own morality. He had become what God wanted in order to fulfill a grander purpose in a bigger scheme. That belief gave him comfort, even when his thoughts stirred up the old memories of growing up literally by his father's side. . . .

Young Malcolm Arno could be invisible when he wanted, a sight so common in a suit and tie normally matching his father's that those on the hallowed grounds of the Church of the Redeemer stopped even noticing him, save for an occasional smile or tousle of his hair. He had grown up motherless, reveling in his father's majesty and wishing to share his every move and manner.

That proclivity had brought him to his father's doorway on so many nights, drawn there by the cries of what he thought was an animal, a sick dog maybe. Malcolm would peer inside at the Reverend Maxwell Arno in bed with one of the young female members of his congregation, none more than sixteen. He would listen to his father's moans and watch his gyrations. This grew into a nightly ritual Malcolm did not regret and, actually, came to look forward to.

One night his father twisted around from the bedcovers and caught Malcolm stroking himself, casting him the slightest of smiles.

"Your mother's passing giving birth to you moved me to lay as I do," the Reverend Maxwell Arno explained to his son the next day. "I felt her death was a sign for me to sow my seed with the younger, those pure and unspoiled so my touch might be the first they feel. Our urges are God's plan for us and there is no shame in that."

Malcolm took that as encouragement to capture more visions through doorways and closets in other bedrooms in the complex, learning that his father's bedding of the young could indeed only be God's work since all the men seemed to be doing it. What he couldn't know then was how such nightly sojourns in both body and mind would adversely affect him later in the succession of foster homes that followed the death of his father.

"Freak!"

"Perv!"

"Faggot!"

"Weirdo!"

The taunts ran into each other, multiplying after his urges led to his forcing himself on a twelve-year-old girl, only to explode even before he got his pants down. He was moved to another home.

It happened again and, again, he was moved, ultimately for a stay in a residential psychiatric facility where a therapist who smelled of cheap aftershave spoke to Malcolm with his eyes on a clipboard all the time.

"Do you think there's something wrong with you?"

No, Malcolm told him. *Do you think there's something wrong with you?*

"Do you consider your behavior acceptable?"

Yes.

"Why?"

God.

"God?"

I'm doing God's work.

"Really? How?"

Like this.

And he stabbed the therapist in the face with a pencil. That made him look up.

. . .

This is still God's work, Arno thought as he entered the Intake Center. He could smell the unspoiled youth of the girls as he moved down the hall toward the rooms they occupied while waiting to be selected. Never did he feel closer to his father than the nights when they joined him.

Like the great Reverend Max Arno, Malcolm was a great admirer of the State of Israel, where the Messiah would someday return. In the wake of the Holocaust, the Jews who came to Israel knew the greatest weapon they could forge against their enemies was numbers. So they had built large families that, in turn, begot larger families, and so on.

On those nights when he lay alone, apart from a young woman blessed enough to be chosen, his mind turned again and again to how the Texas Rangers had emptied his father's dream onto yellow school buses. The Church of the Redeemer's children being stolen away in tears, while handcuffs were slapped on the adults at gunpoint.

Malcolm Arno understood at last why his father had seemed so content that day of reckoning in the parking lot of the Tackle and Gun. He'd smiled at the big, pistol-waving Texas Ranger because he knew his martyrdom was about to be made complete. His dream lost, only to be reborn if he sacrificed himself to a greater cause, thereby solidifying Malcolm's own reckoning as the one chosen to succeed where his father had failed.

The last thing he recalled from that day was looking up and meeting the gaze of the Ranger's daughter, so soft and sweet and even compassionate. But Malcolm didn't want her pity, didn't want anything from her besides the big pistol she'd dropped by her feet so he could gun down her father there and then.

He hadn't, of course, and the hate he felt turned into a weapon. A nuclear bomb of emotions that bled away his youth in a painful, loathsome geyser. That girl, daughter of Jim Strong, had haunted his dreams as she grew up to become a Texas Ranger herself. But in his dreams Caitlin Strong was still just short of fourteen, a bit younger than the young women brought to him here in the world he had built, insulated from the likes of the Texas Rangers and the outside world in general. But it wasn't good enough, because sooner or later they would come for him as they'd come for his father.

Unless he came for them first.

That day was coming, as it had come already in Galveston and elsewhere.

"You say something, Mal?"

Arno swung, not even realizing Jed Kean had come up beside him. "Just muttering to myself, Jed," he said, clearing his throat. "Got a lot on my mind these days."

"That man and woman you've been expecting just got here," Kean reported. "All business, like you said."

"Then let's go greet them, shall we, and get some business done."

55

WASHINGTON, D.C.; THE PRESENT

"My father killed his, the Reverend Max Arno, when I was fourteen," Caitlin said, listening to her voice as if it was someone else's.

Jones's eyes twinkled, flashed, as Caitlin continued.

"And Malcolm Arno's movement, militia, or whatever you want to call it, this Patriot Sun, is based in Midland not far down the road from where his father's Church of the Redeemer had set up shop."

"Your father led the raid that took it down," Jones said, clearly well versed on the subject.

"Along with my current captain, D. W. Tepper. But the gunfight happened a few days later."

"You were there," Jones realized, shaking his head slowly. "Man oh man . . ."

"So was Arno's son. He watched his father die."

"Shot by yours."

"A knife, actually."

"So what was that like, Ranger?" Jones asked, his eyes boring into hers, genuinely curious.

"I felt like a coward, 'cause I wasn't able to help him."

"Well, you've more than made up for it."

"You think Arno's son was the recipient of a billion dollars from the neo-cons?"

"Maybe more and who better? He's got the heritage and more than enough motivation to lead the call to violence. He hosted a gathering at his complex just yesterday, a regular whackjob jamboree. The best advantage we've had against the militia and patriot movements was they've always been decentralized. That's not the case anymore."

"Thanks to Arno."

"Right as rain, Ranger."

"You have anyone inside?"

"Of the groups in attendance? Yes. At the Patriot Sun headquarters? No. We haven't been able to crack that yet. Arno runs background checks on members of his flock that would make the CIA proud, probably with the help of his neo-con pals."

"And that's where I come in."

"Well, the two of you do have a history."

"All the more reason he'll want to keep the Rangers, especially me, out at all costs. My guess is we've avoided the place to keep from appearing provocative and, unless I've missed something, Arno hasn't broken any laws."

"You mean fomenting a revolution doesn't qualify?" Jones challenged. "Give a man who witnessed his father being killed by forces of the big bad State a bunch of bucks and watch what he does with them." His hard-edged stare returned, eyes like daggers of ice stabbing the air. "Even a fraction of that two million number shooting off guns Arno provides them is enough to make us forget shoe bombers and airplane jockeys for a long time to come. Pretty soon they'll be making daily headlines and dominating the news. Courts, women's health clinics, state houses, federal buildings, local government seats, libraries that carry unapproved books, churches that perform gay marriages, lawyers who arrange adoptions for same-sex couples, liberal talk-show hosts, politicians not sympathetic to their cause, schools that teach evolution—"

"I get the point, Jones."

"Do you? Because I haven't made it yet. We're adding soft targets to the expected hit list every day, and we can't possibly watch them all. Plenty of the suspects we're talking about are ex-military who've shot plenty of guns and rigged more than their share of explosives. These aren't yokels liquored up on a onetime dare. Think the Unabomber, the D.C. Sniper, and McVeigh himself multiplied by a hundred, a thousand, *ten* thousand. There's the very real possibility that that's what we're going to be looking at if somebody doesn't put Malcolm Arno on a leash."

Caitlin could only shake her head. "You're a real son of a bitch, Jones."

"Duly noted."

"You want me to call Arno out."

"It's in your DNA, Ranger. I'm just offering you a chance to finish what your father started."

"I was wrong before, wasn't I?" Caitlin said, staring him in the eye as White looked on like part of the wallpaper. "You knew I was there, at the Tackle and Gun that day twenty years ago."

"Of course I did. Your file takes up a whole goddamn cabinet. You've drawn the attention of lots of people who work out of offices like mine."

"They retire their waterboarding tables too?"

"Just put them in storage," Jones said unabashedly. "This right-wing extremist thing goes down the way our worst-case scenarios say it might, the people who made us put the tables away will be begging us to set them up again. These aren't theoretical groups living on millet in the desert and buying explosives with the expiration dates blacked out. These are homegrown fanatics with a billion-dollar-plus bank roll and enough weapons to fight a full-scale war."

Caitlin rose from her seat, suspended between intentions. The floor felt wobbly, her blood pressure rising into the red, and she laid her palms down on the table for support. About to respond to Jones, her Black-Berry beeped, flashing an incoming text message from Cort Wesley:

NEED YOU FAST

"Get yourself another gunfighter, Jones."

"Lots of people are gonna die here, Ranger."

"Then I'd recommend you strap your guns back on."

. . .

After Caitlin had gone, Jones slapped a twenty-dollar bill down on the table.

"What's that?" White asked.

"A bet. I say we're gonna hear from the Ranger again, that she ends up taking the job."

"But she just said—"

"I don't care what she said," Jones told him, casting his gaze out the window as if to watch Caitlin Strong emerge from the building. "You ever hear of Frank Hamer, Bigfoot Wallace, Jack Coffee Hays, Bill McDonald, or the woman's own grandfather Earl Strong?"

"Not a single one."

"Gunslinging Texas Rangers all who had the proclivity to clean up anyplace they happened to hang their hats. Caitlin Strong's no different, a gunfighter through and through. Only difference is the territory has gotten bigger."

"How's that?

"The whole damn country," said Jones, still holding his gaze out the window.

56

SAN ANTONIO; THE PRESENT

The call from Miguel Asuna at his body shop came three hours after Cort Wesley had left him. There were fewer men at work in the bays than earlier in the day, but the scents of fresh leather and rubber told Cort Wesley Asuna had taken some new deliveries in the course of the afternoon.

This time they went into his office, highlighted by a calendar featuring a different naked woman for every month. The calendar was from 2003.

Asuna yanked a beer from a small fridge and tossed Cort Wesley one without asking if he wanted it. "Turns out there's only about two dozen shops who can do a custom job on a truck like the one you're describing. Mike Beardsley found four trucks matching your description and claimed he could account for the owners of all but one. Here, check it out."

Cort Wesley came around to the other side of the desk while Asuna worked a computer keyboard clumsily with his thick fingers. Nonetheless, a black truck with tires somewhere between five and six feet tall appeared on the screen, framed on either side by two men in overalls beneath a sign that read JAKE'S CUSTOM CLASSICS.

Cort Wesley gave the picture a closer look, narrowing his gaze to picture Dylan hiding for dear life in the cargo bed. Hands still bound behind him and scared out of his wits; it made Cort Wesley's flesh crawl, the arrest warrant or whatever it was from Mexico shoved aside for the time being.

"You get a registration?" he managed to ask through the thickness that had settled inside him.

"What, you think I was born yesterday? Yeah, I got a registration." Asuna tore a piece of paper from a pad and handed it to Cort Wesley. "Truck is registered to a hunting lodge in Kilgore. I looked it up just for fun."

"What'd you find?"

"Nothing, because that's what's there: nothing. Just a big empty chunk of land." Asuna's big, droopy eyes tightened on him. "This business, *jefe*?"

"Personal."

Asuna grinned like he knew what that meant—for the truck's owner, anyway. "'Cause I can move a truck like that in minutes. They use them to mount machine guns south of the border. Hey, they could probably fit a Howitzer on this one." Then he looked at Cort Wesley wryly, an old friend and associate again instead of a stranger off the grid for seven years. "So you thinking about coming back to the life? There's more work than ever, if you're interested."

"I got two boys to raise now, Miguel. I think those days are behind me."

Asuna flashed him a knowing grin that stopped just short of a wink. "Sure, *jefe*, whatever you say."

57

Arno approached the man and the woman currently standing in the floral courtyard centered amid the living quarters to create a parklike setting. They could have sat on one of the teakwood benches but had chosen to stand. Perhaps they'd been strolling past the children's swings, slide, and sandboxes. From here they had a great view of the school building, playing fields, and gymnasium—facilities certain to draw more need as the numbers residing inside the Patriot Sun grounds continued to swell.

Malcolm Arno was good at guises, putting on whatever face best suited him at the time. Occasionally, when people looked at him wrong or funny, he wondered if he'd slipped the wrong mask on by accident, getting the same flutter in his gut that came when you find yourself naked in a dream. He needed to be especially cognizant of that today.

The man and woman saw him coming and instantly stood straighter, almost to attention. The man was Chester Singleton, one of the foremost political operatives in the country. Arno hoped the fact that he was the only African-American currently on the grounds wouldn't make him uncomfortable, while the woman already looked uncomfortable. She was tall, basketball-playing tall, towering a head over Singleton, just a few inches short of Arno's six feet even. Her name was Sue Ellen Ward, a take-no-prisoners, win-at-all costs strategist who'd learned the divide-and-conquer strategy from Karl Rove himself as a lowly White House staffer. Ward and Singleton were working together now, having joined forces to climb onto a political tidal wave of a candidate they believed capable of winning the upcoming presidential election.

Drawing closer, Arno watched Singleton remove his sunglasses to reveal slightly crossed eyes.

"A pleasure to meet you, sir," Singleton greeted.

"We were so happy to receive your call," Ward added, pumping his hand.

Arno pulled it back, amazed to find his hand now felt slick across the palm, as if somebody had greased it.

"Well," he said, swiping his palm across his slacks, "I believe we have plenty in common. I believe we want what's best for this country and are in a unique position to make that happen if we work together."

Both Singleton and Ward nodded enthusiastically, looking like robots, albeit highly polished ones.

"That's our thinking as well," said Singleton.

Sue Ellen Ward nodded once more. "Let me add that the governor was thrilled by your invitation. She's been a big admirer of yours for some time now too."

"Do you hunt, Mr. Arno?" the cross-eyed one asked him. "It might be the perfect way for you to get acquainted with the governor on a personal basis."

"Let me tell you something, Mr. Singleton," Arno said, feeling his blood simmer with no help from the sun. "I've got an old musty shirt hanging in my closet I haven't put on in twenty years. I was wearing it the day that Texas Ranger killed my father and it's the one thing I have left from my childhood besides his teachings. It's got blood splattered all over it. I look at it every day and that's the only blood I ever need or want to see, 'sides them that wrong this country bleeding out from sucking wounds that make them linger a while before they die. So if you don't mind, I'd like to cut to the chase here, all of us being busy as we are. I don't see the point in mincing words and making small talk. Not bullshit each other, in other words."

Singleton and Ward seemed to freeze before him, suddenly yanked from their element. Robots for sure, since the sun didn't seem to bother them or raise even the slightest sheen of sweat to the surface of their skin.

"I'd like to do everything I can to get that governor of yours elected president. I got ten million of the most patriotic Americans there are that I can count as supporters, and they're yours along with the leaders they are beholden to who are beholden to me. I got mailing lists, e-mail lists, phone bank records. If you add the largest church congregations in the country I'm aligned with, the number I can deliver is closer to twenty million, or at least fifteen. And, most important of all, what I got is money, a fully legitimate donation thanks to the new finance laws, bless the Supreme Court. I'm thinking a half a billion dollars. You think that might do it?"

"How about fishing?" Sue Ellen Ward said after grabbing her breath back, breaking into a smile that made her look almost human after all.

"I think we could try that," Arno told both her and Singleton, coming up just short of a wink. "See, I'm pretty good with a lure."

The robots tried to smile, not quite catching his meaning, which might explain why they had so much trouble managing the effort. They were holding the best they could come up with on their lips, when Malcolm Arno watched a black truck with tires the size of small planets clear the security booth and drive onto the complex.

58

WASHINGTON, D.C.; THE PRESENT

"No sign of Dylan," Cort Wesley said as soon as Caitlin called him from outside the FEMA building. "But I met up with the lowlifes who took him for a ride north."

"Paz?"

"Paz."

"Lowlifes still alive?"

"Couldn't tell you and don't care."

"Cort Wesley—"

"Don't be lecturing me now, Ranger. Time's not there to spare and I'm working on a lead to find Dylan."

"Where are you exactly?"

"Just had a burger at my favorite joint."

"You're *home*?"

"Thereabouts, but keeping a very low profile."

"Why do I have trouble believing that?"

"I'm not thinking about Mexican jails right now, Ranger. I'm thinking about finding my son. He's alive for sure; I can feel it. Lowlifes met none other than Buck LaChance outside a town called Concepción del Oro the other night. That's when Dylan made his getaway."

"Into the Mexican desert after dark?" Caitlin asked, feeling dread grasp her.

"With his hands cuffed behind him to boot."

"So why is it you sound so hopeful?"

"'Cause I know my kid. Just humor me on this for a minute. La-Chance is the key here and we've gotta find him. One of the lowlifes said there were Texas plates on his truck. I already got something of a make on it but need you to trace it down closer."

"Cort Wesley—"

"Don't say it, Ranger."

"You don't even know what I was going to say."

"If it has to do with that extradition order, I don't want to hear it. You need to bring me in when this is done, we'll cover that then."

"That's not what I was going to say at all."

"Then what were you?"

Caitlin started to speak, then stopped. "It can wait until I get back from Washington."

"What the hell brought you all the way out there?"

"Turns out some folks got a war they want me to fight for them," Caitlin said, her mind picturing Malcolm Arno as a boy staring at her from across the Tackle and Gun parking lot while his father lay dead by his side.

"So what else is new? Your truck gets lousy gas mileage, by the way."

"Advertisements said different."

"Can't believe anyone these days, can you?"

59

"Am I still your only customer, Padre?" Guillermo Paz asked the priest he had brought down from Mexico City to preside over his soldiers.

The priest, whose name had been Juan Jose Morales in another life as a petty criminal and pickpocket until he'd found God, looked at the huge man through the gaps in the mini blinds. "So far, Colonel."

"Easter Sunday's just a few days off. That service will make up for it, you'll see."

"What can I do for you now?"

"Remember that dream I told you about the other day, that vision?"

"Something to do with a Texas Ranger," Morales nodded. "Yes."

"Along with guns and blood. A lot of both."

Morales could see Guillermo Paz scrunched onto the wooden seat on the other side of the blind, his vast size forcing his legs under the curtain covering the cubicle. His skin looked shiny and smelled like motor oil. His wild black hair had the texture of rope, wet with sweat and grease. But his eyes stood out the most; big, empty, sad, and suddenly uncertain, even quizzical. Morales had never seen a pair of eyes so poorly matched to the man seeing out of them.

"I buried two men in the desert yesterday."

"Is that what you've come to confess?"

"No, because it wasn't a sin. They deserved it. That's not the problem."

"What is?"

"These men took advantage of children. Kidnapped them to be sold as slaves."

"*Madre de Dios . . .*"

"Our God isn't always watching, Padre. A lot slips past him, including those two men I buried."

"In killing them you exercised the wrath of God Himself. You were His instrument and, as such, I agree you have nothing to confess."

"Not yet."

"Colonel?"

"It wasn't Mexican officials looking for a way out of their country's mess who put me here, Padre; it was God. I haven't been able to think of anything besides that since I presided over the funeral of those two men in the desert. Those who harm children have to be stopped, all of them."

Father Morales hesitated. He'd heard the confessions of criminals and killers in prison that had turned his blood to ice, not just for the casual demeanor with which they related their acts, but also the utter flatness and resignation in their stares. Colonel Paz was nothing like them and yet far more dangerous to those who didn't meet his moral code or, worse, pushed the buttons inside him that superheated his skin and left him bleeding oil from his pores.

"Everything I heard about you is true, isn't it?" the priest said finally. "That you protected the poor people being victimized by drug lords in Juárez. That they called you Ángel de la Guarda, that you were a spirit sent to help them."

"Well, that last part's not true. Ever read Heraclitus, Padre?"

"No, Colonel."

"He wrote that nothing endures but change. I'm living proof of that. I was a different man altogether before I met my Texas Ranger. I believe everything I've done since has been about living up to her example."

Morales considered Paz's words, nodding. "These men who victimize children . . . they are not kindred souls in the eyes of God and thus not deserving of the same rights as men, His forgiveness, penance, or blessing. Do you read Saint Thomas Aquinas, Colonel?"

"Some."

"Aquinas wrote, 'Justice is a certain rectitude of mind whereby a man does what he ought to do—' "

" '—in circumstances confronting him,' " Paz completed. "My thoughts exactly, Padre."

Morales closed his eyes and muttered a silent prayer to himself. "Then go with God," he said finally, opening his eyes.

But Colonel Paz was already gone.

PART SIX

In response to a request from a reporter for his version of the ambush that gunned down Bonnie and Clyde in 1934, Frank Hamer responded, "Sure I can tell how it happened. We just shot the hell out of 'em."

—Mike Cox, *Time of the Rangers*

60

Dylan couldn't remember a more miserable stretch in his whole life. Maybe sliding out the cramped confines of his mother's womb, if he'd been able to recall that.

From the time he'd somehow managed to hoist himself into the back of the big bald guy's truck and shimmy under one of the tarpaulins for cover, Dylan entered a dark, cramped world of steel and stench. The steel was wrapped in heavily oiled cloths that reminded him of his dad's gun locker in the basement of their house. The stench came from the mildew, mold, and old rust caked onto the tarp like misplaced paint.

After doubling back through the desert, Dylan had squeezed himself in amid the gun sacks, his quivery legs cramping up on him and forcing the boy to bite his lip to avoid crying out. Fatty, the gimp, and Baldy were probably still out looking for him around the stretch of hills he'd run toward before doubling back. But sound could travel for miles in the desert night and he didn't dare let a scream of pain betray his position and plan. A few more hours, maybe less, and his captors would figure him for coyote food.

That's about how long it was before Dylan heard the three men return. The big biker was swearing up a storm, Fatty and the gimp showing him deference and insisting in broken English that they'd find the boy by sunrise. The biker threatened them with something Dylan couldn't discern, then the driver's door opened with a slight creak before slamming closed. The engine raced, roared, and then the big truck tore off.

Dylan felt elated, the first part of his plan having been accomplished. As for the next phrase, freeing himself, he was able to find a part of the truck's steel bed that had creased away from the frame, probably from having something heavy dropped into it by a crane or winch. It wasn't real sharp or jagged, but it was steel and narrow-edged enough to maybe handle the job. So as the truck thumped through the desert night, Dylan shimmied himself into position so his plastic-bound wrists were centered over it.

He got nowhere at first and when he tried to pick up the pace ended up slicing the hell out of his wrists dangerously close to veins and arteries that could leave him bleeding out. So he slowed the pace again, found that place in his mind where he wasn't really here anyway, and fell into a twisted rhythm. Not that he made much progress, especially at first. But the mere sense of the plastic being gnawed at even slightly gave him purpose and hope.

His greatest enemies became thirst, heat once night became morning, and time in general. Through the drive and the several stops along the way Dylan passed it by waiting, gnawing, and dreaming. He slipped off to sleep a few times, further disorienting him from the true passage of time to the point where he lost track of what day it was. The presence of the guns reassured him somewhat, since it seemed to make any ruffling through the bed's contents unlikely at best. They were headed somewhere, all right, a final destination perhaps, and Dylan held to the hope he'd find a way to jostle himself free before being discovered.

Time was quickly eclipsed by the sun's blistering heat. When they'd first set out, the cold was his biggest problem. The night air blowing past him as the big truck hurdled down the road, puckering the tarpaulin and making it feel like ice when it brushed against him. Soon, though, his body heat radiated outward, forming a kind of blanket out of his own smell and sweat. In fact, for a time he felt comfortable, until the sun reclaimed the sky in the morning.

And then, as he continued to shift his arms back and forth, he felt the plastic cuffs snare on an edge of the jagged steel, locking him in place and curtailing his thoughts of escape through the several stops that followed. Dylan fought against panic and focused on working the cuffs free of their bond. But the more he tried, the more the plastic seemed to catch. Dylan felt tears brewing in his eyes and stopped shifting his arms altogether, searching for an alternate strategy to avoid making things worse yet.

But how could they be any worse than this?

The road ran flat for hours, the air smelling of fresh-baked tar until a thunderstorm soaked him through the tarpaulin and he drank rainwater like a dog where it collected in the folds. Peeking out enough to ease this thirst also convinced him he was back in Texas for sure, the big truck cruising down a freeway heading west. Not home, but closer, and that gave the boy the will to restart his efforts to free the flex cuffs from their snare on the bent steel of the bed liner. And finally, finally, somehow Dylan jerked them free. Though the cuffs were still clamped on his wrists, he took solace in his success, however slight, helping him ignore the coppery smell of his blood and the cramping in his shoulders and back.

Then, after more hours than he could possibly track, the big truck slid to a halt and Dylan heard a brief, muffled conversation after which it started on again. When the truck came to a stop next, just a few moments later, the engine kicked off and Dylan heard the rasp of an emergency brake being yanked into place. He heard the driver's door rattle open and the big biker's boots clacking against hard pavement.

"It's about time, Brother LaChance," Dylan heard a new voice greet.

61

MIDLAND, TEXAS; THE PRESENT

"I'm not your brother," LaChance said. "Only brothers I had were killed up in Quebec."

"What's the news on the boy?" Malcolm Arno asked him, approaching the truck's rear.

"Nothing new or good. He hasn't turned up yet. You ask me, he's dead."

Arno's brow crinkled and his lips curled back in something between a scowl and a sneer. He could feel his pulse rate slowing in disappointment. His eyes sought out LaChance's, seeing in their flat acceptance of the world before them a dark evil and fearsome loathing. LaChance had no stake in the boy's fate beyond delivering him here, and it showed. His tattooed skin seemed to radiate static that turned to prickly heat beneath the blazing sun. LaChance favored snakes for his tattoos, and every time he came to the Patriot Sun, a different one seemed to spring to life across his neck or banded arms exposed by a sleeveless denim vest. It had clearly been a jacket once, but he'd sliced the sleeves off, leaving frayed tatters in their place with the right side riding up the shoulder an inch or so more than the left.

Arno was not a man to fear anything, especially in his current circumstance with the world behind him, commentators on radio and television singing his virtues and proclaiming him a visionary to lead a moral movement well into the century. And he wasn't scared of LaChance either, not in those words anyway. It was more like the man flat sucked the strength out of him, his black egg-shaped eyes looking like what his father would have called glimpses of the abyss.

"You should have handled the boy yourself, LaChance," he said finally. "I thought I made that plain."

"Along with the importance of picking up those samples." LaChance straightened his spine, seeming even bigger and more imposing. "Not a good idea to have the boy in tow when I did that."

"You're right," Arno conceded. He could feel himself sweating now and angled himself sideways so the big man wouldn't see it soaking through his shirt. "How about we check out the merchandise?"

"I think you're gonna be real, real happy with what I got here," LaChance said, and threw back the tarpaulin.

62

"You mind giving me that again?" said D. W. Tepper on the other end of the phone line.

Waiting at the gate for her flight back to San Antonio to be called, Caitlin could hear the crackle of cellophane being stripped off a pack of cigarettes. "My old friend Jones—"

"Thought his name was Smith."

"It varies. Anyway, Jones thinks that poor kid from the Intrepid got his legs blown off because he caught wind of a Homeland Security investigation into billions of dollars in cash missing from Iraq."

"Oh, shit," Tepper droned.

"My thoughts exactly. Trail seems to lead to the right-wing militia movement."

"Wait a minute, you telling me those unadulterated nutcases got their hands on that kind of green?"

"Straight from similar nutcase higher-ups in the army, among the original cadre running the Iraqi reconstruction."

Tepper felt as if he'd swallowed something sour. "Meaning they were likely the ones who tried to blow you up down the road from the Intrepid last night. I'll see their asses strung up a flagpole before this is over, Ranger."

"It gets better, Captain. Jones brought up the name Malcolm Arno in particular."

"If your daddy could hear this now . . ."

"What do you know about Arno and the Patriot Sun, Captain?"

The labored breathing returned again ahead of Tepper's voice. "Well, Ranger, lemme put it this way. I wrote the report that brought the FBI to Waco. I scouted the woods on horseback when we took on the Republic of Texas folks, and I closed down the Church of the Redeemer with Jim Strong himself. I'm telling you this 'cause when you look these kind of men in the eye often enough, you get to know the type. I never met Max Arno's son in person, never laid eyes on him up close, but I've seen him on television filling up the screen and that's enough to tell he's as bad as any of them, maybe worse. Not suicidal like Koresh, fanatical like Randy Weaver, or holier-than-thou like his father. And 'cause of that he scares me most of all."

63

MIDLAND, TEXAS; THE PRESENT

"Very impressive," Arno said, regarding the sight revealed beneath the now cloud-filled, late-afternoon sky.

"That was my thought too," LaChance said. "Latest models just off the production line for the same price as the older ones."

"You're a good negotiator, LaChance."

"Must be my charm," the big man said.

Arno pictured a collection of guns like this in the hands of men beholden to those who'd been out to the ranch that week. Let loose on a country in which the kind of action that was coming was long overdue.

"Why don't you get yourself a meal and rest up? I'll meet you in the diner straightaway," Dylan heard the other man say, as the boy pushed himself tighter against the big truck's hot blue finish, scalding his arms. He'd managed to drop out of the bed when neither of them was watching, taking the impact on his shoulder and biting down the pain as he shimmied under the far side of the truck. The exhaust system's chrome pipes steamed heat, roasting him more than the sun. He smelled gasoline mixing with the lingering stench of oily exhaust fumes and baked tar.

Through the long hours of the drive north from Mexico, he'd mostly forgotten about his dick still being out, but now there it was rubbing against his zipper, the boy doing everything he could to get it covered with his shirt even here under the truck's cover.

"Mr. Arno?" he heard Baldy call, voice more distant now. "I'm sorry things didn't work out with the boy."

"Fortune dropped him into our lap and fortune took him away again," said the man named Arno. "I suppose it's God's will, but I'm hard-pressed to figure out why."

They exchanged more words, but Dylan had stopped listening by then. What the hell did the guy mean about fortune dropping him into his lap? Who was this guy and what did he want with him? Could be it had something to do with his father. An old enemy of Cort Wesley Masters Dylan had somehow stumbled upon in his quest to reach Maria Lopez.

The boy tried to angle himself closer to better hear the conversation. But he brushed his shoulder against one of the exhaust pipes as he shifted position and felt his skin singed through his shirt. Dylan bit his lip to avoid crying out but cracked his head good against the crankshaft when he jerked involuntarily away from the pipe.

"You hear something?" he heard the man named Arno say.

64

MIDLAND, TEXAS; THE PRESENT

"No, sir," the big biker said. "Engine fluids just cooling off, that's all."

Arno didn't respond. Dylan could see his legs and felt his breath seize up when the man's knees bent slightly, as if he was crouching down to check under the truck.

"Something else, Mr. Arno," Dylan heard Baldy continue. "The two men who delivered the kid to me in the desert have gone missing."

Arno's legs straightened again. "I would have expected as much, under the circumstances."

"I don't think they ran off. I think they're in the ground. A couple army types showed up in a bar where they were drinking. The men left with them, under some duress I'm led to believe."

"We own the army down there, LaChance."

"I said army *types*. Uniforms, guns. They leave with the Mexicans and the Mexicans drop off the face of the earth."

"Dig deeper. Find out who's holding the leash of these army types."

"Soon as I get back from up north. I missed my brothers' funeral, you know."

"I'm sorry."

"Plenty more gonna be sorry before this is done. You know that stuff they say about feeling it when your twin gets hurt?"

"Yes."

"It's bullshit. They pulled the burned bodies of my brothers out of what was left of that grow house, one shot and the other with a knife still sticking out of his throat, and I didn't feel a goddamn thing."

"A knife sticking out of his throat?" Dylan heard the man named Arno say.

"That's right. Why?"

"No reason. Nothing really."

Dylan listened to Baldy's biker boots finally clacking away across the pavement. He waited for the Arno guy to leave too before shifting out from beneath the truck the same way he'd gone under it. Wasn't easy with his hands still bound behind him and this time his dick rubbed against the hot pavement.

He peered out from the cover of the big truck, registering he was on the grounds of some massive fortlike complex. The Arno guy had called it a ranch but it was plenty more than that. Virtually a self-contained small town—no, more like an army base. From the sprawl, Dylan figured it could accommodate thousands.

Which meant lots of hiding places.

He needed to hide out until he could find himself a phone, maybe a computer. Something to get word to his dad and Caitlin he was here.

Which was *where* exactly?

Dylan hoped the name "Arno" would give them enough of a clue. In the meantime, it was still light out and would be for a couple more hours. So maybe the thing to do was hole up until dark and then find a way out under the cover of night. Get to the nearest main road, and hope somebody picked him up.

Dylan's lips were cracked and bleeding from dehydration. His mouth was a dry sewer bed and his tongue felt like a wad of cotton stuck in his mouth. His stomach ached with hunger, but he needed water more than anything, something else to put on the list.

The building nearest the parking lot looked to be some sort of welcoming and reception center. Dylan watched people he took for visitors entering and then emerging shortly afterward with some sort of badge in an adjustable holder dangling from their necks. They had transplanted some cedar elm and white ash trees to offer shade for the building both front and rear. That rear, he noticed, backed up against an assemblage of exposed piping perched on a berm, like they were having sewer trouble or something. And, sure enough, when the breeze turned right, Dylan caught the scent of human waste and stale manure.

Or maybe drainage was the problem in general, since the exposed foundation at the rear of the welcoming center looked higher than the front. The low-slung windows were outfitted with big wells to soak up the rain and keep it from inside the building. It was the closest structure, sure, but still a hundred yards away. A good half of that could be covered with parked vehicles for cover, which still left half in the open right under the thickening clouds.

Dylan managed the first half without incident, settling himself between a pair of nearly identical SUVs for the last stretch. He wondered what the residents of this place would make of a teenage boy lighting out the rest of the way with hands cuffed behind him and dick swinging free. Then, though, fortune smiled when the clouds opened up, spilling heavy rain that chased workers and strollers away from the outdoors.

Dylan moved out into the sudden storm, feeling it drench him. It felt cool and refreshing, and he imagined himself opening his mouth to it from the cover of one of those window wells. He dropped into the first one he came to, tucking his body in low and tight so it couldn't be glimpsed from casual view. The positioning pressed him up against the window of a subbasement or cellar that looked dark and lifeless beyond the glass. Then he angled himself to the storm, dipping his head backward to drink in the rainwater, opened his mouth and closed his eyes against its cascading torrents.

Suddenly he felt a hand close on his neck and shove him forward against the building, his face mashed against vinyl siding. The strong smell of shit, like the one he caught wafting in the air, assaulted him as a voice found his ear.

"Stay still," Dylan heard it whisper.

Then he felt a sharp knife work its way through the remnants of his plastic bonds until his hands came free.

"Now stay here," the human stench behind him said softly. "I'll come back for you as soon as I can."

And then he was gone.

65

SAN ANTONIO; THE PRESENT

"You run that plate, Captain?" Caitlin asked before she'd even taken the seat before D. W. Tepper's desk. She'd barely slept at all the night before, staying up with Cort Wesley to keep him as calm as she could. Ended up getting even more pissed off than he was, her rage over the still missing Dylan trapping her between tears and fury that left her trembling in a chair.

Tepper's eyes looked milky and bloodshot, a clear sign he was having trouble sleeping again himself. "Rather not tell you what I found, Ranger."

"Why's that exactly? You worried about me going old school again?"

Those tired eyes held hers as best they could. "Not you I'm worried about."

"I can control Cort Wesley Masters."

"No, you can't. Nobody can. Somebody in Austin managed to get part of his military file unsealed—just part of it, mind you." Tepper shook his head dramatically from side to side. "Man oh man, what we know about this boy doesn't even scratch the surface of what he's capable of."

"Tell them to unseal the whole thing."

"Come again?"

"Cort Wesley's a war hero, Captain. Problem is the kind of unit he was part of does everything under the sand. That's the kind of man the

State of Texas is willing to send back to Mexico thanks to a single letter from a corrupt governor."

Tepper weighed her words, tobacco-stained fingers interlaced before him. "Tell me one thing, Ranger. Did he do what they say he did or not?"

"It's complicated."

"Just answer the question."

"Yeah, he did, but—"

"I don't wanna hear no buts right now. If Masters's beef is genuine, tell him to take my nephew's advice and get himself a high-priced lawyer and take it up with the attorney general. Our job is to bring him in and turn him over to the federal marshals. We don't do it, you think Austin's just gonna forget and let this go? And it's not just Austin; we got Washington breathing down our backs to avoid some kind of goddamn diplomatic incident here."

"Tell me about the truck, D.W., the truth behind that nonexistent hunting lodge in Kilgore."

"Jesus Christ, Caitlin, are you listening to me at all?"

"You want me to bring in Masters, we'd best help bring his son back first."

Tepper frowned, Caitlin catching a glimpse of the fresh tobacco stains on his front teeth. "This nonexistent hunting lodge is a front belonging to a shell real estate company that traced back to none other than the Patriot Sun."

"Shit."

"That was my thought."

"Wraps everything up in a neat little bow, doesn't it?"

"In a package we can't touch, Ranger," Tepper said coarsely. "What we supposed to say about what put us onto the truck in the first place, given the way the information was obtained?"

"You and my dad were never ones to stand on ceremony before, D.W."

"This ain't ceremony, Caitlin, it's survival. There's powerful folks out there who count themselves as friends and allies of Malcolm Arno. Hell, there's pictures on the governor's website of the two of them together, for Christ's sake. Used it as his home screen for a time."

"Homepage."

"Huh?"

"It's called a homepage."

Tepper fished a pack of Marlboros from his top desk drawer, tapped one out, and stuck it in his mouth.

"Why you doing that in front of me, Captain?"

"To piss you off as much as you just pissed me off," he said, flicking a match to life.

"Well, since I'm on a roll, try this out: I need to get inside Arno's complex."

Tepper sucked in a deep drag off his Marlboro, then wrinkled his nose. "Private property last time I checked. You'll need cause."

"I was thinking maybe a warrant."

"Not based on what we got on that truck, Ranger."

Caitlin thought back to her conversation with Jones and the man White from Homeland. "My friend in Washington believes Arno's responsible for blowing up that judge in Galveston a few days back."

"Sometimes you really know how to scare me."

"Explosives were pretty sophisticated stuff, Captain. PETN—that's pentaerythritol tetranitrate. My friend in Washington referred to it as military grade, one of the most powerful explosives known to man. You want to send him a sample of what they used trying to blow me up and see if it matches?"

"Your friend willing to go on record with this?"

"Anonymous source."

"Still not enough to get you a warrant."

"How about an interview?"

"Come again?"

"Can we make Arno a person of interest in the Galveston bombing?"

Tepper weighed her words. "You tell me."

"Well, let's assume we had evidence he's got this PETN on the premises."

"Except we don't."

"Arno won't know that."

Tepper pressed out his cigarette in a dish he used as an ashtray since he'd tossed all his real ones the last time he quit, his face looking like he was coming down with indigestion. "Past is gone, Ranger, and better left that way."

"I'm fine with that, Captain, so long as Malcolm Arno is too."

66

SAN ANTONIO; THE PRESENT

"Not sure whether that puts him on our side or not," Cort Wesley said, after Caitlin summarized the salient points of her conversation with Captain Tepper. "Well, yours maybe."

"He's giving us the cover we need."

"Only you, from where I'm standing." He was leaning against the fender of Caitlin's dust-encrusted SUV, looking almost spectral in the darkness around him.

"I'm talking to Arno, somebody's gotta check the grounds."

"What do you think your captain would think about that?"

"I don't really give a damn right now." Caitlin checked her watch. "Come on, we got an appointment across town before we head west in the morning."

"Appointment?"

"Sometimes even the best need backup, Cort Wesley."

Their backup was seated at a shaded terrace table at Starbucks on the Riverwalk. Dressed like a cowboy right down to the Wrangler jeans, fringed coat, and hat beneath which a shock of white hair flowed well past his shoulders. The cowboy took off his sunglasses and rose at their approach.

"R. Lee Shine," he said, extending his hand to Caitlin first before moving it and his eyes on to Cort Wesley.

Caitlin waited for Cort Wesley to finish sizing the man up before speaking. She could see his muscles tensing, regarding Shine as if he were a foe instead of friend. His eyes narrowed, preferring to see a narrower piece of the world he was just reminded wasn't his to control.

"Mr. Shine here's one of the best criminal attorneys in the state," she said, hoping to get Cort Wesley to focus.

"I don't need to be thinking about that right now," he said instead.

"Sit down, Cort Wesley."

His eyes remained fixed on the lawyer as if this was a draw down. "I don't mind standing."

"Let's all sit down."

Caitlin did so first, Shine following while Cort Wesley remained standing with the setting sun hitting him like a spotlight. "Cort Wesley," she prompted.

And he finally sat down, pushing his chair an uncomfortable distance from the table and crossing his arms before him.

"As I was saying," Caitlin resumed, "Mr. Shine here comes very highly recommended."

"By who?"

"By folks in even worse predicaments than you, I suppose," Shine said, facing Cort Wesley and showing no fear or trepidation whatsoever. He had gunfighter's eyes, the kind that never seemed to blink or back down. Cort Wesley met his gaze, seeming to respect that. "Been retired for a few years now," Shine continued. "But once in a while a case comes up I can't resist. The two of you wanna get something inside?"

"Not right now," said Cort Wesley.

"We could go for something stronger instead. My granddaughter's band, The Rats, is playing at a roadhouse just up the road a ways."

Cort Wesley shook his head. "I'll take a rain check, if you don't mind."

"Not at all," Shine told him. "Anyway, I had the privilege to cross paths a few times with both Ranger Strong's father and grandfather and now I'm glad to have the pleasure to be meeting her."

"My dad and granddad both said you were as good with a law book as they were with a pistol. Think it was my dad who said when you addressed a jury even Justice herself pulled off her blindfold to watch."

"Well," said Shine, settling back in his chair, "I won almost all of them, but there are still nights when sleep won't come on account of the ones I lost." He turned his gaze on Cort Wesley. "Ranger Strong asked me to have a look at your case. She also explained some of the circumstances involved, which we'll call irrelevant now far as legal purposes go." He leaned forward, a thin band of amber sunlight splitting his face down the middle. "Let's start with the second most pertinent part of the Extradition Treaty between the U.S. and Mexico: 'The Contracting Parties agree to mutually extradite, subject to the provisions of this Treaty, persons who the competent authorities of the requesting Party have charged with an offense or have found guilty of committing an offense, or are wanted by said authorities to complete a judicially pronounced penalty of deprivation of liberty for an offense committed within the territory of the requesting Party.'"

Cort Wesley pushed his chair forward a bit. "Right now, I got one thing on my mind and one thing only. That's finding my son. 'Til that happens, I'm not going to be much for listening to such crap."

"You said that was the second most pertinent part," Caitlin interjected, so Shine would continue addressing the issue at hand.

"Yes, I did," the old lawyer said, words aimed at Cort Wesley, "because here's the first: 'Extradition shall be granted only if the evidence be found sufficient, according to the laws of the requested Party, either to justify the committal for trial of the person sought if the offense of which he has been accused had been committed in that place or to prove that he is the person convicted by the courts of the requesting Party.' You see the point here?"

"Mexicans gotta prove I did it to make the United States give me up."

"Not exactly. They just have to show a preponderance of evidence suggesting your guilt, and the standard applied, my friend, is America's, not Mexico's. You got a dollar, Mr. Masters?"

"I do," Cort Wesley said and fished it from his pocket.

Shine took it from his grasp and slipped it into his lapel pocket. "We'll call that a retainer. Makes me your duly appointed attorney charged with your representation. Now tell me this: did you kill this man as it is alleged?"

"Yes, sir, I did."

"Were there witnesses?"

"None that were looking once the bullets started flying."

"How far away were you from the nearest witness?"

"Ten feet maybe."

"Facing him?"

"Back turned."

"Inside or outside?"

"Inside. A bar."

"Then we can assume any witnesses were drinking."

"A fair estimation."

Shine leaned back again. "You can see what I'm getting at here. We need to demonstrate in the appropriate federal court that the preponderance of evidence is not enough to warrant granting the extradition request. The problem is that with a murder case most times the court will side with the requesting party unless there are witnesses present to contradict the alleged crime in its entirety. A witness offering an alibi, perhaps. But an affirmative defense, or claim of self-defense, seldom if ever flies at this stage."

"What are my chances?" Cort Wesley asked him.

"Of avoiding jail in Mexico, I'd say fair to pretty good. Can't say the same about avoiding some incarceration north of the border."

"I miss something here?" Caitlin interjected.

"No, ma'am. Once Mr. Masters turns himself in, he won't be eligible for bail because no suspect subject to extradition qualifies under the statute. And the Mexican authorities are notoriously slow in producing the requested material and documentation required for the court to render a decision. Not a verdict, mind you, just a decision whether to grant the request or not. Best chance we got is to make a prima facie case based on the facts alone being in dispute and seek a directed verdict. But I'd be lying if I said I thought I could convince even a drunken monkey of that, and there are plenty on the federal bench who fit that description to a T."

"I don't like the part about turning myself in," Cort Wesley said, stiffening.

"Figure of speech. From what I've been able to gather, this is being pushed at the highest levels so the American, and thus the Texas, authorities have no choice but to act and act quickly."

"You understand granting the extradition request is basically a death sentence," said Caitlin. "Cort Wesley Masters has got no better chance living long enough down there to stand trial than I do of growing a third arm."

Shine processed that with his eyes widening slightly and shifting between the two of them before they locked onto Cort Wesley again, stiffer than the steel chair on which he was seated. "I'm not gonna lie to you, Mr. Masters. This is one big ugly mess, best thing being that I've cleaned up far worse ones and you've got a Texas Ranger vouching for your character. I understand what you're going through with your boy. Got six kids myself and eleven grandchildren. Anybody tried to separate me from them, you know what I'd do?"

Caitlin and Cort Wesley waited for him to continue.

"I'd get me the best lawyer there was with a gunfighter's mind-set who doesn't take prisoners and never misses the bull's-eye."

"That's the problem, Mr. Shine," Cort Wesley told him, his joints cracking as he leaned forward. "Everybody misses sometimes."

67

MIDLAND, TEXAS; THE NIGHT BEFORE

The night before, Dylan had pulled himself up out of the window well long after the man who smelled like a sewer pipe failed to return. It was well past midnight, if he was reading the sky correctly, probably around three a.m. He'd nodded off a few times, only to be awoken by a combination of the hunger panging his stomach and the stench rising off his clothes more fit for a dumpster than his body. He hated the feel of filth all over him and the oil matting his hair to his skin and scalp.

The sprawling complex had fallen quiet and still after dark, though he thought he heard popping sounds coming from under the ground. Could be from slant drilling born of oil wells actually located miles away. Could be this whole complex was built directly over hell itself.

There were guards posted about and others patrolling the grounds in Jeep Wranglers. Dylan also noticed a pair of watchtowers manned by men with spotlights and binoculars that reminded him of prison movies he'd seen. Made him wonder if they had tripod-mounted machine guns up there and just who the tower guards were fixing to shoot if they did.

It helped him to think this way, focus on the goal at hand to take his mind off how miserable he felt. He needed to find a phone to make contact with his dad and Caitlin, and the time had come to do that instead of just thinking about it. The relief over being able to use his hands after the cramped ordeal of the past day, just being able to zip his pants up, had abated, but at least those hands and arms had stopped cramping.

Dylan stayed low as he emerged from the window well, moving in a crouch and sometimes hitting the thick grass when lights of the patrolling Jeep Wranglers splayed his way through the night. He moved toward a heavy concentration of buildings and used them for cover in working his way around to the most outlying structures, where he was least likely to encounter resistance.

One building in particular caught his attention because it was situated totally by itself. There was a guard posted at its front but no one else in evidence Dylan could see. The windows looked to be partially blacked out, or perhaps just covered by dark shades, allowing just the slightest glow of light to emanate from within.

Dylan risked a hundred-yard dash across open ground, glad also for the fact that this far out no security cameras mounted on nearby buildings were likely to catch him. He reached the far side of the building's rear without incident and pressed himself against the dark siding, listening to the steady hum of air-conditioning units that had further disguised his approach. Leaning up against the structure, he heard strange sounds coming from within that made him think of dogs whimpering from fear of a thunderstorm or some other reason humans couldn't understand. But he thought little more of that and busied himself instead with finding a way inside.

This building too was constructed with window wells off the basement windows to add drainage, and Dylan slipped into one not to hide again but to gain access. The window was latched but maybe not locked down. Pushing on it gained him little movement, but hammering it with a closed fist moved it slightly, enough to go back to pushing for the final result.

Click.

Dylan felt the latch separate from its slot and snap downward. The window came open in his hand; not all the way but enough, he hoped, to accommodate him. It was the first time in recent memory he was glad he had his mother's size and not his father's. He managed to snake his upper body through the gap first, then shimmy his lower body down after it. Extending his arms to cushion his drop.

Except there wasn't much of one. The basement was more of a drainage culvert to hold water in the event of spring flooding. The floor was hard-packed gravel with a covering of stones, angular depressions every ten feet or so indicating some kind of pumping apparatus and catch basin.

Dylan's eyes adjusted to the darkness quickly, not scared or hesitant, even when something with tiny claws scampered over the outstretched hands pulling him along. The whole way he kept feeling about the ceiling with his palms, hoping to find the hatchway he expected to be there to provide access to the man-made culvert. When he didn't find one on his first pass beneath the building, he doubled back five feet down, resigned to repeat the process as long as it took for him to find a way into the building above where there had to be a phone.

In the end, it took five trips up and back before he found what he was looking for and then only by accident when he hammered the ceiling in frustration and heard the dull thud he'd been hoping for. He was similarly fortunate that the hatch he found opened both up and down. All he needed to do was yank back the bolt and the hatch would drop, allowing him to climb up.

Without the moon to follow, he'd lost track of time and didn't care about it anymore, his focus changed now. He drew the bolt back and lowered the hatch slowly. Once all the way open, it barely cleared the stone topping layer of the gravel floor, and Dylan eased his upper body into position to climb through it, moving deliberately and agilely.

He was vaguely conscious of a bittersweet smell he couldn't quite put his finger on, the whimpering sound a bit louder now too if he'd stopped to notice. Instead, Dylan was swept by a triumphant glee and sense of relief that comes when you realize the nightmare that just woke you up in a cold sweat wasn't real at all. The misery of the last three days was going to end in this building he began to hoist himself into.

What he'd taken for whimpering sounded more like purring now in the darkness before him, accompanied by strange rasps and rattles that didn't sound human at all. Dylan got his head through all the way, easing his shoulders up to follow as his eyes adjusted to the darkness.

"Oh, shit," he thought at the sight around him, hoping for dear life he hadn't said it out loud.

But maybe he had, because the next thing he knew the world exploded in light and the whimpers turned into screeching wails.

68

MIDLAND, TEXAS; THE PRESENT

She was a good girl, Malcolm Arno reflected, one of the best he'd ever had. He'd let her go into the bathroom after they were finished, passing the time by standing naked before the big bay window looking over the wooded rear of the complex, formed of transplanted trees. He'd had his personal residence built flush against those trees, wanting to feel, with a glance through the glass, that he was deep in the forest, far from the humanity he was dedicated to change forever. The hour after dawn being his favorite time of the day to revel in the view, the glow shimmering off the world a harbinger of things to come that immediately lifted his spirits.

Arno heard retching sounds coming from the bathroom, followed by the toilet flushing. He remained by the window, with only the trees to bear witness to the act now consummated.

He loved being in bed with one of his girls with the blinds open to the dark woods beyond. Reminded him of the few times his father had taken him camping as a boy before the demands of the church became so great and Malcolm had to share him with members and sycophants alike. It had been so long since he'd had his father all to himself, when the Texas Rangers came and set them off on the run together. Malcolm actually enjoyed those days more than he could have possibly imagined.

They hadn't gone far actually—just to a local motel the church owned to wait the law out. Strange how those were such happy memories for Malcolm, the last he held of his father before he was killed in that parking lot by an assassin wearing a cinco-pesos badge. Three days spent watching pay-per-view movies and eating food his father's bodyguards brought in from fast-food joints and pizza parlors. It was like a great adventure.

And then it ended, all too soon.

Arno heard the girl retching again. Flush, went the toilet.

She was a luscious find, but too small and immature in the bones. Underdeveloped thanks to malnutrition. Give her a few weeks here with the Patriot Sun, though, and watch her sprout and blossom. She hadn't been ready for him tonight, but she would be soon. And in the meantime Arno would try out the others, his mind drifting back the whole time to nights spent hidden in closets or peeking through cracked-open doors at men from his father's Church of the Redeemer doing the very same thing.

The toilet flushed again, the door opening to reveal the girl's thin frame silhouetted like a stick figure against the single light reflecting off the mirror. Arno held his gaze upon her, repulsed in that instant by his own proclivities and whims, the shadows revealing this girl to be nothing like the vision conjured up by his fantasy.

He checked his watch, an exact replica of his father's, and found the time for his scheduled video call was just a few moments away. Glad to have an excuse, Arno threw his T-shirt back on and pulled his arms through his bathrobe, tying it tightly as he walked downstairs to his office.

Hardly a wizard with technology, Arno nonetheless much preferred a video call to the standard variety. He liked looking at the speaker's eyes, believing they had far more to say than words. As he settled in behind his computer screen, though, the problem was the other man's features were virtually lost to a spectral blur of colors and dots that intensified with each slight movement. His eyes were no more than black holes chiseled out of his head. All Arno could tell was that the man was wearing a doctor's lab coat, of all things, and he had a nametag pinned to his lapel wrongly identifying him as someone named GILROY.

"Last time I checked that wasn't your name," Arno said.

The man picked at his gray mustache, which looked more silver in the strangely dancing color schemes. "It's been a long couple days."

"I assume that's why we're talking."

"You're going to have a visitor later today. A Texas Ranger named Caitlin Strong."

Arno felt every part of him stiffen. Even his toes seemed to lock into place. "I know the name."

"I thought you might. There are several among us who are concerned by what the subject of her visit might be."

"Concerned?"

"We never authorized the hit on that judge in Galveston, Mr. Arno."

"I don't recall needing your authorization to run the Patriot Sun as I see fit. That is why you came to me, isn't it?"

"My parents were devout members of the Church of the Redeemer. That made you the perfect choice to help realize our common goals."

"So you acknowledge I don't take orders from you."

On the screen before him, the man's grainy visage tightened. "There was no implication either way."

"Why can't you just say what you mean?"

The man angled his face sideways, hardly looking into his webcam anymore. "We tried to deal with this problem for you. Things didn't work out."

"What do you mean by that?" Then, before the man could answer, "Wait, you're not telling me you tried to kill a Texas Ranger?"

"It was deemed an appropriate protocol."

Arno shook his head, hoping the man on the other end of the feed could see his displeasure. "Appropriate protocol," he repeated. "And you're criticizing me for taking out one pain-in-the-ass judge?"

"Sir, I remind you that—"

"No, soldier, I'd like to remind you that your military cabal came to me with the money I needed to do something the Patriot Sun is now well on its way to doing. I listened because your parents were devout followers of my father and I believed our causes were the same. But I also need to remind you that your side isn't the one in charge anymore. You know what you've got for power besides the Tea Party that can't get out of its own way? Me, you've got me. You want the civilians on our side militarized? You want to take full advantage of the tide turning in our direction? Then just sit back and get out of my way."

The man pulled back from the camera, further obscuring his features. "Your past involvement with this Texas Ranger is a concern, Mr. Arno."

"The one you failed to kill?"

"Sir, you need to—"

"I don't need to do anything, soldier. This is my show now and I'll thank you to stay out of it. Maybe next time you want to make a move like taking out a Texas Ranger, it should be you asking *my* permission. Only good thing that came out of your cabal's work in Iraq was the money you funneled to me. So excuse me if I don't profess a lot of confidence in your ability to nation build."

Arno thought he could see the man swallowing hard, his anxiety clear even through all the pixilation on the computer screen.

"You don't understand the complexity of the situation, sir," the army man offered.

"But I understand it's got to be rectified and that's what I intend to do when Caitlin Strong shows up."

The doorbell rang and Arno rose, still angled so the webcam could find him. "There's something else I need to attend to. We finished here?"

"I hope not, sir, I truly do."

"I'll take that as a yes," Arno said, terminating the feed.

He moved into the spacious wood-paneled foyer and threw open the front door to find Jed Kean waiting outside, toothy grin stretched from ear to ear, the first rays of the morning sun framed behind him.

"What are you so happy about?" Arno asked, still irritable and on edge after his conversation with the army man.

"I'd rather show you, boss," Kean said, grinning.

69

As the first public official to ever wage open war against the Mexican drug cartels, Fernando Lozano Sandoval had good reason to sleep in a different bed practically every night. But that didn't mean he had to demean himself or his lifestyle. His position as chief of the Chihuahua State Investigations Agency came with an unlimited expense account—for good reason since it was the only way he could stay alive long enough to win the war he was waging against the all-powerful cartels.

This seaside home at the base of the Yucatán Peninsula had been confiscated from a major drug lord Sandoval had incarcerated along with dozens of others. He found a pleasing irony in making their lavish homes his personal hostels; not so pleasing was the fact that much of his budget stemmed from similarly confiscated drugs being resold to consolidators for whom this business was no different from widgets or surge suppressors. Just another product, a commodity to put out to bid.

Sandoval had gone for a long walk on the beach under the first light of the dawn, finding great pleasure in the smell of the sea air and the waves hammering the shoreline with the promise of an approaching storm. He loved this time of day, the world at its most peaceful where even hope seemed possible. He finally returned to the villa with two of his guards to find the four watching the exterior of his home nowhere to be seen. The men who'd accompanied him on his walk stowed him behind the tree line and moved toward the house. The door facing the water, Sandoval could now see, was cracked open. There should have been three more men inside the house and four watching all points of the access road, in addition to the missing ones who should have been patrolling the perimeter.

From the safety of the tree line, Sandoval neither saw nor heard anything coming from the house. Nothing to suggest something was amiss, but also nothing to indicate it wasn't.

More minutes passed. Sandoval checked his watch to find time had frozen, its battery dead. He took that as a terrible omen, the false serenity the beach had provided vanishing in the same instant that left Sandoval conjuring terrible thoughts about the fate of his wife and his children. Questioning himself over the course of action that could only get him killed with all his vast accomplishments wiped out in a single moment that seemed upon him now. Did he really think he could insulate himself from the same treachery that had plagued his country since the cartels had taken over so much of it? What a fool! He shook his wrist, checked his watch again as if to cling to a faint hope fostered by seeing the time move again.

"It's just after seven," a voice said from behind Sandoval, just as a smell like stale cooking grease reached him. "Time for us to talk."

"Your men are all fine," Guillermo Paz told him when they were inside, seated in chairs overlooking the sea, the waves crashing on the shore looking like bursts of white light against the fog now encroaching on the shoreline.

"You could have just called, Colonel."

"*Suficiente verdadero.* But I figured this was a good way to make my point."

"By which you mean . . ."

"That you can't stop me."

"Stop you from doing what, Colonel?"

Paz responded with his gaze lingering on the sea. "How many places are there like the one in San Luis Patosí where children are bought and traded like coffee beans?"

Sandoval didn't hesitate. "Fifteen. Scattered across the country."

"You have an agreement with these people, of course."

"An arrangement would be a better way of putting it."

Paz turned toward him, his eyes glowing like black rubies in the room's ambient light. "It's time to break it."

"Perhaps you forget that you work for me, Colonel."

"Not at all. But perhaps you forget why you came to me in particular to do your bidding. Another reason why I disabled your men, to remind you."

"What do you want?"

"I think you know."

"I already gave the Ranger San Luis Patosí."

"It's not enough. You brought me in to build an army to help you cleanse the country. Well, that's what I intend to do with these fifteen safe houses, and the quicker I finish, the quicker I'll be able to get back to the task at hand."

Sandoval tried to remind himself he was the one in charge, but all he managed to do was gulp down some air.

"I suspect your friends in the American government have no idea of this arrangement," Paz told him. "Imagine the repercussions if they were to learn of it." He stopped and maneuvered his chair to better face Sandoval. "The man responsible for seeing these children brought home will become a hero, on the other hand."

"I already am a hero, Colonel."

"A much greater one then. Do you read Cervantes?"

"No."

"Not even *Don Quixote*?"

"Perhaps." Sandoval shrugged. "A long time ago."

"Cervantes wrote that a person dishonored is worse than dead. Do you wish to be dead?"

"Need I remind you we're on the same side, Colonel?"

"Answer my question first. Do you wish to be dishonored?"

"That's a different question."

"No," Paz told him, rising from his chair toward a pair of ceiling fans spinning lazily on either side of him, "it's not."

PART SEVEN

He's a strange combination of the old and the new . . . with the glory of the old still clinging to him and shining out with the glory of modern achievement in his line of work. He has of necessity clung to the traditions and methods of a vanishing age, yet at the same time, he is a modern-day scientific investigator, fully schooled in the utilization of ballistics, chemistry, finger-printing, and all the other scientific devices through which up-to-date law enforcement agencies bring criminals to justice.

—The Alamo News, 1941

70

"Your friend didn't give us a lot of reason for hope, did he?" Cort Wesley said after they'd set out on the long drive to Midland.

Caitlin felt stiff behind the wheel, the sun seeming to find her no matter which way the road headed. "R. Lee Shine's not my friend. But he just might be the best criminal attorney in Texas history."

"That how he got to know Earl and Jim Strong?"

"Yeah, by getting off a host of folks they arrested and then buying the beers afterward. And I must've heard a different tale than you did come off Shine's lips."

Cort Wesley looked at her with his eyes catching a reflection of the sun, while not seeming to blink. "I'm not going back to jail, Ranger."

"I don't expect you'll have to."

"I'm talking about even for a day. Once I surrender myself, I lose all control and the next stop could be Mexico."

"Did you hear what I just said about R. Lee Shine?"

"I heard you, but it's not enough."

"Maybe you should've thought of that before you plugged that drug dealer."

Caitlin could see the light sheen of sweat that had risen to Cort Wesley's brow in the mere moments they'd been speaking. "I shouldn't have killed him. It was a foolish act bred of nothing but vengeance. Is that what you wanna hear?"

"No, because it doesn't change anything, including the fact that given it to do all over again, you would."

Cort Wesley turned and stared at Caitlin from the passenger seat until the SUV hit a pothole deep enough to rattle both of them. "Too bad you weren't around to talk me down."

Caitlin stifled a laugh. "So it's my fault now?"

Cort Wesley slumped a bit in his seat, staring out the windshield instead of at her. "You could've turned that task force down."

"But I didn't and look where that got me."

He turned toward her, veins in his neck pulsing. "Ended in gunplay. Sounds familiar, doesn't it, Ranger?"

"I didn't go up there looking for that, Cort Wesley."

"Didn't you? Come on, you going north, me going south—the only difference was you had a badge and I didn't."

"That's not true."

"Oh, right. You killed, what, four of those bikers yourself?"

"You say it like I had a choice."

"I only shot one drug dealer."

"I honestly don't see what your problem is."

"With you thinking a badge gives you license to think you're any different from me. Truth is, at the core we're both just gunfighters cut from the same cloth. We can't get away from it and there's no sense in trying."

This time it was Caitlin who looked toward Cort Wesley. "That's a load of crap."

"Is it? We might as well start putting notches on our guns, Ranger."

Caitlin started to smile, the gesture more reflective than anything.

"What?" Cort Wesley asked, watching her.

"In Washington, Jones said almost the same thing. I think I'm starting to get his point, that our natures allow people like him to use us for their own gains. It's a weakness, Cort Wesley, no matter how much we want to believe otherwise."

"This is about Dylan now. We'd be wise to keep that in mind."

"When the shooting starts, you mean."

They passed under an overpass, enough dark shadows cast to turn the windshield into a mirror, and Cort Wesley thought he saw old Leroy Epps sitting in the backseat shaking his head before swigging down some root beer.

"What are you looking at?" Caitlin asked him.

"Nothing," Cort Wesley said, turning back around toward the front.

"He's still alive, bubba," came the voice of Epps from the backseat.

"You hear that?" Cort Wesley asked Caitlin.

"Hear what?"

"Nothing."

"Pay attention to me here."

"Leave me alone."

Caitlin looked over at Cort Wesley, then followed his gaze into the backseat.

"I'm talking to you, bubba."

"I did so much dumb shit when I was Dylan's age," Cort Wesley said, instead of responding to Leroy Epps. "Any one of a hundred things could've gotten me killed. Take your pick. Dylan does one and we're looking at a nightmare you don't wake up from."

"Don't say that."

"What if it's true?"

Caitlin squeezed the steering wheel tighter. "I watched Mexican druggers murder my mother when I was four years old and can't remember a thing about it no matter how much I try."

"There a point to you raising this now?"

"Sometimes I think me being so willing to use a gun is all about not having that memory. Like the violence of that night found a place in my soul and dug itself in. Every time I pull my gun what I'm really trying to do is dig it back out."

"I still don't see the point, Ranger."

"Both you and Jones call me a gunfighter, but neither of you was there when I stepped out of my dad's truck at the age of thirteen with my grandfather's Colt to stand with him against Max Arno. Ended up freezing to the gravel."

"You were just a kid."

"There's the point, Cort Wesley. So is Dylan. You and me, I don't think we ever really were. He thinks he's like us but he's not. That's not your fault and it's not really his either. He watched his mother die just like I watched mine. Only having hold of the memory hasn't stopped him from plugging the hole inside him just like I do every time I draw my gun."

"That will only mean something to me if we find him," Cort Wesley said, his voice scratchy with defeat and resignation. "If he's still alive."

"He's alive, and we're going to find him."

"*She's right*," Leroy Epps said from the backseat, and this time Cort Wesley just closed his eyes, as Caitlin's phone rang.

71

MIDLAND, TEXAS; THE PRESENT

"Any news on the boy, Ranger?" Guillermo Paz asked, the din of his voice sounding metallic over the SUV's Bluetooth system.

"Not yet."

"He's still alive. I dreamed of him last night. I never dream of any-one who has passed. But there was a lot of crying around him."

"Crying?" Caitlin said, looking at Cort Wesley.

"I don't know what to make of it. It's just what I heard, Ranger."

"Is that what you called to tell us?"

"Us," Paz repeated. "The outlaw is with you?"

"He is."

"Good. Because the reason for this call concerns him. He needs to know that the people who took his son and so many other children will be gone by the end of the day, each and every one of them."

Caitlin and Cort Wesley remained silent, still regarding each other.

"Fifteen locations like the one in San Luis Patosí scattered all over the country. I've dispatched my soldiers to each. They're going to burn the buildings to the ground with the victimizers still inside."

"You got the locations from Sandoval."

Paz said nothing.

"The army you're building is for him."

It seemed Paz was still going to say nothing until, "That's what he thought, me too. Now I realize I'm building it for me. I'm going to make sure all the children are returned safely to their families. But, don't worry, it shouldn't take too long."

"Why would I worry?"

"Because my army will be poised and ready when you need me, Ranger."

"It's not gonna come down to that this time."

"Yes, it is. It always does."

"You sound like that's what you want."

"It's who I am, Ranger. It's who you are."

Caitlin felt something like an emery board scratching down the surface of her spine. "Maybe you don't know me as well as you think you do, Colonel."

"Not you, the battles you choose to fight."

"Maybe they choose me. You ever think about that?"

"You just made my point for me."

"I didn't make any point at all. I just want to get the boy back, that's all. That's enough."

"It's never all," Paz told her. "And it's never enough either."

"What do you mean exactly?"

"Figure it out, Ranger."

"I don't like games, Colonel."

"Do you like chess?"

"It's a game, isn't it? What did I just say?"

"Because I'm starting to wonder if philosophers like Dawkins and James were right, that we are just pawns of the universe. Why else would you and me keep being thrown together?"

"I have no idea," Caitlin told him.

"I'll tell you something else, Ranger. Good and evil are more than just abstract concepts."

"And which side do we come down on, Colonel?"

She could hear Paz chuckle softly. "You'll have to ask the devil that one."

"I think I may be on my way to meet him right now," she said, eyeing Cort Wesley.

72

"I appreciate you seeing me, Mr. Arno," Caitlin told the man seated on the other side of the massive desk.

Malcolm Arno rocked in his chair, studying her without speaking. "You remember the last time we met?"

An old-fashioned clock hung on the wall, marking time with a steady click of the seconds as they passed. Staring at Malcolm Arno, Caitlin had the sense that the length between each became longer, as if time itself was slowing to a stop. The office lighting was dull, casting Arno's face in an uneasy mix of shadows and light sneaking through the windows looking out over the Patriot Sun complex. If she didn't know better, she'd say his skin was actually a blend of tones constantly running into each other with the mix unable to hold. As if Arno wasn't a finished product, a work in progress instead. Formless, wearing what passed for physicality as a Halloween costume. More liquid than solid.

"We didn't exactly meet, did we, sir?" Caitlin asked Arno, his face continuing to shift in and out of the light and dark.

"I suppose not," Arno conceded. "Your father killing mine . . ."

"Mine gave yours every opportunity to surrender."

"Freedom is not something a man like my father relinquishes easily."

"Implying he knew he was guilty, that the Rangers were right in what they did."

Arno leaned forward so fast his chair's back wheels lifted off the hardwood floor and landed back down with a thud. "Is that so?"

"Innocent men don't draw down on Texas Rangers."

"Am I to assume by your statement that the Texas Rangers themselves were without sin?"

"I don't know what you mean, sir."

"Yes, you do. I'm speaking of your father. He didn't come to that parking lot to arrest my father, he came there to kill him."

. . .

Caitlin and Cort Wesley had waited fifteen minutes at the guard station before their vehicle was escorted onto the grounds of the Patriot Sun by a man named Kean. Caitlin parked in a designated area amid several large trucks. She introduced herself but not Cort Wesley, leaving his and Kean's eyes to linger uncomfortably on each other. She didn't notice if he even regarded the Ranger badge pinned to Cort Wesley's shirt.

Kean was leading her past the big freight trucks toward the complex's main offices, when Caitlin stopped suddenly and crouched.

"Something stuck to the sole of my boot, sir," she said by way of explanation and then pretended to pry the nonexistent object free to better inspect the truck's tires. Something about them had grabbed her eye, but she couldn't figure out what at first glance. Caitlin felt Kean growing anxious, though not suspicious yet, and bounced back up, her curiosity satisfied. "Appreciate your patience," she told him, and they had continued on their way.

"With all due respect, sir, that's a load of crap," Caitlin told Malcolm Arno. "We were on our way fishing when Jim Strong got it in his head to check out the Tackle and Gun. Bad timing on your father's part."

"Perhaps the same could be said for your coming here today, Ranger."

"You think I've come here to kill you, Mr. Arno?"

"I suspect if that were the case, I'd be dead already, wouldn't I?"

Caitlin didn't humor him with an answer. "You got call to hold the Rangers in disregard, me in particular. If you'd prefer to deal with someone else—"

"No," Arno told her, "you'll do just fine. As you said, I'm just a, what, person of interest?"

"That's right."

"Based on what exactly?"

"An anonymous tip that someone here in your hierarchy procured the explosives that killed that judge in Galveston. Something called PETN."

"That sounds like a rather flimsy rationale to disturb a man's peace."

"Well, sir, I don't disagree with you there. But we've got to check it out all the same."

"A bit intrusive, wouldn't you say? An example of exactly the kind of interference in private affairs people like me are trying to shake. Is that why I've been targeted?"

"Targeted is the wrong choice of words in this case, sir. Otherwise we would've come with a search warrant."

"Like the Rangers did that Easter Sunday on the Church of the Redeemer, you mean. Tell me, Ranger," Arno continued, leaning his whole body forward now to join his eyes, "would your father have gunned mine down right there on the premises had they met that day instead?"

"If he intended to do harm to him or others, absolutely."

"On Easter Sunday," Arno said, shaking his head slowly. "Nothing seems wrong, even sacrilegious about that to you?"

"The date was chosen, as I understand it, to minimize resistance and thus preclude any loss of life."

"Sounds like you're reading from a field manual, Ranger."

"I'm reading from history, sir."

Arno's head looked as if it were on a kind of tumbler, going from side-to-side again, mixing the light and dark as it did. Caitlin shifted in her chair, suddenly discomfited by how the room's dull light, combined with a cloud that had crossed over the sun, left Arno looking as if he had no face at all she could discern.

"Why don't you tell me why you're really here, Ranger?" he said through lips that didn't seem to move, like he was a ventriloquist letting the air swallow his words.

"I believe I already did that."

"You're lying."

"And you're mistaken."

"Am I?" Arno leaned forward, his features congealing again as the streaming sunlight returned to the windows. "Your father lied to you about that fishing trip and you're lying to me now. You didn't come here about explosives at all."

"Then why don't you tell me what I'm doing here, sir?"

Arno settled back, his chair creaking. "You want this to end the same way it did for your father in that parking lot."

"I'm getting tired of people telling me what I want."

"Your father wanted to kill mine. Nothing was going to stop him."

"You forgetting about those two gorillas drawing first, Mr. Arno? You forgetting about my father giving yours every chance to give himself up even afterward?"

"You really believe that?"

"I was there."

"So was I. And you didn't see the look in your father's eyes."

"Why don't you describe it to me?"

Arno grinned tightly, smugly, his face growing formless once more. "Look in the mirror."

"You saw what you wanted to see then, sir. You're doing the same thing now."

Caitlin realized she could no longer hear the loud clicking of the clock, as if time had frozen along with Arno's features, the intermixed splotches of light and dark locked as they were.

"Why don't you tell me what you see now, Ranger?" he asked her.

"A man I'm going to bring down," she told him. "One way or another."

73

MIDLAND, TEXAS; THE PRESENT

Cort Wesley strolled about the grounds, not being obtrusive but not shying away from the stares of others either. It was strange having a lawman's badge pinned to his lapel. There was ample precedent in the annals of Western history and lore dating all the way back to Wyatt Earp's infamous friendship with Doc Holliday. More modern times had seen Rangers and small-time bootleggers and marijuana smugglers join forces to fight back both Indians and border bandits since they were a detriment to the interests of both.

Still, he found it interesting the way people looked at him, their stares mixed between reverence, revulsion, and something like fear.

He'd spent a good part of his life before the army and even more after it on the other side of things, easily recalling the unease that accompanied an unexpected encounter with Johnny Law. Cort Wesley much preferred the middle where he'd been residing since leaving The Walls and having the responsibility for raising his boys thrust upon him.

All that was gone now. He'd choose any side that got Dylan back to him and right now that side was the Texas Rangers, both literally and figuratively. So he walked about playing the part. Started out by checking the same truck tires Caitlin had to see if he could figure out what had grabbed her attention. There was a strange jagged pattern cut into their surface, as if all four of the truck's outside tires had rolled over something sharp that hadn't quite managed to carve them up. Funny thing was the patterns were nearly an identical match. Even funnier was the tires on the other similar truck showed exactly the same wear in virtually the same places.

And there was something wrong with the grass; not wrong, so much as just not quite right. It was okay here at the center of complex, soft and supple—good ole Arkansas Blue even though it was medium green in shade. The name was actually a reference to its reliability in any climate, its true "blue" nature. But the grass farther out in the recreational fields, beyond a series of drainage culverts built to prevent flooding in the massive spring storms that plagued the state, looked too bright and too green. And when Cort Wesley finally strode out there, the feel of it beneath his boots told him why:

It wasn't grass at all, but some kind of man-made turf. The fake grass laid down in trays used on professional and college sports stadiums. Fabulously expensive to use on this much land and totally unnecessary with an assortment of seeding that tolerated the Texas climate just fine. This just didn't make any sense he could see.

So what would a real lawman make of it, what would Caitlin Strong make of it?

She'd look at Cort Wesley and say, *Only reason they laid field turf was because they knew real grass wouldn't grow.*

Okay, Ranger. Why's that?

Something they did to the land or soil maybe.

That explanation didn't play right with him. *I'm not buying that,*

*Ranger. I can see them working farmland over there on the far edge of their
sprawl. This is something else.*

Like what?

Cort Wesley didn't have an answer for her or himself. He kept walking in the hope one might come, but what he really wanted to find was
some sign that Dylan had been here just like the "D" carved into the
wood floor down in San Luis Patosí. He knew finding something like
that within a complex as big and spread out as this was likely a pipe dream
and an absurd one at that. And so was his certainty that Dylan would
have doubled back from his pursuers in the Mexican mountains to take
refuge in a monster truck registered shell-style to the Patriot Sun. He
had to believe that because it was all he had, and the alternative might
indeed be that his son was being picked at by buzzards in the desert
heat of a godforsaken country Cort Wesley hated with all his heart.
Colonel Paz believed Dylan to be alive because he'd seen him in a
dream. If Cort Wesley had been able to sleep more than a wink in the
past three days, maybe he'd have the same dream and be similarly reassured.

Why hadn't the boy called?

Any solace he took in Caitlin's certainty, Paz's dreams, or the assur-
ances of Leroy Epps melted away in the face of that. It just made no
sense, yet the alternative it presented was utterly unthinkable. Cort
Wesley recalled listening to parents wax optimistic on the fates of their
missing children even after some murderous pedophile had been arrested. Or continuing their futile search in the face of DNA evidence
pulled from a pervert's subbasement.

Cort Wesley circled his way around the buildings now, watched by
Malcolm Arno's private security force, dressed in dark green uniforms
streaked with sweat, at every turn. He cataloged nothing else out of place,
the fake grass remaining stuck in his head like a bad song he couldn't
vanquish. In the end he believed Dylan was still alive, here or somewhere else, because Cort Wesley knew *he* would still be alive, given the
identical circumstances. A boy who could go toe-to-toe with a serial
killer a year ago and escape from a man like LaChance in the Mexican
desert wasn't to be underestimated. Simple as that . . . or maybe not.

The possibility set Cort Wesley trembling.

74

"What is it you think I'm guilty of exactly?" Malcolm Arno asked Caitlin. "Or maybe you're just going to take me down 'cause you want to, like your father did to mine."

"Correct me if I'm wrong, Mr. Arno," Caitlin said, having no trouble holding fast to her cool, "but your father was a fugitive from justice at the time of the shooting."

Arno's face began to liquefy again, his skin nothing more than cover for the different strains of pigment battling each other. It was like looking at a monster from an old-fashioned horror movie showing in black-and-white. And in that moment, Caitlin believed she understood his formless essence, as if the day Jim Strong had killed the Reverend Maxwell Arno had bled him of color forever. The darker portions seemed to be running over the lighter ones now, dominating them.

"And whose justice would that be, Ranger?"

"Do you really want me to answer that question, sir? Is that the way you want this interview to go?"

Arno crossed his arms over a flat, thin chest. "We can put the fact that your father had it in his mind to kill mine all along behind us."

"That what you think?"

"Because it's the truth. No other way it could possibly have been."

Arno's eyes were like his father's as well, too small for his head. Set back in his skull as if they were trying to hide from the rest of his face. Caitlin watched as they seemed to slide forward, growing in the process.

"Your father was guilty of adultery, Ranger Strong," he said suddenly.

"If you're talking about his relationship with Beth Ann Killane, my mother had been dead for eleven years already."

Arno's eyes bore into her, expanding with each beat of his heart. "Gunned down by Mexican bandits."

"Drug dealers, actually."

Those eyes seemed to move forward across the desk without the rest of him. "Tell me, Ranger, did they rape her too?"

Caitlin realized her hand had strayed involuntarily to her SIG. Arno noticed it too, his eyes dipping low for her holster.

"Sir," she started, "I'm not here to rehash the past."

"But the past is what we have between us, I'm sure you'll agree. Allow me to shed some light on it for you. . . ."

75

MIDLAND AND ODESSA, TEXAS; 1990

"Jim?"

"Yeah?"

"Don't let go of me. Promise me you won't."

"I promise."

And, true to his word, Jim Strong had held on to Beth Ann Killane right up to the night before the raid. He'd considered removing himself from the task force more times than he could count, only to have his duty as a Ranger trump his apparent impropriety. The FBI course he and D. W. Tepper had taken at Quantico had warned against this precise eventuality, though not in so many words. All Jim knew was that Beth Ann was the first woman who helped him get through the day without dwelling on the murder of his wife, for which he still felt responsible. It wasn't so much that she eased his guilt as offered it a vent.

The most uncomfortable moments with Beth Ann came not as a result of the task force, D. W. Tepper, or the coming raid, but one Saturday morning when he sat down at his usual corner table at Pancake Alley.

"Somebody I'd like you to meet, Ranger Strong," Beth Ann had said, smiling tightly as she turned to a boy seated at the counter. "Danny?"

He laid the book he was reading down and hopped down off the stool. Spitting image of his mom, Jim reckoned, with a floppy nest of hair hung low over his forehead, wearing his jeans tucked into his high-top sneakers like most boys those days. He must have been two years older than Caitlin but didn't look it. His face was still smooth, unmarked by acne, and Jim was almost certain he hadn't picked up a razor yet. He knew the boy was pretty much growing up without a father around and blessed his own fortune that he'd been son to the great Earl Strong, who had ultimately taken to fatherhood with the same conviction and commitment he'd brought to Rangering. Jim wondered in that moment if he'd been spending enough time with Caitlin and resolved to spend more. Take her fishing as soon as this whole thing with the Church of the Redeemer was done.

"Nice to meet you, Danny," Jim said, shaking the boy's clammy hand.

"You're a real Texas Ranger?"

"I am."

"I've read books on the Rangers."

"Well, we're not nearly as mean as the writers say or as brave neither."

Something in the boy's eyes made Jim uncomfortable, as if he knew about Jim and his mom. Then he figured it was just his own guilt rearing itself up over the poor judgment he'd exercised in sleeping with a woman he had used for his own ends as a Ranger. It made him feel the kind of dirty no amount of showering could relieve, and having the woman's boy standing there made him feel even worse. Danny Killane looked kind of sad and empty, the type of boy who lived inside his head more than out of it.

"Ranger Strong is the one who helped secure your pardon, Danny," Beth Ann was saying and Jim immediately wished she hadn't.

"That was you?" Danny asked him, eyes wide with gratitude.

"It was a pleasure to help justice get done," Jim said, seeing the desperate need in this boy and wondering what exactly he was getting himself into. Until that moment he hadn't really thought of his relationship with Beth Ann beyond the coming Ranger raid on the Church of the Redeemer. Once that came, though, they'd face some powerful issues, not the least of which was the fact that their entire relationship was based on the lie Jim had formed to solidify the poor woman's dependence upon him. He wondered what Beth Ann would think of him once he told her the truth, but his Ranger duty kept him from doing anything of the kind until she'd given him what he needed on the Reverend Arno's stockpile of guns.

I used this woman. I used her and her son.

So what did sleeping with her say about him? The presence of her son in that diner confronted Jim with the weakness and failing of his emotions bred of a life lived on the open road. It came part and parcel with being a Texas Ranger, no ifs, ands, or buts about it. There was a cost to be paid for that, though, and Jim was paying it now.

Still, he resolved not to let his conflicting emotions affect his management of the case and getting the raid ready to go just as soon as he got the intelligence he needed on Arno's guns and final approval came down from Austin. On the former, Beth Ann waited until Danny had taken the bus home to join him at his table.

"I saw the guns," she told Jim Strong.

He leaned forward, waiting for her to continue.

"Reverend Arno took me downstairs, to a part of the grounds I'd never seen before. He was directing me to a storage room where there were supposed to be song and hymn books I could use for the choir come Easter." Beth Ann took a breath to settle herself before continuing. "We passed a door I could see was different from the others, like it was newer. Got a look inside and saw a pair of big men, the reverend's bodyguards I think, stacking up these wooden crates that had just come in."

"You see any guns, Beth Ann?"

She shook her head. "No, just those crates and plenty of others like them. I could only see a bit of the room, though, and didn't want to appear too curious; you know, make Reverend Arno suspicious or something."

"You did good there. What about the smell?"

"Smell?"

"Of the room with the crates. Anything stick out?"

"Well . . ."

"Anything at all, Beth Ann."

"Oil."

"Oil," Jim Strong repeated.

"Not like motor oil, though. Sweeter, almost like the kind you use to cook with. You know what I'm talking about, Jim?"

"It's gun oil. You found them for sure, Beth Ann. You see how the door was secured?"

"It was closed again when we walked past after fetching the song books." She closed her eyes, as if to picture what she'd seen in her mind. "A big lock, the key kind, not combination."

"Any idea where Arno keeps the key to it?"

"Well, he's got a ring full of them he wears clipped to his belt. Lent them to me the other day, so I could look for more song books."

"You think the key to the gunroom could be on it?"

"I suppose," Beth Ann said and then stiffened with her eyes blinking rapidly. "You don't want me to go inside, do you?"

"No, ma'am," Jim said, thinking fast. "I want you to change the lock."

He figured it was the perfect solution. Get the guns out of the Rangers' hair without exposing Beth Ann to any more unnecessary risk. If trouble came to the Church of the Redeember, Jim Strong figured Arno would have men ready to sprint for the guns. They'd rush downstairs at the first sign of the Rangers' incursion and find a new lock for which they had no key. Cutting through it would take time, enough for the Rangers to get both the church and the gunroom itself secured before Arno's men could free up his arsenal.

Yup, Jim Strong had everything figured out, right up to the precise timing of the Rangers' raid on the Church of the Redeemer complex:

Easter Sunday.

It made perfect sense, the only thing that truly did. All Max Arno's followers and loyalists would be in the church, praying and singing while they awaited the reverend's sermon. And Beth Ann Killane taking over as choir head made it all possible, while giving her call to roam the very cellar hall on which the gunroom was located. Crucial since

Jim could in no way let her switch the locks until Easter morning itself. Doing so earlier risked betraying the raid to Arno, who would immediately suspect something of the like was afoot if a mysterious lock suddenly appeared to bar entry to his guns.

But not on Easter Sunday.

"That's just five days away, Jim," Beth Ann told him anxiously, after he'd gone over the plan with her.

Jim didn't reach across the table and take her hands in a gesture of false comfort. Nope, he was done putting on shows and using his personal feelings for Beth Ann to facilitate her cooperation. Instead he looked her in the eye the way he would a young Ranger heading into his first tough assignment.

"You tell him you need more song books as close to the start of the morning service as you dare," Jim explained. "And that's when you slip the new lock into place."

He could see Beth Ann hedging.

"To make sure nobody get hurts," Jim continued. "Rangers are determined to leave our guns in our holsters on this one. But to do that we gotta make sure Arno's men don't show anything that makes us change our intentions."

She swallowed hard. "My son's coming with me on Sunday. I could leave him home."

"Arno asked to meet him, didn't he?"

"He did at that."

"All the more reason to bring Danny then," Jim said, realizing how horrible that must have sounded even as he said it. Made even worse by the fact that Beth Ann didn't seem to gauge his true intentions, trusting him too much to realize he saw an opportunity that could bring the raid that much closer to success.

This time it was she who reached across the table and took Jim's hands in hers. "I'll do it, Ranger." And she smiled.

With Easter just five days away, twelve additional Rangers slipped into town and rented the remaining rooms in the same Odessa motel where Jim Strong had been staying. One of these, an extra-large efficiency with an alcove that allowed it to be advertised as a suite, was turned into their de facto headquarters. As such, its peeling walls were papered with Beth Ann Killane's drawings of the Church of the Redeemer complex. It was big and sprawling, spread out over a dozen acres, which made Easter Sunday an even more obvious choice given how it reduced that daunting scope to the dimensions of a single church building.

With that in mind, the Rangers spent much of the next four days practicing their raid in a nearby church that was vaguely similar in layout and size to the target of their Easter raid. They rehearsed every step and detail, starting with serving the warrant on Arno himself to make his bodyguards show themselves. Serve him right there on the pulpit in the middle of his sermon, spitting out his venom about hellfire and brimstone coming to take those not pure of heart, which the Rangers translated as willing to take girls barely of babysitting age as wives.

Jim had reflected plenty on what drew a stable woman like Beth Ann to such a place, settling on the obvious void her loveless marriage and lack of a purpose, beyond her son, had wrought. She'd been plunged back into the big open world after fourteen years of relative comfort and security. Not happiness—Jim could tell that much as plainly as he could tie his own shoes. Beth Ann had settled for the best she could take out of life and even that had ultimately betrayed her. So she'd turned to the church for belonging, acceptance, a place in the world she could define. Absent his entry into her life, Jim supposed being named director of the Easter choir would have been the highpoint of several lost years.

Thinking of things that way left Jim stiff with guilt until he rationalized he was doing this woman a favor. Making her face the fact that the Reverend Maxwell Arno was every bit as seedy and predatory as the husband who had left her so he could bang with impunity whatever hussies he could get his hands on. He'd renounced his son as a faggot, traded in his station wagon for a Mustang, and off he went, save for the occasional court appearance before a judge who'd once been his golfing buddy. Where else was a woman like Beth Ann Killane supposed to turn?

He'd make all this up to her, Jim swore to himself, once the raid was done, the church shut down, and the not-so-reverend Arno was in custody of the state. Since the whole sordid episode had brought them together, it wasn't all bad, right?

As Jim Strong posed that very question to himself, Beth Ann was fighting to stay calm. The planned Easter morning service schedule had fallen hopelessly behind when the church couldn't accommodate the crowd and had to set up auxiliary seating in a field off the church's rear. Even worse, Maxwell Arno's insistence on greeting all of his arriving parishioners kept her from borrowing his keys again to put into effect the plan Jim Strong had laid out for her. Reverend Arno finally entered to the cheers of his flock, Beth Ann forcing herself to interrupt his reverie long enough to ask for his keys in order to retrieve much needed additional hymn books.

"Don't know what I'd do without you, sister," Arno said, touching her shoulder.

"It's my pleasure, Reverend."

"Is your boy here?" he asked, eyes scanning the VIP area.

"He's right there in his reserved seat," Beth Ann said.

She thought Arno's eyes may have narrowed in her son's direction, but then they locked on her again. "Make sure you introduce us when the service is done, sister." And off he went after handing her his keys, as the organist began his portion of the service.

The lock Jim Strong had given her to replace the one on the gunroom door was rattling around the bottom of her shoulder bag, purchased at a secondhand store just off I-20. And, keys in hand, down the stairs she went to switch out the locks more than an hour after she was supposed to.

She had just reached the cool half-light of the church basement when the Rangers came in simultaneously through all four doors. Pistols and shotguns extended to make sure nobody did anything plenty would regret later.

"Texas Rangers!" D. W. Tepper bellowed hoarsely in his cigarette-labored voice. "Nobody move! You may breathe at your own peril!"

The first thing Jim Strong noticed was that the Reverend Max Arno wasn't delivering his sermon, wasn't anywhere to be seen with the service having not even gotten under way yet. The second thing he noticed was that Beth Ann was not where she was supposed to be according to her depictions of the building drawn to scale.

Which meant the Rangers had no way of knowing whether the weapons were secure or not. Which meant Arno could be on to the whole raid about to go down.

Jim got a powerful paranoid feeling that maybe Beth Ann had double-crossed him. Maybe fell to bended knee to confess her sins to the man she was supposed to help the Rangers bring down. Jim saw it all happen in his head, growing cold over the realization of how much sense the scenario made. He thought in that moment of how proud she was to have her son, Danny, watching from the VIP section but the boy was nowhere to be seen either.

"Shit," Jim said under his breath, just loud enough for Tepper to hear. "This could be going to hell fast, D.W."

"Name the play, Ranger."

That was when a single shot rang out, muffled by the cavernous bowels contained beneath the church, and Jim Strong realized a bad day had just gone to hell altogether.

76

MIDLAND, TEXAS; THE PRESENT

"Where were you while all this was going on?" Caitlin asked Malcolm Arno, captured in a dull blur now as if her eyes were having trouble focusing.

"Upstairs. I was part of the choir. I slipped out once the trouble started. Your Rangers didn't pay much heed to a boy. Met up with my father at a place we'd arranged in the event of an emergency."

Caitlin tried to lock in on his eyes but couldn't find them. "Guess this qualified, from his standpoint. 'Cept he could still be alive today if he'd just gone peacefully, either Easter Sunday or at the Tackle and Gun."

"You really believe that?"

"You got another opinion?"

"Ranger Jim Strong wasn't just staking out that parking lot. He'd caught wind somehow we were coming. He came there to kill my father like I told you."

"I seem to remember him offering your dad and his bodyguards a chance to live. They drew first. Like I told *you*."

"Because they knew what was coming."

"A Texas Ranger gunning down three men in cold blood."

"That's right." Arno leaned forward across his massive desk. "You know, I always knew this moment would come, you and me face-to-face again. Guess you could say we've both come a long way to get here."

"This place has the feel of a fort, Mr. Arno, like you're fixing to fight a war."

"I'm already fighting it, Ranger Strong. A war against the intrusions of a government that have gotten more and more pervasive, a war for freedom. What the Rangers did at the Church of the Redeemer might have been the beginning, symbolically anyway. You'd find a significantly different outcome if you tried that here with the Patriot Sun."

"Your father was no patriot, Mr. Arno, and neither are you."

"You have no idea what I am, Ranger."

Caitlin found his eyes again, liquid pools of black. "That a threat?"

"I could ask you the same question. Are you like your father? Did you come here to throw down and take me on?"

"I was hoping to avoid that, sir, but there is that evidence linking your outfit to the assassination of the judge in Galveston."

"That's the second time you've mentioned evidence without being specific."

"We're just having a friendly chat here. That's why I didn't come with a warrant to search the grounds to see if you're stockpiling weapons like your dad did."

"That what you think, Ranger?"

"I think you're a dangerous man, a lot more dangerous than your father was. I think you are seriously deluded about this country and see enemies where none exist."

When that produced no rise out of him, Caitlin continued in spite of her promise to D. W. Tepper to go easy and not show her whole hand.

"I believe you're up to something here connected to so many bad things, I can't even begin to innumerate them. I think your father was running a cult that was just a few steps short of drinking the Kool-Aid and go out the way those folks in Jonestown did. But you're out to take far more with you than just your own flock. Only beef the Rangers and the state really had with your father besides the tax thing was the polygamy and complaints raised about men having sex with girls wearing cigar bands for rings on their fingers. But you, you're a whole different piece of work, Mr. Arno."

Arno grinned, the pearly white of his teeth running with black. "Then I'd ask you again, Ranger. What are you really doing here?"

Caitlin bit her lip, punishment for already giving too much away, showing too many of her cards. "My job."

"Your calling."

"That's right."

"As I am doing mine. Both of us following in the footsteps of our fathers. You remember the first time we met?"

"I do, sir."

"What did you think when you looked at me covered in my father's blood?"

"I felt sorry for you."

"I don't want your pity."

"I'm not giving it to you anymore."

Arno leaned back, seeming to size Caitlin up anew. "Were you there when your own father died?"

"By his bedside in the hospital when his heart finally quit."

"How'd it feel?"

"How do you think?"

"I don't *think*, Ranger, I know. Take what you felt and multiply it by a hundred and you'll know what I felt. You want to know why I built this place? You want to know what I'm doing here? Making it so no other child has to experience what I did when the government invades our lives just like the Rangers invaded my father's church. I don't kill judges, or abortion doctors, or anybody else who doesn't share my view of the world. But people like you, and what you stand for, are responsible for the people that do. And your father was a goddamn murderer kept from the electric chair only by the badge he wore on his shirt."

Caitlin stood up slowly, sure to keep her gun hand swaying well free of her holstered SIG. "What happened to your mother, Mr. Arno?"

The question drew a flutter from Arno's eyelids, uncertainty claiming his face for the first time. "She died giving birth to me."

"That's what your father told you."

"Because it's the truth."

"No, it's not. I did some checking before I came out here. Your mother was a drunk who ran off with a car salesman when you were two years old. On top of everything else, I guess your father was a liar."

Arno's features finally congealed, looking as flat and expressionless as a marble bust. Caitlin had thought the truth about his mother, and his father's lies about it, might get a rise out of him. But he actually looked calmer, even placid.

"I will pray for her soul."

"You a man of God now too, sir?"

"No, just a man who believes in Him, His word, and His work enough to believe I am doing it now, as my father did before me. Sparing me the pain of my mother's true plight makes me think no less of him."

"Guess that does explain why his taste started running toward young girls after that, doesn't it?"

Arno's expression didn't change, didn't flare, just remained empty and virtually impassive.

"I wonder what else you inherited from him," Caitlin continued, unable to stop herself, "besides the same twisted ambition."

For a moment it looked as if Arno had no intention again of responding. Then his mouth opened, the words that emerged sounding like somebody else's.

"From the time I laid eyes on you in that parking lot, I knew the world wasn't finished with us yet. I'm glad for this chance to set things right, I truly am."

"My father put yours out of business, Mr. Arno, and my intention is to do the same to you."

Arno started to laugh, then stopped. "Look around you, Ranger. I've got an empire here and friends planted so high over you and the Texas Rangers you can't even see how screwed you are."

Now it was Caitlin who smiled. "The problem being that I'm a bit older than the girls you've been stealing down in Mexico. By the way, I got it on good authority that part of your business is about to be shut down, I guess you could say permanently."

Caitlin backpedaled for the door, watching Arno rise deliberately and squeeze the edge of his desk so hard his hands turned scarlet red. "Am I still a person of interest, Ranger?"

Caitlin left her eyes on him, feeling the lip of the doorway under her boots. "I'll be back to see just how much. Thank you for your time, sir," she said, fitting the Stetson back atop her head.

PART EIGHT

Take two men of equal size and arm them with identical weapons. Call one . . . a deputy sheriff and the other a Ranger. Send each out to stop a mob or quell a riot. The crowd will resist the deputy, but will submit to the authority of the Ranger. There is something in the name "Ranger" that makes the wildest cowboy become completely dedicated to his duty the moment he takes the oath of office. He needs no blowing of bugles or flying of flags to make him carry on. He might be out in the chaparral far away from doctors or ambulances and if wounded he would probably, as one old Ranger put it, "lie out there and sour." Nobody would know but he and God, yet he will not flinch from the responsibility.
—W. W. Sterling, *Trails and Trials of a Texas Ranger,* 1959

77

Dylan had never felt more stupid in his life. He spent a solid day stinking in his own sweat and dreaming of getting his hands free, only to get all of himself caught this time.

He sat in the windowless room they'd stowed him in the night before, outfitted with a steel door instead of bars. The walls were painted cinder block and Dylan thought he could still smell the sharp lacquer scent. The room featured a jail-style toilet and a cot Dylan decided to forgo in favor of sitting in a corner with his arms curled over his knees, rocking back and forth like he was a goddamn little kid.

Escaping in the desert and having the presence of mind to stash himself in that truck had filled him with a sense of exhilaration sufficient to get him through a miserable ride. His hands might've been bound but he wasn't a prisoner per se as he was now. All the thinking and sawing in the world wasn't going to get him out of a cinder-block cell. Nope, things might have been as bad as they could get down in Mexico, but they were even worse now.

Thanks to what he'd seen in that building he'd crawled up into. Because of whatever the hell was going on here, enough to make him wonder if the LaChance guy's truck had bypassed Texas altogether and driven straight to hell. Because that building had been full of the last thing in the world Dylan had expected to find:

Babies.

Infants really, residing in cribs alongside twin-sized beds occupied by the women who must have been their mothers. Well, not women exactly—girls was more like it, maybe as old as him but maybe not. A chair to sit in, a bed to lie in, and a crib. Ten or so sets lined each side of the building's floor, divided by the same kind of plastic draping that separated one patient from another in hospital rooms. Dylan thought he remembered seeing some small, wall-mounted televisions, but the sudden wash of light had flooded his eyes and big hands latched on to him before he could be sure.

So now he sat rocking himself from tears, reflecting on what he'd done wrong. What his father would've done different. There wasn't much even in retrospect. He'd thought everything through, only to have the misfortune to enter the absolute worst building possible.

"There's a reason why it's placed on the outskirts," he could hear his dad say now, *"and that's the reason why you wanna choose another."*

Sure, he almost said out loud in response, *but where was that advice last night?*

A couple of brutes wearing dark green uniforms had tossed him in here straightaway, roughed him up a bit mostly because Dylan fought them out of frustration. The door had slammed shut and he heard a lock slung into place. Not long after he heard steps echoing along the concrete hall beyond, the door thrown open by a big man, just as big as LaChance, who remained in the shadows.

"Sit up, boy."

Dylan pushed himself up onto the cot, laying his sneakered feet down on the cold floor.

"Tell me your name or I'll hurt you bad," the man said.

"Dylan Torres." Spoken this time without any threats about who his father was or what he was going to do to the man's private parts.

Even in the shadows Dylan could see the man do what looked like a double take. He'd seemed to be on the verge of another question when he just stood there in dead silence for a long few seconds before closing the door.

The scariest part of the night followed soon after, the door opening again to reveal the same man in the company of a smaller one who took a step forward into the light cast by a single naked bulb recessed in the ceiling. Dylan sat up on the cot again and the man, who was wearing a bathrobe, just looked at him without saying a word. That was what was so scary, the way he looked, more like leered. Like he was sizing up Dylan as some kind of potential prey . . . or something even worse.

The boy felt his bowels turn to ice, glad for the toilet now and knowing he'd need to use it as soon as this man was gone. But he didn't leave right away. He stood there, stare lingering as if to revel in what lay before him. Dylan ended up closing his eyes. Except doing that actually made things worse, the man's stare cutting holes in his flesh like he had battery acid for eyes.

Dylan had shuddered, then shivered.

"Get him a blanket," the man in the bathrobe said to the other.

And then he smiled, showing just a glimpse of teeth. It lingered just like his stare, long enough to make Dylan forget how to breathe until the man backed up through the door and it resealed behind him.

78

MIDLAND, TEXAS; THE PRESENT

"He's got Dylan," Caitlin told Cort Wesley as soon as she climbed back behind the wheel of her SUV.

Cort Wesley looked across the seat at her, Caitlin's eyes rooted on Arno's office window though the windshield, certain he was watching her too. "How can you know that?"

Caitlin gunned the engine and fired up the air-conditioning. "Because I couldn't get a rise out of him."

"Normally you can get a rise out of anybody, Ranger."

"Not Arno. I remember a story I heard once about a half-assed gun-slinger who faced down one of the best guns in the west in a saloon.

Thing was he knew the other guy's gun was empty, giving him an advantage nobody else knew he had."

"So why we leaving?"

"Because staying can't do us any good. There's those truck tires alerting me to something I need to check out."

"And the grass."

"What about it?"

"Can you get your pal in Washington to run a satellite scan of the whole spread?"

"He'll be able to point out the fillings in the people's teeth. Why?"

"Just have him do it. He finds what I expect, you'll know why."

Caitlin reversed slowly, studying the freight carriers one last time before banking the wheel right and proceeding off the grounds of the Patriot Sun. Cort Wesley had lapsed into silence, sitting with his broad shoulders square to the road. He was breathing rapidly for a man who looked otherwise calm.

"I never see my son again," he said finally, his eyes looking like black holes, "I'm gonna take a flamethrower to that place, Ranger. Roast Arno alive."

Caitlin jerked the SUV over to the side of the road. "I think I'm gonna be sick."

79

MIDLAND, TEXAS; THE PRESENT

She climbed back inside after vomiting up a breakfast grabbed at a fast-food restaurant halfway between Midland and San Antonio. Cort Wesley handed her one of the breath mints he'd been downing and the wintergreen rid her mouth of the putrid taste.

"Never met a man in my life who made me sick to my stomach like that," she said, accepting another mint. "I swear Malcolm Arno had oil seeping out his pores. I even smelled it in his office."

"It's the territory. Sticks to the air like gum to the underside of a school desk." Cort Wesley's eyes swept the empty stretch of prairie on both sides of the SUV. "This land used to be nothing but fields when my grandpa was a wildcatter."

"The Masters as an oil family?"

"Just well paid labor, Ranger. We were never much for owning stuff."

"Too bad."

The car's radio cut off and a phone rang over the Bluetooth system, taking over the speakers. Caitlin answered with a touch of a button on the steering wheel.

"Yeah?"

"Ranger Strong?" greeted an unfamiliar voice, slightly hushed unless this was just a bad connection.

"Who is this? How'd you get this number?"

"My name's Killane, Ranger, Daniel Killane. I believe your father and my mother were acquainted. I believe he was there the day she died."

80

MIDLAND, TEXAS; 1990

"Shit," Jim said under his breath, just loud enough for Tepper to hear. "This could be going to hell fast, D.W."

"Name the play, Ranger."

When the muffled shot echoed like a dud firecracker, a cold dread filled Jim Strong like none he'd felt since the call eleven years ago from Austin telling him to get home fast. He couldn't have known then that Beth Ann Killane had taken Max Arno's keys and descended into the old root cellar dug beneath not just the church, but extending via a tunnel that ran under the entire grounds. Branching off like spider veins into a network of possible escape routes.

Beth Ann walked through the thin light toward the gunroom door that was shinier than all the others lining the basement hall on a single side. Even as she shifted Arno's keys from her left hand to her right, she failed to consider how long precisely it would take to find the right one that opened the gunroom. Too long for sure. She owned two watches, one broke and the other had a dead battery. But the clock in her head told her that the Rangers' raid would be under way by now, and if she didn't act fast, it could turn to a shooting fight before too many more minutes had passed. She thought of her son sitting in the midst of it and felt the grip of fear and panic on her insides. She didn't freeze up the way she did when her husband screamed about how she'd choked his life off and he had to leave or risk being suffocated by boredom.

Beth Ann tried a few keys, as many as a dozen before noticing how much play existed in the oversized hasp through which the big padlock had been fitted. Maybe, just maybe . . .

She fished through her shoulder bag for the similar padlock Jim Strong had provided her and tried to work the shackle through the loop of the hasp. It seemed a fool's errand from the start, valuable time better spent on searching for the correct key wasted. Beth Ann started to lift her padlock away.

But she didn't finish, the lock suspended in midair and her in midthought by the fact that quitting was something to which she was all too accustomed. She'd been beaten, battered, and disappointed so often by life that she'd come to accept failure as normal. This would've been no exception, except a Texas Ranger named Jim Strong had entered her life and filled it with new hope. He'd thrown a lifeline to her boy that she caught out of the emptiness. And on top of that his love had offered her a new beginning.

So instead of pulling Jim Strong's lock away from the hasp, she continued to work the shackle and jimmy the lock currently in place, trying to find a gap, a point where she could squeeze Jim's lock through. Her mind told her no, told her to give up. But her spirit, filled with new purpose and conviction, kept her going until the shackle popped through the hasp, grating against the original lock as Beth Ann snapped it closed.

Elation filled her. She'd done the deed, been true to the man she loved more than anything except the son he'd rescued from a certain hell. And that's when she heard the breathing and boots kicking gravel against the hard-packed floor.

"I'm disappointed in you, sister," said the Reverend Maxwell Arno, holding her son, Danny, by the scruff of the neck.

The Rangers moved about the church like clockwork, employing the same precision they'd practiced in the similar building they'd used as a mock-up for this one. They took control of the building in swift fashion unmarred by any resistance, a remarkable success except for the absence of their prime target as well as Beth Ann Killane. Barely a word was uttered in protest until the Rangers began separating the children from their families. At that moment yellow school buses, in accordance with the plan, would be pulling through the gate to spirit the children away to a nearby school where a phalanx of social services and law enforcement personnel were waiting to interview them. As of this point, no one knew for absolute sure what had transpired on these grounds but everyone was fearing, and assuming, the worst.

D. W. Tepper supervised the entire process, Jim Strong having lit out for a stairway he recalled from Beth Ann Killane's drawings at the sound of the gunshot.

Danny looked so small in Reverend Arno's grasp and only then did Beth Ann realize how big a man he was. As if he'd grown larger in the face of a fight the way some animals and reptiles do.

"I'm afraid I've still got the one you're looking for," Arno said, flashing a single key held on a ring in his free hand.

Then his eyes narrowed, hardening on the sight of what she'd done.

"Where's the key to that second lock, sister?"

"I don't have it."

"You don't really expect me to believe that."

"It's true. I don't care what you believe."

"What brought you to do this? Why have you betrayed me?"

Beth Ann swallowed hard, didn't respond.

Arno, wearing an altogether different face that scared her more than any Halloween mask she'd ever seen, jerked Danny forward and back again. "The key for your son. That's what I'm offering you."

In endeavoring to save Danny from one terrible fate, she'd inadvertently sentenced him to an even worse one.

"Let my boy go," she said, finding a strength deep inside herself she hadn't known until she'd met Jim Strong.

"What was that, sister?'

"You heard me."

Arno shoved Danny forward, taking a step with him. The thin light radiating from the naked bulbs swaying above cast his face in a composite of darkness and shadow, his slicked-back black hair still shining as if that were the only thing the light could find. A single cowlick hung down over his forehead, looking like an ink blotch.

"Consider your faith, sister," Reverend Arno said with surprising calm. "Consider yourself in the eyes of your God."

"Is it true what they say?"

"What who says?"

"Is it true the men of this church force themselves on young women little more than girls?"

"Who told you that?'

"The Texas Rangers. They're upstairs right now putting an end to all the pain you've wrought."

And that's when Beth Ann saw Max Arno change. Maybe it was the light or a trick of her eyes tightening their focus in the standoff. But suddenly Arno's face dissolved into a putrid mess of molten flesh that reformed into something dark and formless. Then the bulbs swayed again and his old visage was back, albeit with a hatred that flared his nostrils and curled his upper lip forward.

"What have you done?" he asked in a voice that sounded like the buzzing of a wasp.

Beth Ann saw the pistol flash in his hand, coming up—for Danny she thought until he leveled the barrel on her instead.

Jim Strong was hoping that the sound he thought he heard coming from the basement was an echo of thunder, maybe his ears misfiring or something. But in his heart he knew better. Jim had spent his life around guns and knew a shot when he heard one, no matter how muffled or lost to distance and barrier. He rushed down to the basement with his heart in his mouth, nothing else finding his ears until a boy's soft sobs reached him.

Jim rounded a corner to find Danny Killane holding his mother's head in his lap. He was stroking her hair gently, smoothing it from her face. His hand was wet with blood and his shirt splotched with it from a wound in line with her heart. The light from an overhead bulb framed her face with a radiant glow that made Beth Ann look more beautiful than Jim Strong had seen in their brief time together. Her son didn't acknowledge him as he approached, struggling to catch his breath as the tears streamed down both cheeks, dragging grime the air had pasted to his face. The boy knew he'd lost the only person who truly loved him just as Jim knew he'd lost the last woman he'd ever truly love.

He knelt down on the other side of her body, waiting for Danny to look up before speaking.

"Which way they go, son?"

The boy pointed down the hall where the dangling light bulbs ended in a tunnel of blackness. Jim started to lift the walkie-talkie from his belt, then stopped. The boy didn't need to hear what he had to say about setting up a perimeter, putting out an all-points bulletin, and the like. And the truth was he didn't want Arno and his goons rounded up when they emerged on some distant corner of the property on a preselected escape route.

He wanted them, especially the reverend, for himself. His way. Old school. The way Earl Strong had done it in a bunch of Texas oil towns during the boom and later down in Mexico against drug smugglers and gunmen.

"I heard them talking," Danny said suddenly, his Adam's apple swelled from the hard swallowing. "Something about the Tackle and Gun."

It was the name of a Midland store owned by a church member named Pearsley who Jim figured must've helped Maxwell Arno build the arsenal now stored behind the door Beth Ann Killane had kept safe. Jim had already resolved to share that information with no one at all and handle the stakeout all on his own. If he didn't catch Max Arno there, he'd catch him somewhere else. But he had a hunch Arno would be showing up at the Tackle and Gun before the week was out. And other than that fishing trip he'd promised himself with Caitlin, Jim Strong happened to have the week free.

He wanted to say something to this poor kid who'd just lost his mother, but had no idea what. With a stranger it was easy to find the words because you weren't afraid if they came out a little wrong. Today they needed to be perfect and, absent of that, Jim opted for silence until the boy looked at him, his tears stopped as if someone had shut off the faucet.

"You're gonna get him, aren't you?" Danny Killane asked, a hatred like none Jim Strong ever wanted to see again filling his eyes.

"Count on it," he promised.

"Promise me you'll tell me when it's done, after you do it. Promise me that."

"I promise."

81

Midland, Texas; the present

Caitlin waited to make sure Danny Killane was done before speaking. "I remember him making a call on a pay phone before we left the Tackle and Gun, after Max Arno was dead. That was you, wasn't it?"

"I could hear sirens in the background, so I guess it was. He called to tell me it was done. That's all he said. I didn't even have time to ask him if he was coming to my mother's funeral the next day, but I'm pretty sure he was there anyway. Never heard from him again, though, and that kind of surprised me."

"I'm sorry, Mr. Killane."

"Danny, please."

In her head Caitlin still saw him as the floppy-haired boy her dad had first met in Pancake Alley, small for his age with just a hint of manhood teasing him, instead of a thirty-five-year-old who sounded beaten down by life.

"I moved in with my dad, which wasn't as bad as it could've been, except for the nightmares and him being gone a lot. I never went back to that diner where my mom worked. I wonder if it's still open."

"Where you keeping yourself these days, Danny?"

"Here and there. I know you, though, everybody does. A real gunfighter, a hero just like your dad."

"I don't think I really measure up to him on that account."

"He'd be proud of you, Ranger."

"As I'm sure your mom would be of you."

Silence fell over the line, something as thick as wet tar settling between them.

"I'm the one got her killed," Danny Killane said finally. "It wasn't my mom Arno came down to the basement after, it was me."

"Come again?"

"I followed her. He followed me. Use your imagination, Ranger." Killane paused, the wet tar returning to the line. "I know what he wanted when he came down there after me. I saw it in his eyes and it was the sickest sight I ever saw in my life. I still see it in nightmares that come and go. They been coming a lot lately."

"Where are you, Danny? Let's meet. Pancake Alley's still open in Odessa, right off I-Twenty. I can meet you there."

But the man on the other end of the line, still a boy to her, wasn't interested. "Your dad did the world a service by killing Max Arno in that parking lot, and I was glad I could point him in the right direction. I'm sorry you had to see it, but to those like me that he wronged and hurt, and there's plenty of us, it was like putting down a rabid dog about to sink its teeth into a kid. His son's no different. I should know."

"How's that?"

"I work the grounds for room and board. I got your number off Arno's computer when he was out of his office. He's got no idea who I really am. Thought about moving on a hundred times, since seeing him every day brings it all back. But something keeps me from leaving. Something else you need to know too: Arno's got a boy stashed on the premises."

Caitlin could feel the electricity dancing off Cort Wesley's skin, resuming before he had a chance to speak. "Say that again."

"I found him hiding out the other day with his hands cuffed behind his back. I cut the plastic off him and promised I'd come back, but I got started on the bottle and the night got away from me. Guess I'm not good for much, am I?"

Caitlin kept her eyes on Cort Wesley. "I believe you're judging yourself too harshly. You deserve better than the hand you've been dealt, Danny. Can you tell me any more about the boy, like where they're keeping him?"

"I could ask around."

"Any notion you can provide at all?"

"This place is so big, there's spots in it I've never seen. I work the grounds; that's all. I'll keep an eye and ear out, though. Call you back if I find anything out."

"Don't do anything stupid, Danny. Whatever it is that's kept you with the Patriot Sun this long, make sure it doesn't eat you alive."

A pause followed, during which Caitlin and Cort Wesley could hear Danny Killane's rapid breathing over the SUV's speakers.

"This man killed my mother, Ranger. I think you know what's kept me here."

"Help me find that boy, Danny. It's a better way to even things with Arno than anything else you can do. You need to trust me on that."

"I'll try. I promise I'll try."

"Arno and his father have ruined enough lives. I don't want you or this boy joining them."

"I swear the man's the goddamn devil. All he's missing is horns and a tail. How do you kill the devil, Ranger?"

"You leave that to me, Danny," Caitlin said, feeling Cort Wesley's eyes boring into hers. "You leave that to me."

82

Malcolm Arno walked slowly up the center aisle of the nursery, stopping at each of the curtained cubicles to look in on mother and child. He had fathered all these infants, an even dozen born in the past year to girls delivered to him for the purpose of procreation and no other. It was the best way, the only way, to assure his blood and word lived beyond him.

As far as Malcolm Arno was concerned, his own life effectively began the day Texas Ranger Jim Strong murdered his father. And for the bulk of that broader existence Arno had considered how best to extract his revenge, often settling on Strong's daughter as a target of just comeuppance. He'd lost track of her for the remaining years of his miserable youth, holding only her picture in his memory until she joined the Department of Public Safety as a highway patrol officer. This after graduating from Texas's police academy at the top of her class and then joining four previous generations of Strongs as a Texas Ranger.

Her picture had been on the front page of the *San Antonio News* that day. Her father, the killer of Arno's father, joined her in the shot, his face looking drawn and tired as heart disease ate away at him, making his death a foregone conclusion.

Arno had gone to Jim Strong's funeral, lurking near the rear of the cortege behind even the press. Too far from the graveside to witness Caitlin Strong's mourning, but taking vast satisfaction in the fact that he would pay homage to her passing as well after being the instigator of it. Her face in that parking lot, frozen in his mind forever with her father's truck as a backdrop, had gotten Arno through any number of awful nights that wouldn't seem to end, his misery lengthened by insomnia that plagued him until the Kean family finally took him in.

Arno hated the sounds and smells of the nursery building. Security priorities had rendered adequate ventilation difficult, the heating and air-conditioning systems battling for supremacy as seasons changed and the fickle Texas climate played havoc with the controls. When appropriate the children and their mothers would be moved to a dormitory-style facility that would nonetheless remain insular from the rest of the complex. Then, as the children grew, he would teach them personally, bestowing upon the smartest, most ambitious, and most deserving the bulk of his gifts to assure future generations would not suffer again as past ones had. His work had to go on and go forth. Of the twelve birthed so far, eight were boys—divine provenance serving him yet again.

He knew everything about Caitlin Strong that many did and plenty that almost everyone didn't, including the fact that she'd taken up with an outlaw named Cort Wesley Masters. He saw Masters's son Dylan Torres as the trump card he'd been waiting for all his life, an instrument of fate to make Caitlin Strong at last know the pain he had known since the day her father had killed his. This boy was older than the two of them had been that spring day in 1990, but he looked younger than his years, the symmetry close enough to justify his plans.

Arno wasn't sure yet how it would come to pass, hadn't worked that part out in his brain yet. He only knew that he wanted Caitlin Strong to be there when it happened. Let her hold the boy as the life ebbed from him, let her feel him take his last breath as Arno had felt his father take his.

Someday the infants he heard cooing and gurgling, secure in their mother's protection, would learn how terrible this world could be if they didn't fight for their beliefs and hurt those who sought to hurt them. They'd learn that lesson from their father himself, learn from his own experience of how to deal with an enemy.

Starting with Caitlin Strong.

83

"Why aren't you turning around?" Cort Wesley said, the SUV still parked on the shoulder.

"You wanna go back in there with guns blazing?" Caitlin asked him. "Going up against all of Arno's men, just the two of us, with no warrant or backup?"

"I'm running a little low on time here, Ranger, in case you forgot."

"I haven't, but that might be just what Arno wants."

"You lost me."

"It didn't occur to you that the son of a bitch could be baiting a trap for us?"

"You heard Danny Killane's voice. Man, he still sounds like a terrified fifteen-year-old kid."

"If it really was Danny Killane. We can't let Arno push our buttons or pull the trigger for us."

"This coming from somebody who just puked off the four-lane on account of spending a few minutes alone with him."

Caitlin looked across the seat. "If Dylan is there, what chance do we have of finding him in a place that big?"

"Better than the one we've got if we don't try."

"Oh, we'll try all right, but not until things are lined up right."

And then Cort Wesley realized. "You don't want this to go bad, like it did for your father."

"He deserved better after my mom was murdered. Beth Ann Killane was his last chance at that and Arno's father took it away from him." She looked at Cort Wesley again, slowing the SUV enough to hold his stare. "And, yeah, I don't want his son to do the same to Dylan."

"Boy's place in all this is what I'm still trying to figure."

"Please don't."

"Why?"

"Arno's got no bone to pick with you, it's me he's after. I'm the reason he sent LaChance to San Luis Patosí to pick up Dylan."

"Boy boasted to the assholes who snatched him who his dad was and the hell they'd pay for doing it."

"And Arno made the connection. He made it pretty plain up in his office that he's been following my life ever since that day in the parking lot."

"What the hell he care about me and the boys?"

"People I care about, a way he can hurt me. Information's on the Internet, Cort Wesley. The rumors, anyway."

"Price that comes with being famous, I suppose."

"I never wanted that."

"You got it all the same. Symbol of the new West, which is pretty much identical to the old, except we don't have the luxury of just calling a man out when the circumstances call for it."

"That didn't happen as much as everyone thinks. Neither did gunfights, and the ones that did usually ended with neither shooter hitting a goddamn thing."

"Unless the shooter was a Texas Ranger, of course."

She braked hard and veered the SUV onto the shoulder, tires skidding over gravel and the sensors locking their shoulder harnesses into place. "You wanna go back now and have this out with Arno, say the word. We can shoot him down just like you shot the drug dealer who killed Maria Lopez and her family."

Cort Wesley said nothing, his brow and cheeks shiny with a thin layer of perspiration and his nose looking like it was sunburned.

"You want to play things that way, I'll stand by your side, Cort Wesley," Caitlin continued. "Kill as many of the Patriot Sun soldiers as we can toward no good reason, since their guns'll get us before we even get close to Dylan. Tell me I'm wrong."

"Beats rotting in a Mexican jail," he sighed.

"No," Caitlin said, harsher than she'd meant to. "We do this a surer way that gets you your boy back."

"What's that?"

"Take something away from Arno he cares about even more."

84

"I can't authorize that, Ranger," D. W. Tepper told Caitlin through the cloud of cigarette smoke between them, after hearing everything she had to tell him about her trip to visit Malcolm Arno at the Patriot Sun.

"What happened to this being an ongoing investigation?"

"You leave out the part about it being connected to a task force that wanted me to drop your ass in a meat grinder?"

"LaChance brothers are the key, Captain."

"You want the Rangers to take on the Hells Angels now too?"

"Wouldn't be the first time. You already admitted as much."

"That was over crystal meth and normally with plenty of backup."

"Normally?"

"We may have deviated once or twice."

Caitlin's stare scolded Tepper and he stamped out his Marlboro in an old Alamo ashtray he'd found somewhere that was cracked down the center. "I never felt better since I took up smoking again. Explain that to me."

"I can't."

"Just like I can't see enough of a connection to send you back to the Great White North."

"Not quite that far," Caitlin had told him. "I ran the timeline of the missing cash from Iraq against the surge in drug smuggling across the Canadian border into the U.S."

"Oh boy . . ."

"Arno funneled his money into the best cash crop available, a sure thing investment-wise, not to mention washing all that cash through the mob moving the shit."

"He does this when Mexico's a stone's throw away?"

"The cartels aren't in the market for investors, Captain. They're looking for ways to unload their cash, not bring in more. Arno moved his money north because that's where the opportunity was, the alternative being that this spike in trafficking across that Indian Reservation was just a coincidence."

"You're gonna have to do better than that, Ranger."

"Okay, truck tires."

"Come again?"

"Frank Gage, the DEA man running the task force, took me out onto the ice and gave me the VIP tour of the Res. I noticed a pattern of tire tracks that diverted from the MO he was describing. Big freight haulers riding with chains wrapped around their rubber. Patriot Sun had two trucks in the parking lot with chain impressions in their treads. How's that?"

"Oh boy," Tepper said again, expression mashed so tight some of the furrows in his face seemed to be joining up. "We had water in our radiator, gas in our engine, and bullets in our .45s, your dad and I were good to go. You didn't need to do much thinking against a man who left his belt back in the bedroom of the woman he'd tried to rape."

"That really happen?"

"We made the suspect 'cause his pants were falling down. He started to reach for his gun and your dad fired a warning shot that went right under his privates. No word of a lie."

"I do that to Malcolm Arno, there won't be a warning shot. Authorize me to head north, Captain."

Tepper traced a finger from one cheek across his nose to the other cheek as if he were connecting some unseen dots. Then he retrieved his Marlboro from the Alamo ashtray, but thought better of relighting it. "Toward what purpose exactly, Ranger?"

"Those biker shacks you and my dad busted up in the search for crystal meth dispensaries . . . you inform your captain of your intentions?"

"Not entirely, no," Tepper conceded.

"What'd you tell him?"

"That we were gathering intelligence, maybe working to turn an informant."

"There you have it."

"Have what?"

"My intentions up north, Captain," Caitlin told him. "Put some intelligence together. Meet with potential informants."

Tepper popped out a fresh cigarette and lit it with a match struck against his boot heel. "Suppose you'll be bringing Cort Wesley Masters along for the ride."

"You suppose correctly. And it might be the only way to stop him from storming the Patriot Sun grounds himself."

"Him heading north while his son's a hostage down here doesn't seem likely."

"He knows it's the best way to get Dylan back."

"On account of what the two of you are gonna do once you're back in that ice world."

Caitlin remained silent.

Tepper thought on that as he puffed away. "Things have changed plenty since your dad and I were busting heads. You do this, it's all aboveboard, an official assignment."

"If that's the way it's gotta be."

"And one other condition: when this is over, you make sure Masters comes in even if you have to drag his ass here yourself."

Caitlin stared into Tepper's narrowed eyes.

"We got us a deal, Ranger?"

Caitlin nodded.

Part Nine

Now with three Rangers backing him up, Captain A. Y. Allee shouted to the prisoners [who'd seized the jail on April 3, 1969] that they had until the count of ten to surrender.

"One," he began. "Two . . . three . . . four." Then he started shooting.

"Captain, you didn't get to ten," [Ranger Joaquin] Jackson pointed out.

"Those sumbitches can't count anyway," the captain snorted.

—Mike Cox, *Time of the Rangers*

85

Cort Wesley kept checking his cell phone as they traipsed over the snow-encrusted land of the St. Regis Mohawk Reservation toward the frozen St. Lawrence River that cut through it.

"You expecting a call?" Caitlin finally asked him.

"I keep hoping there'll be a message from Dylan," he said, finally sticking it back in his pocket. "A text or something—that's how he communicates. Maybe you should check your phone. You might have better service up here than me."

A pair of tribal policemen had stopped them once on Reservation land just past a sign that read:

YES "TERRORISTS" COME THRU AKWESASNE
THEY ARE N.Y.S.P. BORDER PATROL
A.T.F. F.B.I. I.R.S. ECT., ECT.!!!

The tribal cops inquired as to the purpose of their trespass to which Caitlin flashed her Ranger badge and leftover drug task force credentials that fortunately weren't dated. The tribal cops acquiesced grudgingly, warning their safety couldn't be guaranteed after nightfall.

Once they reached the ice-covered section of the St. Lawrence that sliced through the Reservation on both sides of the border, Caitlin noticed a figure sitting out on the ice over a freshly carved hole, his folding chair placed to hold the sun on him until afternoon bled into dusk. Caitlin recognized him even with his floppy hat and long coat as the ancient tribal policeman Frank Gage had pointed out when he'd introduced her to the primary drug smuggling route used to ferry drugs from Canada into the United States. She could see no vehicle nearby and wondered how a man Gage had said was near a hundred years old could have negotiated such a large traverse of the ice to reach a point square in the middle, at least a hundred yards from shore.

"Who'd you say this guy was?" Cort Wesley asked, following her out onto the frozen river and nearly losing his balance, his boots like skates on the dull surface.

"Old tribal cop and as tough a man as there is in these parts."

"Old doesn't begin to tell it. I don't think he's moving. You sure he's not dead?"

"Why don't we ask him?"

They continued walking across the ice toward the Indian who had yet to acknowledge their presence.

"Tell me more about the old guy there."

"His name's Charlie Charles. For a time, he was the only law on the Reservation. Carried a tomahawk and a bunch of knives, but no gun until it was mandated by the federal government. The Mohawk lived in fear of a knock from him at the door. Crime was almost nonexistent back in those days. Task force chief told me he's been involved in more car chases than any cop on record, has been shot a dozen times, and was clinically dead twice—three times if you include a heart attack five years ago."

Cort Wesley continued to study the old Indian for movement. He was holding a hand-knotted line in the water between a pair of home-made gloves made of deerskin and bear fur.

"Any idea what he's doing out here exactly, besides fishing?"

"Same thing he was doing last time I saw him, I suspect."

They walked into the stream of sunlight shining onto the old Indian, Caitlin waiting until she and Cort Wesley were directly in his line of sight before calling out to him.

"Officer Charles."

He paid them no heed whatsoever, not even acknowledging their presence.

"Officer Charles?"

Still nothing.

"I told you he was dead," said Cort Wesley.

Which drew a gaze from Charlie Charles, his eyes angling upward from beneath his hat. "Get out of my sun."

Both Caitlin and Cort Wesley stepped aside to remove the shadows from his face.

"And I don't go by that name anymore. I haven't for longer than I can remember, maybe longer than I've been alive."

"What name do you go by?" Cort Wesley asked him.

"Okwaho. Means wolf in Mohawk. It's what the braves called me when I was a young man before I glimpsed the spirit world for the first time. But the women called me something else: Yakohsa. Means horse. Like to know why?" he asked with a grin that ended when his dentures shifted, forcing him to readjust them by massaging his jaws. "Never mind. It was many years ago when I was a much younger man than I am today. Still, both names were well earned. Guess you can call me Charlie."

Caitlin thought of her grandfather Earl Strong living until almost ninety and never seeming nearly as old as Charlie Charles. The Indian's face looked more like leather than skin, as if someone had stitched it over the bone. It was the tawny color of raw fabric and the many scars that crisscrossed it looked more like seams holding the various patches together. A mane of white hair flowed out from under the confines of his old hat, looking thin and stringy in the breeze. He sat so his spine was curved, disguising his true height, regarding them with one dark eye as bright as a boy's and a second crusted over by a milk-colored cataract. His nose was ridged and too big for his face, angled to the right as if the old Indian had broken it on more than one occasion and never had it set properly.

"I was here a little over a month ago," Caitlin told him.

"I remember your gun," Charlie Charles said, eyeing her SIG. "It's easier to remember a person by their weapon than their face, and in these parts one is as plentiful as the other. But I know your kind." Then, with his eye shifting to Cort Wesley, "Both of you."

"And what kind is that, sir?"

"Gunmen. The real ones, not the masqueraders who think the gun makes them tough." He shook his head. "It's the toughness that makes the gun."

"I heard you never carried one yourself," said Caitlin.

"Not until the New York Tribal Council took my knives away. Called them weapons of violence."

"What are you doing out here, Mr. Charles?"

"Same thing you are, I believe."

86

UPSTATE NEW YORK; THE PRESENT

"How old are you exactly?" Cort Wesley asked him.

"Well, my mother once met President Lincoln and my father was a scout during the Civil War. Does that answer your question?"

Caitlin wasn't sure whether to smile in response or not.

"You're wearing a star," Charlie Charles said, noticing the badge pinned to her shirt. "That tells me the law brought you back here. Your eyes tell me something else."

"Just like you're not really here to fish, Charlie," said Caitlin.

"Oh no?"

"I don't see an ice container to store your catch in."

"That's because I let them go after I catch them. All creatures have a right to live out their times."

"Even the drug dealers who use the frozen river on this land as their own private highway?"

"Would've put a stop to it myself before they took my badge away. But you still got yours, 'long with your gun . . . Ranger."

"That's why we're here, Charlie."

"Then I ought to get out of the way before the bullets start flying."

"We've got something else in mind," Cort Wesley told him.

The old man shifted his gaze and held it on him longer this time. "You're no lawman."

"Nope."

"Got the look of a man who would've drove me to drink back in the old times if I wasn't there already."

"Guess I've done that for plenty of others."

"You can't stop them, Charlie," Caitlin said suddenly.

The old man regarded her with both his eyes, the bright as well cataract-covered one.

"That's what you're fixing to do every day when you come out here to fish."

The old man coughed up some cold-reared mucus and swallowed it back down. "I think about what I'd do if I were still Okwaho. But I'm not, not Yakohsa anymore either. But when I come out here like this it's easier to pretend, even though the cold hurts my bones."

Cort Wesley took a step closer to him, making sure to leave the sun a lane to the old man's face. "We don't have to pretend."

Charlie Charles nodded slowly, rotating his gaze between the two of them. He leaned back in his chair, so far and so quick that Caitlin feared it might topple over. Then his eyes left her and Cort Wesley for a place far beyond them.

"The Mohawk have a legend about a young boy who grew into the first eagle to soar in the skies. The Elders must have known he was different and special from his birth because after three moons, the name they gave him from the spirit world was *Ka Bay she go e sayd*, or He Who Walks a Different Path. He became *Ka Bay she go e sayd* because he was more comfortable with animals than people, as if he were too good for folks or existed on a higher spiritual plane. And instead of growing into a man, he grew into an eagle.

"In the midst of his transformation, the Creator Himself appeared to the boy and told him, 'As my view of what happens in this World is different from where I live in the Spirit World, you will spend most of your time in the realm of Father Sky, and view the world below in a different way. As My Vision is unique and different, your eyesight will be keener than any other bird that inhabits the skies.' "

The old tribal cop's good eye sharpened and sought out Caitlin and Cort Wesley once more. "I believe the two of you view the world a different way too. I believe your eyesight is also keener than any other bird that inhabits the skies." His gaze narrowed on Caitlin, the way a gunman does when he's zeroing in on a target. "You ask me why I come out here every day to fish, watch, and wait for something I can no longer change. Maybe it's because I'm waiting for someone who can. Maybe they've finally showed up."

87

MOHAWK INDIAN RESERVATION; THE PRESENT

Chief Dan Tails, duly elected head Elder of the St. Regis Mohawk nation, lived in a ten-thousand-square-foot, two-story log home built on a man-made lake and surrounded by woods. Winter here was an eight- or nine-month ordeal made palatable by the sweet smell of hickory logs filling his home and spilling from the chimney. During the day his home was drenched in sunlight pouring in through the spacious windows. If it weren't for his girlfriend and the children she'd born him, Tails wouldn't have even bothered with shading them from the moon at night, since no one was close enough to peer at anything through the glass anyway. But he maintained a rule that those shades were never to be closed in his study or the den, Tails's way in modern times of communing with nature that included a pristine view of his lake.

The meeting of the Tribal Council had gone late that night, and Tails opened his truck window to the cold near the end of his private drive to better enjoy the scent of the night mixing with his burning hickory. Noticing as he pulled into his integral garage that the shades had been drawn over the section of windows that were never to be covered. Tails pushed through the fire door into his home, prepared to scold his children for choosing a glare-free television screen for their video games over any semblance of appreciation for the old ways of their people.

Tails stormed into the den and threw back the shades, revealing the reflections of three figures in the moonlit window glass. The chief swung, noticing old Charlie Charles seated in a chair flanked by a man and woman Tails had never seen before standing on either side of him.

"Good to see you're still alive, Charlie."

"Had a dream about your father the other day, Chief. He was brewing whiskey from an old still, same way he did back in the days I busted him on a regular basis. I remember when he was born. Bad to the bone from that very day."

"He was eighty-five when he passed six years ago. How old does that make you?"

"Bet you wished I'd joined him already, Chief."

"Who are your friends, Charlie?"

"They come from Texas with some business to discuss."

"They capable of speaking for themselves?" Tails asked, his question directed at the two standing figures.

"I'm a Texas Ranger, Chief Tails," Caitlin Strong said. "Business we have deals with some you've been conducting here on tribal lands, which I learned about when I was up here as part of a DEA task force."

Tails stiffened, standing halfway between the exposed glass and his uninvited guests. "Well, they've got no authority on this land and neither do you."

He was supremely confident of his own power here on land the federal government had no say in managing, the Mohawks being as close to a sovereign nation as it got. But something about the former tribal cop's new pals had him on edge and measuring the distance to the nearest door. Old man just wouldn't die, destined to be a pain in the ass well into the current century.

"We don't recognize outside law enforcement authority here," Tails said to Caitlin, noting her SIG as he reiterated his position. "That makes it illegal to carry firearms on tribal land. I could have you arrested."

"No common courtesy, Chief?"

"You're way out of your jurisdiction, Ranger."

"Just like I was when I served on that task force. I heard it got disbanded after I shot it out with some Hells Angels in a marijuana grow house up in Quebec. You hear anything about that?"

"Can't say that I have."

"Sure," Caitlin said. "Don't know why you would, unless the Mohawk had someone on the inside, one of your tribal cops maybe, who spilled the beans on what we were up to and wanted it shut down."

"You tell a nice story, Ranger."

"Know a man named Malcolm Arno?"

"I can't say that I do."

Cort Wesley looked about the big room, eyes lingering on its exposed beams and seeming to study the finish. "Nice spread, Chief, new too. What, maybe five years?"

"Four."

Caitlin picked it up from there. "Coincides with the time Malcolm Arno received maybe a billion dollars stolen from the reconstruction effort in Iraq by men in lockstep with his point of view."

Tails stood up a little straighter. "I have no idea what you're talking about and I'd like to ask the three of you to leave."

"Listen to her, Chief," said Charlie Charles softly. "She's got it in mind to save your soul."

"From what?"

"Yourself."

"I'm calling the tribal police," Tails said, moving for the phone.

"I already did," Charles told him. "They won't be coming."

"What do you want?" Tails asked, the question aimed at none of them in particular.

"I think you were the recipient of a good portion of that billion dollars, Chief," Caitlin told him. "I think some of that money built the Dan Tails Cigarette Factory and that the rest fueled the rapid expansion of the drug smuggling efforts that use the ice bridge on your land like a private toll road. I think Malcolm Arno funneled the cash to the Mohawk to wash it and make even more to help him fund militia and right-wing extremist movements all over the United States that may be planning to kill lots of innocent people."

"This isn't Texas, Ranger," Tails shot back at her, still sounding resilient. "It's not even the United States really; it's Mohawk land and, as such, I don't have to listen to you or anything else the government you represent has to say. You can't touch me here, nobody can. Just ask the assholes from immigration who keep poking their noses where they don't belong. I've won restraining orders against them in federal court. You really want to push things with me?"

"That depends."

"On what exactly?"

"How much you want to push things with me. I believe, Chief, that the federal government funds this and other Reservations to the tune of the twenty-six billion dollars in aid per year for schooling, medical services, broadband connections, and public transportation from coast to coast. But if those tribes are found to be in violation of federal felony statutes, drug dealing and distribution for example, that funding could get yanked across the board in a hurry until the guilty party can be tried and convicted. Of course, that could take a considerable stretch of time to get sorted out."

Tails swallowed hard enough to force his pursed lips open. "You here representing the government now, Ranger?"

"No, sir. Just myself at the present time. But since the task force I was part of was federal, and the ramifications of this drug dealing stretch all the way to Texas, I imagine it wouldn't be hard for the Rangers to make their case. You'd be well advised to consider that, sir. People tend to listen when we talk."

"Besides," Cort Wesley picked up, "you and the tribe have gotten plenty rich already off all this. Nobody's interested in taking any of that away."

"What we wanna do is stop any more of the drugs from coming in," Caitlin told him. "Finish the job that drug task force started."

"And how do you propose to do that exactly?" wondered Tails.

"That's not your concern."

"Excuse me?"

"What is your concern is what Mohawk tribal law says about proceeds from ill-gotten gains. Charlie?"

"Well," the old tribal cop started, rubbing his chin with a pair of long, skeletal fingers, "we used to burn the homes of moonshiners who built them using *their* ill-gotten gains. I guess that passes for precedent."

"The chief of the tribe back then one of them?"

"No, ma'am, but he was getting paid off to look the other way and keep the locals out, so we burned his house too."

"Are you threatening me, Charlie?" Tails asked the old man.

"No, sir," said Caitlin. "That'd be me. But look at this another way. You might be about to become a hero, Chief." She let him wait before completing her thought. "For helping us put a stop to the drugs coming into the United States over your land."

88

MIDLAND, TEXAS; THE PRESENT

Malcolm Arno was sticking pushpins in a wall map when the call came. He didn't hear his private line buzzing at first, not with his attention rooted on the pattern that was emerging on the wall before him, adorned now with a clutter of multicolored denotations stretching from coast to coast. Concentrated in the parts where the true Americans lived.

That's what his father had called them when explaining the purpose of the sanctuary he called the Church of the Redeemer. True Americans.

The ringing started once more, and this time Arno moved to his desk to answer the phone.

"Yes," he said almost too quiet to hear.

"What the fuck's going on?" demanded Buck LaChance.

"Your language, sir—"

"Fuck my language. The ice up here has melted, if you catch my drift."

"I don't."

"Then try this: we've got a traffic jam of char on what used to be our own private road to heaven."

"Wait, slow down. You're saying—"

"You heard what I said. They're destroying our drugs."

"Who, for God's sake?"

"If I knew the answer to that, I wouldn't be bothering to call because they'd already be dead."

But Arno knew, knew it as soon as Caitlin Strong had left his office, because he'd seen it in her eyes. Not specifically the frozen river she was laying siege to, but a storm she was going to rain down on the world he had envisioned from the moment their eyes met for the first time.

"Someone's taking the war to you," LaChance said. "But I got thirty riders and twice that many guns ready to take it to them."

"No, that's what they want. They'll know you're coming. They'll be expecting it."

"Not the shit storm we're gonna unleash, no. Your father ever give a sermon on the wrath of God?"

"I believe he did."

"Then why don't you come up here, Mr. Arno, and witness it firsthand?"

89

MOHAWK INDIAN RESERVATION; THE PRESENT

Caitlin watched the snowmobiles flying across the ice, three of them running abreast of each other. She was standing in the woods, shielded by branches sprouting leaves in spite of the still frigid temperatures of upstate New York. No need for binoculars, since the snowmobiles were coming so fast, the riders with no sense of what awaited them.

"Always knew I had one last war in me," Charlie Charles said from between her and Cort Wesley, who was standing so still he looked more like a cardboard cutout of himself. "Just didn't think it'd happen this way."

"You should go home, Charlie," Caitlin advised. "Let us handle the heavy lifting."

His one good eye flashed her a look so deep that he appeared fifty years younger. "This *is* my home, Ranger. I'd appreciate it if you didn't forget that."

"I apologize if I did."

"And I'm not going anywhere, since somebody needs to keep the two of you civil. Reasonably so, anyway."

The Indian was wearing a gun belt so old and worn that the brown leather passed for barely beige, creased, and cracking. He had a .357 Magnum with a six-inch barrel tucked in the holster, Caitlin left trying to picture him hoisting it in hands the texture of parchment.

"My dad used to say the only fight worth fighting is the one you know you can win," Caitlin told him.

Cort Wesley's already stiff frame tensed even more, as the snowmobiles sped toward the line in the ice even with them. Their skis hit the oil he'd slicked all over the surface and they spun wildly out of control upon hitting it. They looked like bottle caps twirling on tabletops before going airborne and chucking their riders. Impact on their oversized backpacks spilled a multicolored assortment of aspirin-sized pills across the ice in all directions, the sound like that of hailstones pattering against a tin roof.

"Looks like a rainbow," said Charlie Charles.

"With a street value of maybe a million bucks," added Caitlin.

"Not anymore," said Cort Wesley, advancing onto the frozen river in his ice boots.

MOHAWK INDIAN RESERVATION; THREE DAYS EARLIER

"What is it you want?" Chief Dan Tails had asked inside his big house on the shores of the man-made lake.

"You been looking the other way for those runners," Caitlin told him. "Now we want you to look the other way for us."

"Keep your tribal police from intervening," Cort Wesley added.

"Intervening in what?"

"Better if you don't know that, sir," said Caitlin, "just like it's better if Malcolm Arno never catches wind about this conversation taking place. What you gotta understand here is that we're not out to arrest anybody. We're not looking to issue subpoenas, make deals to turn state's evidence for jury trials that go on forever and end up as a lead item on the cable networks' screen scrawl. Nope, what we wanna do is shut off the spigot now that you've had ample time to fill up your jugs."

"You make it sound a lot simpler than it is, Ranger."

"We'll see about that."

MOHAWK INDIAN RESERVATION; THE PRESENT

Charlie Charles held his Magnum on the injured snowmobile riders while Caitlin and Cort Wesley popped holes in the ice and swept the multicolored pills they'd been hauling down through them.

"You boys can get a move on now," Caitlin told them.

The riders looked at each other, one of them with a knee so torn apart it looked like his lower leg wasn't connected to the upper.

"Better help your friend," she continued. "He drops, he dies."

"We got bosses, you know. We tell them what happened, they're gonna—"

"By all means, go ahead. And you can also tell them this route's been closed. The Texas Rangers own it now."

90

Dylan Torres was being held in an unfinished slab of a building constructed over a mound of earth holding another of the complex's septic systems to better disguise it. Problem was the stench from some water leaching beneath the ground proved impossible for even workmen to bear, so the building's rooms were changed from offices to storage units. A floor of these units was then converted to a makeshift holding area upon Malcolm Arno's realization that the Patriot Sun had made no such accommodation to house unruly members who might otherwise become a distraction. As the group's numbers continued to swell, and the population on these grounds rose, the need for such a facility would become even more apparent. Besides the nursery, the building was the most isolated of any in the complex, out of step with the down-home aura evoked by the other structures with the ever-present smell certain to dissuade the curious from approaching.

Arno held his nose against the stink as he and Jed Kean entered the poorly ventilated building that sat roasting, unguarded by trees, in the midday sun. The stench wasn't as bad as it was some days, especially when they reached the detention floor where a dedicated air exchanger had been added and new ductwork set into place.

A single guard on duty behind a desk on this floor rose at Arno's approach, and Arno acknowledged him with a nod as he passed with Kean by his side. They came to the first room down on the left and Kean worked his key into the lock.

"I'll do this, if you want."

"That's my job, Jed," Arno said, pulling a pair of clippers, the kind used to tend rosebushes, from his belt. "And I'm actually looking forward to it."

91

The first of the trucks came across the ice that night; two of them pickups with oversized cargo beds, one was a long-haul freight, and the fourth a U-Haul seventeen-foot moving truck. In each case, Cort Wesley had plucked their tires from a prone position in the woods with an old Remington rifle complete with telescopic scope leftover from Charlie Charles's hunting days. But it was well maintained, freshly oiled, and the Indian had supplied a box of 30.06 cartridges for load.

The sounds of the tires exploding made Caitlin flinch each time. Each shot sent the trucks jerking wildly before dissolving into wild spins across the ice, not unlike the snowmobiles. They didn't flip, coming to a halt as Caitlin and Cort Wesley trained old assault rifles, first generation M16s, Charlie Charles had never unpacked for the tribal police's armory on the cabs.

From there, Caitlin did the very thing her grandfather Earl had done eighty years before upon confiscating the hauls of drug mules dragging marijuana and black tar heroine up from Mexico: she burned the contents of each truck in a fire pit built atop the thick ice by Charlie Charles. She made the dealers, drivers, or whatever they were watch as the flames crackled and brightened, before heating the ice enough to melt it and causing the whole of the flaming contents to drop through the hole to send a mist of smoky steam flowing up into the air. By the next morning, the hole would have sealed, as if a patch of ice had been fitted exactly to its specifications, save for the lack of snow cover and chipping.

"They're not gonna put up with this long, Ranger," said Cort Wesley, as the fourth fire crashed through the ice and two men made their way back across the frozen river.

"Exactly what I'm counting on, Cort Wesley."

"You and me both. My point was regarding the fact that you haven't exactly explained your plan for dealing with it."

Caitlin winked at him, her smile just visible in the night. "What makes you think I've got a plan?"

92

MIDLAND, TEXAS; THE PRESENT

"Tonight's the night," LaChance said over Malcolm Arno's private line. "We're saddling up and going old school."

"I can't decide whether you're a fool or an idiot," Arno told him.

"I'm supposed to wait around until you come up with a better response?"

"That's the idea, yes."

"Fuck that and fuck you too."

"I'll not have you take that tone with me, Mr. LaChance," Arno said, his shoulders stiffening so fast a spasm shot through his neck.

"Who you think you're talking to here, one of your robot followers? Uh-uh, only way I get my end, the Angels' end, is on delivery of our product, and this Ranger has dumped or burned more than I can weigh so far."

Arno remained silent, listening to LaChance breathing noisily on the other end of the line.

"Cat got your tongue, Reverend?"

"I'm not a minister. That was my father."

"Sure, another fraud. From where I sit, you're fixing to fight a civil war and you can't even put down one Texas Ranger, a bitch no less."

Arno felt a cold rush of icy air up his spine. "This has gone far enough."

"Didn't I just say that? You've got me thinking you've been too busy fooling around with little girls to notice what's going on. You wanna talk patience? How about you wait six months for your next shipment from south of the border?"

Arno ran his tongue around his mouth, trying to relieve the pastiness that felt like cotton wedged along his gums. "Give me twenty-four hours. I've got an idea."

"Sorry. Can't wait that long. Wheels are already turning up here."

"You're playing right into her hands. This is just what she wants."

"She ever take on the Angels in Texas?"

"Her father did, and from everything I've seen she's even tougher than he was. And she won't be alone either; Cort Wesley Masters will be with her."

"That kid's father?'

"That's right."

"So this shit storm is your fault. You insisting on playing things your own way."

"I had my reasons," Arno said, certain LaChance would never be able to understand them.

"But I still like our odds," LaChance told him, absolutely no sense of doubt or apprehension in his voice. "Thirty guns against two. How's that read to you?"

"Just wait."

"Wait for what?"

"I'm sending something to you up there," Arno said, studying the small package on his desk, chilled by the thought of what lay inside. "Something worth more than those thirty guns."

"No such thing, boss."

93

MOHAWK INDIAN RESERVATION; THE PRESENT

"Here they come."

Caitlin watched the big trucks rolling along the frozen river from the Canadian side of the Mohawk land, near spitting images of the ones she'd spotted in the Patriot Sun parking lot. They rolled without lights, illuminated by the moon reflecting over the white surface. As they drew closer, Caitlin could hear the chains wrapped around their tires scratching atop the ice, casting the lower half of the two trucks in a frosty mist of snow and ice pellets.

"Look a bit familiar, don't they?" Cort Wesley said, following their approach through the scope of his rifle. "You wanna tell me what that means exactly?"

Caitlin shrugged. "Guess we're about to find out."

The big trucks were running on double tires, forcing him to fire more shots than he'd planned. It had been a long time since he'd done any sniper shooting and even longer since his ability to fire, jack another round into the chamber, and then recalibrate the weapon for the next shot had been tested.

In Caitlin's mind Cort Wesley had fired four times between a single of her breaths; an illusion of time, of course, but also a testament to his skill and resolve. The trucks were cruising slowly enough to leave their skids more controlled than the other vehicles they'd taken down that had been traveling faster.

The trucks had barely slid to a halt when automatic fire burst from both cabs, muzzle flashes erupting in the still night. The fire was concentrated in the general area from where Cort Wesley had fired. Only neither he nor Caitlin was there anymore, circling around the brief distance to the darkest point of the shore to launch their assault.

The gunmen shot up a storm toward the eastern bank of the river, while Caitlin and Cort Wesley launched their assault from the southwest. They fired high into the windshield, content to leave it at that unless more fire burned their way. It didn't, as things turned out, their eyes having adjusted well enough to the darkness, ready to spot two sets of arms raised in both cabs.

Caitlin and Cort Wesley advanced with the steaming barrels of their M16s cutting twin swaths through the cold thin mist rising off the icy surface.

"Climb out with your hands showing!" Caitlin yelled, hearing her command echo through the cold and dark.

All four men complied, leaving their doors open after dropping down into the night.

"You boys might just live to see the morning now," Cort Wesley picked up, starting toward them.

Both he and Caitlin could see their hands were empty, the weapons with which they'd sprayed the woods left in the cabs of both trucks.

"This is what happens from here," Cort Wesley continued. "You turn around and walk back to the other side of the border. You don't stop, you don't turn around, and you keep your hands laced behind your heads the whole way. Any of you with kids I'd advise to make sure none of his buddies does something dumb, since automatic fire has a tendency to hit people it wasn't necessarily aiming for."

"Now get going," Caitlin added.

When the men started off, she moved around to the rear of the nearest truck, while Cort Wesley held his gaze and his gun on the four men walking off down an illuminated stretch of ice that looked like a narrow ribbon of light. Caitlin slid back the bolt and hoisted up the rear hold, curious to see the contents of this load and, by connection, the previous ones that had surely made their way to the Patriot Sun in Texas aboard the trucks she'd glimpsed down there. The smells of oil and fresh metal struck her hard and fast, no flashlight needed to discern the contents.

"You need to have a look at this, Cort Wesley."

94

MOHAWK INDIAN RESERVATION; THE PRESENT

The weapons were still in their original factory packing crates. Caitlin and Cort Wesley pictured the contents of assault rifles, extra magazines, 7.62mm and 5.56mm ammunition. The larger, more narrow crates held rocket launchers, the kind capable of taking down an airplane or laying waste to a small building.

"See those squatter crates stacked in the back?" Cort Wesley asked, aiming his flashlight that way. "Hand grenades."

"Arno's fixing to fight a war, all right."

"Was there ever any doubt?"

"Only about his ability to acquire the means."

"Well, not anymore."

They heard a brief scratching on the ice, followed by a voice that split the night around them. "Two of you turn around very slowly or I'll shoot you where you stand. Drop your weapons and keep your hands where I can see them."

Caitlin and Cort Wesley did as they were told, coming face-to-face with a big man with a tattoo of an arrow pointing forward on his bald skull. He was holding a twelve-gauge pump shotgun amid a trio of Neanderthals wearing the same black colors and markings of the Hells Angels. Except their hair was crusted with flecks of ice and the back of their black jackets and pants looked like they'd been pelted by a crystal storm.

"Hello, LaChance," said Caitlin.

"I don't remember us being formally introduced."

"I met your two brothers a while back in Quebec," Caitlin started, leaving her sentence off in mid-thought long enough to notice some sort of platform jerry-rigged to the underside of the nearest truck spun round so its back end was facing her thirty yards away. She pictured LaChance and the others clinging to them while the trucks motored across the lake waiting to spring the trap Caitlin and Cort Wesley had dropped straight into. "Right before I killed them," she finished.

Caitlin watched LaChance's features tighten and eyes widen to exaggerate the size of the whites. The shotgun seemed to tremble in his grasp.

"It wasn't the Mounties like you heard," she continued. "I put a bullet in one, used a knife on the other. Can't tell you which was which, of course."

"You wanna die that bad?" LaChance asked her.

"You're gonna kill us anyway," Cort Wesley said.

"Right you are there," LaChance said, acknowledging him for the first time. "But not before I give you a present." He removed a small soft-wrapped package from his pocket and tossed it to Cort Wesley. "Little something from your son."

Cort Wesley held the package uncomfortably in his grasp, as if it were hot or charged with electricity, while Caitlin let her eyes drift to the woods rimming the river on the east and south.

"Got thirty Angels worked into position by now," LaChance told her. "So whatever you've got for backup's long gone."

And that's when the screaming started.

95

MOHAWK INDIAN RESERVATION; THAT MORNING

Charlie Charles was sitting in a lawn chair beneath the overhang when Caitlin and Cort Wesley exited their motel room fifteen miles from the Mohawk Reservation that morning.

"Something wrong, Charlie?" Caitlin asked him, noting the concern in his single working eye that looked sad in the sunlight.

"Back when I was like you, a real lawman, nobody talked. You never knew what was going on until it happened."

"Doesn't sound like things have changed much."

"No, today people talk and, when you're as old as I am, there's a lot of people know where to find me when they got something to say."

"You getting to the point anytime soon?" snapped Cort Wesley. Caitlin had watched his anxiety worsen almost by the hour, culminating the previous night when he slept not a single wink and spent most of it seated in a chair staring out the window at nothing at all. She knew that coming up here to take on the Hells Angels was the only thing keeping him sane, the strategy undertaken to get Dylan returned safe and sound.

Charlie Charles's expression didn't change, apparently in more of a rush than he was a moment before. "The motorcycle bikers who call themselves Angels first showed up on the Reservation when I was still young, sixty or thereabouts. They came to sell drugs and never stopped, even though I sugared plenty of their gas tanks and dropped Ex-Lax into their food while they were jailed before letting them go."

"Look, Mr. Charles," Cort Wesley started, stopping when Caitlin scolded him with her eyes.

The old Indian waited for him to continue and, when he didn't, resumed on his own. "Angels got plenty of enemies too, on both sides of the border. One of them was a mother to one of them who detested her son for the filth he'd splattered on the family name. She's a great grandmother now, spry woman of near ninety. We still talk from time to time, last night being the most recent."

"What is it, Charlie?" Caitlin asked, after he stopped.

"She's got a great nephew rides with the Angels these days. Hates him as much as she did her own boy the Mounties put in the grave after he robbed his eighth liquor store. This morning she called to tell me a bunch more Angels slept at the kid's house last night, which is across the street from hers. Word is they got an army massed ready to come across the border."

"Guess we know the war they're fixing to fight," Cort Wesley said, his tone more restrained.

"I've been up against them before."

"Gonna take more than sugar in their gas tanks to win this time, Charlie."

"I know, Ranger," he told Caitlin. "That's why I figured I'd come down here. We need to get an early start."

Back on the shores of the frozen river, Caitlin and Cort Wesley spent the rest of the morning following his instructions in what implements to gather from the woods, a laundry list of sorts recited from ancient memory through lips formed into a reflective smile.

"You've done this before," Caitlin noted, watching the old man's arthritic, knobby hands suddenly seem to straighten again as he nimbly worked them through twinelike vines, branches whittled by Cort Wesley to a razor-sharp edge, and rocks packed in snow to be laid across low-hanging branches.

Charlie Charles didn't miss a beat on his work as he replied. "When I was a boy, when the people of this land were even poorer, moonshining was our parents' sole source of income. Some criminals from downstate took issue with that, thought we were cutting into their liquor business. We weren't ready for them the first time they came, but we were the second."

"I'll bet there was no third," said Cort Wesley, carving the ends of more shaved stakes into lethal wooden daggers.

Charlie Charles just grinned again, looking as serene and content as the first time Cort Wesley and Caitlin had glimpsed him fishing through a hole in the ice. They watched as he twisted various nooses and nets out of nettle fiber and basswood-fiber twine lifted from the seemingly bottomless pockets of his deerskin vest and old trousers that bagged on him like a sack.

"When I was a boy, to guarantee the success of a hunt," he explained to Caitlin and Cort Wesley in a voice suddenly lacking in age, "we fasted and sacrificed before going into the forest. And we carried what we called hunting bundles on us that included charms shaped like animals, medicines, and talismen passed down from our ancestors."

Charlie Charles paused long enough to remove a fresh spool of homemade twine from his vest. He rose to his full height, which seemed suddenly taller, and measured off some lengths against the distance from the base of a tree to its lowest hanging branch.

"My father preferred the more traditional techniques, such as moose and deer calls that imitated the sounds that fawns make, dangerous if a wolf or wildcat came instead of the doe. We also hunted deer at night, when they came to the stream or lake for water and to eat the pads and stems of water lilies. Used a jacklight, torch, or lantern set on a special wooden platform in the front of a canoe with a darkened backstop to freeze them as they stood. Later, 'deer shining,' as it was called, was outlawed by the U.S. government except for Indians on federal reservations."

"With all due respect," said Cort Wesley, "hunting's not what this is about."

Charlie Charles didn't smile this time. "Isn't it?"

96

In the moments that followed, the mere lapse of time between breaths and heartbeats, Caitlin saw it all happening in her mind in conjunction with the screaming. The first line of defense they'd laid in the woods were Charlie Charles's own deadly version of the old deadfall traps used to snare game animals.

"How do you know they'll be coming this way?" she'd asked him.

The old Indian had grinned at her. "Because I cut back the woods thirty years ago to make sure their fathers would."

The traditional deadfall trap was a simple mechanism made of sticks supporting a heavy weight pivoting on the tip of the more upright one. A trigger would be planted at the base of the lower stick that, when jarred, would collapse the weight atop the animal. Charlie Charles's more modern version used the identical principles with triggering branches instead of sticks and foot-long wood tips shaved to a thin, pointed edge instead of mere weight. Come that night, the Angels unfortunate enough to trip these outlying traps would send the others scurrying through the dark in shock and confusion.

The first series of screams told Caitlin that that was exactly what had happened an instant before a pair of arrows buzzed the air, seemingly within milliseconds of each other, downing the armed Hells Angels standing on either side of LaChance. One of them fell backward into a fourth man, his pistol jerked into the air and the shot he managed to get off was sent skyward.

Caitlin lurched toward him, as Cort Wesley charged LaChance, jerking his shotgun into the air. Caitlin saw him struggling with the bigger biker, the two men battling for leverage and control of the shotgun, while she pounced on the pistol-wielding Angel just lowering it into firing position.

The horrible screams of the men impaled by the deadfall traps continued to pierce the silence of the night. Fresh wails joined those as more Hells Angels, funneled into what was essentially a layered obstacle course of pain and death, fell victim to more of Charlie Charles's old-fashioned traps.

Storm-downed limbs, lashed high between trees with heavy rope, dropped in a speed-gathering arc once the camouflaged rock holding them in place as a contact point was struck.

Buckets of road tar heated by open flame, and then nailed on a swivel atop branches, would spill their thick, oozing contents upon anyone who so much as jostled the lower hanging connected branches.

The hardness of the earth rendered the old covered hole trap infeasible, so Charlie Charles opted instead to hammer more razor-pointed wooden spikes into the ground camouflaged by brush and snow. Add to these what amounted to tripwire strung in tight strands of twine and tied between stakes. Those lucky enough to avoid that could still find their boots and feet pierced by the sharpened spikes, and those who fell victim to the tripwires were almost certain to fall forward into the deadly snare waiting to pierce flesh and muscle as if they were pudding.

Other than the deadfalls meant to inspire panic, Caitlin had seen no real rhyme or reason to the way Charlie Charles had set his traps. But she knew he had one all the same, just as she knew he'd be able to detect which traps had been sprung with every cry of agony or scream for help. The latter would come mostly with the simplest snares, basically just a wire noose suspended in the likely paths of the Hells Angels rushing desperately through the woods. Once a boot hit the center of the noose it would snap into place, tightening over the foot or ankle the more the man tried to free himself. Unless the victim decided to chew his own leg or foot off, the wire would hold him for as long as need be. Charlie Charles had also rigged some lifting snares that would actually jerk their victims into the air, but professed to have far less confidence in their functionality.

Caitlin took advantage of the screams that were coming with virtually no pause at all, glimpses at the edges of the woods caught in the moonlight of black-garbed figures caught by snares, impaled by spikes, slammed by heavy tree stumps, or covered in road tar that steamed over them. She struggled with the much bigger and heavier man, letting him think he had regained control of his pistol before jerking it around toward him and adding her finger to his over the trigger. He looked puzzled when the shot resounded, hitting him like a swift kick to the gut, before his eyes locked open, his weight collapsing atop her like a piano.

Cort Wesley and LaChance, meanwhile, continued to fight for control of the shotgun, the chambered shell exploding from the barrel with an ear-numbing roar and piercing the nearer truck's fuel tank. Gasoline flooded out, first splashing and then rapidly spreading across the surface of the ice in a glistening pool.

Screams continued to split the still night air, Charlie Charles's traps working as well as his skill with a bow. Caitlin continued to struggle to get herself out from beneath the bulbous frame pinning her in place. But she couldn't find enough traction on the ice to change her position or push the biker off and ended up doing her best to shimmy free as his blood pooled around her, mixing with the spilled gasoline.

Ten feet away she saw Cort Wesley finally gain the upper hand, LaChance's grasp on him slackening after taking blows to his face with the shotgun's butt. Even through the dark, she could see Cort Wesley's eyes inflamed with rage, certain to batter the kidnapper of his boy to pulp if she didn't intervene.

Caitlin thought she could hear the sickening *thwack* of bone mashing, a sound curiously like that of stepping on a fallen ice cube. LaChance keeled over backward to the ice, Cort Wesley on him in an instant, continuing to hammer away with the shotgun butt that was now cracked and coated with a thick wash of gore. She fought to free herself from the dead man still pinning her, wanting to stop Cort Wesley from murdering this man and finding himself tumbling into a pit of violence and despair even Dylan's return might not be able to vanquish.

Caitlin finally slipped free of the body, the ice at once frigid beneath her again as she scrabbled sideways, struggling to regain her footing.

"Cort Wes—"

Her call was interrupted by the clacking of gunfire and the sight of the Hells Angels who'd managed to avoid Charlie Charles's traps approaching the ice with weapons firing away in their direction. Their bullets pinged off the ice, narrowly missing the stream of gasoline spreading across it like spilled milk on a tile floor.

Where was the old Indian, the arrows that were supposed to cover this precise contingency?

"Cort Wesley!"

He looked up from the pulp LaChance's face had been reduced to, just as flecks of ice exploded around him from the shooters slipping and siding toward them across the ice. Caitlin continued scrambling for the pistol she'd dropped on LaChance's command, Cort Wesley righting the shotgun on the advancing bikers and racking a shell into the chamber.

Not much good the twelve-gauge was going to do from this distance against eight, maybe ten Hells Angels. But Cort Wesley fired it anyway, barrel angled downward for the ice instead of the advancing shooters.

BANG! BANG! BANG!

Caitlin wasn't sure which of the shots ignited the gasoline; maybe a lethal combination of the heat and spark generated from all three. Either way the flames caught and spread as fast as they could devour the gasoline spilled from the truck's massive tank.

The flames were waist high by the time they reached the bikers, fresh screams erupting that were worse than any of the others had been. Some tried to make it back to shore. Others rolled over the fuel-splattered ice in a futile attempt to put out the fire that was eating them alive.

Caitlin wanted to clamp her hands over her ears, wanted to be somewhere far from this place, away from ice and drugs and death. The stench of burning flesh, hair, and clothes, claimed the air, the noxious odor of the burned-up gasoline all but gone. As the bikers dropped in the spasms and throes of death, she imagined their blood boiling inside their ravaged skin, felt her mind ravaged by a degree of prolonged violence worse than any gunfight she'd ever experienced. She realized she'd actually found her gun and had taken it in hand with no one left to shoot at, something that suddenly seemed surprisingly civilized compared to what she'd just been party to.

She wanted to vomit again, just as she had when disgust forced her onto the shoulder of the four-lane beyond Malcolm Arno's complex. It was the sight of Cort Wesley that stopped her. Standing tall and erect over LaChance's still form, silhouetted by the orange glow of the flames that seemed afraid to consume him. Shotgun still in hand, he looked past Caitlin toward the burning bodies along the shore and lingering screams deeper in the woods. He stood like a silent sentinel—emotionless, more statue than man. She stared at him and wondered if this was the man he'd been before his sons came into his life, the man who'd done things in Iraq he still couldn't talk about. He'd come home to work as a mob enforcer laying waste to the Mexican gangs who ended up seizing the drug trade a few years later anyway. Wondered if this was the man he'd stay if Dylan were lost to him forever.

But Caitlin glimpsed hope in Cort Wesley in the form of the revulsion that twisted and turned itself onto his expression after he finally acknowledged the smells that had almost sickened her. He became man again, the machine vanquished and the man recalling the small package LaChance had tossed him before blood trumped the night.

Caitlin watched him pluck it from the ice and unwrap it, watched him shudder violently, the pain and desperation stretched across his features sucking the hope from the world, as the last of the screaming finally faded in the night.

97

MOHAWK INDIAN RESERVATION; THE PRESENT

Caitlin found her legs again and moved to him. Cort Wesley didn't look up, didn't seem to even be present until he extended the unwrapped package to her as if it contained something fragile.

"It's Dylan's. I know it," she heard him say just as she took the package and regarded the tip of a finger inside, nail and all, looking more like a movie prop than something real.

"We're going home, Cort Wesley. Call in every Ranger we can." Her voice sounded like someone else's. She knew she was speaking but didn't remember forming the words. She coughed from the stench in the air flooding her lungs, as if the whole world had gone sour. "Just like my father did when he raided the Church of the Redeemer."

· · ·

"I broke my leg, you can believe that," Charlie Charles said after they found him shivering amid the frosted brush into which he'd managed to crawl. "Sorry I wasn't as much good to you as I should have been."

They covered him with their coats to ward off shock and exposure.

"We've gotta go, Charlie," Caitlin told him.

"Far as I'm concerned you were never here."

Cort Wesley seemed to be studying the horizon for the sight of flashing lights, while Caitlin's gaze turned on the smoldering flames finally giving up their hold on the night that still smelled of death.

"Gonna be tough to explain all this," she said to the old Indian.

Charlie Charles forced out a smile through his chattering teeth. "I'll tell them it was the spirits of my ancestors rising up to fight by my side one last time."

"You figure they'll buy it?"

The old Indian shrugged halfheartedly. "When you're as old as me, people don't listen much to what you have to say anyway."

"You've got your gunfighter, Jones," Caitlin said to the man in Washington as soon as she and Cort Wesley were on the road heading toward Albany International Airport a hundred and fifty miles away, the Reservation and all it had wrought shrinking behind them.

"What made you change your mind, Ranger?"

"Malcolm Arno is a turd that needs flushing. Let's leave it at that."

She could picture Jones smiling smugly on the other end of the line. "Whatever you say."

"You get those satellite imaging reports back yet?"

"Got the shots, and the bill, right here. This was a seven-figure recon job, all the retasking I had to pull off."

"We get our money's worth?"

"The outlaw was spot on, Ranger. There's a whole warren of underground bunkers, a few the size of football fields, running beneath Arno's land."

"Why the fake grass?"

"I was getting to that. Thermal dynamics in the satellite shots reveal a heat signature that would make it impossible to grow normal grass over what they're doing down there."

"Don't tell me, some kind of shooting."

"Constantly, as in all the time. Shooting up a storm. Heavy, heavy training by the look of things."

"Looks like you were right about that war Arno's fixing to fight."

"Just like I was right about the gunfighter who can stop it. Problem is, Arno's not fixing to fight it, he's fixing to *lead* it. Those weapons you found inside that truck? Picture them distributed to right-wing hate groups from coast-to-coast."

"A weapon for every wacko."

"A billion bucks' worth buys you a lot of heartache, even with inflation. That's why it's a good thing we've got a gunfighter on the job now."

"I could use those satellite feeds."

"They can't be e-mailed but I can messenger the spreads to you via private jet."

"Bit pricier than FedEx, isn't it?"

"You're about to wage a war, Ranger. I think I can justify the expense."

"You being straight with me, Jones?"

"About what?"

"About no bomb that's gonna mysteriously fall on Arno's complex. No mysterious accidental launching of a cruise missile."

"That's a good idea. You just think of it?"

"Arno's holding Cort Wesley Masters's son in there. Sent us a tip of the boy's goddamn finger to prove it."

"Then the cruise missile's already en route."

"Come again?"

"You, Ranger, and there's absolutely no stopping it."

Caitlin's next call was to D. W. Tepper. "Captain, I—"

"Don't say a word, don't say a goddamn word."

She could feel the anger and resignation in his voice, words pushed out between drags on a cigarette carving an indentation into his fingers he was squeezing it so hard.

"We're dealing with a shit storm of epic proportions," Tepper continued. "A Category Five by the name of Caitlin."

"I'm on my way back now, Captain. I can be in the office by noon maybe."

"Forget the office. Shit Storm Caitlin might as well have swept it away as far as you're concerned. We gotta meet somewhere else."

"Name the place."

"How about the Alamo? Can't think of anywhere more fitting under the circumstances."

PART TEN

HOUSTON—Special teams of Texas Rangers will be deployed to the Texas-Mexico border to deal with increasing violence because the federal government has failed to address growing problems there, Governor Rick Perry said Thursday.

"It is an expansive effort with the Rangers playing a more high-profile role than they've ever played before," Perry said of the Department of Public Safety's elite investigative unit.

—The Associated Press, September 11, 2009

98

"You're going to be getting a call," the man told Guillermo Paz over his satellite phone.

"I know."

"You have our blessing, Colonel."

"I don't recall asking for it."

"I'd like to get you the specs of the site. Where should I send the messenger?"

"Out here?" Paz asked him, mystified. "Don't bother, I don't need them."

"Don't need them?"

"I saw this place in a dream. I know what must be done."

"In a dream," the American repeated.

"You don't believe in such things?"

"Mister, I try to believe in life and death, but death keeps getting in the way."

There was a pause, Paz listening to the man breathe against the backdrop of a mechanical whirring sound, as if he were on a treadmill or something.

"Sandoval complained about what you did to those safe houses."

"Safe houses," Paz repeated. "That's what he called them?"

"Look, unofficially I applaud your work. It's just that this isn't a well-funded operation, everything sub rosa."

"Sub rosa?"

"Under the radar, Colonel, and the payoffs to keep those houses operational financed a good portion of your weapons."

"Tell me which weapons, so I can destroy them right now."

"Colonel—"

"I won't fight a war for you on the blood of children, *Señor* Smith."

"I told you, my name's Jones. And this particular war wasn't in the original plans."

"Not yours, perhaps."

"Who's then?"

"You're not a believer, so why should I bother with an explanation? Our fates are entwined because of Caitlin Strong. You should have known it would come to this."

Another pause came. More whirring that slowed finally and then cut off, the American's breathing finally sounding normal.

"And I'm glad it has, Colonel. This is a more important war, much more."

"All wars are important to the people who fight them," Paz reminded.

"Especially when you win," said Jones.

99

SAN ANTONIO; THE PRESENT

Tepper was already standing in the Alamo chapel in front of one of the display cases when Caitlin entered through the heavy double doors of the famed facade.

"I thought I warned you about Malcolm Arno having friends in higher places than we can reach."

"Must've slipped my mind."

"Well, slip it back in. He claims you threatened him with bodily harm and conducted an illegal search and seizure."

"He's lying."

"The threats are on tape."

"Made by him toward me."

"Not according to the governor's office, Department of Public Safety's Office of Professional Responsibility, the Midland police, the FBI, and the federal marshals who took the computers out of our office this morning."

"What?"

"Shit Storm Caitlin, remember? They're looking for evidence of abuse and conspiracy against Arno and the Patriot Sun."

The Alamo Chapel, the one structure to actually survive Santa Ana's assault mostly intact, had been converted into a museumlike shrine to the famed battle when fewer than two hundred defenders had managed to hold back an army of four thousand for thirteen days. Various display cases dotted a floor that stretched sixty yards from front to back. Plaques memorializing various participants in the battle and portraits of the defenders, along with scenes frozen from the battle, hung upon the stone walls.

The reconditioned building was, of course, far stronger structurally than its predecessor. Instead of adobe, it was built of concrete and stone with a yellowed stucco finish eerily close to that of the original. The building's remaining windows, seven in all including the three in the alcove wings, were simple yet majestic and let just enough light in to bring the interior to life without creating the kind of glow that would have detracted from the reverence. Besides the sun, the shrine's sole lighting came from a trio of dangling, period-accurate chandeliers.

As always when she visited the Alamo, Caitlin found herself reconstituting the battle in her brain, inserting herself into it with a 7.62mm minigun to mow Santa Ana's troops down as they laid siege. There were fortified rooms in three of the chapel's four corners, one of which had been the hiding place of the women and children who lived to tell the original tale of what had transpired, spread through the generations since.

"You seen the paper since you landed?" Tepper asked her, swinging away from the display case featuring one of Jim Bowie's original knives that bore his name, although not one of those actually recovered from the premises.

As Caitlin suspected, he'd been smoking up a storm, evidenced by the brown stains painted on his fingers and nails along with the smells of nicotine and tar clinging to his person like a shroud. But he looked more alive somehow, his eyes bursting with vitality and anger.

"No."

"Don't look. We're on the front page and not in a flattering light either. They're calling this a near Waco. They're calling you a trigger-happy loose cannon who's got Arno in her sights to settle old scores."

"It was my father killed his, not the other way around."

"Media has a way of twisting things, don't it?"

"Goddamnit it, D.W. . . ."

"Have you ever once heard the word 'patience'?"

"It's somewhere in my vocabulary."

"Not lately. You need to stay out of this until I can get things properly sorted out."

"I can't."

"Did I just hear you say that?"

"Arno's holding Dylan Masters hostage at the Patriot Sun. While things get sorted out, the sick son of a bitch could be trimming off more of the boy's body parts."

"Will you do as I say just this once, Caitlin, for God's sake?"

"I'm telling you Malcolm Arno's just like his father, D.W. Crazy as the day is long with an army of followers who think just like him and can't wait to turn their insanity and hatred into a shooting war."

"Well, Ranger, some of those followers come with titles like 'senator' and 'congressman' in front of their names, and Arno's got all of them raising holy hell. Haven't you been watching the news?"

"I've been a little busy."

"Right, that was the last call I took before coming here, something about you blowing up the whole Mohawk Indian Reservation."

"Not exactly."

"Then try this: obstruction of justice, trespassing, civil rights violations, unlawful entry, unlawful search and seizure, unlawful possession and discharge of a weapon, kidnapping."

"Kidnapping?"

"Then there's a hundred-year-old Indian who claims the ghosts of his ancestors killed a dozen Hells Angels and put maybe two dozen more in the hospital. One of the dead ones happens to go by the name of LaChance, although there wasn't much recognizable left of him. Any of this sound familiar?"

"Some."

"Tribal chief ID'ed you, Caitlin. Said you extorted him into giving you what you wanted."

"Yeah, the details of the drug shipments coming in across the border over tribal lands," Caitlin conceded.

"The operative word being *tribal*," Tepper snapped at her. "Since when do the Texas Rangers have jurisdiction on land the federal and local authorities don't even go near? Hell, the Canadians pulled out all their monitors and guards three years ago."

"Which means nobody is doing a damn thing about fifty billion in dope coming across that border. Sound familiar?"

"Different border altogether, Ranger, and different times."

"You talking about the same Rangers I am, chasing bandits and druggers across the Rio Grande with guns blazing?"

Tepper turned back to the display case, Caitlin studying his suddenly flat reflection in the glass. "Lots of bodies buried in the desert on that account."

"Now it's frozen rivers. Only difference I can see, Captain."

"Where's your evidence?"

"Burned or under water, except for the guns."

"What guns?"

"I called it into Jones. Homeland Security's got them now."

"*Our* Homeland Security?"

"Is there another?"

"Don't crack wise with me, Ranger. You're not exactly banking a lot of friends these days as it is."

"I need to get into Arno's compound, Captain, and I need the Rangers with me."

"You need to lay low or risk being arrested by any of five different agencies on any of a dozen charges. More probably before the day is through. I can't even keep track anymore."

"I've got a source who puts the boy on the premises under duress. And if that's not enough, I've got the tip of Dylan Torres's finger on ice. You want a DNA match, I'm sure I can get it."

"Look, Ranger, I know you wish these were Earl Strong's times when all you needed was a hunch to ride roughshod over the world. But they're not. Internet and the twenty-four-hour news cycle subjects us to a scrutiny we can usually dodge down here in our little corner of the world. But you've expanded your territory to the whole damn country."

"Not me, Captain—Malcolm Arno. He gets his weapons distributed and extremist army in place, and anyone who doesn't abide by his beliefs or convictions can consider themselves an endangered species. That judge in Galveston was just the beginning."

"And you wanna take him down?"

"Hell, yeah."

"Then let the system do its job. I'll ride with you all the way to Austin on horseback if that's what it takes to make people listen."

"You're not listening to *me*, D.W. Arno figures as long as he's got Dylan Torres as a hostage, I'll stay out of his hair. Give him the time he needs to move his plans to the next stage."

Tepper spun toward her again, his actual face looking craggier, more pitted and gaunt than its reflection. "How many trained men you figure he can muster with arms in that compound?"

"Three, maybe four hundred seems a safe bet, almost all with military backgrounds to boot."

"Unless this goes Waco. Then we're talking, what, three, four thousand innocent bystanders on top of that?"

"Something like that, I suppose."

"A potential massacre, in other words, if we go in with guns blazing."

"You tell my father the same thing before the Church of the Redeemer raid?"

"I didn't have to."

A couple snapping pictures joined them by the display, so Caitlin and Tepper slid sideways to a larger case featuring original art from the era depicting the battle as it was believed to have happened at that time.

So much had been lost to myth and legend that nobody was really sure of all the details, when and how all the principals had died. Caitlin and Tepper fixed their eyes forward, speaking squarely to each other's reflections now.

"Right, Captain, because Jim Strong came up with a way to minimize the casualties."

"What's your point?"

"What if I could do the same thing?"

"You and Masters alone, some kind of half-assed commando mission?"

"Yes or no, Captain?"

"You're not asking for my permission, Ranger, so don't expect me to give it."

"Anybody give Jim Strong permission to stake out the parking lot of the Tackle and Gun twenty years ago?"

"That was different."

"No, it wasn't."

"You know your problem, Ranger?"

"Oh boy . . ."

"Shut up and listen. That day in the parking lot, watching that gunfight, screwed up something inside you, messed up your balance and left you seeing the world a different way. If your granddad Earl was still alive at the time, he would've counseled you on the pain that goes with it. But your dad wasn't much for that kind of talk and figured it would pass. Only it didn't, and I get the sense you've been waiting for this day ever since. That you and Arno glimpsing each other across that gravel set you on a course of violence that could only lead to this."

Tepper's comments stung Caitlin with the harshness of their disapproval, especially since she couldn't dispute a single one of them. Two forces had indeed been born that day outside the Tackle and Gun, meshed on opposite sides of the spectrum until the time they were destined to converge again.

"Jim Strong had a plan, Captain," she said to spare herself further pondering on the subject.

"I was there, Ranger."

"Easter Sunday's just two days off."

Tepper turned from his scrutiny of a drawing of the Alamo wall being breached. "Tell me you didn't just say that."

"Can't."

"Your dad and I had a dozen Rangers. You're gonna need an army."

"I know," Caitlin told him.

100

SAN ANTONIO; THE PRESENT

Cort Wesley sat outside the entrance to the Alamo on a park bench in the grassy plaza, the ghost of Leroy Epps next to him with absolutely nothing to say. Could be Cort Wesley's imagination couldn't conjure up any intelligent words for him to impart or could be old Leroy was at as much of a loss here as he was.

Cort Wesley remembered Leroy once telling him he had no desire to get out of Huntsville. The world had just gotten too big, nothing seemed to go right, and nobody seemed happy. Inside, life was laid out for you and you were spared any decision-making, most of which had turned out bad for him. He figured his transformation into a better man inside the brutal prison known as The Walls was due primarily to that burden having been lifted from him so he could turn all his attention inward since there was no place else to look.

For the first time, Cort Wesley figured he knew to what Leroy Epps had been referring. Relationships were the problem. Nothing ever came from them but pain, no matter what you tried to tell yourself.

"Nothing to say, champ?" he said out loud. "You never been at a loss for words before as long as I've known you."

Epps finally grinned. *"Got one of those root beers, bubba?"*

"Sorry, no."

"Then I got nothing to tell you."

"I'm happy to do the talking, champ: I'm gonna get my son back."

"Glad to hear that."

"Normally you'd have something critical to say on the subject."

"You get me that root beer, I'll see what I can do."

The old man turned away, as if he didn't want Cort Wesley to see the thoughts lurking behind his milky, bloodshot eyes. Cort Wesley found himself fearing Epps knew something bad was coming and didn't want to pass any hint of it to a mere mortal, at least not for less than a root beer. Funny thing being, Cort Wesley probably would've gone and bought him a bottle, if Caitlin Strong hadn't emerged through the Alamo's big double doors. Anything to get some worthwhile advice from one of the few people in the world he trusted, dead or alive.

"Well?" Cort Wesley asked when Caitlin was close enough to hear.

"Captain Tepper told me I'm gonna need an army."

It was all she needed to say, the statement's implication, coupled with her dour expression, saying the rest.

"So what do we now, Ranger?"

"We take his advice."

101

Midland, Texas; the present

The workman who doused himself in cheap aftershave to cover the sewer smell that hovered over him like a cloud had been waiting outside Malcolm Arno's office for three hours when his receptionist finally relented and sent him in.

"What can I do for you?" Arno asked the man, after opening a window in spite of the air-conditioning.

The man remained standing before his desk, soiled hands scraped raw from futile washing held by his side.

"You can sit down."

"No, sir, I can't," the man said. "I don't deserve it."

"And why's that?"

"Your daddy was a preacher."

"He was a minister."

"But you're not."

"It wasn't my calling."

"So you can't hear my confession."

"We've got two reverends and a priest on the grounds to handle that."

"It's not them I've wronged, sir, it's you."

The first wave of the man's smell reached Arno, tolerable for the moment. "You work for me here?"

The man nodded. "You were kind enough to take me in, give me a chance after I fell into the bottle for some years."

"We all have our demons."

"I've done you wrong, Mr. Arno, and I can't live with that no more."

"What's your name?"

"Daniel, sir, Daniel Killane."

Arno felt his heart skip a beat in the very moment the rest of the man's stench hit him like a freight train, nearly spilling him out of his chair. What he'd just heard, though, was more than enough to keep him upright and listening, his recognition of the foul odor pushed as far back as his mind would hold it.

"I believe our families have a history between them."

"What are you doing here, Mr. Killane?" Arno asked, feeling as if he was listening to himself talk.

"Like I said, you were kind enough to—"

"I mean in my office now. What's this wrong you've committed?"

"I cut the bonds off a boy's wrists and then I called a Texas Ranger to say he was here."

Maybe it was the air-conditioning, or a chill blast of air pushed through the window by an advancing storm, but Malcolm Arno suddenly felt cold enough to shiver. "What Texas Ranger?"

"Caitlin Strong."

Arno wasn't sure if Daniel Killane was still speaking or had stopped. He gazed across his desk and saw this soiled mess of a man as the young boy his father had followed down into the root cellar to pretty much end both their childhoods. He wanted to feel hatred for him but all he felt was . . . nothing, until his thoughts turned back to Caitlin Strong.

"Her daddy was the one who killed yours after yours shot my mama."

"Sit down, Mr. Killane."

"I—"

"Please."

Killane finally took the chair, easing himself to the edge to leave as much of the upholstery free of him as possible.

"What did you tell this Texas Ranger?"

"I'm sorry, Mr. Arno, I'm real sorry."

"Just tell me what you told her."

"Everything she asked about this place, mostly about its defenses. How many guards, what kind of guns . . ."

"Where to find the boy?"

Killane squeezed his eyes closed before nodding. Arno thought he might be finished, but then they snapped open with a pleading desperation like none he'd ever witnessed before.

"She's coming, Mr. Arno, she's coming with an army probably led by that boy's father. They're planning a full frontal assault. Storm this place like it was the beach at Normandy with plenty of men and guns both."

"A full frontal assault," Arno repeated.

Killane nodded again, leaving his eyes open this time.

"The Ranger tell you when it was coming?"

Killane's eyes did the nodding this time. "Yes, sir, so I could make myself scarce, maybe take flight if I so choose." Those eyes growing moist now, even his tears seeming to stink. "I didn't know what I was doing. When I saw that boy, it brought everything from that day back—"

"Mr. Killane . . ."

"—how much it hurt when I found my mom shot, so I—"

"Mr. Killane . . ."

"—did something bad without thinking on it, just like the days when the only friend I had was the bottle. But you changed all that. You took me in, gave me a chance, and this is—"

"Mr. Killane!" And this time, Arno snapped upright so fast he jostled the items atop his desk blotter.

"—how I repay you."

Daniel Killane lapsed into silence, having spoken his peace.

"You still haven't told me when the assault's coming," Arno said.

"Easter Sunday, sir, sometime just after midnight."

Arno felt suddenly unsteady on his feet, grasping the edge of his desk for support. *Easter Sunday* . . . History repeating itself to a T. This Ranger wasn't only a master of irony, but also an adroit strategist, just like her father.

"Can you forgive me, sir?" he heard the human sewer ask him. "Can you find it in your heart?"

"Forgiveness is for God."

"Maybe if we prayed together, maybe if we prayed. . . ."

Malcolm Arno was thinking instead about lifting the .45 from his top desk drawer and putting a slug in the man. Right in the face to obliterate his desperate eyes and teeth half rotted by crystal meth. Drown the man's very identity, leave him with nothing to take to the grave with him.

"Could we pray, sir?"

Then again, he might be of some use yet.

"I'll leave the grounds. I'll pack up and be on my way," Killane continued, hanging his head so low it looked disconnected from his neck.

Arno circled around to the front of his desk and lay his hand down on the man's shoulder, the shirt beneath his touch wet with rancid perspiration that nearly made him gag.

"You'll do no such thing, Mr. Killane," he said, channeling his father more than he ever had before. "Now, let's pray together, you and me. . . ."

102

ODESSA, TEXAS; THE PRESENT

"It's good to see you again, Colonel," Caitlin said, rising with Cort Wesley as Guillermo Paz neared their table in Odessa's Pancake Alley restaurant right off I-20.

"I've dreamed of you a lot lately, Ranger," Paz said. "I knew you'd be calling."

"Wanna thank you for the help you extended to Cort Wesley down in Mexico."

Paz studied them both briefly. "It wasn't enough, apparently."

"Not yet."

"I need your help, Colonel," she'd told him over his satellite phone the day before.

"So I've been told."

"By who?"

"We have mutual friends."

"Jesus Christ . . . Don't tell me—"

"Who do you think set this all up, Ranger? Who do you think put me together with Sandoval?"

Caitlin thought of Jones manipulating the scene, arranging a private army for Sandoval to wage war on the drug cartels to eliminate further incursions over the border. Homeland Security indeed.

"This army you're building is gonna wipe out the cartel druggers."

"That was the plan."

"*Was?*"

"Until something more important came along," Paz told her.

Paz looked around the old coffee shop, Caitlin still wondering how much this Pancake Alley resembled the place where her father had met Beth Ann Killane, allowing him to save many lives while losing the one he cared about the most. Fresh-baked pies were on display in a case with a mirror back. Various pastries, almost surely homemade as well, sat in cake stands with a plastic cover. A single waitress roamed the booths and tables wielding a Bunn coffeepot, ready with a smile and a refill. For a moment Caitlin saw her as Beth Ann herself and half expected to see Jim Strong seated at his regular back table where he'd turned her as an informant against the Reverend Maxwell Arno.

"Where are your men, Colonel?" Caitlin asked him.

"En route over land via a route cleared by our mutual friend in Washington. Their weapons are coming here separately." He looked outside as if to read the sky. "They'll be arriving anytime now."

"I've got the satellite imagery right here," Caitlin said, reaching for the photo arrays laid across an open chair.

"No need, Ranger," Paz told her, seeming disinterested. "Our mutual friend has already briefed me." His eyes moved to Cort Wesley. "Your son is inside this place."

Cort Wesley nodded, very slowly. "Yes, sir, Colonel."

"It will be my pleasure to help free him."

"How many men you bringing?"

"I was told to expect two hundred soldiers, so I planned for three hundred. But I wasn't told how many of them had seen actual combat."

"From what we've heard about the Patriot Sun, plenty," Caitlin chimed in.

"Have you ever read Foch, Ranger?" Paz asked, the chair beneath him creaking from the strain of supporting his bulk.

"Who?"

"Ferdinand Foch, a French military theorist. He wrote that victory is a thing of the will."

"Well," said Cort Wesley, trying to smile, "we got plenty of that."

103

MIDLAND, TEXAS; MIDNIGHT, EASTER SUNDAY

Malcolm Arno watched the throngs of those living within the complex walls pouring into the meeting hall for the midnight service his father had so looked forward to every Easter. Said he enjoyed it more than the sunrise and morning sessions that followed. Said he could never remember a single Easter mass where the weather didn't cooperate, convincing him his fated blessing had come from the very power he worshipped.

True to that form, tonight's weather was clear as a bell. A cold front had passed through earlier in the evening, carrying the promise of rain that never actually fell. The humidity and desert fog it had wiped from the scene would make it impossible for Caitlin Strong's army to approach the complex surreptitiously, commando-style. And if they tried, one of Arno's many spotters or the early-warning security systems he had already in place, would betray their presence and make them easy fodder for the snipers and gunmen his field commanders had placed in the towers and wall—all camouflaged so as to make sure nothing deterred the enemy's approach. The bulk of his best-trained troops were already concentrated outside the walls, prepared to prevent the enemy from fleeing and to come up on their rear flank to catch them in a deadly cross fire.

Greeting his followers, the flock that worshipped and revered him, was nonetheless difficult with each passing minute that could see the first crackle of gunfire. Arno hoped the attack, and its far more brutal counter on the part of his men, would not come until all those attending the service were safely settled in the meeting hall within cinderblock walls reinforced with steel sheeting. For the spillover, the service was being piped into the cafeteria as well as every room in the complex outfitted for television via wireless technology, if that didn't beat all.

Arno wondered what his father would make of all this, how far Malcolm had advanced his dream. But that thought spurred others of the great man's ultimate downfall at the hands of a traitor and his own lecherous desires.

He'd long known the truth behind Max Arno's descent into the church basement on Danny Killane's trail; he'd seen it in his father's eyes when they fell on the boy up in the front rows reserved for special invitees. But he'd managed to resist accepting that truth until that boy, now a stench-riddled human excrement of an adult, returned to his life.

The force of that reality should have made it easier for Arno to clip off the tip of the Masters boy's finger out of spite and rage. But then he'd met the kid's big dark eyes, same color as the hair that swam past his shoulders. Something stirred inside Arno, a longing buried deep enough to push back with a gush of self-hatred and guilt. He saw him through his father's eyes and the boy became Daniel Killane at the age of sixteen. Past and present swirled together, merging, the son struck by the same predilections as the father, now threatening to become the ruin of both of them.

"Mal?" Jed Kean's voice had shocked him back to the present and shook his eyes off the boy. "Why don't you let me do it?"

"No," Arno shot back at him, "this one's mine."

And he'd held the boy's eyes as he fitted the clippers into place and drove the blades together with a squeeze of his hand. The sound was like that of a branch giving way, a single crackle as the clippers bit through bone. The boy winced and clenched his teeth, but didn't cry out as heavy tears rolled down both his cheeks. He kept staring at Arno, never looking down at his finger, and Arno couldn't remember a pair of darker eyes ever in his life, filled not with terror but an unbridled hatred.

In the end he'd finally left the room utterly unnerved and unable to get Cort Wesley Masters's son out of his head. Was this how his father had regarded young Danny Killane? Was the Arno line doomed by a sinful nature that threatened to overcome the just ends both father and son had sought?

Malcolm Arno had drank himself to sleep that night, awaking the next morning with nothing more than a foggy recollection that made denial all the easier to bear.

"Everthing's set," Kean said, having come up alongside him without Arno noticing, on the steps of the meeting hall.

"You going to the service, Jed?"

"I'm going wherever you go."

Kean's already big torso had been made even thicker by the Kevlar vest he wore under his jacket. He had an M16 slung around his shoulder, none of those passing by them paying it much heed, even on Easter Sunday, since guns here were as common as dog leashes in the outside world.

Arno swept his gaze about the towers and walls where armed men viewed the perimeter through night vision goggles and telescopic scopes. Sixty of his best, all military with actual combat experience, were concealed by the camouflage of ground and brush cover outside the wall. The pattern of their concentration was meant to quell the expected invasion by funneling the attackers into a narrow corridor so the anticipated cross fire could better chew them up. Might all be over so fast that those enjoying their Easter service would never know the difference. All the gates had been closed, barred, and reinforced, along with all other points of entry to guard against any of the attackers somehow making it through or around the laid ambush.

"I think my father was a weak man, Kean. I think he gave into temptation and let it destroy him." Arno held the big man's stare longer than he'd intended to. "I've never shared that with a single soul."

"I appreciate the honor."

"We must be strong where he was weak. We must protect all we have built."

Kean nodded, while beyond him long lines of Patriot Sun members continued to stream into the meeting hall.

"I'm giving the sermon myself tonight, Jed. The topic is how bones heal stronger after they're broken, a lesson I've applied to my own life. Appreciate your opinion when I'm done."

"Be my pleasure."

"And this Texas Ranger's got no real evidence that boy is on the premises, other than the word of a drunk," Arno said, feeling that same stirring again. "So however this goes I want him disposed of with the rest of the trash by morning."

"That'd be my pleasure too," Kean nodded.

104

MIDLAND, TEXAS; EASTER SUNDAY

Malcolm Arno took to the pulpit at one in the morning sharp after a lavish introduction from the old priest who'd baptized him and presided over the funeral of his father. A smattering of applause filled the meeting hall at that, neither dignified nor appropriate for the occasion, but he enjoyed hearing it nonetheless.

There wasn't a seat open before him, the overflow pressed up against every wall leaving only the doorways free. Barely room to breathe, much less move. But the cool breeze easing in through the open windows made the packed confines tolerable, even pleasant. Jed Kean stood in clear view just to his side on floor level, facing the audience with the curled cord of his plastic earpiece worn as unobtrusively as possible.

Arno felt his emotions rising to a crescendo even before he began his sermon. Just gazing out at the wide-eyed faces that had come because they shared his beliefs and his dream filled him with satisfaction. These were the people with whom he'd be celebrating the transitional events of the coming months, transitional because America could never think of itself the same way once his masses rose to take back what was theirs. Arno didn't care whether it was called a civil war, a revolution, or whatever else. To him it was a moment in time that would mark the passing of one age to another. In this moment of triumph, he grasped how far he'd come, how far beyond the Church of the Redeemer he had taken his movement. And then he knew what he had to tell these people, beginning his sermon to them by utterly diverting from his planned remarks.

"You are not zealots, or cultists, or dwellers on the fringe," he spoke into the microphone. "You are Americans in search of an America thought gone forever, stripped from us by those who fail to appreciate or grasp the core values on which this country was built. They drown us in debt and turn freedom into a punch line, a talking point to be hoisted up the flagpole when it suits their needs so they can face and salute it even as they turn their backs on those like you and me. But that cannot be allowed to continue. That cannot—"

Thwamp . . .

Arno stopped suddenly, the sound that reached him from outside not right, a trip wire triggered in his mind. Could have been anything, most likely the product of his overly amplified senses honed to a razor's edge by the excitement and unique circumstances. He felt he had won, even though he couldn't define his own victory.

Thwamp . . . thwamp . . . thwamp . . .

There it was again, the sounds like the first patter of heavy rain atop a roof.

"That cannot be allowed to debunk or debase the true America or the true Americans who reside within." Arno had forced himself to continue, stealing glances through whatever windows he could find as he rotated his gaze. But he couldn't see anything amiss. Maybe it was just rain. Maybe the cold front had brought the residue of a storm with it. "In 1836 proud Texans fought for their liberty and their rights inside an old fort called the Alamo. We are the modern version of those settlers, and our task is just as hard, the stand we're making here equally vital. Us, and the millions of others who think as we do, have drawn a line in the sand this government, its offshoots, and sycophants must not cross, because if they do . . ."

Arno paused again, the audience likely believing it was for effect when the truth was something had skirted across his field of vision through one of the windows. A figure dashing through the night, hunched with arms extended and something dark clutched in its grasp. Could have been one of the men Jed Kean had posted around the meeting hall. If so, though, where in hell was he running?

"If they do," Arno resumed, looking down to see if Kean was holding a hand to his ear to better listen to a message, but he wasn't, "they will be met with a fire and fury like none they've ever seen. I speak not of them just breaching our walls, but of them breaching our values and the country they have forsaken that we continue to hold close in our hearts."

And then he heard it, a series of quick popping sounds like the kind of firecrackers children set off on the Fourth of July. A soft, uneasy murmur spread through the clutter of bodies squeezed into the meeting hall. Arno figured he'd better get talking again, until he realized the source of the discomfort was not his silence or the crackling noises outside. It was a figure standing in the center aisle, halfway between him and the door, halfway between heaven and hell. A figure wearing a pistol holstered on her hip and a Stetson tight over her balled-up hair.

The figure of Caitlin Strong.

105

"You're taking a terrible risk here," Caitlin had told Danny Killane two days before. "I'm not going to lie to you about that."

"I don't care about my own life no more, Ranger. I belong in the sewers I tend."

"Through no fault of your own. If anyone got dealt a bad hand, it was you. I won't have this added to that lousy draw."

"I'm not doing this for you," Killane told her. "I'm doing it for me."

And that solidified the plan Caitlin and Cort Wesley laid out for Guillermo Paz: the satellite scans of the property had revealed not only the underground bunkers and firing ranges, but also a network of warrens that could only be escape tunnels. Just as Arno's father had laid beneath the Church of the Redeemer grounds in far less elaborate fashion.

The plan was for Killane to tell Arno of a multipronged frontal assault undertaken by a veritable army. In fact, Paz had brought only fifteen men north of the border with him because that was all he figured he'd need under the circumstances.

The only thing missing from the satellite scans was the actual entry points to the underground tunnels, but these Cort Wesley had found the same way he'd excelled at uncovering rabbit and prairie dog burrows when out hunting as a boy. Almost always alone to escape his father who was normally out all night. Reeking of booze when he came home and made even more violent by the hangover when he woke up. Cort Wesley wanted more than anything to be a better father to his boys, making the most of the opportunity that had thrust them into his life.

He led Caitlin, Paz, and Paz's men into the network of bunkers beneath the Patriot Sun complex, wearing a flak jacket and carrying an M16 supplied by the colonel. Caitlin opted against both, having her reasons.

The lighting along the underground corridors was dull and hazy, shed by lighting somehow wired into the ceiling. They passed under the meeting hall just before the service got under way, emerging up through a trio of buildings emptied by the mass gathering. Malcolm Arno had not yet begun to speak when Paz led his men into position and Cort Wesley slid through the night toward an outlying building where Danny Killane had told them Dylan was being held.

Caitlin, meanwhile, waited for Paz's men to gun down the guards around the meeting hall with quick four-shot bursts rendered silent by the sound suppressors affixed to their barrels. These men and the rest would now move onto the next phase of the colonel's plan, while Caitlin sliced through the night toward the building entrance. Waiting until the next round of gunfire began before simply pushing the double doors open and stepping inside.

106

MIDLAND, TEXAS; EASTER SUNDAY

"Malcolm Arno, I am placing you under arrest for the kidnapping of Dylan Torres."

Arno couldn't believe what he was seeing, hearing. Time wound backward, history repeating itself. Another Arno being taken down by another Strong.

Not this time, *goddamnit*!

He saw Jed Kean jerk his M16 into firing position, a blur of motion partially concealed by his great coat. In his mind he saw Kean gunning down Caitlin Strong, already concocting a rationale about a rogue Ranger operating on her own. But his eyes registered Caitlin Strong's gun clearing its holster and blowing fire from its barrel before Kean managed to pull his M16's trigger.

Her bullet slammed into his Kevlar vest and punched him backward into the pulpit, M16 barrel tilted low toward the floor.

"Don't do it," the Ranger said when she saw it starting to come up again.

Kean tried anyway, leveling his assault rifle back into firing position. Caitlin shot him in the wrist and he dropped to the floor with the M16 shed from his shoulder.

"Now come with me quietly, sir, so no one else gets hurt."

Amid the cries of shock and confusion that followed, Caitlin stopped fifteen feet from Malcolm Arno. She looked at him the very same way her father had looked at his from across a parking lot twenty years before. Another pair of gunmen, wielding assault rifles, lunged out into the aisle behind her. She turned and met their stares impassively, her SIG held in as unthreatening a fashion as she could manage.

"You boys wanna drop those or you'll die for sure."

The men looked at each other, both dropping their rifles and raising their hands into the air. Caitlin swung back toward the pulpit, glimpsed Arno ducking through a curtain. Her ears were stung by screams of panic that erupted after the spray of gunfire began to flow nonstop outside. She could hear it in the corner of her mind, picturing Paz's soldiers taking out the guards watching the front of the complex and posted all over the grounds.

Thanks to Danny Killane, the bulk of Arno's forces had indeed clustered beyond the gates and walls. Waiting in vain to ambush the invaders they had every reason to believe would be attacking in traditional fashion. Now Paz's men would claim the superior defensive positions that would allow them to cut down Arno's soldiers at will from the gated wall and towers.

Caitlin surged through the curtain with both hands on her SIG, half expecting Arno to be laying in wait. But he wasn't and had left nothing in his wake, besides an emergency exit door opened to let in the cool of the night.

107

The sewer stench hit Cort Wesley as soon as he drew to within sixty feet of the unfinished building, the remaining distance to be covered in the great wide open. He didn't hesitate, didn't stop. The time for subterfuge was done.

It was time for guns.

In that moment, as the M16, with a second magazine duct-taped to the first, started to dance in his grasp, Cort Wesley felt he was back in southern Iraq mowing down Republican Guardsmen in complete violation of his orders. Watching them fall like digital characters in one of his son Luke's video games, figuring if he could save even one life from the betrayal by the U.S. government it would be worth the price he'd have to pay.

He couldn't leave these people, not after prepping them for a revolution that never came. Then the Republican Guard had come with a convoy of men and vehicles that stretched as far as the eye could see to quell the uprising. Did he expect to kill all of them? Did he intend to let them kill him as punishment for his country's reprehensible act of betrayal?

In the end, Cort Wesley fought as long as his ammo lasted before moving off to the forward position he was supposed to withdraw to hours before. The other Special Ops personnel said nothing to him at all, just as they said nothing to their superiors about what he'd done. Not that it mattered. Cort Wesley knew he was finished with Uncle Sam, having come to feel that a government that couldn't keep its word wasn't worth fighting for.

But getting his son back was. The M16 felt comfortable in his grasp, in spite of the fact he hadn't done much shooting with one since leaving the service. All the soldiers Paz had brought along were needed to secure the main area of the complex, leaving Cort Wesley on his own. Not that that bothered him; it was what he wanted, to find Dylan and put an end to this himself.

The first enemy fire reached him as soft spits in the night, the reports drowned out by the louder exchanges coming from the main area. It was accompanied by the brief flares of muzzle fire behind bullets chasing his slithery form moving in a zigzag. Cort Wesley thought he heard the familiar *rat-tat-tat* of a minigun well behind him, could only hope it was friendly fire courtesy of Paz's men taking the towers as planned.

He heard the hiss of bullets whipping past him, thought he could feel their heat scratching at his face as well. He didn't return the fire until he had a sure bead on the shooters' positions both outside the unfinished building and from behind window shells within it. He set the M16 on full auto, not about to chance shooting on the run to single or even four-shot bursts.

Cort Wesley could hear the screams echoing from behind the missing windows, more like loud guttural grunts of shock that often followed the mashing of bone and muscle by 5.56mm slugs. The muzzle flashes continued to pour from in and before the building, the shooters turning from dull shapes to actual men as he drew closer with his eyes adjusted to the darkness now.

Cort Wesley felt several smacks to his torso and sides, the flak jacket saving him from all but a bullet that actually cut a crease through his right ear and left a stinging pain for residue. He could feel a lump of dislodged skin flapping as he ran, the pain further charging his adrenaline-fueled body. He jerked the magazine out, spun it around, and slammed the second home in less time than it took him to take a breath. Then, maybe fifty feet from the building, he simply stopped dead in a black patch of ground ignored by the moon, and started firing off single shots until the return fire stopped altogether.

Figuring more of Arno's soldiers could be laying in wait, baiting a trap, Cort Wesley advanced slowly with the tip of the M16's barrel cutting the air before him, avoiding the slew of bodies he'd dropped. The entrance to the unfinished building was a swinging, barely hinged door. He spun through it to find no one waiting and mounted the unfinished wood-plank stairs toward the fourth floor where Danny Killane had indicated Dylan was being held.

Cort Wesley had entered that special zone in which senses heighten to an almost precognitive level. Sounds became sights, telling him who was where, his shots sure to be an instant ahead of theirs. But those senses yielded nothing for him until he crashed through a fire door that turned out to be just leaning in place and dropped in his path. There, in the center of the hall, a man in uniform sat on his knees with his hands in the air.

"Please! Don't shoot! I surrender, I give up!"

Cort Wesley approached, wary of the open doorways on either side of the hall. He stopped with his M16 angled low.

"Where's the boy?"

"Gone."

"Where?"

"I don't know! I swear it!"

"Does Arno have him?"

"Arno? Why would he . . ."

Cort Wesley continued holding the rifle on the man who swallowed hard.

"Don't kill me."

And finally Cort Wesley tilted the barrel slightly upward. He knew the man was telling the truth, just as he knew Dylan had been here. It wasn't the scent of his clothes or hair gel, nothing like that, so much as an inexplicable residue of presence, the same way Cort Wesley knew his son had taken his truck without permission upon climbing into it himself.

"Looks like this is your lucky day, hoss," he told the man still kneeling before him. "But you better hope it's my boy's too, or I'm gonna gun down every last one of you."

108

MIDLAND, TEXAS; EASTER SUNDAY

Malcolm Arno saw it all coming apart. In trying to be the antithesis of his father, he had fallen prey to the very same proclivity of letting his weaknesses consume him. His obsession with Caitlin Strong had proven to be his undoing, just as a vastly different one had been his father's. If he had left well enough alone, if he hadn't ordered Masters's son brought here to make the daughter of Jim Strong suffer, the Patriot Sun would have been spared the wrath being visited upon it now.

So much lost, squandered. For some reason, though, Arno still wasn't pondering how to hold it together, how to get out of this in one piece and continue his stewardship of a movement flourishing all over the country. The Tea Partyers might be weak, insignificant larks, but the same vitriol they displayed fueled the groups beholden to Arno, his cause, and his money. He would arm them with guns like those contained in the shipment squandered up north, just as he would arm the right candidate with enough money to bring the true America into the mainstream come 2012.

Only he didn't care about any of that anymore. All he cared about was causing pain to Texas Ranger Caitlin Strong, to see the agony stretched over her face as she had glimpsed it on his the day her father had killed his. If there was a future for him and the movement to which he'd dedicated his life, it would come after that.

Arno stormed up the stairs of the central office building that coordinated an empire bigger than anything he'd ever imagined. His office door was open and he surged through it so out of breath that he had to drop his hands to his knees to quell the hammering of his heart. Once he'd caught his air, he moved to the closet and threw open the door to reveal the huddled, bound form of Dylan Torres nestled on the floor. Huffing in his breaths, staring up at him with pure hatred. His bandaged finger, cuffed behind him with the others, had bled through the gauze and soaked the back of his already filthy jeans. Arno was glad for the gag in the boy's mouth since he couldn't stomach any words from him right now, afraid they'd move him to choke the life out of the kid here and now even though Caitlin Strong wasn't around to bear witness. He continued to glare downward, relieved the stirring had not returned in a place inside him he neither recognized nor acknowledged.

For another brief moment, as he stood over Dylan Torres's frame, logic settled and Arno wondered if he might yet be able to spin this whole mess to his advantage. He had friends in places so high they could see God on a clear day, friends who understood the impact he could have on their mutual pursuits and weren't about to let him go down. But then the emotions that had been simmering ever since that day in the parking lot of the Tackle and Gun resurfaced. He reached down and yanked Dylan Torres out of the closet, jerking him to his feet. He could see the inside of the door was peppered with scuffs, indentations and fissures indicative of the boy trying to kick himself free.

Arno pulled a ceremonial reproduction of a Bowie knife given to him by the governor from a wall mount and stuck its tip against Dylan Torres's throat.

"Fight me and I'll kill you, I swear I will," he said in a voice muffled by the hate surging through him, as he steered the boy toward the doorway. "Now let's go."

109

MIDLAND, TEXAS; EASTER SUNDAY

Caitlin lost track of Malcolm Arno, but not Guillermo Paz. She'd glimpsed enough of his men's eyes to know he'd culled them from the most violent the Mexican Special Forces had to offer, all at the bequest of Fernando Lovano Sandoval with the complicity of none other than her friend Jones in Washington.

Most of Paz's men were concentrated in the courtyard fronting the meeting hall and cutting all the way through the main gate. She'd followed them attacking the soldiers of the Patriot Sun in relentless fashion without mercy or compunction. And Caitlin had lost count of how many fallen bodies she'd spotted or stepped over in her pursuit of Arno.

True to Paz's plan, his soldiers had managed to capture both guard towers and had turned the 7.62mm miniguns on the Patriot Sun soldiers beyond the walls charged with repelling the frontal attack that never came. The nonstop cacophony of churning fire from the six rotating barrels burned Caitlin's ears and left her picturing the men outside fleeing that fury if they were smart, or falling to it if they weren't.

Caitlin saw Paz himself dashing across the courtyard, veering toward her position so fast he didn't notice a Patriot Sun soldier steady a rifle on him from behind a shack advertising free lemonade. He ran with an assault rifle coming up, steadying on a spot beyond her.

She spun her SIG on the gunman taking aim at him.

Paz fired.

She fired.

The gunman with a bead on Paz dropped dead to the earth, just as did a Patriot Sun soldier ready to shoot Caitlin from the gap between the two nearest buildings.

Paz ejected both magazines from his A4 assault rifles and slammed fresh ones home.

"The boy?"

"He wasn't where we thought. Cort Wesley's headed back now."

"We'll find him, Ranger. In my dream an eagle swept from the sky and scooped him to safety. My dreams are never wrong."

Caitlin gazed back out from the two buildings she'd taken cover between. "Arno's men are running for their lives, Colonel."

Just as she said that, though, one figure emerged into the center of the courtyard dragging another.

"Oh, shit," said Caitlin.

110

Malcolm Arno slid through the night dragging Dylan before him, knife tip pressed as far into the boy's neck as it would go without punching a hole. Ground mist swallowed both their feet, Caitlin catching glimpses of the boy's sneakers, which were dirty with mud.

"Caitlin Strong! Texas Ranger Caitlin Strong, you come out here! I got something that belongs to you."

"Tough shot," Paz said, trying to measure one off.

"Leave this one to me, Colonel," Caitlin said, easing his hot barrel down with one hand while the other holstered her SIG.

Paz looked almost offended and swallowed hard, as she advanced into a thin spray of light to make sure Arno could see her.

"Right here, Mr. Arno." Her hand was poised close enough to her SIG to draw it fast without appearing threatening. But even if she managed to hit Arno like this, reflex would drive the point of his blade the rest of the way home and Dylan would bleed to death for sure.

Arno's eyes sought hers out. Caitlin had been on the scene of prison riots a few times and had assisted local authorities in the apprehension of escaped mental patients a few more. And the eyes of the man now standing before her with Dylan's life balanced at the end of his Bowie knife were as mad as any she'd ever seen.

"Come closer," he said, a thin smear of blood appearing under the blade's tip.

Caitlin did as she was told.

"Stay back!" Arno ordered the big man she'd shot in the wrist inside the meeting hall. He'd stepped out of the shadows holding a pistol in his off hand, the other one wrapped in a torn shirtsleeve, breathing hard through his mouth. "This is between the Ranger and me, Jed Kean. Isn't that right, Ranger?"

"Sir, I'm not going to say anything to humor you and that's all I've got in mind right now. So I'm just gonna keep quiet."

"Sir," Arno repeated, mocking her. "Mister . . . Your father called mine sir. I believe he called him reverend too. Are you Rangers supposed to do that, show a man reverence before you gun him down?"

"Let the boy go, Mr. Arno."

"You can stop now."

Caitlin did.

"This is how far apart we were in that parking lot, Ranger. Right when our eyes met after your father killed mine."

"They both made their choices."

"And now I'm making one too. Evening the score. Killing this boy, taking his childhood the way your father took mine. Making your life a study in misery as long as it lasts."

"Your father was a sick man, Mr. Arno. I don't believe I'm telling you anything you don't already know."

Arno was squeezing the hilt of the knife so hard his hand was trembling. Around him time had stopped, the world frozen solid. The shooting had ended, the remnants of Arno's surrendered forces with their hands in the air being watched by Paz's handpicked soldiers for whom taking lives was no different from picking fruit off a tree.

"I'm making a point here!" Arno yelled, his voice echoing through the cool night. "I'm gonna kill the boy, Ranger, and you're going to kill me. And tomorrow the groups that follow me, the people intent on taking back this country, will have their martyr. Their war will go without me and I'll be smirking at you from the grave. Because in the end I'll be the winner and you'll have nothing."

Caitlin heard the swift pounding of boots across the ground and turned to see Cort Wesley drawing parallel with her ten feet on the right, his M16 raised and ready.

"Cort Wesley!" she started as Arno twisted Dylan more toward him to deny Cort Wesley any chance at a shot, while opening the slightest sliver of one for Caitlin.

"No, not you!" Arno screeched at him. "It's gotta be her!"

"Go ahead," Cort Wesley said to Caitlin. "Take the shot, Ranger, take the goddamn shot!"

Caitlin eased her hand closer to her pistol, watching Arno smile at the sight, his eyes gleaming.

"Draw your gun, Ranger! Make me the martyr of my movement! Help me fulfill my fate!"

Still a tough shot by any stretch of mind, an inch bad and Dylan could catch the bullet instead of Arno, who was pressing the knife hard against his flesh, the tip ready to pierce flesh as soon as she went for her SIG.

"I'll take it, if you don't," Cort Wesley said, voice slightly muffled.

Then a new figure stepped into the light splayed from a pair of utility poles. Danny Killane was holding a pistol in hand, a revolver, walking straight for Malcolm Arno from the rear, stopping maybe ten feet behind him.

"Do what she says, Mr. Arno. Let the boy go."

"You betrayed me, Daniel," Arno said hatefully without turning toward him. "You brought this on all of us!"

Caitlin tried to make Danny Killane regard her, catch his eye with hers, but no such luck. Danny Killane, his life destroyed by the father, who'd agreed to plant false intelligence with the son about the attack. He'd promised Caitlin he'd flee the premises right afterward.

"You're a traitor, Daniel. You'll be the first to be punished."

Killane raised his pistol in a shuddery hand, not even seeming to see Dylan in the picture. Out of the corner of her eye Caitlin saw the big man named Kean bring his left hand around, hearing fresh shots blaring in the night in tandem with muzzle flashes spitting from his barrel.

Danny Killane spun around like a marionette attached to some invisible puppet master.

Cort Wesley blew a burst from his M16 into Kean, staggering him.

And Malcolm Arno twisted that way as Kean fell dead in the same moment as Danny Killane, exposing himself for a shot. Caitlin drew her pistol, finger taut on the trigger ready to fire.

But she didn't fire. Looking at Danny Killane's body splayed in the street, a portrait in futility and despair bred of the violence that had destroyed him a long time before it had killed him.

"Take the shot!" Cort Wesley yelled.

"No," Caitlin said, eyes on Arno and the knife he held against

Dylan's throat as she holstered her pistol and started forward. "I won't do it."

Arno looked bewildered, lost, uncertain, knife quivering in his hand.

"It's what he wants." Caitlin kept walking. "You hear that, Mr. Arno? Forget martyr." Caitlin stopped ten feet from Malcolm Arno, trying to reassure Dylan with her eyes. "Drop that knife now or all you'll ever be known for is killing an innocent boy."

Arno's eyes bled rage, hatred, but also something else she hadn't glimpsed before: weakness. The mask of his power ripped off, exposing the twisted soul beneath.

"Either I arrest you for kidnapping or for murder, sir. Your choice."

Arno's grip tightened on the knife and for a moment, just a moment, he seemed ready to plunge it home. But then his fingers opened and let it drop to the pavement. It clanged, bounced once, and stopped.

Dylan broke away from his slackened grasp and ran toward Cort Wesley, leaving Caitlin and Arno staring at each other. Neither breathing until Caitlin yanked her handcuffs from their belt pouch and covered the rest of the ground between them, while father and son collapsed in each other's arms.

"You are under arrest, sir."

As she jerked Arno's hands down and behind him to slap the cuffs on, Caitlin glimpsed the body of Danny Killane. Killane's eyes glazed yet somehow hopeful, as if restored of the innocence stripped from him so many years before. Kean's bullets had shredded his torso and the fall had torn his shirt to expose his shoulder and a tattoo painted over the flesh in the most vibrant ink colors Caitlin had ever seen.

"What is it, Ranger?" Paz asked, approaching with both assault rifles slung from his shoulders.

Caitlin held her gaze on the tattoo. "An eagle, Colonel. It's an eagle."

Epilogue

I believe the common thread from the first days of the Rangers until today is pretty much the same. Their job one hundred and eighty years ago . . . was to protect the innocent . . . citizens against the people who take advantage of the weak and defenseless. We are still doing that today. We still have that passion.
—Texas Ranger Senior Captain C. J. Havra, 2002

While Malcolm Arno was being arraigned on a charge of felony kidnapping before a surprisingly sparse crowd at the 142nd District Courts in Midland, Danny Killane was being buried next to his mother, Beth Ann, in a tiny cemetery on the outskirts of Odessa. Caitlin, Cort Wesley, and Dylan were the only ones in attendance besides a paid minister who kept pronouncing the kid's name wrong.

But he wasn't a kid, Caitlin reminded herself. His childhood had ended right around the same time hers and Malcolm Arno's had. Just like Dylan's effectively had now. He'd insisted on attending the funeral and stood impassively between Caitlin and Cort Wesley, as if searching for the right expression of what he was feeling.

When the minister closed his Bible before completing the final prayer, Cort Wesley flashed Caitlin a look and then led Dylan down an embankment into a sun-drenched section of the cemetery so the boy wouldn't have to look at R. Lee Shine's ancient, elegantly restored Lincoln Continental. They stopped in a rare open space amid gravestones squeezed so close to each other as to remind Cort Wesley of the flagstone walks he'd laid while working construction as a boy about Dylan's age.

"You understand why I gotta do this," he said to his oldest son.

The boy pursed his lips and blew the hair from his forehead. "Not really," he said, as the strands flopped back down.

"I killed that man."

"He deserved it."

"Irrelevant in the eyes of the law."

Dylan frowned. "No such thing down in Mexico, Dad, and you know it."

"Which is why I'll be home so quick you won't even miss me."

Dylan looked down, then up again, kicking at the ground where someday a fresh grave would be planted. "You did it for me."

The boy's statement took Cort Wesley by surprise, left him stammering for a response until he settled on the truth. "I did it for me, son. Ease my guilt, make me feel better about how I handled things when I got word about Maria and her family. That doesn't make it right. What it does make it is not your fault. You keep that straight in your head if this starts to weigh you down. If you'd asked me to gun the son of a bitch down, I would've said no, absolutely not, since that isn't the way civilized folk go about things."

"You saying you're not civilized?"

"I'm saying violence and me seem joined at the hip. No matter how much I want to change that, I just can't shake it. And that's why I gotta go with the man in that old Lincoln. 'Cause if I don't, all I'll have left is that violence."

"You'll still have me," Dylan said shyly.

Cort Wesley laid his arms atop the boy's shoulders, feeling the sun-baked heat radiating off them, hot enough to burn his hands. "Not the way I want, not if we gotta go on the run. You'll have Caitlin around 'til I get back."

"She's the same as you and you know it."

"No. I would've gunned Arno down for sure. Fact that she didn't exposed him for the coward that he is, and that's a hell of a lot worse than a bullet. The day the jail door gets slammed behind him he'll be forgotten for good."

"I would've shot him too."

"Guess we can both learn something from Caitlin Strong then, can't we?"

. . .

R. Lee Shine leaned up against the front fender, boots crossed casually on the sun-bleached asphalt. Caitlin and Cort Wesley walked slowly down a slight embankment toward him, arms wrapped about each other.

"Wish I knew how this ends, Ranger," Cort Wesley said, less surely than she'd ever heard him say anything before.

"They end up jailing you down there, I'll bust you out."

"That a promise?"

"From one gunfighter to another."

"A gunfighter as good with brains as she is with bullets."

"Easier to aim, as it turns out."

Cort Wesley touched his bandaged ear and winced. "Still hurts like a bastard."

Before Caitlin knew it, they were kissing and she didn't want it to end. And in those moments it honestly seemed like it wouldn't until Cort Wesley eased her away and held her at arm's length, smacking his lips.

"I'm gonna remember that taste."

"That almost sounds romantic."

"Close as I can come anyway."

"I'll be in court for the hearing."

"Only after you get the boys off to school. And if Dylan gives you any lip or starts his misbehaving again . . ."

"Want me to shoot him?"

"In the leg, Ranger."

"Still hurts, Cort Wesley."

"Doesn't everything?"

Caitlin watched R. Lee Shine's Lincoln pull off, arm draped over Dylan's suddenly stiff shoulder. Her eyes misted up, but she fought against wiping them as the big car cleared the rise and disappeared. She turned to say something, spotting Guillermo Paz standing in the old cemetery's one real shady spot thanks to a nest of Texas red oak trees. Unarmed, dressed in civilian clothes, and mopping his damp brow with a sleeve. Dylan glimpsed him too and slid out from under her arm, his eyes freeing Caitlin to approach the man who'd helped saved his life.

"The last time I cried was when I came home for my mother's funeral," Paz said, as she neared him. "Sometimes I wish I could cry again."

Caitlin stopped a few feet before him. "Thought you'd be back in Mexico by now, Colonel."

"My business here isn't finished. There's something I'm supposed to pick up: two truckloads of weapons recovered from an Indian Reservation in upstate New York."

"Our friend Jones, no doubt."

Paz let her comment hang in the air between them.

"What else have you dreamed lately, Colonel?"

"Aristotle said hope itself is a waking dream."

"I was looking for something more specific."

"About the future, perhaps?" Paz cast his gaze off into the distance, as if to look for R. Lee Shine's old Lincoln. "I don't need dreams, Ranger, to tell me you and the outlaw will stand side by side again."

"When?"

Paz shrugged. "Sometimes my vision confuses this world and the next. Sometimes I'm not sure it matters. It seems like there's always another war to fight either way."

Caitlin felt her eyes moistening up again. "Can't argue with you there, Colonel."

Caitlin called Mark Serles from behind the wheel of her SUV.

"Had the first fitting for my legs, Ranger," he told her. "Don't mind telling you standing upright again brought tears to my eyes."

"You're a brave man, M.J. You deserve a fresh start."

"I wanna apologize for any bother I caused you."

"I can't begin to explain how important the information you gave me was. I'm calling to say that what happened to you over there wasn't for nothing. Your story saved more lives than you can possibly imagine."

"How?"

"Watch the news. It won't be hard to figure."

The dead air filling the line made Caitlin wonder if Mark Serles had hung up until his voice returned, cracking a bit. "Thank you, Ranger."

"No, Sergeant, thank *you*. And I mean for everything."

Back in San Antonio, Caitlin and Dylan stopped at Mission Burial Park, the cemetery located on the San Antonio River where her father and grandfather were buried in clear view of the historic Espada Mission. They didn't exchange a word about his father, and Caitlin felt the boy take her hand when they got to the gravesites of Earl and Jim Strong, squeezing it tight and unconsciously gazing down at the bandaged finger now missing its tip.

"I understand why you didn't shoot him," Dylan said, "but I still wish you had."

"Part of me does too."

"Well, I wish you'd left me someone to kill," he said, his remark not as scary to Caitlin as the thin, sure smile behind it. The words, meant to be funny, turning out anything but. "My dad's going to jail 'cause of me," he added suddenly. "'Cause of me pestering him and him figuring he had to do something after that guy killed Maria and her family."

"Oh, almost forgot," Caitlin said, turning toward him. "I got your boots in my truck."

Dylan smiled, a boy again for the moment, and squeezed her hand tighter as he pressed his face against hers.

"Your father pulled them off the feet of a Mexican cop who must've thought we wouldn't notice."

The boy broke down, tears cascading down his face as he hugged her tight. She squeezed him back, not about to let go, her gaze drifting over Dylan's shoulder to the matching graves of Earl and Jim Strong.

Caitlin couldn't say exactly what had drawn her to Mission Park today. Maybe it was the hope of seeing the ghosts of her father and grandfather standing under one of the many beautiful cottonwood or flowering dogwood trees on the grounds. She'd caught similar glimpses of them before that always seemed to set things in their proper balance and leave her enriched with the sense that there was a greater purpose to whatever she was doing.

Today, though, there was the only her and Dylan, their sobbing borne witness to by no one from this world or the next, other than an eagle soaring overhead in search of its next prey.